After Julius

Born in 1923, Elizabeth Jane Howard was awarded the John Llewellyn Rhys Memorial Prize for her book *The Beautiful Visit*. Her subsequent novels were *The Long View*, *The Sea Change*, *After Julius*, *Odd Girl Out*, *Something in Disguise* and *Getting it Right*, which won the Yorkshire Post Prize and was made into a film. She has also written a collection of short stories, *Mr Wrong*, fourteen television scripts, a biography of Bettina von Arnim with Arthur Helps, a cookery book with Fay Maschler (reissued by Macmillan as *Cooking for Occasions*), two film scripts, and has edited two anthologies and published a book of ghost stories. Her most recent novels, written as the Cazalet Chronicle, are *The Light Years*, *Marking Time* and *Confusion*.

ELIZABETH JANE HOWARD

After Julius

WITH AN INTRODUCTION BY
SELINA HASTINGS

PAN BOOKS

First published 1965 by Jonathan Cape Ltd

This edition published 1995 by Pan Books
an imprint of Macmillan General Books
Cavaye Place, London SW10 9PG
and Basingstoke

Associated companies throughout the world

ISBN 0 330 33833 1

1 3 5 7 9 8 6 4 2

A CIP catalogue record for this book is available from
the British Library

Typeset by CentraCet Limited, Cambridge
Printed and bound in Great Britain by
Cox & Wyman Ltd, Reading, Berkshire

DEDICATED
TO KINGSLEY

CONTENTS

INTRODUCTION

ELIZABETH JANE HOWARD is a writer with a remarkable talent for intimacy. She makes a confidante of her reader, privately revealing the thoughts and feelings of her characters, particularly of her female characters. Howard is in the tradition of novelists such as Jean Rhys and Rosamond Lehmann, both of whom possessed an almost extrasensory understanding of the shocks and subtleties, the often painful dissimulations inevitable for women living in a man's world. She has a fine feminine sensibility, and we come to know those lovely, untidy girls, those elegant but wretched wives and widows, in detail that is as true as it is poignant. As in two of her earlier novels, *The Long View* (1956) and *The Sea Change* (1959), Howard shows herself an expert in tracing the effects of deceit and disappointment in human relationships, and yet such is her appetite for life, her creative vigour, that there is nothing sour in her outlook, nor is she in the least restricted by her alliance with her own sex. Her scope is wide, her horizons large. She has a strong sense of period and place, a sense that significantly informs and supports all her fiction.

From the start of her writing career Elizabeth Jane Howard showed herself master of a sophisticated technique, expertly dealing with a large cast and effecting difficult changes in time and location. First published by Jonathan Cape in 1965, *After Julius*, with its complex structure, is no exception, the focus moving from London to Sussex, from the early years of the Second World War to the 1950s, from one generation to the next. The protagonists are the widowed Esme and her two daughters, Cressida, known as 'Cressy', and Emma. Esme's story is told partly in flashback, although the unfolding of the present plot takes place over one week-end. Howard's use of plot to reveal character and chart the shifts in a relationship is highly accomplished. Esme's husband, Julius, has been killed in the war, shot in the course of heroic action during the evacuation from Dunkirk. For Esme this is not the tragedy it might have been. Julius, a publisher with a passion for poetry and public causes, stands on an altitude unattainable to his pretty but ordinary young wife. It is poetry that distances Esme from Julius. 'In all moments of emotion he resorted to poetry; and this included making love to her. She had pleaded ignorance, but this only provoked hours of tender instruction, and every time he reached out for some slim calf-bound volume from a shelf, or threw back his head and half shut his eyes (he knew a fantastic amount of stuff by heart) the same wave of unwilling reverence and irritated incomprehension swept over her.'

After her two children are born, Esme falls seriously in love for the first time, her lover, Felix, a charming and cultivated man some years younger than she. When Julius is killed, Esme's passionate hope is that she and Felix may marry, but Felix, unfortunately inspired by Julius's noble example, himself goes off to join up and disappears from Esme's life for nearly twenty years.

At the time the novel opens Esme, now fifty-eight, is in a state of high tension, waiting in her pretty house in Sussex for Felix to arrive for their first meeting since the war. Her first sight of him does little to allay her anxiety: 'He had matured so well, while she had simply decayed as little as she could contrive.' Also expected for the week-end are Cressy and Emma. Cressy, a not very successful concert pianist, is a beauty with a messy love life characterized by unhappy affairs with married men. She is in the middle of one such affair now, yet again trying to find the resolution to bring the miserable business to an end. Emma, on the other hand, sensible and good, has so far shown little interest in the opposite sex. It surprises everyone, therefore, that it is she who turns up with a boyfriend, the disconcertingly unconventional Dan. Daniel's eccentricity is vividly established by his first act on entering the house. 'Daniel moved to the fire, picking off a blackberry from Esme's elaborate flower arrangement. "Frostbitten," he said and spat it neatly into the flames.'

Cressy, the elder of the sisters, has been briefly married and, like her mother, widowed during the war. Howard makes brilliant use of period and place deftly to define the pathos of the childlike Cressy's hopelessly inadequate relationship with her husband, Miles, an amiable fellow far more concerned with the building of the motor torpedo boat over which he has command than with his homesick young wife. Miles takes Cressy with him to the Isle of Wight, where for a time he is able to live with her ashore. The first morning Cressy wakes up in their hotel bedroom, 'sleepy, warm as a bird . . . it took her at least five minutes to understand that he would be out for the whole day – would not see her until late in the evening. "But what shall I *do*?" she had asked in panic. He looked nonplussed. "I should look at the Island. It's very pretty, really," he added: he had sailed there before the war. "But how do I have lunch?" "Go down to the dining-room and ask for it. Damn!" He was shaving fast with a cut-throat razor, and the simplicity of her question had made him cut himself. "Really, darling!" he had said, as he stuck a piece of cotton wool to the blood.'

That comfortless hotel in Cowes, where Cressy sits dismally in the lounge with old copies of *Yachting World*, tellingly conveys the state of her marriage. Such significant detail is employed also in the description of Esme's house in Sussex. The reader's first encounter with her takes place in her bedroom, a room that tells us nearly all we need to know about Esme. 'She lay on her side, her head neatly shaped by the Lady Jayne hairnet which tied under her chin. The room, which was zagged with oak beams (genuine, but with that look of hypocrisy that ensued from efficient worm-treatment), had four fussy little windows with ugly steel frames, peach chintz curtains and frilly pelmets. A great many photographs were tilted about the room: her parents, the house in Portugal where she had been a child, herself being presented (black lipstick and fat, white gloves); her husband; darling Sambo with an idiotic ribbon round his neck . . .'

Equally effective is the description of the tiny London flat shared by Esme's daughters, typifying the dingy flavour of genteel urban poverty immediately after the war. The flat has linoleum on the floor, a nasty stain on the ceiling and a bathroom painted the colour of tinned peas. "[Emma] got up, lit her gas fire which was a contemporary of the earliest Baby Austins; small, roaring, resolute – gallantly pouring its drop of heat into the bucket of room – and went to the window . . . Rows of back gardens, with battered lawns, an old pear tree now bleakly articulate and dripping; air like fudge, a pimento sun and an unexpected seagull – at its best in its moving distance – wheeling about in aimless expert circuits. It was cold and there might be fog.'

Elizabeth Jane Howard is a marvellously sensual writer, responsive and alert to her physical surroundings, to texture, colour, sound; she is intently aware of the natural world, interested in animals and birds and observant of their habits. Here, for example, is the cat belonging to the cook, Mrs Hanwell: '[the cat] was edging his portly fur through the hedge back from one of his abortive excursions. Mrs Hanwell pretended that he was worth keeping because he was such a good hunter, but he was far too cowardly to catch anything but butterflies in summer which he crunched up like fairy toast, and then jostled her all over the kitchen for square meals.' Square meals are a speciality: there are some mouth-watering menus in *After Julius*. For dinner on the first evening of the week-end, there are 'chickens, plain roast, with bread sauce, mashed potatoes, Brussels sprouts with chestnuts and thick chicken gravy, followed by a plum tart – bottled plums – and Mrs

Hanwell's husband's cream'. This feast is insufficient for Dan, who in the middle of the night goes downstairs to visit the larder. 'He found a wedge of blackberry-and-apple pie – just enough for one, and a piece of rather hard, greasy and slippery cheese. He was examining a white can covered by a dear little piece of muslin with blue beads weighting its edges, when he heard a noise.'

One of Elizabeth Jane Howard's finest qualities is her unerring instinct for psychological truth. She is frequently very funny, with a good line in delicate irony, but at the same time she never flinches from the depiction of humiliation, of disappointment and despair. When Esme, for example, finally realizes after a scene of nightmarish misunderstanding that she has lost Felix for good, she bleakly turns back to her empty life, its emptiness crucially summarized in one unforgettable detail. Esme, having watched her lover leave, slowly walks from the hall into the drawing-room in search of occupation. She looks over to her desk, 'neatly crammed with letters she had already answered'. That tells it all, and there the chapter ends.

The novel's climax, a *tour de force* brilliantly balancing comedy with an almost savage sense of desolation, takes place during a dinner-party given by Esme on the Saturday evening. The guests are Dick Hammond, who is Cressy's married lover, his wife, Jennifer, and a much-ridiculed but touching local widower, Major Hawkes. Cressy is appalled when Dick walks into the room, but tries to save the situation as best she can. We, however, know it is unsaveable as soon as we are introduced to the unknowingly wronged wife. '[Jennifer] was wearing a low-necked beaded sweater and a terrifically hairy skirt. She [Cressy] smiled. It felt like a smile – and offered Jennifer a cigarette. "How *super*! I'm not in the least musical, but honestly, I should adore to hear you play. I'm so stuck with the children these days, that nothing ever improves my mind."' The scene is perfectly paced, with the fact of her husband's deception gradually dawning on Jennifer, while Cressy, watching her lover's patronizing behaviour, begins to feel that she herself may be over the worst. 'Dan and Emma had gone ahead to light the candles on the dining-room table. Thus Dick was able to hang back, and as she [Cressy] straightened herself up from the fireplace, he made a quizzical face – helpless and conspiratorial dismay. She met it with an expression of impassive good humour. He tried harder.

'"You look so wonderful, darling: God, I'm sorry about this: she insisted on my coming . . ."

'[Cressy] brushed the lichen off her hands and said: "Don't let it worry you," as she started to move for the door . . . She felt about ten feet high and fifty miles away. Good heavens, it was *easy*.'

Elizabeth Jane Howard is an enormously gifted writer, with a rare understanding both of human nature and of the power and poetry of the English language. Although *After Julius* is in a sense a novel in a minor key, all her remarkable qualities are evident within it: her humanity, her wit, her powers of observation and description as well as her stylistic grace and technical expertise. This novel marks an important stage in the development of one of the finest practitioners of our time of the sophisticated comedy of manners, a genre in which Howard was to attain near perfection in her magnificent tetralogy about the Cazalet family completed in the 1990s.

Selina Hastings, 1994

PART ONE

FRIDAYS

CHAPTER 1

EMMA

OW it is a Friday morning in November.

She woke at exactly quarter past seven in a back bedroom on the top floor of a house in Lansdowne Road. In fourteen minutes the telephone would ring, and a man's voice – charged with that sense of routine emergency that she associated with war films: 'enemy bearing green 320' – would tell her that it was seven-thirty, which of course, she would know already. But when she tried cancelling the telephone, she didn't wake up at all. These fifteen minutes, which in a sense were some march on the day, could surely be put to some use or pleasure, but almost always she lay rigidly governed by her anticipation of the tearing ring, and when it came, she picked up the receiver so quickly that there was always a wait for the man's voice.

Then she got up, lit her gas fire which was a contemporary of the earliest Baby Austins; small, roaring, resolute – gallantly pouring its drop of heat into the bucket of room – and went to the window. It was an attic room, almost the kind which in the country would have been used for storing apples and old finery; and the window had been slightly enlarged by some pirate builders who regarded draughts as a natural hazard of any alteration. Cold thick air streamed purposefully in from the edges of its frame, but the view, when she had dragged the rusty linen marigold and butterflies together (her mother had given her the curtains) was pretty for London. Rows of back gardens, with battered lawns, an old pear tree now bleakly articulate and dripping; air like fudge, a pimento sun and an

3

unexpected seagull – at its best in its moving distance – wheeling about in aimless expert circuits. It was cold and there might be fog.

The stain – like spilt coffee – on the ceiling seemed to have got larger in the night. She would have to tell the Ballantynes, which was doubly awful, because the roof was their job, and they couldn't afford it, so they got the frightful builder Bill Ballantyne had known in the war, whose face was congested with good living and his chronic, unreliable smile. He smiled and smiled, and agreed to any suggestion; then weeks later he botched up whatever he had been asked to do and broke something else. He must make a fortune smashing things up, and nearly all his customers were people who'd known him in the war which made a mysterious difference to their view of his character: like Bill's, it was always based on some kind of fancy nostalgia.

The bathroom was all the colour of tinned peas, but as it had been painted and tiled by Mr Goad, the tiles were cracking and the paint lay in huge bubbling blisters. He had also chipped the bath quite painfully when he installed it, but when Bill had remonstrated about this he had countered with a nine months' wait for a new bath, and the fact that he had bought it cheap – as a favour to Bill – from a job lot of exports rejected by Venezuela.

She turned on her bath and then went back along the passage to the door opposite her room. It was shut, and when she opened it, a stale haze of smoke, old warmth, and suspended crisis assailed her. It was their sitting-room, and as she switched on the light she knew that Cressy had been having one of her scenes.

It was really a very nice, enormous attic, with sloping ceilings and a squat black stove – now out. For a moment she looked at the cushions all over the floor, the large, white handkerchiefs crumpled and crushed into creases of the sofa, the cups of untouched black coffee and the piano open, thanked goodness it was the week-end, and took the coffee pot to the kitchen for breakfast.

Her sister, as usual, was difficult to wake. She had dumped the breakfast tray, lit the electric fire, drawn the curtains and turned off the light before there was the slightest movement. Cressy lay on her front with her head turned to the wall, but as the light went out, she muttered something, threw out a beautiful arm and unclenched her fingers: another crumpled handkerchief fell on to the floor.

'Coffee,' said Emma briskly – but her heart sank.

Cressy turned in bed and looked at her. She did not speak, but her eyes, which seemed already full of tears, brimmed over and momentous drops slipped down her face. 'Oh Lord!' She sat up.

Emma picked up the handkerchief: it was sopping.

'Do you want another one?'

Cressy shook her head, and reached out for a faded old pink cashmere cardigan which she put round her shoulders and wrapped across her like a shawl. Then she took the sherry glass filled with lemon juice that Emma faithfully squeezed for her every morning, and drank it. Emma, whose teeth could not bear her to watch this, began pouring coffee and wondering whether it was better for Cressy to talk and cry more, or shut up and probably cry later. She exchanged the sherry glass for a huge Wedgwood mug of black coffee, and said rather hopelessly: 'Are you warm enough?'

Cressy nodded, and a flurry of tears fell out. Then she said: 'He's going to Rome for the week-end. *Rome!*' she repeated bitterly.

'Couldn't you go with him?'

'He won't take me. We might be seen. After all these months of looking forward to this one week-end, which God knows isn't much to ask, there's suddenly a conference in Rome.'

'I don't suppose he could possibly help it.'

'Oh, I know that. That's just Life!' She said it with a kind of

5

savage intimacy, as though she had always known it lay in wait to wreck her: 'He could have taken me with him if he'd wanted to badly enough. But if things are at all difficult, he simply doesn't care enough to cope.'

And if they weren't difficult, *you* wouldn't care enough, Emma thought uncontrollably; but like everything about Cressy (and probably everyone else) this wasn't strictly true.

'When does he get back?'

'Sunday night – he thinks. It's just that I did so desperately want – so terribly – just – '

'A bit of time with him.'

'It's odd – they don't seem to mind at all. Like going to a concert, but never practising. It's like an entertainment – kind of fringe on life, but not the actual stuff.'

'If he wasn't married would you marry him?'

'Marry,' she repeated dreamily: 'I don't know. I've tried to be realistic about it, you see, and he's always been married. That's the point.'

'But, if you could find the right person, you would like to be married to them?' Emma felt a sudden panic that this question might be answered the wrong way – leaving no way out, and spoil all sympathy, kindness or anything that one could feel.

But Cressy said immediately:

'It is the only thing I really want in the world. If I could find the right person, I'd do anything to keep things good and make them better. I just feel all wrong by myself: you don't; I suppose that's why I have affairs and you don't? But *you* would marry, wouldn't you – if you found someone?'

She shrugged, because an almost tangible weight of hopelessness descended with this question. 'Oh – I expect whoever I was supposed to marry got killed in the war.'

Cressy looked shocked. 'Really, Em, that's just pure neurosis. You've got plenty of time. Ten years younger than me – phew!'

'I'm much older than you were when you were married. Anyhow, I'm not so sure as you are that it would make me so terribly happy. Look, I'll have to go in a minute. Are you coming home for the week-end?'

'Perhaps – I'll think – there might be a fog – I don't know – I'll ring you.' She suffered from the chronic disability of the lovesick to make any plan outside that orbit. Emma left her – out of tears, at least, and combing out her coarse, black, glossy hair which hung in pointed waving locks to her shoulders, like a young witch. She certainly didn't look her age.

Poor dear – she really *was* unhappy, thought Emma as she dressed. Probably not for the reason that she imagined, which she felt, after all, could be changed, but for a much worse, deeper, more creeping reason. I suppose people who are invariably serious about something end up by boring the other person about whatever it is. She tried this theory out: food, poetry, politics, love; well, it seemed true of the first three and so – but of course, being really serious about something would mean seeing it all round, in which case there would be some part of it to take lightly. Perhaps Cressy wasn't serious *enough*? If one took oneself seriously, on the other hand, one never found anything to laugh at, which implied a partial view. That is what I would like, she thought, turning off her gallant little fire which seemed to have had some sort of fit in her absence and was purple and flickering. I would really like to find more things to laugh at. I'd like people to come up to me and say, 'This is a laughing matter', and mean it.

She had dressed in a pleated skirt, a heavy navy-blue boy's jersey and her new navy-blue openwork stockings in which she felt both warm and dashing. She hauled her heavy red coat out of the cupboard, checked the typescripts in her music case and looked out of the window to see whether it had begun to rain. The seagull was now sitting on a chimney stack, looking dank and dirty and lonely; it wasn't raining but the air was loaded with greasy black moisture; she could imagine the drops beading its feathers, and got out a thick woollen square for her head. Her head made her remember the ceiling, and she went back to Cressy's room.

Cressy was standing at her window, barefoot, shivering, and as she turned towards Emma, streaming again with tears.

'Thought you'd gone. It *does* look like fog, though. There's some hope. Or do you think it's *craven* of me to want there to be fog?'

'Of course not. But if there isn't *do* come down. It would be a popular move. You could come back on Sunday.'

'I know. I'd thought of that. Have you got just *one* cigarette? Dick smoked all mine last night.'

While she hunted in her large, packed handbag, she said: 'If you see either Ballantyne, could you mention my ceiling? It's getting bad again – different place to last time. Oh dear, I'm afraid I haven't. Ask Bill for one.'

'So that I'll be sure to remember the ceiling. Do you really want Goad padding about your room when you're away?'

'No, but I thought next week – I *must* go. Leave it – never mind. 'Bye. *Don't* despair. Every silver lining has a cloud. Think of your career. I'm catching the four twenty if possible.' And she escaped.

Down the stairs, past the aura of steamy Floris bath oil, the cracked yellowing paint and the dark-green linoleum of the bedroom landing, down another flight with a dreary etching of some different part of Venice at each step (what Venice had to put up with! – like the Gospels and Mozart and the sky on calendars), into the hall, coffee-coloured unless the light was on; past the sensual smell of other people's breakfast, and the hall table thick with bills and a city hat; past the guns, golf clubs and German helmet (first world war) and an angry, dusty badger's head sticking out from the porridge wall like a furry gargoyle. The fanlight had the number of the house painted on it: backwards it had a misshapen, outlandish air. She could never open the front door with one hand, which meant dumping everything. Down the crazy path, past sodden privet to the gate which seemed always malevolently covered with machine oil. Down the street, which in spring and summer was edged by front gardens flowing with lilac, laburnum and cherry, with pyracanthus, plum, iris and may, and well-to-do cats packed between the railing spikes, and very old men being strained on a stroll by ancient Victorian terriers. She remembered this crowded, streamingly scented scene with longing as she hurried through the cold beady air to the Tube, but forgot the summer misery of being trapped in an airless office throughout the few really ravishing days. She was late for the office in any case, and being late always makes one forget anything else that has happened.

She thought about her sister on her way to Holborn. In spite of her rather foolish unthinking question about marriage being answered in such a way as to allay her immediate anxieties about Cressy, she did get waves of panic about Cressy's future. Thirty-seven seemed to her – although of course she would never have breathed it – an interminable age; it was difficult to be a promising pianist at thirty-seven, and precarious to be crying your eyes out over detached but married men: the trouble was that the men got in the way of the music, so that it had never seemed to get established enough to be the comfort and inspiration that Emma was sure it was meant to be. Had Cressy, she wondered, really been unhinged by her early, disastrous marriage? By her father's death? Of course, she had married after their father had died – perhaps it had been some kind of Oedipus rebound that had made her marry, suddenly, a man whom she hardly knew. Poor Miles: he had been fifteen years older than Cressy – struggling with the Wavy Navy: 'Irregular hours, filthy food, appalling seasickness' he was quoted as having said on one of his brief leaves. The marriage lasted barely a year because he had been killed on the Dieppe Raid. She remembered the guns shaking up her tummy and backbone as they sat on the lawn in Sussex with Cressy – pale-green –

9

skinning rabbits. She had been eight, then, and it had seemed extraordinary to have a raid in the middle of a fine summer's day. 'I'll make you a pair of gloves, Em,' Cressy had said, and she had watched while Cressy pegged out the skins on a board in the sun, and showered them with some white powder. But afterwards she had simply cried a lot and played the piano – sad, stormy, dreary old Brahms – she quite forgot about the gloves. The guns before that had been Dunkirk. Really Emma couldn't remember before the war at all, excepting isolated pictures of her father, which were always the same, always memories in the middle of something – never the beginning or the end. 'We were just looking for a ball in the bushes at the end of the lawn.' Couldn't remember it being lost, or finding it, but the sudden delicious smell of her father's silk handkerchief when he wiped her face – lavender and lebanon cedar and the silk as smooth as bottle glass: 'You blackamoor,' he said. The long grass had come up to her chest – she couldn't have been more than four. Then, doing something called 'ducks on mud' with his hands holding her cheeks: she had never heard a duck on mud, but she used to think it was a terribly funny and difficult noise to make. She had been seven when he died, a few days after her birthday. He had simply gone to London one morning and not come back. 'He's gone to London for the week-end,' she had said the first breakfast that he hadn't been there: these were Wednesday and Thursday, but the week-end for her meant two nights – she hadn't noticed that they always started on a Friday. The worst thing about that had been her mother's face, which afterwards she felt had seemed to be charged with something more than grief, and the dreadful, racking sobs which she had woken to hear coming from her room at night, and which had frightened and horrified her so much (her *mother* – at such a loss?) that Emma had not wanted to touch her for days . . .

This was a long way from Cressy and her problems. The advantage of a disciplined mind was supposed to be that if you chose, you could think one thought for a very long time, but apart from not having such a mind herself, she didn't think that she had ever met anyone who had. Most people's thoughts, even when they were supposed to be concentrating, hopped about with the tame apathy of domestic rabbits. The best she had ever achieved had been when she had been able to think in waves – coming in, draining away, coming back just a little farther about every third wave. That had been when she was trying to paint, and only sometimes then, with a particular picture: years ago. And now, having failed to do anything which she privately thought worth while, here she was, trying to be a reliable reader and editor in the family business. Holborn. She got up and walked the routine yards to Great Queen Street.

The packers in the basement and the back of the ground floor were hard at it, with the Light Programme twice life-size. The girl on the switchboard had finished her salmon-pink jersey and was doing the ribbing on something acid mauve with a lurex thread. The smell of new books – like very distant daffodils – plus central heating and a whiff of Californian Poppy, were always in the tiny ground-floor hall. She said good morning, and started the long climb up. The first floor was the Accounts Department – a seething mystery with which she had nothing to do excepting when Miss Heaver, who had been with the house for twenty-eight years, came round with a donation list for a leaving present for somebody. On the next floor – the last with nice ceilings and unspoiled chimney-pieces – were her uncle, his partners, and their secretaries. Up again to what must once have been a bedroom floor, now housing Production, Art Department and Publicity, all jealous of one another's rooms. And finally – and really it was quite a haul – up to Editorial at the top of the house – three small rooms for them of which one was hers, and one smaller, a kind of box room in which once a week the travellers held their smoke-ridden and unexpectedly hilarious conferences: for what on earth book travellers found to laugh at week after week she simply couldn't think. But like the packers, they were always cheerful, at least when she saw or heard of them.

Her room faced south on to the street and there was a parapet where pigeons sometimes sat and ate the dull pieces of bath buns. It was very small, permanently dirty, and either stuffy or freezing, depending upon the window, but as she had apparently no creative ability (her efforts in other directions besides painting had made this agonizingly plain), this was the place where – apart from her bed – she spent most of her life.

The scripts that morning presented a choice of a romantic and powerfully unconvincing novel about the Aztecs; an account of crossing the Sahara in a pre-war London taxi (a saga of homespun inefficiency which it made her yawn to think of); and the ruminations of a sullen young man who was living a life of such self-imposed freedom that nothing whatever happened to him, a fact which he resented on every single page. And there was plenty more where that came from. Oh, give me somebody good, she thought: just let one writer occur today whose capacity matches his heart, and who isn't entirely living on other people's experience . . .

CHAPTER 2

ESME

HER bed was like a nest, large and soft and warm as
though it had been made of feathers. Her paunchy
pillows were so downy that she needed three of them:
all the bed-clothes were peach pink, and a bed-jacket edged with
white swansdown lay at the foot of the eiderdown quilt. She lay
on her side, her head neatly shaped by the Lady Jayne hairnet
which tied under her chin. The room, which was zagged with
oak beams (genuine, but with that look of hypocrisy that ensued
from efficient worm-treatment), had four fussy little windows
with ugly steel frames, peach chintz curtains and frilly pelmets.
A great many photographs were tilted about the room: her
parents, the house in Portugal where she had been a child,
herself being presented (black lipstick and fat, white gloves);
her husband; darling Sambo with an idiotic ribbon round his
neck, and her children at various ages; the ones of Cressy were
always good, and of Emma always disappointing. The dressing-
table was painted buff and apple-green with tiny pink rosebuds
and an artificially cracked surface, and was littered with pink
enamel, silver and organdie. The rest of the house – excepting
for her passion for anonymously flowered chintzes – had
somehow slipped past the 'thirties, was much more the result of
family accumulation, prosperous, thoughtless and good-
natured, but no amount of teasing either from Julius or
subsequently the girls had shaken her conviction that hers was
the prettiest and comfiest bedroom in the world, and she adored
waking up in her delicious bed.

She nearly always began her day with twenty minutes' cosy

dreaming about the past – not because the whole of her life had been so very happy, so much as that she needed to reassure herself that it had been worth while before starting upon another day. As she lived mostly alone, this rather curious habit had easily taken root, so that now she felt rather cheated if the telephone or people interrupted her. She called herself 'she' in these dreams – it made her feel less egocentric.

After a time, she would switch on her electric kettle to make tea on the tray beside her bed, and when she had drunk one cup, she would put on her feathered mules and tap downstairs hopefully in search of post. She was a great letter-writer, and her letters were surprisingly shrewd and funny and observant. If there were no letters she would make lists: lists of people to ask for week-ends, lists of bedding plants, lists of things that she wanted to get mended in London, lists of books she wanted to read, lists of programmes she wanted to hear on the wireless, lists of household stores to be ordered from Battle, lists of odd jobs that she thought Hanwell should do when it rained too much for him to work out, and things that she meant to say at the next WI meeting . . . she could always find something, she had had so much practice.

This morning she lay longer than usual, partly because the room was a little cold, partly because it was Friday – the beginning of a week-end, the beginning of what after all these years she still felt was a tiny holiday. On Fridays Mrs Hanwell stayed and cooked until the washing-up on Sunday evening. On Fridays she got in drink, and did the flowers – it would be chrysanthemums and berries today – and got out soap and arranged suitable bedside reading for her guests. This week-end was a quiet one – just the Hammonds and Brian for dinner on Saturday, and of course Emma. She usually re-read three Austen novels each winter; at the moment it was *Pride and Prejudice*, which meant that whenever she thought of Emma she worried about whether she was really just like Mrs Bennet (about this daughter), as the one thing that she wanted for Emma was that

14

she should make a good marriage; nothing spectacular, but something charming and secure. At twenty-seven (Mrs Bennet would have given up *years* before) Emma showed no signs of marriage, or even of any particular interest, and she felt that this was anxious-making and unnatural. It was possible, she supposed, that Emma led some kind of secret life in London, but if she did so it was ineffective – she came regularly every weekend, and she never looked, as her mother privately put it, 'enhanced' in any way. Just neat and calm and much too pale. She wasn't a beauty, like Cressida, but she had a nice little face – a lot of people found odd eyes most attractive – and pretty legs and a lovely skin ... 'But she didn't seem to find the *excitement* I used to have when I was young.'

The excitement had come out of the secret, perpetual clash between her desires and her as passionate love for appearances, and only when it was raging did she feel really alive. On those stretches in her life when it had subsided, she felt that she had 'given in' to something – was either vegetating or going to the devil. Life, she felt, had to have this edge on it, and if, as once it had, the edge became too sharp, well, in retrospect, at least, it was all part of the excitement. From the age of sixteen she had simply adored being in love. Competition for young men had been pretty strong in those days: so many of them were dead, you had to be fun if you wanted a gay time. Dancing with somebody new and attractive – the inquisitive bantering compliments and the provocative defence, with the possibility of that thrilling moment when one might get a message in oneself telling one to go ahead ... Then, the exquisite, suspended boredom of the times between meeting, enlivened only by whatever subterfuge was necessary, for in spite of many and unbelievable risks she had kept her actual reputation mysterious. And of course there were the longer times when she had had to live on recreated moments of somebody's voice or hands, or to exist in a dreamy state of erotic curiosity about what would happen next. That was when she had been living with an aunt in Chester Square, going to classes for household management and learning French; long after her parents had died, after she had done her Season and worked for the Red Cross. Of course, all those years she had hoped that someone really stunning would turn up; sometimes for brief moments she had even thought that they had − somebody who would change every-thing and begin a new life for her. Once she had thought that she had started a baby, and oh! the unspeakable terror of it! She had taken castor oil for three days running, and somebody had said that boiling up parsley was a good thing and she had tried to do this in the middle of the night in the cavernous kitchen at Chester Square, had been caught, and pretended that she was making some preparation for her skin. Thank goodness that had been a false alarm because she felt that her aunt would have died of horror if she had found out, and a good deal of the time Esme loved her. (It never occurred to her that her aunt had had a shrewd idea of what was going on, felt that it was high time that Esme married, and had set about collecting chances until they accumulated into a fate.) It was at the fourth dinner party given by her aunt that Esme met Julius; back from the war three years now, but still with any provocation at all describing himself as 'the one that got away'. It was years before she understood the self-derogation implicit in this remark, which had seemed to come out with a kind of jovial cynicism that she had privately labelled bad taste. It was odd, but she could remember Julius exactly at their first meeting and exactly on that last morning when he had caught the 8.32 for London, but only with difficulty in between.

At first sight then, he had struck her as romantic and interesting, although what precisely she meant by either of these descriptions she was afterwards not sure. His appearance had about it that faint, natural carelessness − all features arresting and none perfect – and his manner that touch of civilized bravado which is often confused with originality, at least by young girls of nineteen. He was of medium height, with dark hair which was trying to curl behind his ears, a forehead with a high, oval hairline which balanced the long upper lip, large black-brown eyes with almost girlishly fine eyebrows – but these made resolute by the large, rather beaky nose, and by ears whose sheer size would have looked eccentric on a woman. He had a melodious voice, but laughter was an inappropriately muscular effort, and he held himself so erect that his neat, economical movements were significant and attractive. He was a publisher, in his uncle's house, she discovered that evening, unmarried, and just thirty-two. When he asked her whether she enjoyed poetry, of course she said yes. When, a few weeks later, he sent her a poem written out in pen and ink she dutifully read all the words of it until, nearly at the end, she realized because it described the dress she had worn that first evening, that he had actually written it about her – an exquisite shock to her vanity! But if he hadn't put the dress in she might never have known and goodness knows, everything might have been different. They married when she was twenty, in May, and it was not until he cast himself upon her with lines from a sonnet relevant to that month, but to little else, and which anyway turned out to have been written by Shakespeare, that it dawned upon her that it was poetry that was his prevailing passion. This was a discovery upon which the sun never set. In all moments of emotion he resorted to poetry; and this included making love to her. She had pleaded ignorance, but this only provoked hours of tender instruction, and every time he reached out for some slim calf-bound volume from a shelf, or threw back his head and half shut his eyes (he knew a fantastic amount of stuff by heart) the same wave of unwilling reverence and irritated incomprehension swept over her. By the time she was having Cressy, she hit upon a counter-interest with which he might at least sympathize. She had developed a passion, she said, for really good novels (and she found, after a certain amount of perseverance, that this became true).

The publishing prospered, a partner retired and Julius succeeded him; they bought the house in Sussex and kept a small flat in town; went for trips to Paris and Rome and New York, apart from ordinary holidays. Julius adored his daughter: it was he who had named her Cressida as a compromise between their disparate choices of Zenocrate and Joan. Everything was very pleasant, and if you had stopped her in the street, or driven her into a corner at a cocktail party, she would have been most unlikely to admit that poetry had spoiled her sex life with Julius – although this in fact was the case. What Julius had felt about it, she had never really understood.

When they had been married about ten years, however, she had begun to see the contrast between what she wanted and what she was expected to want, in a light which was both lurid and alarming. She took to Russian novels, but the discontent of the sad and beautiful creatures she discovered in them had either some quality of resigned melancholy with which she felt herself out of century, or a spirit of sheer recklessness which part of her, jealous of their heartfelt opportunities, could only deplore. Out of all this, because she was primarily a physical creature, because Julius so much adored their daughter, because she felt uncomfortably detached from her body and because nobody then appeared to sweep her off her feet (which in this sense were beginning to kill her), she conceived the desire for a son. Once envisaged, this seemed a perfect solution, providing physical engagement, using her affections, and certainly not running counter to the society which was her world. She was thirty-one; still a year younger than Julius had been when they married.

And so, early in September, on the night train to Inverness, she lay in her bed and called to him in the adjoining sleeper. They had dined, with a bottle of burgundy; it was the beginning of a short holiday, and for a while she had lain simply enjoying the rhythmic rocking of the coach and beneath it the wheels racing over the track with a mathematical roar. The charm of sleeping compartments, she thought, was entirely masculine; the white paint and much mahogany, the navy blankets with scarlet stitching, the heavy glass water-bottle and coarse white linen floor drugget – everything was ingenious, simple and solid, and surprisingly satisfactory. But when she called to Julius, he didn't answer – he was in the next compartment, after all, and the communicating door was only just ajar. Suddenly, she leapt out of her bed, spilt some scent down her neck, took off her wedding ring and knocked on his door.

'I wonder if I might trouble you for a light?'

'But of course.' He had been hanging up his suit and was in his dressing-gown.

'You must think it funny of me, barging in like this, but I can't do without a last smoke before sleeping.'

'Not at all. Do take a seat – Miss – '

'Upjohn: Ruby Upjohn.'

'What a pretty name.' His face was impassive as he handed her his case.

'What a pretty case!'

'You think so?' He gave a modest laugh. 'As a matter of fact if that case could talk, it could tell us a thing or two.'

'Ooh – could it?'

'To cut a long story short, it was given by King Edward to my father in gratitude for some highly confidential service. Do you see?' And he showed her the ER (the case had been her engagement present to him in the days when she was Esme Roland).

'You must be ever so proud, to own a valuable thing like that.'

'Naturally I wouldn't have told you if you hadn't seemed so interested.'

In a minute he would start asking her questions, so she

crossed her legs, blew out her smoke in a manner which she hoped was beguilingly inexpert and said:

'Actually I'm running away!'

'Miss Upjohn!'

'Oh do call me Ruby –' and she launched into her tale about a cruel theatrical manager, at the end of which he exclaimed with glowing eyes:

'Ruby, what a splendid little girl you are! I think this calls for a drink.' He had unscrewed the cap of his silver flask, and handed it to her: 'Let's drink to the brave new life opening out before you in Inverness.'

As she drank some, and choked prettily, he added: 'Don't ask me where the flask came from: it conjures up painful memories never far from my mind, which I should be happier to forget.'

'Ooh, I am sorry: I can't imagine a man like you having troubles.'

'Little Ruby! How touching that you should think that.' He gave a bitter laugh and stared moodily between her breasts.

By the time he had finished telling her about his wife whose whole nature was given to her rock garden, and who consequently had not a spare second over for beginning to understand him 'and I'm a funny, complicated sort of chap' the brandy was drunk, and she could say that it was funny they'd met wasn't it, both lonely, both in trouble. Well – she stood up – she thought that perhaps she'd better be getting back to her bed now. Ruby – Ruby – he had seized her in a vice-like grip, wasn't there anything else she couldn't do without before she went to sleep? 'Captain Fortescue!' 'Call me Valentine!' and she swooned neatly on to the bed, pulling him with her . . .

Sixty miles further north she murmured: 'Dear Captain Fortescue: I like trains –'

'And?'

'I like no poetry –'

'And?'

20

'I want a son not called Valentine.'

And that was when Emma was conceived.

But after that, everything seemed to tail off into a mist of routine, fatigue, anxiety and hectic, immemorable celebration. He grew perceptibly more concerned with the state of the world: he worried about unemployment, disarmament, and Hitler and the monarchy; he insisted on Cressy being educated at home; he worried about China and Spain and Abyssinia; he would not let either of the children listen to the wireless. A good deal of this was reflected in his publishing: he stopped building up his list of young poets for which both he and the house had begun to be distinguished, and started upon symposia of political thought, aspects of international economy, the effects of science and philosophy upon industry, the distinctions between racial and religious prejudice, the psychological implications of leadership and freedom – books which she couldn't even try to read and which in any case hardly sold at all. (His brother, Mervyn, kept the whole thing going with what Julius described either as nice novels or pot-boilers.) He seemed to work harder and harder, had chronic indigestion, slept badly and was only occasionally fun – with the children. By now she had grown accustomed to his ways and the mechanics of their domestically hectic life: traffic out of London at week-ends was becoming frightful, and two households were a perpetual strain. In the end she left Cressy and her governess in the country, and very often Emma as well. No son was a private, nagging refrain, and for the rest of her functions she sometimes felt as though she was endlessly laying an elaborate table for a meal to which nobody in the end sat down. On top of this, some people, at least, began talking of the possibility of another war. It was too much: to slip quietly into middle age without a son, without a husband whom one could any longer meet as a stranger on a train, without a lover . . .

And then, the first May of the war, the last morning of her married life. She had woken early, opened her eyes, and gone down alone, out to a milk-and-gold morning, a pale and tender sky, declining dew, and the sun still rising higher above the exclaiming birds, opening roses with fresh pangs of light, exposing the shabby backs of airy bees and devouring the night sweat of the ground with radiant consolation. She was never in her life entirely to forget the earthly delight of being in such a morning. Afterwards, she thought: a seed, perfection; a drop of mercury, some drip from a celestial sphere, and she looked up at the sun and felt blissfully of no account.

When at last she went back to the house and up to her bedroom, he was standing with his back to her, staring out of the window with a newspaper in his hands.

'Did you hear the guns?'

She had not heard them. There was a long, choked-up silence, and he did not turn round.

'Esme – '

'What is it, Julius?'

'*Don't you know?* "Now all the youth of England are on fire." *Can't you imagine?*'

He turned round, and she saw with an ugly shock that he was crying. The sun from another window shone on him; he stood grey faced, a little paunchy, balding – two deep lines dredged from his nostrils to below his mouth – a worn and ageing creature now rubbing the dry freckled knuckles of his hands in his eyes – incompatible with his anguish which seemed to her only unlovely and discomforting. She felt a surge of anger at the discrepancy between his appearance and his feeling, at the pathos of his uselessness; it didn't *matter* what *he* felt and there was something contemptible in his showing it: he had had his war – why, he did not even have now to face her illicit fears! Aloud, with soothing cruelty she said: 'There's nothing *you* can do.'

'Are you glad of that?' he answered quietly, and a thrill of uncertainty and fear shot through her and was gone. She didn't know.

He picked up the newspaper which had fallen to the ground, and folded it up. 'I must catch my train.' Below them, the sounds of Cressy's morning practice had begun – fine, heroically measured scales, four octaves, the beginning of her three hours. 'Well,' he said again, 'I must catch my train.' He had blown his nose, his eyes were no longer naked; he had withdrawn into his ordinary appearance distinguished by nothing in particular.

'Have a good day. Look after yourself.' Now that he was asking nothing, she was trying to seem ready and kind. She kissed his cheek: he had cut himself shaving. 'Wait a minute: you look awful with blood on you.' She ran her handkerchief under the cold tap and dabbed him up.

'It would be awkward if I looked better. Don't let Emma on to the main road with her bike. She shouldn't do that until she is at least ten. Good-bye Esme.'

She heard Cressy break off in a scale, and imagined her flinging her arms round his neck: she was going through a dramatic phase. With the piano stopped she could hear an aeroplane – limping on one engine by the sound of it. And every now and then, that casual, throaty rumble of the guns which she had not heard when she had been in the garden. She went to the window where he had been, trying to put out of her mind the picture of him which part of her was ashamed of having found distasteful.

The piano had begun again. He would have gone – unless he was saying good-bye to Emma. She began to walk to the telephone; the day had become simply another fine one, and exciting. Had he gone? Something made her go back to the garden window, and he hadn't; he was holding the back of Emma's bicycle, pushing her along towards the garage, his head bent over her stiff little pigtails. She could not stop watching them, feeling so little that either of them felt: Cressy, she knew, adored him, but he adored Emma. At the garage Emma got off her bike, leaned it against the water butt, and threw her arms round his waist until he lifted her up; the bicycle collapsed to the ground behind them, but neither of them took any notice.

She sighed – a tremor of anticipation, of regret, of danger and satisfaction; the tightrope of longing and secrecy and play-acting was quivering for her, and she picked up the receiver.

The room was still the same room, and still too cold. She got up, pulled on her pink mohair dressing-gown as quickly as possible, and went to the same window where he had stood and wept – what was it, twenty (*twenty?*) years ago. The sloping lawn declined from the house, the wide border against the wall, even most of the trees were unchanged. One or two had blown down, one or two had been planted; the rest continued in their apparently ageless prime. This morning there was a heavy white mist above the crystallized grass; the sun was like an enormous frozen firework. There might well be fog, and Emma's train would be late. She put on her mules, and clacked downstairs for the post.

There was one letter. She knew the writing immediately, but it was still an extraordinary shock, and she simply held it for a long time in a kind of mindless amazement, before going upstairs to open and read it.

CHAPTER 3

DAN

HE woke to the pulverizing roar of the washing machine, which seemed to be operating in or on his outer ear. His mouth was like slimy gravel and his eyes like small pieces of scorching plush. The thin, jazzy curtains were letting in light of a second-rate kind and he could hear kids outside. He heaved himself up, found he'd been sleeping with his head pressed against the rotten little cardboard wall – because the bloody machine noise got less at once – and waited to see whether the inside of his head was going to keep still or not. Tea was what he craved: a good strong pot of tea, but she wouldn't hear if he yelled; you got privacy these days with machine noises instead of properly built houses. Nevertheless, he yelled – once – just to see if he still could, and while the noise was still bucketing through his head like some rocks being chucked down hill, she came in, her face all pursed up with ready-made shock.

'Sir Walter Scott awake! Well what a surprise! Do you happen to know the time by any chance incidentally?'

'I don't,' he said carefully, 'happen to have it on me. Oh go on, Dottie – be a sport – make us some tea.'

'You needn't think you're getting it in bed.' She twitched back the curtains and began a kind of useless, irritable tidying of the room, which meant, he knew, that she was nervous as well as angry.

'Look, Dot. You can say anything you like to me if you'll just get the tea first. *Don't* do that to my books.' She was

25

throwing them into his cardboard brown suitcase which lay by the settee on which he was wedged.

'You're a nice one to worry about what other people do with *your* property: it comes well from you that kind of fuss after your lazy *sodden* uproar last night with people banging on walls, and that cat one floor down asking me whatever was the matter last night.'

'Don't answer her – lazy bitch – she's not worth your golden breath.'

'I didn't say: "It was nothing, Mis Green, only my brother got drunk and beat up my husband before my own eyes".' She left the room on this, and he heard the washing machine stop and taps being run.

Oh dear oh dear, he thought. It was a bit hard on poor old Dot – he didn't care a bugger what Alfred thought of it; it was Dottie he loved – his favourite sister – in fact none of this would have happened if he hadn't been so shocked at what Dot had got herself into. Alfred was a little security-loving pipsqueak with no more go in him than a waterlogged ball in the cut. He swung his legs over the settee, and while waiting for his head to subside, looked gloomily round the room. Everything about it seemed terrible to him: the walls covered with three kinds of fidgety wallpaper, the heavily varnished bilious walnut furniture, the art mirror with a wrought-iron frame, the paper flowers nasty, greedy overfed-looking roses in the green vase shaped like a girl wearing a transparent dress which she held up in a festoon on one side, the chair covers made of something which looked like waitresses' greasy hair-ribbons machined together, the zigzag mottled buff tiles where there wasn't a fireplace, and the semi-circular rug – a cubic design in pea-green, saxe and old gold – the telly, the wedding pictures in chrome frames, the mags which were all Dot read now she was married and the collection of Disney china animals, the streaky carpet – modern again – as Dot had proudly pointed out, black, yellow, red, grey, black, yellow, red, grey, black . . .

'Whatever are you doing?' She stood with the tray hitched against her stomach trying to glare at him. She had eyes as violently blue as cornflowers, but there was nothing dreamy about them, he thought: either they were fairly snapping with merriment, or stormy with unshed tears of rage. The love-light in *her* eyes would be something, but trying to make the adjustment was too much for him. One's sister was known: whenever one could see that she was attractive, one wasn't feeling that way. 'I wouldn't catch me breath with a hand on *her* breast – tickled her too often when she was a kid.' Aloud, he said:

'Dot, you're a lovely girl. They don't breed 'em like you in these concrete boxes. They need room for that sort of thing. Some air, and reality, and none of this sex tied up with where's-my-next-meal-coming-from and everything in cans and twin beds. There's more of *you* than meets the eye – you're not the least anybody can do – '

'The last thing that will go with you will be your talk. Jaw, jaw, jaw – your teeth will fall out, and your hair fall off and you won't have a bladder you can call your own, but will you talk!'

The twin beds had made her angry: Alfred didn't like the idea of sharing a bed. She had poured his tea and now she banged it down so that it slopped. He seized her tied-back hair, which was rich and dark-brown and hung well below her ample waist. 'Dottie, listen to me. Drink a cup of tea and let me explain.'

'Wait then, while I get me a cup.' Pride had forbidden her to bring two in the first place. While she was gone, he drank half his scalding cup and pulled on his trousers – he had slept in his shirt. I must be tactful, he thought: I must exercise great tact. It had a shady, foreign sound: plain speaking was his forte, but you couldn't go around knocking women about – even your own sister.

He waited while she poured him another cup and one for herself; he could hear three separate radios. When she had sat

27

down on a hard chair at the table – this was the living-room –
rested her rosy face on one hand which was wrinkled and white
from washing, and was looking elaborately unconcerned and in
a different direction, he knew she was listening and ready.

'About last night, Dot – I'm sorry, and that's all I can say.'
He knew that she would disbelieve a graceful apology; it had to
be wrenched from him for her to accept it. So he added
grudgingly: 'I mean it.'

She said stiffly: 'You'd no call to go losing your temper.'

'I know it, Dottie.'

'Making a beast of yourself, and using brute force.' She was
gaining spirit now: if he could appear unpardonable, she could
forgive him. To aid this he said:

'I didn't drink such a lot, but I didn't have my dinner or my
tea. It was just meant to be a kindly argument.'

'There's no such thing in your language, Daniel Brick. If
people don't agree with you, you always knock them up, and
what's kindly about that? And if they do agree with you, where's
the argument?'

'That's my girl! What a mind for a woman!'

'I'm the only one who can stand up to you and keep you in
your place, and you know it.' She finished severely, but he knew
she was pleased.

Simple, dear girl, he thought. All the complications of
women were on top – a kind of patina; underneath they're as
simple as can be. The trick is never to let them know it. And if
it's a choice between my skill and their simplicity, I know what
suits us both every time: even with my sister. I may not be
tactful, he thought, but by God, I'm cunning. He held out his
cup to her. 'Well – Dot?'

'Well – once more then.' She was deliberately ambiguous
about whether it was forgiveness or another cup of tea. Watching her drain the ugly trashy little square pot with sunken lid
and stunted spout, he suddenly remembered the last real
celebration at home – in the butty boat, with Dot flushed and

lovely, wielding the great brown Measham pot with its decorated glaze of posies, pink and blue flowers and LOVE AT HOME on a white swag around it. When that pot was full, you had to have arms like Dot to lift it. Their mother only used it for occasions . . .

'Will I fetch some hot water, Dan?' She was smiling at him, and for the first time he noticed smoky smudges under her eyes, and wondered if that little bastard had taken it out on her afterwards.

'No. Listen – Dot. I said things all the wrong way last night, but that doesn't mean what I said was wrong. This *is* an awful life, and if Alfred calls this progress and civilization, he must have had a right time of it before. No – *listen*. He's living as though the point about it all is that some day he'll be weak and old and maybe dead – he wants to feather his nest long after he won't be laying in it. He can't *enjoy* that job! He *can't*! So why does he do it? So you can live here in this awful labour-saving little concrete box with hundreds of others above and below and around you like a flock of battery fowls. You don't want half the things you've got, and you certainly can't buy what you need in a place like this. And meantime, while you're waiting for you and Alfred to wither into a bag of bones with a stomach attached, you don't have any fun, any adventure; there's no beauty or entertainment in a dump like this. And, Dot, you're only twenty-five! Think of it! You've got forty years before you'll be sitting in the sun – before you need be thankful for small, hygienic mercies. Your mind will go to seed. You'll get potty with all the days the same and nothing in them.'

She was staring at her cup, but he knew she was shaken, because her eyes were closed and choppy, like a lake with a storm coming. Then she said:

'My days *aren't* all the same.'

He said nothing, knowing that she would flounder in his silence.

'We're saving *up*,' she said; 'we aren't going to stay here all our lives. Alfred wants a house with a garden. He's very fond of roses, and we can't keep a dog here. That's why we're so quiet now.

'We're saving for a car as well. Then Alfred can take me to the country, Sundays.

'We may even travel abroad for a holiday! It isn't just our old age!'

'You didn't used to need a car to get to the country, Dot.'

'I know what you're thinking of! It's time you got those fancy dreams of life on the cut out of your head. We were on a coal run – remember? Dad wasn't a Number One – he wasn't in a position to choose what we carry. It was coal or nothing, right through the war, and after it. All right – a proper man's job, you'll say. But do you know what that was like for our mother? It was every single thing black, with soot and that grease that's always at the back of coal, into everything – over us children, all our clothes, the cabins, you even had a job to keep it off the marge. Every single drop of water to be carried in the cans, all the water to be heated for washing, and however much she washed us or our clothes or the boats, it was never clean for five minutes because the coal dust was always there, over everything. And it wasn't just the coal. Don't you remember the winters? I remember when the lines were frozen stiff in the morning – take the skin off my hand – and standing at the tiller in the butty with a head-wind hours on end; cups of tea and bits of bread at odd times, and nowhere for the young kids, and down in the cabin it hurt getting warm. That's what I remember, and when I think of our mother's life, struggling to feed us on the rotten rations – kippers and cut water – not even what they gave to the rivermen, and working on boats with Dad as well, and she wasn't brought up to it, she wasn't born on the cut, she wanted us all to go to school – she was just so tired out with it all, she didn't have the energy to *think* about anything, just bringing the lot of us up was all she could think to do. When I think of all she went through, I *hate* the boats –

I said I'd get out of them if it killed me. If I'd married Sam Brownie I'd be like our mother by now with my life one long battle against time, and money, and dirt. That's the country for you, in the boats. Do you remember when that inspector came down, Dan? To find out which of us could read and write? And Mam said about me, "She can write lovely, but she can't read what she writes." I was twelve then and I hated that man for trying to get at her, and that's the only reason I wanted to learn to read, so if he came again he couldn't say anything. *I* had no other fancy to read.'

'You learned all right when I taught you – sharp as a needle you were.'

'I notice *you* didn't stay with the boats, Dan, for all your talk about what a wonderful life it was, and the fuss you made when I came ashore to work in the caff. I sent Mam money each week you know – ten bob every week.'

'I know Dot – she told me.' It was just in his throat to tell her about his books then, but he'd planned the surprise for so long that he wouldn't spoil it now. Somehow, her long outburst about their life when she had been his young sister – all true, but only the half of it – had taken away his energy for making the proposition to her that he had been milling about in his mind since the previous night. But his head ached, and he had also gone to sleep with the feeling that this Friday held something fateful in store for him: feelings of this kind were rare, and he never questioned them. So, in the end, he asked her. She *was* his favourite sister, and he couldn't bear to see her being wasted on that little, mincing bureaucrat.

Still heaving from effort, she watched him with open, anxious eyes, until he reached the end, when they darkened; she made the deliberately angry gesture of folding her arms and cried:

'You've no *call* to say such things of Alfred! Where's the harm *he's* ever done to you?'

'It's you I'm thinking of, Dot.'

'I can see you're not thinking of him!'

'It's just that there's so much more to life than you imagine – than you'll ever get in this – '

But she leaned towards him with a smile which suddenly showed the true colour of her gaiety and said: 'I don't imagine it, Dan – it's here! Imagination's what you fall back on – like a piece of cold bacon.'

This time, he could not admire her – he was too genuinely astonished. Her lovely, capable arms were still folded across her body, and looking down at it she said in tones of practical comfort: 'Anyways, I've no longer just myself to please – I've a baby on the way, to be born the first week of May.'

An old, natural, innocent triumph – he could only retreat from it. 'Looking at her with mixed feelings,' he thought, as he recognized another printed label remark attaching itself to his life. The idea was an outrage to him. She ought to be the Virgin Mary – *how* he would have cared for her then! She had no idea how kind he could be with a good reason for it.

'Alfred makes me think of baked beans,' he said aloud and absently.

She eyed him warily, not knowing how to take this: she liked baked beans.

But Dot made him feel about lovely, rolling women in pictures he had seen at the Tate Gallery by the river: firm, candid, festive girls; hot-summer, Sunday women – out to enjoy themselves, in to be enjoyed: creatures about whom one felt a kind of sporting sentiment. He would rather Dot had married anyone than that little runt; if he hadn't been in hospital at the time, you wouldn't have seen Alfred for dust. Poor Dot – perhaps women just couldn't tell the difference between one man and another.

'Well – all I can say is I wish it was mine.'

'Don't let me ever hear you say such a thing. The idea!' But he could see that secretly she was not altogether displeased.

'Will you name him after me, Dot?'

'Alfred wants to call him Clarence, after his Dad.'

'*Clarence!*' He was almost too shocked to jeer.

'And Mabel if it's a girl.'

'I'll have a word with him about that!'

'No you won't, Dan. He wants you to go.'

'He . . . *wants?* . . .'

'He doesn't want you here any more. He wants you gone when he gets back to his tea. He says he and you don't see eye to eye about anything. He says you ought to have a proper job and writing's no good if nothing happens to it when you've written it. 'Tisn't any good arguing when he gets upset, it goes to his stomach. He says he won't have you eating his food and insulting him. He says poetry was for olden times and people don't want it any more. He says you got gypsy blood . . .'

'Shut *up!*' he yelled. 'I don't want to hear any more of Alfred's second-hand opinions third-hand from you. You must be mad to live with anyone so awful! He's like some silly little bit of machinery, ticking away, turning out hundreds of the same trashy little objects nobody knows what to do with. He hasn't got any blood at all! Squeeze him and all you'd get'd be a few drops of Wincarnis which wouldn't stop a postmistress from getting 'flu. Give me Romany blood any day. Alfred's got no more tradition than a paper clip – he's not worth an inch of your hair on a Friday night. If you come with me, *I'll* look after the child – the both of you – I can do it easy. It's your whole life, Dottie – you'd see something of me you don't know about –' but he saw from her kinder face that she was stubborn, and felt tears like pain in his eyes.

'You got no job, no money, Dan.'

'About six miles from here, I have only to walk in to a building and ask, and they would give me fifty pounds.' That impressed her, and to rub it in, he added: 'I could ask for more – another fifty – but I wouldn't – they'd have to pay what I asked, and that's what I'd ask in one go.'

She seemed to believe in him then, but it made no difference,

so he had to leave. She cried when he went, and begged him to
write to her: this emphasized their separation as though one of
them was going on some journey – which was funny, because
she was stuck in that awful flat for life as far as he could see, and
he didn't know *where* he was going, because he hadn't anywhere
to go. And so, as he hadn't anywhere – he'd had to give up the
room when he got sick of the job – and as it was one of those
mornings when the air, like mildewed chain-mail, was gripping
his chest so that he moved slowly and swallowed a good deal in
order not to start coughing – and by God, the taste was like
sour bacon rinds – and as he seemed mysteriously to have only
three and tenpence and the beginnings of a forged season ticket
which he'd got tired of making because he couldn't make up his
mind what would be the most useful journey, he got rid of his
suitcase and went, meekly paying his fares, to Holborn, to Great
Queen Street, to his Publishers (they always had a capital letter
in his mind), they being the only people left in London after
Dottie who knew who he was.

It was awkward at first: they didn't seem to know. He had
announced himself with a flourish to a motherly old peach who
sat by a switchboard knitting in a colour that he could have told
her wouldn't suit a rabbit in a Disney film. She looked blank:
asked if he had an appointment with anyone. He said he never
made appointments, which was true, he'd never made one in
his life. Who did he wish to see? He named his editor. 'He's not
in this week,' she said, but he could see that he'd made his mark
by knowing a name she knew. So he named the first name on
the imprint. 'He's dead,' she replied in the same neutral voice,
and then looked as though one of them had dropped something.
He had begun to sweat: 'Well, someone,' he said. He couldn't
be kept waiting, and so palpable a lie seemed to strike her as she
began to fiddle with the switchboard.

'You go right upstairs to the top and the first door on the
right.'

'You don't happen to have an extra strong peppermint on you?'

But she shook her head, looking dazed: 'I'm sorry.'

He took the stairs slowly, and in order to take his mind off coughing, he concentrated upon mourning Dottie. He wasn't used to stairs. When he reached the top, the door on the right was open and a girl stood in its way. The first thing he noticed was her legs, because she was wearing stockings like some of those pictures that had reminded him of Dot. But she wasn't like Dot – she was a skimpy little thing with a pale London face and she was holding out a hand and saying in a small cool upper-class voice: 'How do you do?'

'How d'you do?' he muttered, and wondered how she knew he'd come off the boats.

There was hardly space in the room for both of them to stand, she remarked, but he was suspicious of her, and thought she managed to make even this sound like an advantage.

'My name is Emma Grace: I believe you were asking for my father. Did you know him?'

He shook his head. 'It was just a name. I had to say someone.'

She frowned and he noticed her extraordinary eyes – funny, he'd never seen that before – poor girl – he wondered if it made her feel a freak . . .

She was offering him a cigarette. He shook his head, and watched her light hers. The door behind him burst open and a woman in a blue overall reached round him to put a cup of tea on the table.

'Sorry dear – the saucers all get used on the cats.'

The tea already had the cold fog of cooling milk – funny what a lot of drinks were brown . . . She was asking him whether he would like some. He shook his head again: there was getting to be a fog on the whole enterprise. The woman disappeared as explosively as she had arrived, and there was a short silence while the murky air settled and the papers she had all over the table lay down. She cleared her throat: it didn't sound as though she was used to doing it.

'Now, what can I do for you, Mr Brick?'

'I come about the money.'

'What money?'

'All that money you owe me. It runs well into a hundred pounds, but I don't want all of it today. Just some, and a few questions answered, so I know where I am.'

'Mr Brick, I'm sorry to seem so stupid, but do we publish you, because I don't seem to know . . .'

'You've got two books of mine and six agreements to publish them.'

'Yes? I mean I'm sure we have, of course, I'm awfully sorry I haven't read your work; we divide it up you see, so not everybody has to read everything.' She took a sip of her tea, and added rather hopelessly, 'Things *get* divided up: that's why I didn't know about you.'

He wasn't used to admissions and began to feel sorry for her. He felt in his pockets for the neat packed-up lump of sugar he'd taken from London Airport. 'I don't suppose they put sugar in that tea. This lump has probably travelled miles in an aeroplane.' He put it by her cup. 'Packed against damp, I shouldn't wonder.'

'It's very kind of you, but I don't take sugar, actually.'

'Don't you *actually*? Well, I'll have it back then.' He wouldn't have taken it in the first place if he hadn't particularly liked it. 'It's wonderful the trouble they take nowadays about details: they have a bird's-eye view of the lot. It all goes with splitting the atom: there's detail for you, if you don't look at the consequences. In the end I expect they'll freeze people in squares and travel them in paper with the Company's name on it. Anything might come out of a detail like this.'

She was staring at him, each eye equally amazed.

36

'It wasn't rude,' he said; 'your voice is so – orderly – I had to see if I can copy it.'

'And can you?'

'And can you?' he echoed. 'Not yet, but I will in time.'

'Time,' she said, shaking her head as though to empty it. 'Your money. I'll have to go downstairs.' She got up. 'Do you mind waiting here?'

When she had shut the door (couldn't she *afford* proper stockings?), he hurried through an examination of everything that lay on her desk. Rather like a teacher's – nothing nice, except for a marbled green pencil with wood that smelled good and foreign. He put it in his pocket, turned to the telephone and picked up the receiver. A girl answered it, and when he said nothing, asked what he wanted.

'The Tower of London.'

There was a pause, and she said, who was that, and was it a joke.

'It's on the River Thames and no joke. This is the Head Beefeater. I've written a book about the Life of a Beefeater, so naturally I'm here and it stands to reason I want to speak to them.'

'Want to speak to who?'

'Any other old Beefeater you can knock up. Hurry, my dear, or they may become extinct.'

There was another pause, and then she said: 'It still sounds funny to me.'

Trying to copy Emma, he said:

'In a job like yours you should be grateful for entertainment of any kind.'

'Replace your receiver: I'll call you when I'm through to them.' Her voice sounded icy, but beaten, and he put back the receiver grinning. Real green penguin dialogue that – quite a job to shift it into actual life. Actually, actually, euacherley – he couldn't get it dead like her. He'd never been able to conduct his telephoning sitting down before – he only used telephone boxes for some fun, like other people used squibs.

She was a long time. But then, *he* wouldn't cough up a sum like fifty pounds in a hurry. He took a sheet of paper, got the green pencil out of his pocket and wrote: '"Is anybody there?" said the Traveller.' 'The shadow of an ordinary man' (*Alfred* – to the shadow). There was a pause while he digested his dislike of that jumped-up little cock-of-the-concrete-roost: then he wrote 'Journeys end with lovers meeting', 'So come into the garden Maud', and put it on the table where she would see it. That would show her he knew a thing or two. Just as he was wondering if he couldn't have done better at this game if he gave it a bit more thought, she came back, and glided round him to her chair.

'Sorry if I seemed a long time. I had to go down to Accounts.' She handed him an envelope.

'Here – what's this?' It felt suspiciously thin, and he opened it. A single piece of paper, with printing and writing – some sort of money order – not a bit what he had in mind, but before he could think of how to deal with this piece of crooked dealing, the telephone rang, and he watched her face change from attention to mystery and then suspicion as she listened to whatever was being said. Finally, and with dangerous sweetness, she said:

'Mr Brick, I think this call is being made at your request. Which department of the Tower of London do you want, because they all have different telephone numbers?'

He felt himself getting hotter under the collar and tried to outstare her: *she* wasn't one to see a joke, and with all this gap he'd lost his taste for it.

'Me? How could that be? *I* don't know anyone at the Tower of London: I don't come from this town at all.' He coughed, on purpose, and then couldn't stop. 'Excuse me – '

By the time he had managed to stop, she had finished with the telephone and was staring at him and looking so anxious he had to smile. He rubbed the sweat off his forehead and said: 'It's all right. I expect with all the books you read you get fancy ideas about TB; well, I have the laugh on you there. Have you by any chance got a nice strong peppermint handy?'

She jerked open a drawer and hunted about.

'Only fudge, I'm afraid.' She held out a battered paper bag. 'It's coffee.'

'Kept it too long, haven't you?'

'It's home-made,' she answered stiffly.

'It looks like furry sand.' He put a piece in the side of his mouth and waited for the scalding, salt taste to settle down his throat. 'See here. About this.' He waved the piece of paper.

'It's a cheque, made out to you for fifty pounds. Isn't that what you wanted?'

'It's not what I came for.' He had begun to feel both angry and frightened: he didn't like girls having the upper hand about life and he'd never seen a cheque before – how was he supposed to know what to do with it?

Suddenly, she smiled, for the first time, and he felt that there was something somewhere the same about them: this made the difference enjoyable and mysterious. She was younger than he – a London girl who worked indoors with books and money . . .

'If you can wait until my lunch hour, I'll come out with you and we'll cash it. That is, if you've got time?'

'I've got time.'

'If you like, we could get a hundred ten shilling notes.'

He looked at her sharply, but she just wanted to please – she wasn't making fun of him.

'Are you lunching with anybody?'

He shook his head.

'Because I'm allowed to take our authors out to lunch sometimes. It's lovely for me, because then I get a much better lunch. We could go to the bank afterwards.'

'All right. I'd be pleased to.' He noticed how, when she seemed unsure of herself, she used the same word twice: she

must have done this before, or he wouldn't be noticing it
now . . .

'Would you like something to read?' She was indicating the
dusty shelves crammed with books which were sooty and
warped, and made him think of prunes laid out to dry.

'I'm not much of a reading man.' But he got up obediently
to look for something while she started writing. He ought to
have been feeling rather fine: fifty pounds for the asking and a
meal thrown in *and* a girl of a kind he'd not ever had much to
do with, but he had begun to suffer from the sense of shock
which nearly always follows an escape from something: the
alternative to this cheerful situation blared in his mind. Supposing he had just got the fifty pounds? Supposing he hadn't even
got that? The day outside was the same, and, like it or not, it
was one of his days, to be followed by a chain of others which
bound him to his life. At the moment they presented an
enormous void, marked only by daylight and street lamps. What
was the point of money – of this great place where he knew no
one? He hadn't just been thinking of Dot – he'd been clinging
to her. The damage of two years in a hospital in a cocoon of
weakness and irresponsibility, wrapped in events over which he
had no control, was suddenly manifest. 'It's not what happens,
it's when you realize it.' All that time he had lived within the
prescribed goal: this would be good for you, this would be bad,
this was something you had to be careful about. Eat well, don't
smoke, and a fuck was equal to a five-mile walk. That had all
been on the landslide of being able to take one's body for
granted, when one was still rejoicing in the extreme, merciful
difference, when one could remember exactly what it had been
like to be just a hulk of pain – agony smudged by drugs –
complaining, trying to joke, crying because one was ashamed of
having complained, sullen because one had been weak enough
to cry – no days and nights then, just time with no size or shape
to it – the occasional sparks of gratitude when their kindness
reached him, the nightmare troughs when they seemed to be

urging him to move, to drink, to do anything which seemed beyond his bounds of endurance . . . He was sweating from the memory. Occupational therapy – that was how he'd started writing – a psychological accident – surely not how most people started to do such a thing; and this jolted him back to his present, these few hours of sitting in her office with her, having a meal somewhere posh and going to the bank – it was like the last bit of ground, the overhang of a cliff over nothing: 'Good-bye,' she would say, 'pleased to have met you'; no, that was like Alfred, although he never was pleased to have met anybody, but she'd say something, and then disappear back into the orderly privileged life she looked as though she had.

When he turned round to her, he found that she was already regarding him: was neither writing nor reading. Surprise at this, and some idea of his own dilemma, provoked him into asking:

'What do writers *do*? When they're not writing, I mean. How do they spend the rest of their lives?'

'It depends whether they're rich or poor. Most of them have some sort of work.'

'What sort of work?'

'Oh – a lot of them have literary fringe activities. Some of the women have houses and children and things like that.'

'I'm not a woman,' he said sternly.

She didn't smile – just said: 'Do you mean what do I think *you* ought to do?'

'I mean what *is* there?'

'Oh. Well – what did you do before you started writing?'

'I was brought up as a boatman.'

'A boatman?'

'Have you ever heard of Fellows, Morton and Clayton?'

She shook her head. She didn't know everything, then.

'Well they were the biggest canal carrying company. My Dad worked for them. The whole family worked for them.'

'Do you mean like Painted Boats and Emma Smith?'

'I don't mean for a lark in an emergency: I mean it was our life – my Dad; his Dad and on back – before engines when they had Number Ones and mules, before railways when everone needed the boats. That's all history; I'm talking about this day.'

'Where do you live now?'

'I don't. I had a job at the airport, but I couldn't find the enjoyment in it so I give it up.'

'What were you doing?'

He sat down: the thought of it made him tired.

'Bricks. I was carting bricks in a barrow. It wasn't a whole job. If they give me something to build I might have found the sense in it. But I just moved bricks from one part of the site to another part – never saw where they came from or where they went to. It was just a meal ticket – no life to it.'

'I do *see*,' she said earnestly. 'It's what most people feel about their work.'

'Oh *no*!' He felt something like panic at her understanding so easily. '*You* don't know anything about *that*: hundreds – thousands of people have no idea of it: they have fine lives filled up with change and success and concern – once you've discovered the trick of what you are, you just have to live up to it. That's it, isn't it?' He felt frantic for her agreement: this attentive silence was simply blotting out his horizons. 'Take – anything! Take trees, for instance. They're on the move all their lives – moving up, in air, and down in earth, changing, making growth, they never stop until they get chopped or fall, and I'm not talking about murder and death. I'm just talking about how one is from day to day. All life must be some kind of movement or other, only we're meant to see why we're going, it doesn't just happen to us – *we* – *move* – isn't that the point?'

He had been speaking with his eyes fixed on her face, wanting her to argue, to understand, to be the exception, to show him that he was one; and while these, and many other requirements of her divided, dissolved, and recurred, she started to speak, checked herself, and got to her feet.

'Give me my coat.' She indicated the back of the door. 'You'll have to hold it for me – I get stuck with this thick jersey.'

He followed her down the stairs, past the knitter at the switchboard and out into the street in a silence charged with protest. She set off purposefully, walked fast for a few minutes, with her hands in her pockets and little streams of warm white breath drifting round the edge of the scarf which obscured most of her face. Then, in a voice too quick for the casual words, she said:

'I usually go home to Sussex for the week-ends. I catch the four twenty from Charing Cross. If you've nothing better to do, you might like to come too?'

CHAPTER 4

CRESSIDA

WHEN Cressy was alone, she became quite good, and very different company. She had a strong sense of ridicule, and found herself a continuously rewarding subject. In company, she was a serious romantic, applying her mind to aspects of life which do not depend on thought for their success. She therefore struck emotional attitudes and then found it difficult, or impossible, to keep still in them: people pushed her and she wobbled, which few attitudes will stand. Although she was usually entertained after the event, at the time (and her life attracted endless variations upon no more than two themes) whichever it was loomed so large that she had no proportion about it – became a straw in a whirlpool, the only pebble on the beach: played desperately to the gallery and forgot completely who she was. Nobody had ever really enjoyed the best of her, and it was this that made her sift and search through even unlikely material in her constant pursuit of someone with whom she could communicate, could share her amusement, could be herself whoever she happened to be at the time. She was amiable, physically attractive, possessed of small private means and connected with the arts, and although one would have said that these advantages perfectly equipped her for settling down with some pleasant, overworked, civilized man (somebody whose illusions had been knocked off him, like the celebrated corners at school), this had so far never been the case. Her own nature and one or two unfortunate early events blocked the way. Leaving these aside, her very advantages were, of course, capable of more than one direction. All men, and very many women, hold the view that women are designed to please – an idea of elastic luxury: Cressy, with her amiable temperament, was incapable of forgoing the attempt at least, often with insidious success. Pleasing meant approximating to the man's idea of the sort of woman his position and intelligence owed him, and as there is nothing more rigorous than anybody's idea of their rights, the image could never be sustained. Her physical attractions made this part of it worse: she was sometimes beautiful in that dark, restless, desperate manner which encouraged heroics, the classical dishonesties arising out of situations which had been provoked by appearances rather than desire or experience. She looked as though she ought to be, had been, might be somebody's major love, and for many men who had earlier bitten off exactly what they could chew, this was an irresistible challenge. Her private means simply offered her a wider variety of opportunities, and the fact that she was a – very minor – professional pianist meant that each man returning to, or embarking upon, the cud of married life could console himself with the fact of her Art – such a comfort, so constructive. If it was not a solace it damn well ought to be.

For twenty years she seemed to herself continually to have been starting something, with the idea, the intention, the hope of it lasting, until sheer duration had become an abstract quality that she applied instinctively, indiscriminately, to any new relationship. In the wake of her desire for an emotional structure, however rocky, she towed her career, feeling sure that it could only fulfil the promises of her early dreams about it if all else was running smoothly (a man in love with her and with whom she was in love). When love failed her, she nearly always turned to music (after a period of nightmare vacuum) and met the next man with the appearance of being committed to it. She would have been working steadily for weeks, months, occasionally even a year, and the impression she gave was unintentionally quite false. An attractive, serious, dark girl with a pleasant talent, trying to make the most of it; unattached and with enough money for her lessons, a beautiful instrument, and clothes of ravishing simplicity and elegance for recitals at the Wigmore Hall. Had been married; husband killed in the war. No children. Sad, but infinitely intriguing – and convenient. Surely there must be a lover lurking about? Some cynical, selfish fellow who ruined sensitive intelligent girls by spending two evenings a week with them – preying upon their finer feelings with anything from money, the right sexual touch to downright lies about the future? But there never was, for Cressy was passionately monogamous. So whoever it was took possession, spent two evenings a week with her (and sometimes more, but they couldn't be sure from week to week – they'd telephone anyhow so don't go out: and, poor fool, she never would), and preyed upon her feelings with whatever equipment they could bring to bear.

'The world's sucker,' she thought standing by the window of her bedroom. 'I believe everyone. There is absolutely nothing that any of them say that I don't instantly accept as the truth – only varnished a little because I also believe that they don't want to hurt my feelings.'

She had remained where Emma had left her: her tears had stopped, and the urge to telephone had begun. It always started as a casual thought: 'Why not ring him up? You'll tell in an instant by his voice how things are' – and was always sharply dismissed: idiotic; lack of pride; taking things too seriously. Back it came: 'I *am* lacking in pride; I always take things too seriously – if this equates with being idiotic, that's what I am.' What harm could it do? He would be alone in his flat; never got to the office before ten. If she was married to him, she would be making those delightful, domestic, *little* plans with him that she was certain married people (in love, of course) made with each other. Even when she *had* been married, she had not been able to make them. Occasionally, she and Miles had tried to imagine their life together after the war, but they had been large plans – deliberately vague and grandiose. They had always been shy of each other – had never parted, she realized, without the distinct and real possibility of it being for the last time, and this fear – which was almost never, and then only obliquely, mentioned – smothered their marriage into something composed of second thoughts, short-term arrangements, and shallow, crisis acceptances. She had married at eighteen, in a trance of shock: her father had only just died, and there was no one else to prevent her. She had married at all costs to get away from a place with which all her associations had become unbearable; where all those nearest her had suddenly, without any warning, stepped out of their familiar roles and revealed themselves as horribly unrecognizable – stark in their treachery.

She had been seventeen – dreamy, untried, her mind narrowly contented, her preoccupations simple, the older parts of her taste and experience concentrated upon music. There were no finer shades of feeling then: there was good, some bad, and then mystery; there was love and there was nothing of the kind; people meant what they said and said all that they meant; one moved along one's enormous lifeline to some splendid but unknown destination, but the direction was none the less laid, like railway track. To be a pianist, to have parents who were the landscape of one's society, a sister so much younger that she accentuated the delightful privileges of being grown up, and *then* – to discover the incalculable joys and agonies of being secretly in love . . .

Afterwards, she used the abrasive comfort of at least not having made a fool of herself. Nowadays, another part of her wondered whether she had not compensated for this by making a fool of herself ever since.

Emma's question about whether, if he was free, she would marry Dick, had produced her stock reply (the question was one to which she had for many years now accustomed herself), but later, inside, it woke her out of a stupor into some confusion. This morning, knowing that with Dick she was on

47

an extreme edge, that the layers of scenes and reconciliations were almost worn through (although he would, of course, return from Rome, and to her), she tried to see where any change in what had become a painfully familiar situation might be made. But he would return; defensive, truculently overtired, patronizing, breezy: 'Well? How have you been amusing yourself?' and would be met by a coldness which inadequately concealed the violence within her. The breezy lies would be rejected, the angry justifications denied, she would be stripped of her assumed indifference and stand exposed in her resentment, like a horrible fancy dress. And what lay beneath the resentment (mutual by now, as it was frighteningly contagious: he would have held out his hand for hers, she would have touched it with icy, unforgiving fingers)? What for years she had called love – with variations admittedly – but she had always ennobled these situations with that word: now she was beginning to recognize them merely as various translations of a longing to appear before one person, at least, as she wished both to be seen and to be. It was from *this* position that she had always imagined herself loving: to be pronounced rich before giving; to be given all the benefits of her own doubts; to be always within the understanding sight and earshot of another person – this would engender love, and meanwhile, surely the imitation of any virtue was not so much a dishonesty as an encouragement? But the whole thing broke down because neither she nor Dick (nor Edmund, Joe, René, Gilbert, Tom, Sebastian, Nils, Graham nor Harry) had ever managed to preserve their illusions about one another (had always failed at different points to sustain the beloved image they had been practising to become, and were *ad interim* trying to present). Only love, she felt, was worth seeking and then keeping: but she seemed to have been hampered by not being quite sure what it was, and had therefore attributed it to everything to be on the safe, dangerous side. If she had remained married, would none of this have happened? But the difficulty about those months was that, apart from their brevity, none of her memories of them seemed to be connected in the least with marriage, and Miles dying had set a seal of unreality upon the whole affair.

If she had been asked what was her sharpest memory of those few months of being married to Miles, she would unhesitatingly have answered 'homesickness'. (She never *was* asked, as people made a whole set of false assumptions, based on sentiment, lust, and a kind of jingoistic nostalgia for the brave boys and their splendid little wives and widows of the last war, and mere homesickness would have shocked them.) It had come as a shock to her, and at the time, of course, she suffered it without a word to Miles – or anyone else.

Miles had been commanding an MTB which was building at Cowes, and until the trials were completed, he was able to lie ashore with his wife. This meant that he could at least dine and sleep with her, leaving her at eight o'clock in the morning, sleepy, warm as a bird, and, he fondly imagined, contented. But Cressy had never stayed in an hotel in her life. The first morning it took her at least five minutes to understand that he would be out for the whole day – would not see her until late in the evening. 'But what shall I *do*?' she had asked in panic.

He looked nonplussed. 'I should look at the Island. It's very pretty, really,' he added: he had sailed there before the war.

'But how do I have lunch?'

'Go down to the dining-room and ask for it. Damn!' He was shaving fast with a cut-throat razor, and the simplicity of her question had made him cut himself. 'Really, darling!' he had said, as he stuck a piece of cotton wool to the blood.

She had lain in bed watching him cover himself with expert speed: vest and pants – he looked like somebody in the Gaumont British News; black socks and suspenders added a circus air as he jabbed his cuff links through the starched holes of a clean white shirt: buttoned into it, he became like the charming dope in a glossy American film comedy; a pause while he combed and parted and smoothed his fine blond hair, and then, after knotting the rather greasy black tie, stared into the shaving-glass with that intimate but curiously unseeing gaze that congeals to intensity in certain kinds of self-portraits. He seized the black trousers that chinked of money, and dragged them on: the braces hitched added an appearance of outrage or farce. It was not until he was in the black jacket with its two wavy rings of gold lace that he assumed his usual daytime recognizable anonymity. She had watched him, begging inside that he wouldn't be so quick, and wondering how on earth to get through the day on such scant information; then he had bent over her, kissed her ear and a strand of hair – 'Have a good day' – and gone, and she was watching the shut door. 'Like dogs,' she thought. 'It isn't that they love people so much: they're just lost indoors without them.'

She had lain on her back for the first crowding minutes of his absence. Lying on her back was not natural to her; she slept like that, and the position – since everything that Miles did to her occurred in the dark with the additional unreality of no intelligible sound – simply engendered thoughts of death, thence the war, the facts that Miles might get killed and that she was now married to him, and finally, that she was committed (among other things) to the mystery of living in an hotel. It was only five past eight: very nearly twelve hours had somehow to be spent. The bedroom was not particularly small, but she had the uneasy feeling that one was only meant to be in bed in it. Better get up and go out to look at the Island.

But outside were nothing but men: in fact – she later discovered – about sixty thousand of them, although they seemed more because there were hardly any women. She made her way through the narrow main street of Cowes with the notion that if she reached the river, she might see Miles on his ship; but the sheer weight of masculine interest, both strident and irresponsible, turned her back. Being stared at by people she did not know was far worse than the whistles, cat-calls, unintelligible asides and the kind of laughter which implied greater knowledge of her than she cared or dared to have of them. Thoughts like: 'My legs are bare', 'My hair is too long', 'Well, anyway, I'm wearing a ring', 'I could do up another button on my shirt' succeeded one another with discomforting speed. ('I don't know anybody on the whole island excepting Miles, and I don't know where he is.') All these men, unassailably sheltered behind the distinction of being men and the anonymity of wearing the same clothes, presumably knew who they were and seemed to know what they thought about her . . . Her legs were trembling above her steps as though she wasn't quite sure how far away the pavement was; she felt breathless and there seemed nowhere safe for her eyes. She wasn't seeing the Island at all: better go home. ('But I can't spend the whole day in *bed*!')

Turning back involved encountering some of them again: now they pretended that they knew her, which was different, but worse. Round a sharp corner, she came upon a small sweet shop: the door was open and because there was an old woman behind the counter she went in and decided to buy pear drops. They were the first thing that she had bought with Miles's money and she wondered whether he would mind. 'Perhaps I needn't tell him.' He didn't like sweets, but ninepence wasn't much.

When she got back to the hotel, the chambermaid was doing their room; she wandered down to somewhere marked Lounge. *Lounge*? It was filled with very uncomfortable chairs, large framed photographs of J-class racing yachts labelled *Rainbow*, *Endeavour*, *Astra* and so on; there was also an upright piano which was locked. She sat down with an eight-weeks-old copy of the *Yachting World* – and she didn't see how it could have been very interesting when it came out – and a pink pear drop. There was a clock with a boring tick. It was a quarter past nine, and as her hair caught in one of the brass studs on the back of her chair, she suddenly felt sick, and longed for home, for Emma, her own bedroom and their yellow Labrador, for the

beautiful, gentle Blüthner that had been her father's last present
to her, for the known intimacies of family life when privacy had
been an adventure instead of this out-of-her-element isolation
marked by visits of a friendly but incomprehensible stranger.
That was how the home-*sickness* began – and it actually made
her feel sick as well as frightened and sad. Perhaps it was the
war that made it so difficult to see the point of marriage; after
all, dozens – probably *millions* – of people got married when
they were eighteen. 'It can't be my age.' Well, she *couldn't* have
stayed at home, so it was silly to be homesick. She got the pencil
out of her pocket and began making a list of possible things to
do out on this limb. 'Read books; knit pullover for Miles; see if
piano will unlock; go on trying to go for walks.' She couldn't
think of anything else, and it was twenty past nine . . .

It was ten o'clock, and Dick would now be at his office: she was
safe from being able to telephone him. She had a bath, and
steeled herself to go into the sitting-room, where they had spent
that interminable, circuitous evening – round and round something so painful, and true and *small*, that neither had the
courage to touch it.

'I hate the way *things* stay the same,' she thought, when she
had opened the door. Cushions stayed dented; handkerchiefs
thrust and crumpled, the sugar in the bottom of cups, the
Haydn sonatas open at the F major: it could all stay like this for
a hundred years: tactless, immutable, triumphantly inanimate,
lending itself to the pathetic hysteria of people like Miss
Havisham and Queen Victoria. She cleared up the room with a
burst of energy which became progressively more savage, until
she reached the F major. But you couldn't, she found, after
trying, be savage with any opening statement of such graceful
confidence: she stopped playing and read the rest of the open
pages. Haydn defied ill nature. 'I love him,' she thought: 'it's a
calm, respectful business.' If only, last night, she could have

simply said: 'Do you love me?' then, perhaps, he would have been able to say, 'Not enough.' Why hadn't she done that? Perhaps then she would have found that it was all right – even better – with his not loving her enough, so long as they both knew it: better than this emotional jockeying for even more precarious false positions. He wanted her, and he was the kind of man who was rather proud of feeling affectionate about people he wanted: 'I'm *so* fond of you!' he would say, with an air of near complacent surprise, as one showing off a rare talent just discovered: *his* back and her head. Well – she was no better. She wanted him, and she wanted him to be in love with her, and her failure nagged at and damaged all pure feeling, consideration – let alone love – for him. He was not – and she knew it – honestly the man for her, but when she was with him, or even talking to Emma *about* him, something (perverse? starved?) insisted on pretending that he was. She wanted attention and pity for that because her real deprivation ran too deep for anyone to see, and alone with it she became extremely frightened. 'Anything really good has the appearance of ease,' she thought sadly, and resolutely turned her attention to Haydn.

The telephone rang at twelve. She had worked two hours; that muscle in her right forearm was aching again – working too long on the four-bar trill had done it – and anyway, she had to lunch with her sister-in-law. She picked up the telephone and spoke to it: there was a pause, and then she heard the button being pressed and the sound of coins dropping. Dick! She was back where she had started her day.

'Cressy? Is that you? I thought you'd like to know that the conference is due to end at four on Sunday afternoon: I'll try to catch a plane back about six. See you then. Don't be disappointed if I can't make it.'

'No – I won't be.' Something fiendishly stupid in her made her add: 'But you will try, won't you?'

'Of course. Everything fine?' It couldn't be less than that: couldn't just be all right.

'Yes.'

'Good.' He sounded heartily unconvinced. 'Things always seem better in the morning.'

Oh no, they don't. She said: 'I don't know.'

'Take care of yourself.'

'I'll probably go ho – away for the week-end.'

'Splendid idea. I shall have had dinner on the plane, so don't worry about that.' She knew that he called living alone in the flat moping: she was *hating* him – simply *hating* him.

'Anything you'd like me to bring you?'

'A bottle of Alpestri.' She knew that that would be a nuisance.

'Alpestri?'

'Al-pes-tri.'

'Do my best. Must go now. Is it a scent?' he added.

'A drink. It settles the stomach.'

'What's wrong with your stomach?'

'Nothing. My stomach's all right. Fine.'

'Fine,' he repeated. 'Well – I must be off.' Where *to*? For God's sake, at twelve o'clock, where *to*?

'Have a good lunch,' she said, and put down the receiver. That had not been at all all right. I'm turning into a first-class bitch. I just hate him when he's breezy; I can't be breezy back: only bitchy or hurt. And I bet he prefers me bitchy. This has got to stop: it's no good each of us wanting the other to be somebody else. But I wish he was, she thought later, rummaging hopelessly in her untidy drawers for a belt: I wish we were both quite different: completely different, and madly in love.

Miles's sister was called Ann Jackson. She was tall and bony and faded: even as a young girl (which was when Cressy had met her) she had had that hopelessly muted appearance described by women who don't like competition as good taste. Her hair, fine like Miles's, but lifeless brown; her eyes neither blue nor grey and inhibited to a minimum of expression; her voice both quiet and flat, her body in the main spare and shapeless, good ankles and beautiful hands failing somehow to redeem it. When Cressy had first met her she had been married to a Major Jackson for six months. She had been wearing a pale-blue lambswool sweater, a grey flannel skirt with an uneven hem, and a string of graded, rather small pearls. Her husband, a Commando, was away, and somebody – probably Miles – had commiserated loudly that she had only spent three weeks of her marriage with him. Afterwards, Cressy had sharply remembered Ann's quiet, unemotional voice as she said: 'Actually, we were really awfully lucky to have that.' Major Jackson had been on the St Nazaire raid under Ryder's command: he did not return with the task force and was reported missing. Ann waited until somebody hesitantly got the news to her that somebody else thought they had seen him on board the Hunt class destroyer mined to blow up in the harbour. It was certain that the destroyer had blown up – with no survivors. So she went down to the beach near Lewes one evening and walked steadily into the sea, and it was only because a fisherman noticed her neat, well-made shoes on the shore that she was collected at the last possible moment and dragged back to life. Cressy remembered how astonished she had been by this: how profoundly it had upset her views about people's appearances, about love, about death – and not least, about Ann herself. Then Major Jackson had returned: it must have been extraordinary for him to live with somebody who had demonstrated that she would rather die without him, and Cressy had found herself so obsessed with this speculation that she had always felt shy with them. Two years later he had died of double pneumonia in an assault ship bound for the Mediterranean. Miles had also been killed by then; from that moment Ann had treated Cressy with a kindness as ferocious as it was unacknowledged, and when Cressy saw that she was necessary to Ann as an unwitting example of how to go on existing with a sense of continuous, total and agonizing loss, she had been able by degrees to return the kindness. Cressy had no other friends like Ann, Ann had no other friends like

Cressy, and in twenty years they seemed to have discovered very little of their essential differences: but they knew almost everything that happened to each other. Cressy respected Ann while secretly thinking her life unbearably dull (a Magistrate in the Juvenile Courts and a great deal of work for blind children), and Ann felt protective about Cressy while feeling that her life was a fast-moving series of glamorous and nerve-racking events.

She was late for lunch, but only the amount that Ann had known she would be. They kissed, and Cressy looked apologetic: Ann waved her towards the sitting-room where a low table was set for lunch before the fire, in front of which lay Ann's brown Burmese cat in an attitude of affected abandon.

'Have some sherry,' Ann called from the kitchen.

As she clinked the bottle against the sherry glass, the cat lifted his head and looked at her with the famous insulting topaz stare he reserved for total strangers: then dropped his cheek back on the rug; he did not like sherry. Cressy suddenly remembered that she had been wanting a cigarette since she woke up, and took one out of the silver presentation box given to Major Jackson by his regiment on his unexpected return after St Nazaire. The flat was full of things like that. Ann chain-smoked, and came out of the kitchen now carrying a tray, with a stub expertly poised between her lips. She said anxiously:

'Has Saki been nice to you?'

'He's pretending we've never met, as usual.'

Ann picked him up; he strained in her arms, looking martyred and highly strung, and licking his lips as the only possible well-bred expression of distaste. Cressy felt bound, for Ann's sake, to stroke his rich chocolate fur – a gesture he endured with majestic disapproval.

'He doesn't like the weather,' Ann said, sitting in an armchair one side of the tray.

'He doesn't have to go out in it.'

'But he knows it's there. You're looking tired, Cressy.' Cressy knew that whenever Ann said that, she meant, 'You've been

56

crying too much.' Now, as they began their lunch, she also began:

'I ought to leave Dick.'

'Leave him, then.'

'You know it's not like that.' Ann looked obediently expectant, but it was the obedience that struck Cressy.

'You must get sick of my problems.'

'I never really understand them.'

'How do you mean?'

'Well – are you worrying about leaving Dick for his sake, or for yours?'

Cressy finished her sherry. 'Mine – I suppose. It's all got so – nagging – and unimportant.'

'If it isn't making you happy, I should stop.'

'What *does* make one happy? That's what I want to know. Not knowing makes me inclined to hang on to what I've got. Rather a miserly view.'

'Do you wish you could marry him?'

Here it was again. What was it – a moral question? A solicitous one? Did everyone – well, all women – think that all affairs had to be worth their weight in marriage? She said flatly:

'He doesn't love me: it would be hopeless. In a year's time I'd be sitting in a dear little Georgian gem in Sussex wondering why he had to work so many evenings in London. Why do you ask?'

Ann lit a cigarette, and blew the smoke away from Saki's sulky face.

'I don't know – it's a kind of gauge I suppose. If you love someone enough to marry them, you can stand being made unhappy by them; if you don't, why put up with it?' Unless you partly like being unhappy, she added, but she did not say this.

'Unless I think that one can't be in love *without* being unhappy.'

Ann's faded eyes met hers with a look of shrewd affection.

'Seriously – what would you do, if you were me?'

'You don't want me to take that question seriously, do you?'

Cressy persisted: 'I *said* seriously.'

Ann put out her cigarette, and cut a piece of Camembert.

'Have some? Well – what about the rest of your life? You're a pianist . . .'

Cressy interrupted: 'I'm no *good* at it: I operate on the level of near-competence – that's all.'

'Still, it's something to do. You enjoyed teaching when you tried it. Don't interrupt: you asked me.' She gave her Camembert rind to Saki, who ate it sideways with a grinding purr. 'I mean that most people's lives are divided between what they do by themselves and what they do with other people. I should have said that you have a rather lonely life where other people are concerned.' She looked at Cressy, and then too quickly, somewhere else. 'I mean, people like you and me are always having to arrange their lives on the wrong scale: you know – how to make a success of living alone, *or* how to be some kind of public administrator – often both . . .'

She went on talking in this vein: with a careful kindness that confused what she meant, until, with a pleasantly self-abusive laugh, she admitted the confusion and went to make coffee. But Cressy knew what she meant. She hadn't meant that people did things *by* themselves, or with other people. She had meant *for* in both cases. If you asked Ann how she was, or indeed for any news about her life, she almost certainly told you something about one of her blind boys – that she had succeeded in getting one sent to an ordinary school, that she had taken another swimming for the first time in his life: that she had had a most rewarding discussion with the man chiefly responsible for designing new symbols in Braille with the result that another one who wanted to be a scientist stood a fair chance of getting into a university . . . If you persisted, 'But how are *you*?' she probably told you something about the insufferable Saki; what she really was, or felt about herself, was something she seemed hardly to consider, and certainly never discussed: just as nobody had had the slightest idea that she would try to drown herself.

When Ann came back with the coffee, they both spoke at once.

'I *ought* to leave Dick.'

'You *ought* to get married.'

Ann put down the coffee tray. 'I didn't say you ought to leave Dick: I said – '

'It can't be any good: look at the kind of conversation we've had about it: the thing is – what am I to *do*? It isn't that I mind what I'm like: I mind not enjoying it. I keep living in some kind of immediate future that makes everything dull when it happens; like recognizing every single telegraph pole from a train window. I want an occasion to rise to – even an awful one, if there aren't any others available. I'm perfectly aware of how self-absorbed – and – *boring* I sound – well *am*, but I don't seem to find anybody, and I'm simply no good at purposes without people. I mean, if I could find a man who even *thought* he was saving the world, I wouldn't mind washing his socks, but everybody seems just to be keeping going and making money for that. I never go to sleep feeling even kind or *useful* – just twenty-four hours older, or anxious about something which doesn't matter, and knowing what waking up in the morning will be like. Teaching! I'm no good at that because I don't care enough about people *or* music. I don't seem to have anything to lose – that's what's so frightening. I only get unhappy at the kind of rate I can get used to – a kind of chronic tolerance: if there was just something to be *for*, I could manage the against side of it?'

It wasn't a question, but she was trying not to start crying, and this made her voice sound like one.

There was what seemed like an interminable silence. Ann pushed a cup of coffee across the table to her, opened her husband's cigarette box, lit both their cigarettes. Then Cressy said:

'Could I come and work with you, do you think?'

'Of course you could: I don't think you'd like it though.'

'That doesn't matter: it would probably be very good for me.'

Ann said gently: 'But you see, about that sort of thing, I have to think of *them*.'

Cressy stared at her a moment, and then, with her eyes full of tears, began to laugh. 'Oh my God! I *am* far gone, aren't I!'

And Ann, relieved by this mild hysteria – which was, after all, simply Cressy laughing at herself some time after one would have thought it possible – said mildly: 'You're all right: I think you've just thought it out too much. Anyway – you have to start by being *for* yourself.'

Cressy took her hands away from her streaming face: 'Do I?'

'Not just you: everybody. You have to start by finding out what would suit *you*; otherwise, one's no use.'

'You're a much *better* person than I am.' She blew her nose. 'You think about other people all the time; you're *practical* as well as being kind.'

'I've got no sense of humour, you see: I simply can't afford to think about myself; the only times I tried it, it never made me laugh.'

This was tacitly the end of the conversation. Cressy said that she was going to Sussex: might she call Emma at her office to see if she wanted a lift? But Emma was not back from lunch – at a quarter to three.

'Perhaps she's having a nice lunch.' Ann was always hoping that Emma would get married. Cressy told her what Emma had said that morning about whoever she was supposed to have married being killed in the war, and Ann, with no conviction at all, said nonsense: the idea struck at her most painful superstition and made her brisk.

As she went, Cressy said: 'I shall leave Dick. I'll do it on Sunday night. There now – that's one thing.'

And this was chiefly why, when the telephone rang on three occasions while she was packing for the week-end, she did not answer it.

CHAPTER 5

FELIX

'**P**ASS Dr King the marmalade. No – on second thoughts
– don't.'

Felix looked from godson to mother. The godson's
features instantly decomposed to resentment and froze there: he
drew an interminable breath at the end of which his face looked
as though it was half-way through an explosion. The howl, like
terrible thunder, was still delayed: he had his audience cold, and
was taking his time. Mary passed him the marmalade, and said
briskly: 'Finish your cornflakes, Barney.'

That did it. A sound which Felix felt was out of all
proportion to his size burst from Barney just as his father came
into the room. 'Christ!' he said with good-humoured disapproval; 'Christ!' He picked up his son. 'What have you been
doing with him? Oh don't be so awful, Barney.'

The baby, in a high chair, took one look at her father and
then dug her hands into her porridge and thrust them lovingly
at his neck as he bent to kiss her. Barney – midway between a
real howl and an artificial one – aimed a surprisingly expert kick
at his sister. The porridge was deflected; the baby howled; the
telephone rang. Mary, six months pregnant, went to answer it.

'All meals in this house should be taken in a boiler suit and
ear plugs.'

'This is Dr Lewis's secretary,' Mary was saying, opening a
loose-leaf pad with one hand and uncapping a Biro with her
teeth.

Felix went to help her. Jack Lewis had given the baby a
lump of sugar, and put Barney back on his chair. With shaking

61

hands he was pouring coffee. They had been up very late the night before. 'Always get your secretaries pregnant,' he was saying: 'then they have to stay with you.'

'I should think it will be about an hour,' Mary was saying. 'He's visiting now, but I'll get a message to him. I should keep him in bed until the doctor comes.' She put down the receiver, said: 'Mrs Halloway. I'll get your eggs,' and went to get them.

'Damn and blast Mrs Halloway. She gives us Milk Tray for Christmas,' he added moodily. 'Milk Tray!' He retched absentmindedly. 'She must know we loathe it.'

'Do you hate all your patients?' Felix felt, as usual, detached, curious, made up of visiting interest: it was a very long time since he had actually lived anywhere.

'Good Lord, no! Some of them are quite reasonable: they die, or one cures them or something. It's the ones who go on and *on*, getting 'flu, measles and things – the kind of people you're bloody glad you're not ever seeing at their best.'

Jack Lewis had been through Medical School with Felix: in so far as Felix had one, Jack was undoubtedly his closest friend. He was – had always been – a man of passionate kindness, which he inadequately concealed by a flow of cynical and defeatist statements. He had married, while Felix was in Korea, a young Jewess: 'a physicist,' he had written, 'doing research on transistors for General Electric – but don't despair – picture enclosed – it takes all sorts to understand a transistor.' The picture had been of a girl in a sleeveless sweater and jeans sitting on a park bench pushing back long straight hair with one hand. 'Mary Black', Jack had written on the back. '24 years: 38 23 38.' The picture had been bad enough for Felix to take the proportions, with her alleged beauty and intelligence, on trust. 'Congratulations look forward to being a godfather,' he had cabled, and now, six years later, here he was in their pleasant but rather uncomfortable maisonette in Bayswater, with the monster, Barney, aged five, thoroughly mobile but only, as his mother said, spasmodically reasonable, fiddling about with his cornflakes and staring with frightful, impassive concentration at Felix. Felix was used to babies, or young children, in quantity: faced with the blown-out bellies and dreadful lethargy of their near-starvation, he had felt, in the beginning at least, not only a shocked desire to relieve their suffering, but a conviction of its being his right and duty to do so. His fall from this position of righteous ignorance had been a slow, painful trail, blazed by pieces of uncomfortable self-knowledge, the culmination of which had been that he simply had not loved his fellow men enough: if they were merely wounded or starving, he was able and willing from his personal foxhole of health and strength to help them; if, in their desperation, they lied, cheated or otherwise employed any available resource to help themselves, he despised them, was irritated by their stupidity, disgusted by their fear and shocked by their continuing selfish interest in their own existence . . .

Barney, though, was a new experience for Felix. To begin with his health was on a scale which commanded respect. Felix had unwisely tried to fling him over his shoulder practically on meeting: Barney's bones seemed to be made of pig-iron and his limbs upholstered in shot; he was utterly solid and of astonishing weight. His hair, his skin, his eyes, shone with well-being, his nature was both arrogant and resourceful; he really seemed as though, Felix thought, he felt sure that whatever he did would be all right. Just now, as a simple means of gaining his godfather's attention, he had laid his cornflakes spoon on Felix's sleeve and was saying (clearly for the second time), 'Did a poisonous snake sting you?'

Mary said: 'Bite, Barney, not sting. Snakes don't sting.'

'Did a poisonous snake bite you?'

'No – not actually.'

The telephone rang. Jack groaned and Mary answered it.

'Put your spoon down, Barney. This is Dr Lewis's secretary.'

Barney put his spoon down without taking his eyes off Felix. In spite of the fact that Mary was speaking on the telephone, he created his own silence. Then he said: 'Why not?'

Jack pushed back his chair and got up. 'He's crazy about snakes. I'll be down in a minute. Tell her to get two lots of vaccine out of the fridge, will you, Felix?'

The baby wanted to get down. To this end, she suddenly hurled herself sideways, so that the top half of her body hung over the side of the chair. Mary indicated the need to release her: but when Felix reached her he found that although she palpably had no waist, her body seemed to have a vast hinge in the middle which now seemed locked. She turned tomato-coloured but remained immovable. '. . . just fluids, until the doctor has seen him,' Mary was saying. 'Yes – some time this morning: right, Lady Birdneck, goodbye.' She put down the receiver and sped to the rescue. 'Really, Felix – you're hopeless: she's caught her foot, can't you see?' She could say this kind of thing, Felix had already discovered, and simply engender general affection – no rancour at all.

'She should have more feet,' said Barney, 'or a lovely scaly tail.' He turned to Felix. 'She's got nowhere for peeing as well. It all comes sloshing out on nappies' – he spread his hands dramatically – 'from *any*where! She should be slain.'

'That'll do,' said Mary. 'You were awful when you were a baby.'

'Was I? How was I? How was I awful?' He was delighted.

'Silly and dirty' – she was undoing his back trouser-buttons – 'and you couldn't say anything – you couldn't even sit up. You were a complete washout. Just a silly old baby. Up you go, and shout when you've finished.'

Mary began clearing breakfast. The baby had edged herself off the carpet and was making very good time across the linoleum towards a saucer of tinned cat-food by the sink. The telephone rang again; Jack appeared; Felix watched while Mary spoke to a patient, extricated the vaccine from the fridge and gave her husband his list of morning calls.

'I'm off: good-bye ducks. Have a nice week-end, Felix – Christ! What *have* you *let* her get hold of now?'

The baby had reached the cat-food which she was cramming on to her face with those slow-motion movements that in babies betoken real interest and pleasure.

'Let!' said Mary pouncing on her: 'let!'

'Roll on next week,' said Jack. He bent to kiss his wife's ear and looked at his daughter with loathing. 'Little vitamin-packed *pet*! I'll prolong your active life for you.' He ran a casual hand over his wife's belly. 'Isn't fecundity wonderful!'

'I've finished!' roared Barney from above. 'I've finished!' he yelled as though he had thought of something else, or something quite different had happened.

Mary heaved the baby on to her right hip and followed Jack out of the room. Felix was left alone in the large kitchen. It was also the Lewises' dining-room, but had clearly been converted to these functions: the children's night nursery in a Victorian household had probably been its original use. Two large sash windows with bars outside; a big fireplace with blue-and-white (and nasty) tiles, and heavy, old, fitted cupboards either side; high ceiling and an elaborate frieze of acanthus leaves swollen and muddled by years of repainting. Walls and ceiling were now covered with yellow emulsion paint which made the fog outside look like evening. Felix walked to one of the windows. It was the kind of day which in the East he had thought of with morbid nostalgia: dank, windless air with that intoxicatingly evil taste when one inhaled it through the mouth: the sun like a scarlet moon but seeming to burn cold instead of monotonous heat; frost and fog and London soot and sidelights on cars. He thought of his drive to Sussex with pleasure. The drive, anyway – he was uncertain about what he expected at the end of the journey; was not, indeed, at all sure why he was going. Duty? Curiosity? Part of this new and extraordinary need to attach himself to a situation which cut him down to size? He'd had enough of king-sized situations, he'd only to watch Jack and Mary in their small, overworked world to see that it took a remarkable amount of energy and intelligence to hold down a personal place in the scheme of things. Now, instead of trying to combat famine over hundreds of square miles, he was going to spend two weeks of his professional time giving an old friend the first holiday he had been able to have with his wife since they were married. The children were going to Mary's sister, and he was acting as unpaid locum for Jack who had never been able to afford one. This wasn't much to do for anybody, but on the other hand there hadn't seemed to be anybody else to do it. Jack had insisted upon buying a private practice from a doddering old tyrant who had reluctantly retired just over two years ago. While he had retained any control, he had refused Jack a holiday, and since Jack had taken over, his debts were such that a holiday had been out of the question. Felix had come to distrust his own motives so chronically that now he wondered whether he hadn't taken on the job of locum (to begin on Monday) simply in order that he should have a cast-iron reason for escaping whatever he might find in Sussex. She had not been the kind of woman whom it was easy to imagine either ageing or poor: but all he had been able to discover about her (by an anonymous telephone call to her husband's firm) had been that she had not married again, and lived in the same house. And so he had written to her saying – untruthfully – that he was going to be in her part of the world and wondered if he might come and see her. She should have got the letter yesterday, and she was to telegram or ring up if it was not convenient – i.e. if she did not want to see *him*. She had done neither. He had stayed in the whole of Thursday evening to make sure: the telephone had been working because Jack had had a late night call, but there had been nothing from her. The clumsiness of these arrangements struck him again, exactly as they had done last night. Jack had put down the telephone saying: 'I'm genuinely sorry that call wasn't for you. I'm off. Watch her: she gets very sexy when she's pregnant. Leave me a shot of your lovely Scotch.' When he had gone, Mary had said: 'Give *me* a shot of your lovely Scotch,' and held out her glass.

She was lying on their battered old sofa, barefoot, and wearing Jack's ancient camel-hair dressing-gown and the plain gold ear-rings Felix had brought back for her as a wedding present. Her hair was tied back with a limp piece of crimson chiffon; she looked wholesome and somehow glamorous and astonishingly young.

'You look tired,' he had said.

'Can't remember when I last felt untired: isn't it frightful? I expect all I'll do on the holiday is sleep and sleep and sleep – hey – that's enough.' She gave her gentle sly smile and added: 'We must seem such domestic vegetables to you.'

Felix thought of the facts that she had worn the ear-rings without stopping ever since he had presented them, and that, according to Jack, she had not slept at all the night after the holiday had been planned. 'Not at all,' he said.

She smiled again, stretched, and said: 'It's ages since I had several drinks, and even longer since I could lie about doing nothing but talk to an attractive man who wasn't my husband. Jack's quite right. Pregnancy has all kinds of erotic undertones. The Scotch is going quite literally to my head. So do tell.'

'What shall I tell you?'

'Oh! If the lady telephoned, would it be good or bad? Do you want to see her, or do you feel you ought to want to? Why did you stop trying to save the world and come back here to save Jack and me? Why aren't you married? Why are you a doctor? Do you feel detached and superior, or attached and frightened?'

'What do *you* feel?'

'It's simple for me. I love Jack, you see: I don't have to think where that leads me – I just go. You didn't have to *save* us,' she added hastily, 'you're just making things much, much easier, and God, or something, bless you for that. Oh! *you* talk! Tell me a story: I won't know the people, so you can say anything about them.'

'No, you wouldn't know them: this was way back in my youth.'

He told her, conscious of the omissions: but also aware as he talked, of how much more he remembered than the private, casual, package memory the affair had ever provoked in his mind. It was the detail that astonished him; not the basic bone-structure of events – meeting her at Nice Airport when he had been trying to buy scent for his sister – but things like the way in which she had said: 'Yes, that is a delicious smell – here!' and held out an arm. She had been wearing a white jacket, with three-quarter sleeves, and short white gloves which stopped at the wrists; it was the bronzed gap which she offered him. He could exactly remember the wave of apprehension and excitement and challenge as he bent to smell her burnished skin. This was no tortuous young girl tinkering with those long division sums of her Experience, Virginity and Future. This was a worldly, womanly woman – what he had imagined his life being full of all through his adolescence . . . 'Are you travelling to London?' she had asked. 'Yes: with you.' 'How do you know I am alone?' 'You're not alone.' He remembered dancing in the gents as he ran over this incredibly sophisticated dialogue. She had laughed – but she had not been simply amused. Still in the gents combing his hair, fiddling with his tie, trying to look forty, and tragic and experienced; experimenting with a little world-weary smile which he somehow could not get to play round his mouth, and being rudely interrupted by an immense foreign gent who had walked in, taken off his fur-collared overcoat which he gave to Felix to hold, and vomited with operatic gusto for what seemed like hours. 'Cara mia!' Then he had patted his stomach – one of the largest Felix had ever seen – said, 'Nott-a-somuch,' and started to trim his moustaches with a tiny pair of scissors extracted from a miniature lizard-skin case.

It had been a landmark in their intimacy when he had known that telling her about this incident would amuse her. These details! He apologized for them, but Mary said:

'Don't. That's what's so fascinating. You must have been in love.'

'I don't know. I was terribly young – infatuated . . .'

But she interrupted him: 'No, in love. Because when that happens you don't just notice and remember the other person, you notice everything round them. Then what?'

'Oh – then. We flew back to London together. Had dinner in a small restaurant. I felt she knew all about me by the time we got to brandy, in spite of the efforts at mystery that I made. She wasn't only a good listener, she was really good at asking questions.'

'Better than me?'

'I don't know,' he said with great affection. 'How can I know that?'

'Where did you spend the night?'

'She had a flat in London. Her husband was away. I'd sort of hoped there wasn't a husband around – I mean I realized that she must have one – she wore a ring – and when I found he was still about, I decided he must be a brute.'

'He wasn't?'

'Far from it. She told me he wasn't from the start. That didn't suit me at all, and I sulked – it didn't go with my romantic notions of rescue and indispensability. Then I found she had children, and decided that whatever he was like, she stayed with him for their sake. He certainly neglected her, and she was certainly someone who repaid attention. Anyway, I was twenty-three, and the mere idea of having a mistress was intoxicating. She was shrewd, entertaining, pretty and neat, and vulgar though this may sound to you, she adored going to bed with me.'

'What about you?'

'I was quite simple about it all. I could just conceive of having an affair with somebody when you only went to bed, but the moment I found myself enjoying her company as well, I got confused, and assumed that I was irrevocably in love. I hadn't envisaged the possibility of *liking* the women, you see – I had been brought up to think that apart from any casual sex I could arrange for myself, I'd inevitably find someone who made me feel I *had* to spend my life with her. Of course I thought she was the one.'

'Did you see a great deal of her?'

'Not to begin with. We wrote to each other a lot. She lived mostly in the country, and there were days when I could send letters when her husband wasn't there. She was very good at letters. She used to tell me things that were happening; she went to a lot of parties and was good at describing people: if she told me things that involved her husband, I used to make scenes.'

'Bore for her.'

'At first it was. In the end I think she came rather to depend on them. She made me go to their house in the country when he was away, which he nearly always was. I didn't stay there, of course, because of the children: we used to take picnics and go to vulgar desolate places like Camber Sands and Pett Level – that was in the spring of 1940: all the winter before she met me in London, or places like Tonbridge in tea shops. We used to sit with a frightful plate of mixed cakes between us, wishing we could go abroad. I failed my first lot of exams that year, because I spent so much time either with her or thinking about her.'

'What about the war?'

'What about it?'

'Didn't it make any difference? You haven't mentioned it at all.'

He thought for a moment. 'Of course, it must have. At the time it didn't seem to – except perhaps to excuse things one did on the grounds that one wouldn't be able to do them for very long. No – of course it made a difference. The morning that war was declared – I mean old Chamberlain and the Germans – she rang me up. I was living in digs in London – Victoria – and the telephone was in a passage so I always felt that everyone could hear everything she said. She said: "Felix, don't stay in London tonight." And I said: "Where else can I go?" And she said: "Come here. You can stay here. They'll bomb London, and if they're going to do that, they'll obviously do it tonight. You *must* come. Everyone will understand; it's an emergency." Then, without the slightest warning she put her elder daughter on the telephone – the schoolgirl one – so shy I never remembered getting a word out of her before: she said, "You can have my bed to sleep in if only you'll come, Felix." Then *she* was speaking again – a thousand bombers, she said – London would be flat; she'd explained to her husband that I was coming – nothing else, just that I was the son of an old friend of her aunt's – the bombers would be flying straight over their house on the way to London – she couldn't watch that – and suddenly I thought, "Perhaps *she* will be killed, and I shan't see her again," and I went.'

'What about your family? Or do you regard that as a very Jewish question?'

'They were in Easter Ross. I'd had rather a quarrel with them – failing to get into Aberdeen, and then failing my first year exams. They weren't too pleased. The thing was that *all* the menace seemed to be directed upon London – one didn't think of people in the rest of the country as in immediate danger. I sent them a telegram and drove to Sussex. It took hours. Anyway, that's how I met the husband. Digging an air-raid shelter in the garden.'

'What was he like?'

'It's funny: after all my histrionic fantasies about him, he turned out just to be a man digging. Much older than me, of course. He'd been digging all day – with the gardener, and the younger child with her sand spade. The older child came out soon after I started digging, and *she* brought us drinks and stuffed olives and things like that.'

71

He was silent, frowning absently, turning his empty glass round and round in his hands. To Mary it seemed as though there was suddenly much more than he could tell her.

'That night, at dinner – I only stayed one night,' he said at last, ' – he asked me what I was going to do. I simply hadn't thought at all. Then *she* said something about my being a medical student, and wasn't that a reserved occupation? Then he asked me how old I was: I told him. He said, 'My God, I wish I was your age.' That was the first time in my life that I realized I seemed to have absolutely no sense of public responsibility. *I* hadn't made the war – it was nothing to do with me. But *he* was minding because he was afraid he was too old to be any use at all – that was how he put it – the use part, I mean.'

'Was he much older than she was?'

'He was twelve years older: he was forty-nine.'

The telephone rang; she answered it, and it was Jack. She spoke briefly to him: said that he'd been putting an appendicitis into hospital, and then, as she returned to the sofa, he said suddenly, and much louder than he had been talking: 'He was killed returning from Dunkirk in a small sailing boat the following May. It wasn't his own boat. He didn't know much about sailing. He collected three men off the beaches. It was the only way he could think of to be useful. He died and I joined the Army.'

She couldn't understand his defiance. 'That's nothing to be ashamed of, surely?'

He didn't reply; got up rather clumsily, and poured them more Scotch.

'Sorry – I'm being dense.'

'*You're* not dense.' He smiled at her and sat down. 'Oh – well.' It was a full stop to the confidence rather than the end of the story.

'What about the lady who hasn't telephoned?'

'It's the same lady.'

72

'Felix! She must be . . .'

'Fifty-eight last July.'

She was staring at him with something like incomprehension or incredulity, he wasn't sure which. He held her eye and said slowly, carefully:

'I'm not sure. Perhaps I ought to have been married to her for the last twenty years – that's the thing. That's why I have to go and see.'

She started to speak, checked herself, took a swig at her glass, and then the front door shut. Jack had returned.

'Oh dear, oh dear. I should like to have come back weary from my tense, medical crisis (a straightforward case of appendicitis diagnosed correctly for me by the child's mother) to a scene of illicit and unbridled passion – my best friend in the arms of yet another wife.' He collected his empty glass and made for the bottle. 'You can see why I'm forced to the movies week after week: my home life's so unemotional – human nature simply doesn't function here. Everything goes on being *all right*: why is that, I wonder?'

'You're not being funny: don't.'

He turned round from pouring his Scotch.

'Something might go wrong about our holiday,' she said. She looked up at him. 'I honestly couldn't bear that.'

'Oh yes you could. But it won't go wrong.' He put his hand round the back of her neck and Felix saw her little shiver of pleasure and her face soften from anxiety.

'I promise you, as far as I'm concerned, nothing will go wrong about your holiday,' he said. Committed. Not to disappoint one nice girl about two weeks. You're coming on, King: you've made a start; in a month you managed to make two personal decisions and get your teeth fixed – oh yes, and buy a second-hand car and a couple of warm suits . . . I suppose that by this time next year I may be irrevocably settled – as I would already be if I'd married Clara. Until he'd met her he would have thought it impossible for anyone to be a sexy prig – I should have told Mary *that* story – that would just have made her laugh . . .

Mary returned, and he came away from the window to help her with the breakfast things.

'What have you done with them?'

'The baby's in her pen and Barney's spending the morning in the bath. He's got his aircraft carrier you see,' she added as an explanation. 'He plays battles and shipwrecks: I just have to warm up the water from time to time and he's perfectly happy. What time are you going?'

'Afternoon. I'll do the shopping for you if you'll make a foolproof list.'

'Oh Felix. Then I can do all the house and keep the telephone switched on here.'

'You lucky, lucky girl.'

She gave him a battered purse and a list in her clear, rather masculine writing. 'Get two more herrings if you want lunch with us. Sorry it's a long list, but it's groceries for the week. You know where to go, don't you?'

He knew. In the purse were three pounds: much less than he would spend on giving dinner to a girl. This was the kind of thing that Clara had never stopped pointing out, although she was always on the being-given-dinner side of the question: she would state one of these discrepancies with sentimental formality, and try to make him feel responsible for it. At first, she had succeeded. Whatever it was that had decided him upon working in the hospital of a camp for Korean refugees was fed by her smug determination that together they were good enough (i.e. chronically better than all these thousands of people who had been so ignorant and stupid as to get turned out of their homes without visible means of sustenance) to save the world. It was her contempt for what they were supposed to be saving that in

74

the end had so disgusted him (and thereby brought him to his senses). The final, frightful scene he had had with her when he had unleashed all his pent-up resentment and dislike on what she thought and felt and was, had confoundingly presented him with a self-portrait of hideous completeness and accuracy. Afterwards he had realized that their association had been founded on the most nauseating kind of mutual flattery; something like Orwell's pigs trying to be angels – scratching each other's backs in vain for wings . . .

The supermarket was full and dazzling, impregnated with creamy music, and the shoppers, pushing their wire perambulators along the highly polished floors, looked from the street as though they were swimming in light, but the moment one was inside, it was the street people who looked like dim fish in a dirty tank. With list in hand, Felix settled down to the grim business of finding the goods Mary wanted: in spite of the music, this was not soothing. He rammed his perambulator against a stand and large packets of detergent fell, in slow motion, to the floor where they seemed to take on new life and skidded for yards. The pot of jam he chose was mysteriously sticky. He simply could not find any sign of pearl barley, and by the time he was in despair about this, felt too self-conscious and unpopular to ask. He got stuck behind a woman with a large walking child, and every time he bent down to take something from a shelf near the floor, the child tickled him with a plastic daffodil. The first time this happened, he turned round with what he hoped was an appearance of cooperative *bonhomie*: but the child's expression was impassively grim. After that, he tried to pass the woman (this was when he rammed the stand), and after that, he tried not to bend down much. In the end, he gave up the pearl barley, and queued to check out. He had spent two pounds, seventeen and fourpence. With laden baskets, he staggered to the fishmonger. It did not seem a very good shop. The fish had the strained worldly expression of people who have had to keep still for too long, and the fishmonger looked startlingly like a fish, which seemed to Felix the wrong way round. Then he went to a small grocer and bought the pearl barley, a Fuller's walnut cake and two bottles of Mâcon. The grocer looked sad and tired, but was working hard on the personal touch. 'Doing the shopping today, I see.' Later he said that it seemed they were in for fog, and that he could see that Felix had his hands full. This was when Felix was trying to ram the Mâcon, one in each basket, without the grocer noticing that he had clearly bought most of his groceries elsewhere. A bottle punctured the barley, which was in a weak blue paper bag, and he heard it pouring steadily into the basket as he backed out of the shop, opening the door rather cleverly, he thought, with his foot and a bit of his shoulder. He had meant to buy Mary a bunch of chrysanthemums, but unless he carried them home between his teeth it was out of the question.

The Lewises' maisonette started on the second floor of the house, and he realized, as he trudged up, stabbing the electric time-switch buttons with his right elbow, that if he was Mary, he would have been doing all this in the company of Barney and the baby, and except that Barney might have been a useful counter-ploy with the plastic-daffodil torturer, the prospect seemed almost insurmountable.

Mary received him with rewarding gratitude.

''Fraid I broke the barley. The cake and the wine are from me. What would I do next if I *were* you?'

'You'd have a strong cup of Nescaff while you did the vegetables for lunch. Oh, Felix – she rang up.'

'Who?' He wasn't thinking.

'You know. Your lady you told me about. She said she'd only got your letter this morning, and that she'd love you to come for the week-end.'

He smiled and sat down. 'I don't know how to do vegetables.'

She put the coffee in front of him. 'They're done. Felix, I know it's none of my business, *really*' (what did she mean by *really*, he wondered indulgently), 'but you won't rush into anything, will you? I mean, you will *think* – you know what I mean.'

'Would you say I was an attractive man?'

'Why?'

'Well, here I am, jobless, homeless, practically friendless: I'm not much of a catch, am I? And the last woman I had anything to do with told me she loved what was inside me – she wasn't interested in my appearance.'

'I bet she *was*. Weren't you interested in hers?'

'Oh I loved what was inside her – but not where she meant. So you see I need reassurance: otherwise, who knows, I might throw myself gratefully on anybody who'd have me.'

She was not sure whether he was teasing her or not and started to blush.

'Of course you're attractive,' she said angrily, 'and doctors can easily get jobs, and you've got us and you can always stay here.'

'You make me sound more pathetic and dependent every minute. Come on, Mary, am I an attractive man?'

But it was no good: she was blushing too much and too cross about it.

'You and Marlon Brando,' she said as bravely as she could.

'A lot of Jews have red hair you know: you ought to like me.'

At this point Barney appeared round the kitchen door. He wore a loofah strapped on his forearm and Mary's bedroom slippers, and carried a sodden number of the *British Medical Journal*.

'I've finished,' he said: 'the paper floated badly. I'm hungry.'

'The only good thing about *lunch* with the Lewises,' said Jack, 'is that there are fewer Lewises present.'

Barney and the baby had been fed at twelve thirty and were

now resting, although resting up a child of Barney's physique seemed to Felix to be asking for trouble. The bathroom, as his father had remarked, was like the Everglades. The grownups had eaten their herrings, mashed potatoes and sprouts, and were now engaged upon the best rice pudding Felix had ever eaten. Most of the practical problems of Felix being locum had been discussed; Mary was going to make an explanatory address book, and Jack was going to go through the patients' files to give him the low-down on their characters – 'in some cases, very low indeed'. This was for Sunday night.

'You'll be back by then?'

'I'll ring you if not. No, of course I will be.'

Mary was anxious either about her holiday or his week-end: he wasn't sure which.

She planned to take the children to her sister in Esher on Sunday, spend the day there to settle them in, and come back in time to be taken out to dinner by Jack and Felix. 'Where does she want to go?'

'Last time she was going on about it, it was to be Wheelers, but she's bound to change her mind. You know what they are.'

'Indecisive little creatures.'

'They only like to pretend to choose things.'

'Have to let them have their head sometimes.'

'After all, their brains weigh much less than ours.'

'Still, they make a lovely change from men.'

'You don't make a lovely change from children,' said Mary, blushing with rage. 'Either of you.'

As soon as lunch was over, Felix said he'd better be off. It was Friday, and the fog might get worse, he said. Really, he was beginning not to want to go at all. This established family life was softening him up to the point when his intentions were starting to seem anything from deliberately silly to dangerously absurd.

CHAPTER 6

ARRIVALS

THE house was very quiet, in spite of Mrs Hanwell in the kitchen. On most winter evenings, when she was entirely alone, Esme used the radio a lot. She hummed to herself; she never thought of the whole *house* – simply whatever room she happened to be in. Floorboards creaked, logs crackled; she turned the pages of a book and unwrapped the silver paper from a chocolate, while outside the windows, weather of one kind or another made larger, more distant sounds which prevented her from feeling cut off in a domestic vacuum. But on Fridays, when she always had people to stay, she noticed the silence: the house seemed too big for her – too spasmodically inhabited. About six o'clock, she would go round to see that everything was ready for the week-end. She would begin with the main double spare-room and check that it had its preliminary hot water bottles (she had her generation's terror of damp linen), flowers, suitable books, rich tea biscuits in a padded chintzy tin, and the bedside lamps working. A glance at Emma's room – a stranded beach of all her childhood – filled with objects that had become family landscape and which Mrs Hanwell (who approved of possessions) kept rigidly and symmetrically regimented. Cressy's room was crammed always and only with her immediate past: clothes she couldn't decide what to do with, programmes of the last concert she had given, postcards and photographs of the last foreign holiday she had had. At least once a year Cressy indulged in a moody clean sweep, which left her room belonging to nobody. There was no photograph of Miles, which, when she remembered him, Esme

79

found faintly disturbing. Either Cressy cared about him so much that she couldn't bear to be reminded, or she didn't care at all, and neither of these feelings was comfortable when one was thinking about somebody else. The room that had been Julius's dressing-room she changed so much that she need not remember how it had been. Now it had fashionably ornate flowered wallpaper, a white venetian blind, built-in cupboards and the fireplace blocked by an electric heater that Cressy had condemned as hideous. There were two more small rooms where the maids had slept before the war, but nowadays they were hardly ever used. Generally, at this point of her tour, she would go downstairs to talk to Mrs Hanwell, but tonight she felt far too strung-up. She went back to her own bedroom, sat down in front of her dressing-table, and from the back of her sewing box took out once more the small dog-eared photograph. She had taken it herself, at Pett Level – made him wind down the front window of the car and lean out of it towards her – and the sun, of course; snapshots then were always taken with the maximum sun direct on the subject's face, with the result that his eyes were screwed up with smiling and the light. He wore an open-necked shirt with a silk scarf which she had given him; a lock of hair lay across his rather square forehead; the angle of his head showed his high cheekbones and pointed chin, but the slight, accommodating smile with which, on demand, he had provided her, had obscured the shape of his mouth, just as you couldn't see the natural contours of his eyes (hazel, they had been, with absurdly long, dark lashes). But then, in the photograph, his hair was not red, there were no freckles visible, and his habitual expression of expected amusement was missing. She had never understood this expression. To begin with she had thought that perhaps he might be laughing at her, or worse, at himself *about* her, but he had early displayed all the sensual devotion, all the petulance of incipient jealousy, all the day-to-day uncritical approval which ranged him on her side. Esme, as any of her friends would have said,

80

was a practical creature; laughter meant that one was not
serious, and apart from Noël Coward and P. G. Wodehouse
and stories told by people about friends whom they did not
really like, people who seemed to have an aimless desire to find
life amusing were simply frivolous – which meant light-hearted
in the wrong way. You could be funny about 'characters', and
she was definitely not a character. She wanted life to be unreal
– and earnest: and with Felix it had been both those things. He
had seemed gravely involved with her. The only fault he ascribed
to her was the one which all lovers find essential to their self-
respect: that before him, she had chosen the wrong man – in
this case to marry. She was an intelligent, charming, discrimi-
nating, sophisticated, sensitive, entertaining creature, but she
seemed to have made the fatal pathetic disastrous mistake of
marrying a brute, boor, bore, man-who-wasn't-able-to-appreci-
ate-her, man who cared nothing for love, for woman, for human
relations, above all for her. It would not be true to say that he
revelled in her suffering (he had had to temper his opinion of
Julius who ascended from brutishness to callous indifference),
but in the end he had had to pay more attention to the dramatic
facts of her situation than to the character of a man he had
never met. And by the time they had both settled for this, her
situation *had* begun to weigh upon her; her need for Felix was
consuming her life. The rest of it had become a dreary, practical
dream where she did the same practical, meaningless things over
and over again, always just out of emotional earshot as it were,
and nobody could ever hear what she was. But now, she was
simply staring at the snapshot which she had once known by
heart. Felix – he looked so – oh! more than anything, he looked
so *young*! Involuntarily, she looked up at the mirror. Large,
grey-blue eyes, slightly protuberant; a very good, fine skin;
small, neatly defined nose and mouth, an enormous forehead –
wonderful for arranging hair; delicate but unremarkable eyebrows – these were all things she could always have observed.
But the marks, lines, blurring, fore-knowledge, fatigue, the

81

harness of boredom, of minutely perceptible physical decay – the descent from 'good lines' to 'good features' with no discernible line attached – had all occurred about ten years ago. She touched her well-preserved throat with elderly hands: her body was now neat but shapeless – at least she was neither scraggy nor fat and her legs were still good. She was an attractive, elderly middle-aged woman whose heart, at the moment, was refusing to keep up with her times – was thudding with obtrusive, irregular haste. She was fifty-eight. She looked again at the snapshot: he would be older too, but this, from her memory of him, would only be to his advantage. She knew he had become a doctor, and she had read in the newspapers that his parents had been killed in a car accident. 'Mr and Mrs King of Easter Ross . . .' Mrs King; she wondered whether in all these years there had been a Mrs Felix King: if there had been, she was certain, from his letter, that Felix was now alone. Why was he coming? After all these years of silence, of cutting himself off completely, why did he suddenly decide to come? She could no more stop asking this question than she could think of any contenting answer. She looked once more at the snapshot, put it away, and reached for her Arpège – a touch more of that to give her confidence. A car was coming up the drive – she hurried to the landing window: it wasn't Emma's taxi – it was a car.

She opened the door to him. The light was behind her and shone full on his face; his eyes were screwed up, dazzled by it. For a second he looked exactly as she had remembered him – very young, charmingly tentative about his reception; then he stooped to kiss her cheek.

'Esme!' He was carrying a suitcase, and a mackintosh slung over his arm.

'Felix dear – it's lovely to see you again.' She remembered that she had always felt breathless on meeting him, but now she couldn't afford the silence that had gone with it.

'Come straight in and have a drink. Did you have a frightful drive? How was the fog? And of course Fridays are always awful.'

He put down his suitcase and she saw his fleeting glance round the hall. Everything was the same – excepting her. Mrs Hanwell appeared from the kitchen, and she asked for ice. He followed her into the long, low sitting-room where apple logs were blazing and the drinks tray winked and gleamed on a table behind the sofa.

'What'll you have?'

'Some whisky, if I may.'

He had moved to the fireplace and seemed much occupied with warming his hands.

Mrs Hanwell came in with ice. 'Good evening, sir.' She did not know Felix, but she was a countrywoman, and would have thought it discourteous to encounter anyone at any time of the day without greeting them.

'This is Mrs Hanwell, Mr – Dr King.' Esme saw Mrs Hanwell's expression dilate a little with the spark of respect. Her opinion of men was triumphantly low: she knew they were awful, and she liked to be right about them, but doctors were a cut above the ordinary run: in matters of real interest about life (and this included death) they were the ruling class.

'No sign of Miss Emma, then,' she said.

'Her train will only just be due,' said Esme. Her hands were trembling with the whisky. 'And it'll probably be late because of the fog.'

'Very likely,' said Mrs Hanwell, and left the room. She disapproved of travel, knowing that it was quite unnecessary if people would only stay in the same place.

'Ice?'

'Please.'

'Soda or water?'

'Soda.'

He came towards her to take the glass, and for a moment their eyes met. 'I feel terribly nervous,' he said. She realized that he had grown up a great deal.

'It is rather queer, isn't it? Such a long time, and not knowing anything about each other.'

'That was my fault. I didn't know how else to do things. I suppose now we're both older and wiser.'

'I'm older, and you're wiser,' she answered. He looked at her, feeling that she meant exactly that, and her absence of bitterness touched him.

She sat down opposite him, crossed her knees and reached for a cigarette. He noticed the movement: it was the first thing about her he had seen which hadn't changed at all – her pretty legs with elegant knees.

She said rather desperately:

'Tell me about yourself.'

He smiled then, and settled himself on the corner of the fender.

'Not yet: *you* tell me. If she is arriving in half an hour, tell me about Emma. Is she married?'

'Oh *no!*'

He laughed outright. 'That was really a motherly cry. What a shocking thing! And she all of twenty-five, I suppose?'

'Twenty-seven. It's not her not being married. It's her having no men around. She works in the family publishing business and shares a flat with Cressy. She comes down practically *every* week-end and simply *reads* and goes for walks and washes her hair!'

Felix repressed a smile at these criminal activities. 'And Cressy?'

'Well – Cressy – you know she was married, of course?'

He shook his head.

'Of course – it was just after – after you joined up: after her father died. She married a naval officer called Miles Egerton. He was killed in less than a year after the marriage. No children.

84

She went on with her music. She's terribly restless, has unproductive affairs. She was always rather intense – do you remember?'

'Yes, I do.'

'Secretive too. She's much better-looking than Emma, but I can't talk to her. I don't think she likes me, really.'

'Is she coming this week-end?'

Esme threw her cigarette into the fire (she never smoked them to the end, he remembered) and got up to pour them more drinks.

'One never knows. Probably not, but she simply won't make plans about anything. She always has some half-made arrangements she's waiting to hear about. Another?'

He took his glass over to her. She looked up at him as she took it. 'That's the children,' she said, and they both discovered that talking about them had only made things easier while they were actually doing it. Questions rose like bubbles in both their minds and exploded unasked in the silence. Standing facing her with the new drink in his hand, he said abruptly:

'Did you miss Julius? I mean – later – after the first shock?'

She looked at him steadily, thinking honestly about it.

'I missed what he stood for in my life. The children's father: a man in his own house; the other half of being a couple. But in myself – I didn't, you see. It would have been far less lonely if I could have missed him like that. And of course, I felt that I'd let him down. That showed me that I didn't love him.'

'I don't get that at all.' He was thinking how much he'd felt – still felt – that he'd let her down.

'You can't feel that about someone you *love*. Someone you pity – feel responsible for – all that. But otherwise, it doesn't come in; it simply isn't possible.'

He felt a familiar rush of admiring affection for her. Ten minutes of her company after twenty years, and she was still showing him something.

'Esme, darling, what a lot you know!'

'That, my dear, is a remark which flatters you far more than it does me. You mean, if I know *anything* that you don't, I must know a great deal. Well, *really!*'

'It's very good to see you again.'

And she answered in a carefully social voice: 'You should have come before.'

Then they both heard the taxi, and Felix felt a pang of irritation at the prospect of being interrupted. There were voices in the hall, and Esme had time to say, 'She's brought someone with her,' and Felix to mutter, 'A *man*, at last,' before the door opened and Emma came in with Daniel.

'Mother, this is Daniel Brick. He's come for the week-end. I did try to ring you this afternoon, but you must have been out. Having your hair done, I see now. It looks super.'

'How do you do, Mr Brick: I'm delighted you could come. Emma, this is Felix King.'

'It sounds awful to say it, but I last saw you in pigtails when you were about seven.'

Emma looked at him clearly, and he remembered her extraordinary eyes. 'Well – neither of us could help that, could we? Mother, we've brought you a peace offering – a kind of bribe for having Dan at such short notice. Where's the box, Dan?'

Daniel, who had shaken hands without speaking, pulled a surprisingly large box out from under his jacket. 'I was afraid of the damp for them,' he said.

'How very kind of you. Darling, give yourself and Mr Brick drinks.'

But Emma, Felix noticed, stood her ground, willing her mother to take the paper off the box. Esme was not insensitive: it worked.

'I must open this before I do anything else.'

The brown paper was torn off to reveal coloured pictures of what looked like explosions.

'It looks like a set,' said Daniel; 'but 'tisn't: they're all hand-picked for value.'

86

'Fireworks!' cried Esme faintly.

Felix turned to Daniel: on his face was a look of serious generosity; Emma seemed both excited and protective: only he knew that Esme hated bangs. 'Terrific,' he said: 'Mr Brick and I can set them all up tomorrow when it's light, and you can watch them in majestic comfort from the french windows.'

Esme remembered that he remembered. 'What a perfect plan! Thank you *so* much, Mr Brick.'

'We bought them after lunch,' said Emma. 'You have to know a lot about them to buy really good ones, and hardly anybody does.'

'Like Chinese meals,' said Daniel. 'They make a fortune up in London filling people up with bits of rice and egg and that and calling it meal H. You have to know a thing or two to put them to some trouble and get your money's worth.'

'We had a Chinese lunch, so now we're starving,' said Emma. 'What room shall Dan have?'

'Perhaps he could have the nursery: Cressy hasn't turned up but she might, and Felix is in the dressing-room.'

Felix offered to do drinks while Esme went up with Emma to see about rooms.

Daniel moved to the fire, picking off a blackberry from Esme's elaborate flower arrangement.

'Frostbitten,' he said and spat it neatly into the flames. He seemed entirely out of place, and entirely calm about it: and Felix began liking him very much.

'What'll you drink?'

'A bottle of Bass if it's handy.'

'I'm afraid it isn't.'

'Rum and ginger?'

Felix looked carefully. 'Try again.' Daniel, he saw, had taken the sheet of silver paper out of Esme's box of a hundred cigarettes and was making it into a cup.

'I dunno,' he said. 'I suppose there'd be port in a house like this.'

'I expect there is somewhere: there's some sherry here. How about that?'

'Yeah; and when *she* comes back – the girl I mean – you can put some in this for her.' He had made a perfect little cup, with a stem and base. 'Most people can't get them to hold liquor,' he said. His rather large, pale-blue eyes met Felix's. 'There's five pounds' worth of fireworks in that box, you know. Not many people get that laid to their door.'

'No, I should think not.'

Daniel accepted the sherry. 'Then I had a fancy for them myself. Still – you don't give presents you don't care for, do you? That's for weddings and such. You're not a married man, are you?'

'No,' said Felix, surprised. 'Are you?'

'I've not had the time for it. Takes time to find the girl; time to hunt her down – it's a life in itself; then I like a bit of mystery – and that slips through your fingers when you get to know anyone well. That's why I'm fond of filling in forms.' He drained the sherry. 'Glasses are on the small side aren't they?'

'Have some more. I hate forms: why do you like them?'

Daniel nodded in acknowledgement of the drink and drank it. 'Mystery,' he said. 'They don't tell you a thing about people: they just look as though they do. I got a shocking temper – you never get that on a form and I've run into a good many in my day.'

They both heard Emma calling him. He put down the glass.

'They live in all this house, do they?' he asked, making for the door.

'Yes. Sounds as though she's upstairs.'

'Stairs again,' said Daniel and went.

Felix felt himself smiling with curiosity and pleasure; the whole week-end was going to be far less portentous and more enjoyable than he had thought. He began trying to fill the fragile silver cup with sherry from the heavy ship's decanter – difficult – the cup trembled and nearly lost its balance and sherry spilt. He was interrupted by Esme. She shut the door, and almost ran into him.

'My dear, he's a *poet!*' Her dismay was so dramatically transparent that he had to straighten his face.

'I mean he keeps writing poetry.'

'Perhaps he writes a spot of prose from time to time as well.'

'You don't understand! It's frightfully difficult to live with! They only met this morning, and Emma's brought him straight down! That's serious, don't you think?'

'I *don't* understand. Are you worrying about his being penniless, or is it simply that the pursuit of poetry strikes you as raffish?'

'Of course I don't mind whether he's rich or poor,' she said, putting it another way – and then, proceeding to outline all the prejudices she had precariously overcome, she went on: 'And I don't mind his accent – *is* it Sussex, do you think – or West Country? or his having no luggage – he hasn't *any* – not even a brief-case' there Felix did laugh: the idea of Daniel with a brief-case as minimal equipment was too much for him 'or even the fact that honestly he doesn't look very healthy – oh you know what I mean, Felix, fearfully pale – not at all a good colour. Do you know what he did when Emma showed him the old nursery, where he's to sleep?'

Felix waited.

'He got straight on to the rocking horse! And all those fireworks! A *man!*'

'Leaving out the fact that he's a man, I think you're jumping to conclusions.' Severity was having a good effect upon her, he noticed. 'You have no reason at all for supposing that she wants to marry him. You were complaining about her never bringing anyone. Why are you so against *poets*, anyway?'

For some reason that he had no idea of, Esme blushed.

'I'm not against them *en principe*,' she began, when they were again interrupted by Mrs Hanwell.

'The chickens will be past their best in fifteen minutes, madam,' she said. 'What about Miss Cressy?'

'We won't wait for her,' said Esme.

'Very good; I notice Miss Emma's brought a gentleman down.'

'Yes. He's staying, and we've put him in the day nursery.'

'He'll be needing his dinner first though. There's a car coming: it'll be Miss Cressy.'

'I can't hear anything.'

'I've got wonderful ears,' said Mrs Hanwell, and left the room.

Felix said: 'It's like a frightful IQ test. "Past their best in fifteen minutes' time" . . .'

The car could easily be heard. It drew up with a dramatic jolt, seemingly outside the windows, and a few moments later, Cressy entered the room.

'Sorry, darling, I tried to ring you – ' she began, and then she saw Felix and stopped moving as well as speaking.

'Do you remember Felix King? Dr King, he is now.'

'How do you do?' said Felix. She seemed unable to say anything, so he held out his hand. She looked at it and took it uncertainly. She was wearing a lemon-yellow roll-neck jersey and rather faded blue jeans. But she's *staggering*! he thought. Her hand was very cold.

'He used to come and see us just before the war,' said Esme.

'I remember,' said Cressy. 'Goodness, Mother, what *have* you done to your hair?'

The childishness of this attack was so startling that Felix saw it was ineffective, like stabbing somebody with a bargepole.

'Had it set in order to look my best for my old friend,' she said with gallant accuracy. (*How* old was Cressy? Well over thirty, surely?) 'Have a drink, darling, I'm sure you need it. Oh – Emma's brought a strange young man for the week-end.'

'Do you mean we don't know him, or he's odd?' Cressy was pouring whisky rather sloppily into a glass.

'Both, I think, but Felix likes him, don't you, Felix?'

Before Felix could reply, Cressy, who seemed now to be behaving as though he wasn't there, said: 'She told me this morning that she thought whoever she was supposed to have married probably got killed in the war.' She took the drink and prowled to the fire with it. 'Well, if he's young, at least you can't say she's looking for her father, which we're all supposed to do from morning till night.

'Although, it's a very silly thing to say when you come to think of it. It's not so much that women are looking for their own father in other men, as that every now and then they want a man to be fatherly to them: utterly different – unless they've got a mother complex and want to be in love with their son.'

'The same thing probably applies there,' said Felix.

She looked at him then with an insolence that was really too studied for someone of her age. 'What do you mean, exactly?'

'I mean, that from time to time, they might want a man towards whom they could feel maternal,' said Felix patiently. She had the kind of eyes usually attributed to young Italian beauties.

'Oh,' she turned away, and edged a log further into the fire with small, well-polished idlers. Her feet were bare in the shoes, he noticed.

It was a relief when Emma and Daniel rejoined them and they all trooped into the dining-room to eat Mrs Hanwell's chickens, plain roast, with bread sauce, mashed potatoes, brussels sprouts with chestnuts and thick chicken gravy, followed by a plum tart – bottled plums – and Mrs Hanwell's husband's cream. Emma got a wishbone, and Daniel dried it for her over two candles. Cressy went to bed quite early, but the others stayed up till midnight or thereabouts. The week-end had begun.

PART TWO

SATURDAYS

CHAPTER 7

DANIEL

H E liked the room they had given him so much that he
hadn't in the least wanted to go to bed. She was a
dear little thing: she had brought him to the door of
what they called the nursery, and asked him anxiously if he
wanted anything. No, he had said: it wasn't at all that he
couldn't think of things that he wanted, it was just impossible
to know what she was expecting him to want. So he had stuck
to nothing. Well – good night, she had said, and walked away,
and although he felt somehow that he had deprived her of
generosity, there wasn't one thing he could do about it. The
room was fascinating. It would take him all night to go through
everything in it, but as he also had a lot on his mind he cast
himself on the bed for a start. He could see that if you had to
stay in the same place it stood to reason that you would need
more room, but the quantity of places that you could be in this
house were none the less startling. That dining-room now – did
they really only eat in it? He'd eaten so much that he was
beginning to feel hungry, so he laid off thoughts of dinner; it
had been so good that any thought of it brought those fruity
juices to his mouth. What he couldn't make out was how much
of an *occasion* the whole evening had been for them. Sometimes
he had felt that it very much was one: when the mother had
asked that doctor to open the wine, his eyes had travelled from
one face to the other and he'd felt that something serious and
shifty was going on. He didn't trust doctors anyway – he'd
nearly made off when Emma had told him upstairs. You *couldn't*
trust them, as he well knew: full of what looked like good will

one minute and then jab! into your chest with a needle or sawing away at your rib bones with you enjoying the full privilege of a 'local'. *They* told you you needed it: how were you to know? The last thing he'd do to anyone who felt as rotten as he had felt would be to saw off bits of his ribs. For a bit he pretended that he felt too ill, or wasn't allowed to get up off the bed: knowing he could was a private luxury, although that shouldn't mean just being pleased about something awful that wasn't going to happen. It wasn't a cheap bed at all. Nothing here was like that. From two chickens for supper onwards, the whole set-up was regardless. Why did she work in an office then? Something he would never do in a million years minus a million meals he ought to be getting. For a moment the idea of being rich going with things being boring skimmed his mind; he simply couldn't bear it: if you could enjoy life without much, it must be ten times better with ten times more than not much. Otherwise, where was everybody going to? Naturally you chose what you wanted – you didn't just get things to keep like that silly sod Alfred. If Dot could see him now! All she'd worry about was his not having any pyjamas – 'luggage' as Emma had said. She had seemed surprised. It wouldn't strike her that he felt *exactly the same now* as he would have felt if he'd been lying there with a pair of pyjamas under his hand. He couldn't be cold, because anyway he wore an extra lot of clothes, and that was what blankets were for at night – to keep you even warmer. Where was he? Occasion. Well, that sister of Emma's would make an occasion out of a milk shake on a wet Sunday afternoon. She hadn't seemed to like the doctor either; but then he'd never seen anyone treat their mother as she had done – downright discourtesy if ever he'd seen it: crossed in love, he had no doubt, and nearly on the shelf on top of that. No wonder the poor thing was edgy. Of course, the father had died, and a houseful of women without a man to crack the whip always made them soft and restless. Women couldn't do without a living grievance, a chronic reason for being too tired, over-

worked, having no time to themselves; children provided that
for a bit, but they grew out of needing the attention – resented
it as soon as they learned how. But a man could be a satisfactory
nuisance for as long as he lived: he remembered his father
having to be undressed on Friday nights on the good weeks
when they'd been on the beer run (better pay for the load, and
a spot of free liquor); or his angry, aimless gloom when they
had to wait too long for a load, and on top of trying to stretch
the money for food, his mother'd had his general sense of
injustice unleashed on her. And when *she'd* died, Dot had had
to take over. But Emma's mother – there she had sat all alone
in the lap of luxury with just the two girls to bring up – no
wonder she wanted a bit of male company, even a doctor; no
wonder that older sister was out of hand, and Emma still a child
– in many ways more like Dot at fourteen for all her office
working. He'd enjoyed that meal with her, even if there hadn't
been much body to the food. The place was exotic – dark, with
paper lanterns and candles on the table under the bowls of food.
Chopsticks were offered and the waiters had been foreign all
right – tight yellow faces and fathomless eyes. He had had a
moment's panic when they sat down, and he had thought that
perhaps she ate Chinese food every day, but she said no, egg
and tomato sandwiches, this was a treat for her, and she had
looked as though it was. They'd had jasmine Chinese tea – you
could see the flat dead little flowers in bowl cups with green
dragons on them, and she'd asked him about his writing which
had made him foreign too, as though he was someone else he
happened to know better than anybody else he knew then. He
hadn't wanted it to stop because he wasn't sure what to do
between dinner and catching the train. But it had been easy.
They had wandered along the narrow street looking in shop
windows choosing what they fancied until they'd come upon
the shop filled with tricks and noses and beards and fireworks.
It was she who had suggested buying some, and she had wanted
to pay, but it shocked him to see a woman spending money

except on food. The Publishers had paid for their meal, and at the bank he had got a great book of notes with a brand new elastic band thrown in round them – also two paper clips and some practically new blotting paper he'd picked up: those wide counters and iron grilles cut both ways and they couldn't see what went on. No, he had bought the fireworks, chosen them too. Then they had passed an animal shop, and he had asked whether her mother had a canary: he suddenly felt he ought to take a present and a canary struck him as suitable. But Emma had said her mother didn't go in much for birds and he wasn't spending thirty-five shillings on what they called a Belgian hare for someone he hadn't even met, so that was that and they had walked on. They'd called it Belgian to put the price up, he shouldn't wonder. It was still raw and cold, and they had talked about what it would be like to live on an island with white coral sand and palm trees. She was very nice to walk about with; not a giggling deadweight where you had to provide all the entertainment for two, and not bossy or patronizing because she lived in London and worked in an office. It was more like going with a friend than a girl.

Every now and then he copied her voice and she said he was getting better at it, and he said copy me, and she laughed and wouldn't. They passed a stationer and he looked there a long time, and she said why didn't he go and buy himself something nice there: he made some excuse; he liked to come by his stationery – paying for it out of a shop was not his line. She was no fool, because when they went back to her office to fetch her 'luggage' she showed him a small cupboard in her room filled with the stuff and told him to help himself, but this wasn't how he liked to do things either, so he'd only taken one or two things he hadn't wanted, to be polite.

He'd enjoyed the train. They'd had tea and biscuits on it and she'd told him about her father: it was the nearest he'd come to a hero and he felt a respect for her being related. It was then that he'd decided to give all the fireworks to the mother, to cheer her up. And now, here he was, in the nursery; it struck him as queer to have a different room for being a child in, but he supposed in a house of this size, you'd get worn out thinking of what to use up all the rooms for. Tomorrow they would actually see the sea: she'd promised to take him; he'd told her that unreliability put him in a rage, and he thought she'd stick to her promise. He could do with a cup of tea now. He sat up and looked round for something to take his mind off food. Another turn on the rocking horse? – but the trouble with that was that it was so nearly like he imagined the real thing, that you got bored going nowhere. He looked like having to fall back on those old books, and when he opened them, the first thing he saw was a coloured picture of some teddy bears having a birthday party – jellies and buns and an enormous cake with simple candles. The picture had been coloured in chalks so all the food was yellow and orange . . . food again. He knew he wouldn't sleep without some sort of a snack, so before he had time to think too much about it, he started off in search of the kitchen. The passage was dark, but he found a light and put it on long enough to see where the stairs began. A clock some-where ticked so loudly that the tick sounded irregular. The kitchen was a nice square room with a big table in the middle and a big stove against one wall. There were several doors along the third wall and opening them he found successively a room (just for washing up in!), a place (just for keeping brooms in!), and a larder with stone floor and marble shelf, and rows of bowls and bits of things on dishes in wire cages. This was very promising. He found a wedge of blackberry-and-apple-pie – just enough for one, and a piece of rather hard, greasy and slippery cheese. He was examining a white can covered by a dear little piece of muslin with blue beads weighting its edges, when he heard a noise. I'm found out, he thought, feeling that he really was in strange country because he had no idea how much they'd mind: people never liked finding you where they didn't expect to – he knew that, even if you weren't doing anything wrong wherever it was. Honestly hanging on to the piece of pie he turned back to the kitchen.

It was Emma's sister, with her black hair waving round her face, wearing a very grand white quilted dressing-gown and scarlet feathery slippers.

'Oh,' she said, and waited.

'I had so much supper, you see, I'm hungry now.'

'*You* can't sleep either.'

He shook his head.

She looked at the pie in his hands.

'Is that what you want?'

He nodded, and sat at the table. 'There was a piece of cheese.'

'Have it! Have anything! Shall I make some tea? Or coffee?'

'I'd rather tea.'

He watched her lift the round lid off one of the hot plates on the Aga, and move the kettle on to it. The kettle responded at once.

'Magic,' he said. 'I'll get that cheese, if you don't mind.' They had been talking very quietly, which, in a funny way, had made them sound as though they knew each other. When he came back to the table, she was warming the pot.

'My sister's got a fridge,' he said to keep the conversation going. She wasn't the company he would have chosen for this meal.

'Most people have, haven't they?'

'I can't answer you there.' He started his pie. Immediately, she fetched him a plate and a blackberry slipped out and fell on it – just in time. He looked up to thank her and saw a tear roll over the edge of her face into the air.

'What'll you eat then?'

'I don't know. Nothing – I don't think.' She was collecting cups and spoons and sugar.

'I know where the milk is: you sit down.' In the larder, he looked desperately for something she might like. There was some cold rice pudding, and on one shelf higher a jar marked 'quince jam 1959'. When he came back, she was sitting with her elbows on the table, holding her hair back from her face with her hands.

'You only picked at your supper,' he said encouragingly. 'Rice pudding's best cold in my opinion.' He pushed the jar towards her. 'Try some of this with it.'

'How do you know I didn't eat much?'

'I was there. Pour the tea and let's have a feast.'

She smiled and picked up the pot. He liked her hands: they looked soft, but not just soft, without fancy nails. She liked the fact that he'd noticed she didn't eat: women always liked that sort of thing. I must entertain her, he thought; take her out of herself a bit. 'Do you often make tea?'

'In the middle of the night? I don't think so. I heard you come down – at least I didn't know it was you, and I've run out of sleeping pills.'

'Do you take 'em every night?' (How the rich *lived*! Everything done for them by someone or something else!)

'No. Just sometimes.'

'Nervy, are you? I'm nervy myself: it's awkward, because you can't put your finger on it – what's wrong, I mean. It's a nice cup of tea you've made. Who did you guess it would be then, when you heard the noise?'

She looked warily at him for a moment: she wasn't at all like Emma. 'Not you,' she said. She pulled a packet of cigarettes out of her pocket and a small gold lighter. 'Want one?'

He didn't smoke.

'Who could it have been?'

'Emma – most probably. My mother wouldn't eat in the night: she'd worry too much about her figure.'

He wanted to smack her for that. 'What about that doctor?'

She looked at him for a moment without speaking, said coldly. 'I've no *idea* what *he* does,' and then, without any more warning, burst into a flood of tears.

101

He waited a bit, amazed, and then fetched one of the drying cloths from the rack over the stove.

'What's upsetting you so much then? Poor girl: what's making you so angry – and sad?

'Use this – it's nice and warm to mop you up.

'Have another cup of tea.' He had poured it out. 'Strangers don't count: you can talk to them and no damage done.'

When she had given over gasping and streaming, she told him. It was a queer tale and more than anything else he found it confusing. All about her mother and this doctor (he *knew* you couldn't trust them) years ago. When her father had been alive – before he was a hero. The doctor had been much younger than her mother – he hadn't been a doctor then – but he had seduced her; or, as the poor girl cried, her mother had seduced the younger man. With the father in the house and all. *She* thought that this was why he had gone off to get himself killed in the war: it had been so awful for him. And she, a young girl of seventeen, she had known about it – she'd heard them in the garden one night when they thought she was asleep in her room. Up till then, she'd just thought he was a friend – you know – someone who came and went – she hadn't noticed that he seemed always to come when her father wasn't there – was working in London. But the things she had heard in the garden had made it all abominably plain. And her poor father had got to know of it – never *mind* how she knew that! She just knew it; and then there had been Dunkirk and he had gone off one morning when she had been practising, and she'd just kissed him like any other morning only he hadn't come back. And then she had realized that it was because her mother had made his life so terrible – not worth living – that he had gone off in a little boat and got killed. Now he saw, didn't he, that for her to walk into the room twenty years later and find this awful man there with her mother was too much?

He listened, and nodded – more to show that he was listening than to indicate agreement or even understanding. He understood that she was not happy all right, and of course, if people felt like that, they spent nearly all their time trying to find the reason for it, and he knew that he wasn't there to find the reason *for* her, just to provide comfort – a little ignorant warmth in this awful life of hers, jam-crammed with ideas and disaster and with no man to account for it or take her mind off herself.

When she had no more to say she asked him what he thought. He thought.

'Twenty years is a long time. Even if your mother fancied him then, she wouldn't be picking up her skirts after him now. After all, twenty years ago she would have been what?'

She did some rather sulky calculations then, and said thirty-eight.

'Only a year older than you are now,' he began, but she interrupted with arrogant astonishment:

'How on earth do you know my age?'

He looked sly, but resisted the temptation to tease her.

'Your sister told me. You don't look it,' he added. 'But I don't suppose your mother did either. Come now, you've been a married woman – haven't you ever been in love?'

She blew her nose on the tea towel. 'Of course I have.'

'Well, then.'

'Have *you* ever been in love?'

Trust a woman for turning the tables. 'Yes,' he said promptly: 'with Rita Hayworth. It lasted eighteen months and broke up for lack of occasion.' That got him out of any real confession. He'd never told anyone about Violet and he wasn't starting now.

'That's not what I mean.'

'She died,' he said, without having meant to at all. 'Anyway, you can see that there's nothing unnatural about falling in love: I'm not talking about rights and wrongs or morality of any kind – just how people are. You can't go on blaming her for that. Is there someone you care for at the present time?'

'I don't know. I mean, you can go to bed with someone for *months*, can't you, without really knowing what you feel about them?'

This threw him. To conceal his amazement and curiosity he took her untouched rice pudding. 'Do you mind if I finish this for you?'

She shook her head. 'Of course, one calls it love because one can't think what else to say.'

'Does one?'

She glanced sharply at him, but he stared back guilelessly. Then he filled his mouth with rice pudding and quince. He was thinking furiously. She took his silence as an invitation for further confidence.

'Everybody's *married*, you see. They're always weighed down with wives and families and awful, arduous jobs to pay for their boring lives. I'm just light relief – only I'm not a light person, and they don't relieve me. I met Dick *with* his wife on the train from here to London . . .'

He heard what she said, but he wasn't taking it in much. He had too much on his mind. If one of the hazards of living a rich life was that you couldn't call your wife your own, he would have to think again about his entire future. He had the sick, familiar sensation of sliding imperceptibly into a jam. Already it looked as though he'd got stuck with a career that left you wondering what to do with a lot of your time. He knew all right that you could spend weeks without a poem coming your way, and he didn't get at all the same kick out of any other kind of writing. In between times he'd thought that having enough money would mean that things like new blades for shaving and making a proper job of it, affording stamps and sticking them on envelopes, frying sausages exactly right how you wanted them, would be pleasant enough while he was waiting for any great adventure. But beyond, or within his dreams and his day-to-day habits, lay a number of convictions which he didn't want interfered with by the facts of other people's lives, thanks very much. He didn't at all like his idea of respectable girls and tarts being interfered with by people having too much money to need to be paid for it.

'. . . half resents me being a pianist and half expects it to fill my life when he's not there . . .' she was saying. Was her being a pianist the point? After all, he hadn't met any of them before – perhaps music made them a randy lot. Or perhaps it was because she was a widow: that wasn't her fault, after all.

'Once you're sure that the other person doesn't love you, you have to stop – don't you think?'

'Perhaps you should get married again,' he said hopelessly. Who on earth would marry a tart of thirty-seven? She didn't seem too sure either, for she said immediately:

'It's all very well to say that, but one has to find the right person first. I want a man I can respect: someone who is at least trying to help other people – you know – with ideals and at least one principle I can understand and admire. Not just making a little more money this year than he would have dreamed of needing last.'

'Last what?'

'Last year.'

Of course she didn't *look* her age. That was something to do with the rich which fitted in with his scheme of things. Without the slightest warning he was engulfed by a huge yawn. This meant, he knew, that he wanted to get out of a situation – not just because he was getting bored, but because it made him anxious. He used to yawn and yawn the days before his operations; he'd tricked them there: they all thought he was being cool. Luckily for him, she yawned too.

'Caught it from you,' she said. 'You've been very patient, listening to me like this, Dan – I suppose I may call you that?'

'Try and stop you,' he thought. 'It's my name,' he said.

She put her hand over her mouth to yawn again. That's why her fingers were nice – all that piano-playing.

'I'd like to hear you play the piano,' he said.

'Why do you think he's come back here after all this time?'
She was off again. 'Who?'

'Dr King. Why would he *want* to come?'

He sensed some sort of trap here: like smelling fire without knowing where it came from. 'Perhaps he wanted to see how you'd all grown.' She couldn't quarrel with that, surely? And she didn't.

'I suppose he might have wanted to do that. I'll play for you tomorrow. Do you write good poetry? I should think you might.'

That was a fool question. That was more like a woman than she'd been being for some time. 'It's not something you have much say in,' he answered with better-humoured care. 'Supposing you know in the first place. It wouldn't be at all like playing the piano – where you have all your notes laid out . . .'

'I know that,' she interrupted – very rudely, he thought. 'But do *you* think it's good? When you've finished it, I mean.'

'They're making a book of it,' he answered stiffly: 'they don't pay me for my opinion.'

She looked abashed, and much the better for it. She hadn't the face for gaiety, he thought – the very opposite of Dot – she looked her best with trouble brewing, more like those record sleeves of grand opera. She'd look just right coming down some draughty stone steps in her nightdress yelling out some royal secret.

They went to bed in the end: she didn't clear up much – said Mrs Hanwell would do it, and his opinion of her dropped further still. However, he wanted to get back to the strange and crowded privacy of his room. They were quiet on the stairs, and she did all the lights. 'Good night, Dan,' she said. 'Good night, then,' he answered, and she slipped off down the passage.

In his room, he took off his jacket, shoes, trousers and his top jersey: quite enough in a strange place. Then he shut the windows as he never fancied air coming in at him all night, and got into bed. He tried to get to sleep before what had been making him anxious came into words in his mind but he couldn't do it. He was afraid that Emma might turn out to be like her sister: he didn't want that, but they were likely two of a kind. It stood to reason. I must test her so she won't know she's being tested, but I have to know. I'll think of a test first thing tomorrow – something cunning that she won't know what it is . . .

CHAPTER 8

ESME

S HE had had a wretched night. She should never have drunk that cup of coffee after dinner. Only then she had thought that perhaps the girls and that strange young man would go to bed, or go to play the gramophone in the library, and she would have Felix quite naturally to herself. But it hadn't turned out like that. They had all sat so long over dinner that she had sent Mrs Hanwell home and she and Emma had done the washing up. When they had joined the others, it was to find Cressy gone to bed, and Mr Brick teaching Felix some extremely complicated patience game. As she had come into the room, and seen Felix's red head bent over the cards, she had resisted an absolutely mad impulse to stroke it. Naturally, one resisted one's impulses, but that didn't stop one feeling frightful about having had them in the first place. Perhaps she just felt maternal about him now. But much later that night, as she tossed in a bed which she felt Mrs Hanwell could not possibly have made properly since it had seemed cold and lumpy from the word go, the idea of her feeling maternal about Felix made everything much worse. It underlined everything that she had lost and everything that she had never had. He had matured so well, while she had simply decayed as little as she could contrive. At dinner she had got him to tell her something of his Far Eastern experiences, and even while he was being most interesting about how long it took to rehabilitate a starving child, she had wondered – in a manner which she drearily recognized as incurably vulgar and frivolous – whether, in true Somerset Maugham fashion, he had contracted some quasi-marriage with a beautiful illiterate half-caste.

Even if he hadn't done anything of the kind, she thought, switching off her bedside light for a third attempt at sleeping, he must have slept with other women since me: perhaps dozens, perhaps just two or three serious ones. But while the thought of an anonymous crowd of girls was painfully bearable, the idea of two or three mistresses (such as she had been) was not. In the dark, when one had the double ostrich sensation of neither being seen nor being able to see oneself, it was easy for memories and sensation to flood her stranded body so that it became what she felt. Now, she was not feeling so old: just parched and abandoned, overcome by simple longing for him to press his hands each side of her waist, to stroke her shoulders, to sharpen her nipples with his fingers until she was ready for him to come slowly into her (as she had taught him, because then he had been too young to wait long). Afterwards he would kiss her – the best time for it; they would admire each other's eyes, intent, affectionate – nothing to gain at those moments because they each had everything of the other; he would admire her ears, her knees, her wrists (which he said was the first thing he had noticed about her), and she, more secret in her admiration because really it was more than that, would adore his neck and the shape of his head and the polished skin over his back. His skin had smelt wonderful, 'of warm grapes', she had said, and he had said 'nonsense', but she had felt his young man's vanity examine the remark and accept it as a compliment. He had been such a darling, and nothing about him seemed changed except to make him even more attractive. She shifted from lying on one side of her back – she seemed to be burning hot and her body ached. She was back where he had left her, twenty years ago, and, she had bitterly discovered, in love for the first time in her life, and without him – only now he lay a few yards away. Being in love meant that one could not do

109

without the physical presence of the other person: without it, one forgot everything; had no proportion about time since it all seemed indiscriminately endless; one did not notice anything very much and one did not in the least care about not noticing. All this, she knew, would make some kind of people assume that all she wanted was to be eternally in bed, with Felix making love to her non-stop. She had wanted to be eternally with Felix whatever either of them was doing, and of course, sometimes it would have been making love. But she knew that loving someone entirely was, for her, at least, centred upon their being there – hearing them, seeing them, touching them only sometimes. And all this, when she was thirty-eight, had burst upon her – with someone who was fourteen years younger than she. Then, she had been able to say that this difference did not really matter: she had been remarkably attractive and Felix had set the seal on her attractions: she had the kind of figure that in the 'twenties had been described as 'boyish'; and impeccable skin (which meant not just her face) and an emotional energy unimpaired by domestic chores or tensions. It had not seemed impossible then. She had imagined marrying him; having their children; providing him with all the structure for a happy and successful career; and even, she remembered now, putting up gracefully with his casual infidelities which she had reckoned would have started just about now. Some time when he was over forty and she 'was older'.

The plain fact was that she wanted him – now. Not just as much as she had ever wanted him – possibly even more. Twenty years of celibacy had not helped this at all. It seemed simply to release a weight of feeling which should never have been allowed to accumulate. And if she was so much older, why should her body go on behaving in exactly the same way? *Why?* He had once asked her whether, when she wanted him, the feeling started from the top and went down, or the other way round: then, almost immediately, he had touched her, and she had said the other way round – like an arrow, really, a kind of burning thud; and he had hummed a bit of 'Jerusalem' and said he'd known the bit about arrows was pornographic, and she had said why was a woman wanting a man always considered more pornographic brackets absurd, and faintly improper brackets than the other way round. He laughed and said that he supposed men had had more practice at dressing up their lusts, or alternatively, no need to clothe them.

She was not naked and she seemed to be either feverishly hot or covered with a cold sweat and sometimes both at the same time. She sat up in the dark and immediately her arms and shoulders were cold. One spent a great deal of one's life learning to act truly on what one felt. What could she do now? She sat, for a moment or two, allowing herself to want him, as though he was in London, or she had the curse badly, or Julius was there: any respectable, irresponsible reason – anything at all which let the thing stay just how she felt. Then she turned on the light. Then she could not help seeing bits of herself. The absurdity, the shame, the imagination of people controlling hearty laughter with social compassion and the most secret indictment – what, indeed, she might well have felt about someone else, a friend, in her lack of position – flooded over her. Here she was, a woman of nearly sixty, struggling with embarrassing lack of success over a situation which any outsider would have dubbed sheer lust; than which, if it failed, there was nothing more funny and disgusting. It was hateful to be in a position that could neither be ignored nor put a stop to. And he would be asleep: she was certain that he had no idea how she felt.

She got out of bed, but even then, she was so governed by her sense of appearances, that she stopped at her dressing-table. For some reason, she had not put on her hair-net, or any face cream. She turned on the dressing-table lights and three impressions of her appeared. She was amazed at how harmless, blurred, insignificant she looked. 'What you need is a night's rest,' is what she would have said to these poor muddled

111

impressions. Staring at herself she started to cry. Nobody could afford to hate themselves in this kind of way for long; self-pity was the only possible descent from such a pitch. She had been alone for a very long time: most women did not have to live without a man from the age of thirty-eight. And if the man suddenly turned up after all this time, it was perfectly natural that she should feel like this. It didn't mean anything. It simply hurt. On top of feeling unhappy, she felt dreadfully humiliated: it was very unfair to be made to feel so ashamed at her time of life: she would feel much better for a good cry that would get it out of her system. So, like a peevish child, she indulged herself in as much of a show as she could put on, until, snuffling quietly, but with not a tear left, she crept shivering and exhausted into bed.

But this had not prevented her from waking very early – at least an hour before her usual time. Her head throbbed and her bones ached and the thought that this was only Saturday morning hung over her. She switched on her electric kettle and got out of bed. Two cups of tea and a very hot bath helped. Then she settled down to make herself 'presentable', which meant, as it always had, as attractive as possible. Her favourite tweed suit and some new, rather fashionable stockings further raised her morale, and by the time she drew her curtains to see what kind of day it was going to be, the sun was up and out. There had been another heavy frost, but the mist this morning looked much less purposeful than yesterday; the sun was pale-yellow and the sky ice-blue; the lawn glittered and smoke from village chimneys in the valley was the colour of dog violets. She loved these mornings: a cock pheasant swaggered about in the field of stubble at the end of the garden; there were two perfectly new mole-hills in the front of the main border just where she had planted a new batch of grape hyacinths, and Mrs Hanwell's cat – whom she privately thought of as plain dotty – was edging his portly fur through the hedge back from one of his abortive excursions. Mrs Hanwell pretended that he was worth keeping because he was such a good hunter, but he was far too cowardly to catch anything but butterflies in summer which he crunched up like fairy toast, and then jostled her all over the kitchen for square meals. This morning she felt actually comforted by the sight of him and the mole-hills and the pheasant. It was eight o'clock, and she went down for the post.

Emma was the first down for breakfast, looking neat and pretty – and nervous at finding her mother alone. Esme asked her what she planned to do.

'I thought I'd take Dan to see the farm: Hanwell's, I mean.' She had her back to her mother while she poured coffee at the sideboard. 'He's nice, isn't he?' she added.

'Very nice, dear,' answered Esme, and this meaningless exchange seemed to ease them both; Esme returned to *The Times*, and Emma, after some counting, took two poached eggs.

Felix was next. He said a few things like wasn't it a lovely morning and how nice and English they both looked and yes, he'd slept like a log. It was easier seeing him than she had thought. She had expected actually to blush and not to be able to meet his eye; but it was all unemotional and quite cosy, really. Things always seemed worse at night. The whole atmosphere was getting like the first act in those plays before the war that Julius had so much despised: 'dull and worthless people eating endless breakfasts,' he had said.

Mr Brick arrived, apologizing for being late. He brought three large and beautiful mushrooms wrapped in a handkerchief. 'Where did you get them?'

He'd been out, he said. He presented the mushrooms to Emma who took them out to Mrs Hanwell. Mrs Hanwell adored her, and would love cooking them. While Emma was out of the room, and Mr Brick was at the sideboard, Felix looked at Esme and winked. This brought utterly unexpected tears of gratitude to her eyes: she felt counted, in league with him; sure that he had come to see her after all. She pushed her cup towards him. 'Give me some more coffee, there's a dear,' she said.

Cressy arrived just at the same time as Emma's mushrooms. Cressy was one of those few people who, even when no longer a young girl, could arrive at breakfast unmade-up, not seeming to have combed her hair: in fact, she would have sat up in bed, dragged the four garments she wore on Saturday mornings towards her and somehow got out of bed twenty seconds later with them on. And she looked unkempt, careless and magnificent. Esme felt both men's attention on her as she said, 'Morning all,' and downed her lemon juice. She looked at Emma's mushrooms and made a mock Bisto face. 'Where *did* you get those?'

'Dan found them.'

'I say you are a forager.' She yawned. 'Night and Day, You are the One.'

Emma said:

'What on earth do you mean by that?'

'Dan and I had a midnight feast: but don't worry, not in the dorm.'

'*I* wasn't worrying.' Emma had gone a uniform bright pink and glared at her mushrooms.

'Oh dear,' thought Esme: 'she hasn't woken up in a better frame of mind.' Aloud, she said: 'I've got to go into Battle this morning.' She was looking at Felix as she spoke. 'Anybody like to come?'

He immediately said, yes, he'd love to see Battle Abbey again, but before she could clinch it, Cressy said:

'You needn't, Mother. I've got to take my car to Mr Monk. I'll collect the meat, etc. And there's plenty of room for a sightseeing doctor.' She turned to Felix. 'From one road, you can see the carp pond or whatever it was that one of the owners of the Abbey drowned himself in. It's cursed by fire and water, you know. I suppose modern curses would be by Gas and Electricity:

fire and water's so general. I mean lightning counts, and one year a marquee caught fire at a flower show: they counted that in the curse, of course.'

Emma said: 'Perhaps Mummy *wants* to go to Battle.'

'Well, do come if you want to. I only meant that I've got to go, because Mr Monk has my new battery and I need it badly.'

'No.' Dignity was not just important at her age, it was essential. 'You take Felix: I've got plenty to do here.'

Cressy looked at Felix. 'If he wants to come.'

'I'll come with you,' said Felix. His face had a total lack of expression which, she remembered exactly as though it was yesterday, preceded anger.

So that was that. When everybody had finished breakfast – including Mr Brick, who had concentrated upon food with speechless, unwinking attention – they all dispersed. It was while she was in the sitting-room finishing her list for Cressy that Felix came in.

'Is she always like that?'

'Who?' But she knew perfectly well who he meant.

'Your elder daughter.'

'No – not always. I don't know what's the matter. I'm sorry she's so rude to you.'

'I wasn't thinking of me. It's you she's intolerable to.'

She made a gesture – resigned, dismissive – really to conceal her pleasure in his interest.

'Do you mind if I tell her where she gets off?'

She didn't know what to say to that. 'She's not a child, you know.'

He gave one of his Scottish grunts. 'She behaves like one.'

'Well – see if you can find out what's the matter.'

He said he'd see and took her list. Minutes later, she heard them leave, and Mrs Hanwell claimed her attention.

Mrs Hanwell was in an obscurely bad mood, and it took Esme some time to discover that this was because someone had eaten some pie reserved for Hanwell's elevenses. Mrs Hanwell did not *say* it had been eaten: she simply reiterated that she could not think where it had gone: listing with mounting resentment a number of improbable things which could not possibly have happened to it. In vain did Esme suggest that it had been eaten by Cressy: Miss Cressy would not *touch* blackberries; it was the same with Whiskey – he never fancied anything sweet – unlike Hanwell, who had a sweet tooth, and liked his pies cold and in the morning. 'Well, now, what could we give him instead,' and Esme started to rummage through the larder followed by Mrs Hanwell pointing out all the things he couldn't have because they had not got them. In the end they were settling for half a green jelly rabbit and some custard on to which mixture Mrs Hanwell said she would crush some home-made gingerbread to give it body, when the telephone rang and Esme thankfully escaped to answer it.

It was Jennifer Hammond. Her husband had been unable to go on his Continental business trip because of the fog, so might she bring him to dinner with her this evening? From her voice, Esme knew that Jennifer was speaking with her husband in the room. He has to go to London early tomorrow afternoon for a conference, Jennifer said. Had she been alone, she would have asked Esme what she thought this meant and then, without waiting for Esme's reply, told her. So Esme simply said it would be wonderful to see them at a quarter to eight and rang off. Jennifer Hammond spent all her spare time wondering whether her husband was unfaithful to her. Esme was her nearest confidante. Richard spent two nights in London every week, maintaining there a one-roomed service flat which was almost insultingly uncomfortable for two on the rare occasions when he invited her to share it with him. He also went on foreign week-end business trips; the only time when he had really pressed her to accompany him had been to Glasgow last February. She hadn't gone because her older child, Timothy, was getting whooping cough and all the pipes had frozen up. 'But *Glasgow* – in *February* – I *ask* you!' she had said to Esme in her little nasal, clipped drawl. She had been married for about five years now, but the highlight of her career had been before then when she was doing her season and working in a poodle salon in Knightsbridge: 'Girl With Double Mission' the *Express* had said of her on the Hickey page, 'Miss Jennifer Templeton-Urquhart-Chance does not let the grass grow under her feet either at the Savoy or in Sloane Street,' etc. What Esme was unable to make out was how much, if Jennifer was right in her speculation, she minded. 'Looking a perfect fool' came fairly high up on her list of anxieties, and it might only be that. Esme had advised her not to find out for sure, and to take comfort in the fact that husbands who made regular, if clumsy, attempts to conceal their behaviour did not really want to break up their marriages. Jennifer had stared at her with hurt, dry eyes, and said: 'I think that's terribly cynical – dn't you?' The vowel in 'don't' got lost these days like some of the final consonants of her youth. However, some of the advice seemed to have stuck, since Jennifer frequently told Esme that she had finally decided not to make a scene.

That would make eight for dinner. She must warn Mrs Hanwell to make even more of both stuffings for the goose. On her way to the kitchen she remembered wearily that Cressy had condemned both Hammonds as dull. Oh dear.

She could not stay long in the kitchen because Hanwell had come in for his elevenses (he usually began them soon after ten) and he was so paralysed with shyness that it was cruelty to use the kitchen when he was there. In spite of having known Esme for fifteen years, he would still start like someone being given an awful fright when she appeared, and then subside into a trance-like stillness, unable even to masticate – food froze in his mouth and his eyes rolled in slow frenzy round the kitchen in desperate and local effort to escape her presence. Meanwhile his neck changed colour from Georgian to Victorian brick. Eventually he would be reduced to staring at his hands laid on the kitchen table as though they had alarmingly changed size or were the wrong number, while Mrs Hanwell, in a loud high voice, gave vent to his alleged opinions. He managed a very small farm about half a mile away and helped part time with the garden. He had once been to London, to the Zoo, but hadn't enjoyed it much, and Mrs Hanwell said he wasn't going again – wouldn't dream of it. She got out of the kitchen as soon as possible and said she would make some beds.

She made the beds, and tidied up, and it was still just after eleven. She could not expect them back before twelve. Thoughts of Felix were again banking up in her mind; nothing coherent – simply the sense of his being here, returning to see her in this same house. Before she had really noticed it, she had taken out the picture of him and was looking at it, to see how he had changed. He looked now much more resolved, steadier than this picture, indeed, all the things one might expect him to have grown into, but this had increased his charms – for her, at any rate. He was now a qualified doctor; he had been to the wars, he had travelled in the course of his profession (she wondered what had induced him to go off to the East like that? If he had stayed in England, he would now be doing very nicely in private practice in London – just the right personality and appearance to make a great success). It was really rather like Julius – that going off into the blue to help mankind. A noble gesture: but like most pieces of nobility, one needed to be the right distance from it; otherwise it would be like standing too close to somebody who cried 'Friends, Romans, Countrymen' and getting a clip on the ear. She'd had that once in her life; well – twice: first Julius, then Felix. The similarity of their behaviour struck her for the first time. Both had set aside their private lives to serve an uncertain, unknown quantity of humanity. In both cases, it had been she who had suffered: she, who had never for a moment seen or understood life in these terms. Was this a sexual distinction? Was this the heroic equivalent of men working and women weeping? Would she, in fact, at any point, have risked her own life for anyone? This was too large and loose a question; she must be found dishonest, or found wanting. But, of course she hadn't wept at first – not about Julius. That was what was so awful. When the news had come, Julius's brother, Mervyn, had rung her up, and gone to see her in the London flat. She had been there because she had an assignation with Felix that evening in London. Mervyn had broken the news so gently, that for some time she hadn't understood what he meant. Then he had given her Julius's letter. It had been very simple. He felt that this was something he *could do*, he had said: and one must do what one could. He hoped she would understand. (The implication here was that if she didn't it was just too bad.) Then followed some anxious details about the children: and instructions to apply to Mervyn in case of any difficulty. Finally he had said something like, 'Thank you for my daughters. Be happy.' Mervyn had insisted on taking her out to luncheon: she must eat; she must not be allowed to be alone. And she had gone; had listened as though in some kind of meaningless, not good, not bad, dream, about how, although she would have to choose between London and the country, there was quite enough money for one place. He had made over all his shares in the firm to her, with provision for the girls when they married. Finally, Mervyn had said that she was taking it wonderfully: call him any time (he had seemed daunted by her calm: he was himself deeply shaken by his brother's death), and left her in the empty little flat. She had rung Felix: he had been out. She had sat, trying to understand her position and trying to have the right feelings about it. But the awful thing had been that the most she was able to feel about Julius was regret tinged with faint pangs of anger (knowing as little as he did, how *could* he reconcile abandoning her and the girls with helping people?) and a distinctly uncomfortable amazement that his death was not making her feel more unhappy. Inside, or below these expressed feelings in her mind, was the extraordinary *light* sensation of excitement about her being free. She knew, or felt, that this was wicked – a wicked fact about her, but she could not stop these rockets of excitement and relief which kept exploding in the roof of her mind, illuminating briefly an immense future of marvellous love. For, by then, she knew that Felix was the only man she had actually loved – for whom she would do anything, give or become what he willed.

It was not until she was getting ready to meet Felix (his telephone was not answered when she rang it) that she began to wonder how *he* would take it. He was young: it would be a difficult situation for him. He would, she realized, not be at all sure how *she* would be feeling, and he would make decently sombre gestures about Julius: she would love him less if he didn't. She must be gentle and enigmatic: let events run their course, but run by him, not herself. She must not impinge on his new and touchy manhood. This would not be dishonesty, it would be tact. I must be very wicked to be able to think so much about it all, she had thought, while trying to decide what one should wear in these circumstances. That shows you. In no play, or book, would anybody think what I'm thinking unless they were totally bad: i.e. unable to love anyone. '*All* she worried about was what she should wear the night after her husband had died when she was going to meet her lover.' But I don't want to be a mean and frivolous creature, because that isn't good enough for him – for my darling love. I would never have done anything about it: would have stayed with Julius and brought up his children as long as he expected me to. I didn't arrange what has happened. But the thought of being able to spend every night with Felix openly, by right – to know that she would always see him, could have his child, made her feel faint with joy and longing for the most simple and direct celebration.

It was a marvellously fine, golden evening: the news-stand placards were still chalked with 'Dunkirk Latest', but all the evening papers had been sold. People hung on news and being nice to each other in the streets and needing to hear Churchill's voice on the wireless. There was not much traffic, but a great many people walking about. Their flat was in Adelphi Street, and she was going to meet Felix in the Charing Cross Hotel which was large, dingy and anonymous enough to be safe.

He was waiting for her, got slowly up from his chair with a look of barely suppressed excitement, nearly smiling, but trying to look as though she was simply an acquaintance. He had a newspaper in his hand.

'Do you want this?' he had said.

'Why should I?' She wondered irrationally whether the paper had something about Julius in it, but then she was sure that it hadn't, because he simply said, quite cheerfully:

'What would you like to drink? Supposing that they've got whatever it is?'

She thought for a moment, and chose brandy.

He put the newspaper down on the table. 'I say – is there some sort of crisis?'

She shook her head. 'I'll tell you when you've got the drinks.'

Obediently, he rushed away and she sank into his chair. As she did so her eye caught the headline: '100,000 of Our Boys are Back'. Felix had put his gas mask under the table: he would leave it behind if she didn't put it in full view. She tried to visualize a hundred thousand men and failed. Felix came back with the drinks eventually: probably after a long time, but she didn't know how long; her impatience to see him had evaporated and she felt only an increasing apprehension about the extra half hour in their lives.

When he returned and put the glass in her hand, he pressed the top of her wrist with two fingers. 'I want to kiss you,' he said. Their eyes met with a mutual candour. There wasn't another chair near, so he sat on the arm of hers.

'Julius is dead,' she said.

He gave a violent start, his beer slopped on to his hand and he put the glass down, and then looked at her as though he wasn't sure that he'd heard what she said.

121

'It's true. He was killed yesterday. I only heard this morning.'

'Oh God. How do you mean *killed?*'

'In some sort of boat: fetching people from France. He was shot. But the people who were with him are in hospital and they aren't up to talking much yet. I tried to ring you, but you were out.'

'I was at School all day,' he answered mechanically, and then burst out: 'I can't believe it! I just, can't – take it in.'

'I had to tell you.'

'My poor darling. You shouldn't have come!'

'Why not?'

He had looked at her then, and then quickly away.

'I had to come: for one thing I wanted to tell you.'

'How did he come to be in a boat fetching people? What made him do that?'

She said almost irritably: 'I tell you I don't know. He didn't say a word about it. Just caught the train to London on Monday morning and didn't come back.'

'Terribly brave of him.'

'He doesn't know a thing about boats.'

'That makes it more – ' he stopped.

'Courageous?'

'Yes.'

There was a long, uncertain silence; then he said: 'My God!'

She offered him a cigarette. 'Thanks.'

There was another silence, while he smoked, staring at the hideous railway carpet, and she tried nervously to feel what he was thinking.

'I find it pretty hard to take in too,' she offered at last.

'I was thinking about what he said at dinner that night.'

'What?'

'He said: "My God, I wish I was your age." I see now what he meant.' She didn't remember that, but she didn't say so.

Then he said: 'Let's get out of here,' so they did.

Outside, he said: 'Don't let's go out to dinner'; and she agreed. They walked silently back to the flat. She had half a bottle of whisky, and while she was getting soda and glasses he wandered restlessly round the small living-room, fidgeting, bumping into things, until she wanted to snap: 'Oh, for heaven's sake, sit *down*!'

She handed him a glass and said: 'Come and sit by me, darling.'

He sat obediently, with his long legs stretched out, holding the glass in both hands, and she thought, 'What beautiful hands he has.' Then, without looking at her, he said: 'You don't think this has anything to do with us, do you?'

She did not see what he meant.

'I mean,' he said, with a patience both cold and embarrassed, 'do you think he'd found out that you were unfaithful to him, and that made him go off?'

Although she could not reasonably object to it she did not like the way he put this. 'I'm sure he hadn't any idea of it. Anyway, it wouldn't have been the point with him.'

'Why wouldn't it?'

'Oh – because he didn't *do* things like that.'

'You don't have much practice at dying before you do it.'

'I mean that he always – or always tried – to do things from larger principles, not out of what *he* felt about people, or any particular people, but what he thought *people* ought to feel about – humanity. He wasn't really interested in people singly or personally.'

'You mean he had a public conscience?'

'That's what I was trying to say.'

There was a silence, and then he said: 'He really had, hadn't he? I mean, when somebody actually goes out and dies for something, you do know that they always meant it.'

'I suppose so.'

'You don't seem very impressed.'

'*Impressed?*' She got up quickly and fetched the whisky.

'I'm sorry: you must have had an awful shock!' But he sat quite still.

She poured them each a stiff drink – she was beginning to need it – then, sitting across the room from him she said: 'If Julius *had* found out about us, it wouldn't have affected his going to Dunkirk. Supposing I had been utterly devoted – faithful – it wouldn't have made any difference to him about going. He would simply go because he would think it more important than his private life: he would just go because he thought it was the right thing to do. So you needn't worry about that.'

'Worry about it! You don't understand! You don't seem to realize what a remarkable man that makes him.'

So began their first and last quarrel. She had the nightmare sensation of being pushed into arguing on the wrong side – or if not the wrong side, arguing from a completely dishonest position. It was all very well for other people to admire this gesture, she said: but what about *her?* What about his children? Had he any right at all wilfully to jeopardize their family life – to leave them without a father simply because he wished he was a younger man and able to fight? Surely, if one undertook marriage and fatherhood, one's first responsibilities lay there?

Did hers? he asked with cutting intensity. Was that how she had been behaving about her responsibilities? If he *had* been a younger man, he had gone on, he would have quite possibly been at Dunkirk anyway. And supposing that he had guessed about their affair? Very few men would have utterly disregarded that factor: it must have made him feel he had less to live for had he known . . .

They didn't know that he knew – had no reason on *earth* to suppose that he knew . . .

It wasn't as though he had left them paupers, was it? A man like Julius, he was sure, would have arranged everything very carefully in the event of his not getting back . . .

'You've always been *against* him,' she cried.

'I never realized what he was like. You never told me!'

'I simply told you that I didn't love him!'

And he had looked stony and incredulous, even about that. As though, she cried, he didn't believe her, or it wasn't possible. They had left the facts of the matter far behind: it was not a composition of shock and guilt – she had never envisaged his capacity for guilt. It was he now who filled their glasses – contemptuously. Julius, she said unsteadily, after a swig of lukewarm, neat whisky, Julius hadn't loved *her*, so it was useless and cruel to put all the responsibility for indifference on *her*. You didn't love people out of intellectual admiration for their behaviour, and for years now he had been so concerned with the state of the world that he had entirely forgotten that she was an infinitesimal part of it. Couldn't he *see that*?

Not infinitesimal, he corrected (he had more trouble saying the word than she), she meant a tiny, if you like, but none the less real part of it.

All right, she meant that.

Anyway, she wasn't keeping to the point. Caring about humanity didn't rule out personal affections: it was simply that different occasions required different scales of concern . . .

No! no! *no!* People could always suit occasions to their temperament! And Julius had always been a man for the larger, more distant occasion.

Did she not think that the world needed men like that?

She thought they had been talking about marriage – not the state of the world.

It seemed to him, Felix had said, pouring the dregs of the bottle into his own glass, that this was a time for worrying about the state of the world.

All *right*, she had said: perhaps it is – in fact it obviously is: we may be invaded next week. But you can't expect that to alter my feelings about somebody I've been married to for eighteen years.

There was the first silence of the quarrel, then she picked up the telephone pad on the table by her empty glass and saw it had Julius's handwriting on it. They had been sitting in the dusk, and it was now too dark to see his face across the room. As she got up to do the blackout, he said, from miles away, 'We don't understand one another.' He got up and left the room. She did the blackout with meticulous, despairing care: there were two windows and the black blind stuff could only just be made to fit. Then she switched on one of the small lamps. Seeing the small, empty room, she had the first surprising, painful stab of loneliness — of being on her own now with nobody entitled to care. She listened, but could not hear a sound of him. Perhaps he had gone? The second this occurred to her, she was sure that he had. He'd just walked out in an angry huff. She would be alone all night in this flat which had really belonged to Julius . . . She ran to the door and into the hall, and in the dark she ran straight against him. 'Felix!' The panic that he might have gone, the fright of running into him, the relief that it was he, were too much for her and she burst into tears. She sobbed and sobbed, clinging to him, unable to say anything coherent or to move until he half carried her into the bedroom and laid her on the bed. He was all kindness, all tender concern: he sat on the bed and held her in his arms and comforted her. She was really unhappy and he was truly kind and it was all real again. 'Don't go tonight — please don't leave me.' He would not dream of it, of course not.

He undressed her and put her to bed: and for both of them the absence of eroticism was another layer of discovering love. He was almost like her father, but she had never had a father whom she could remember. Then she had got frightful hiccoughs — the whisky and emotion and no food, and he had propped her up and made her sip water and repeat some nursery formula after him which he swore could cure her and it did. When he joined her in bed, it was he who commanded the situation; she enjoyed the voluptuous confidence of utter passivity . . . She went to sleep holding his hand as though he were leading her to it.

And in the morning, as she was afterwards never able to forget, everything seemed very calm, and gentle, and sunlit. Once she had tried to speak about their quarrel, to assume apologetic responsibility for it, to explain quietly in this more temperate climate of affectionate intimacy, but he would not allow it, and she still felt he was so much wiser (older?) than she that she was grateful, really, to desist. She was going down to Sussex, to the children, she said: she must tell them. Of course, and he would take her to Charing Cross. He had waited until the train started, and she had watched him standing on the platform, his hair ruffled by the departing train. She had watched until his face was a blur and his hand, raised in farewell, had dropped. Then she had turned anxious attention to the separate problems of telling Cressy and Emma that their father was dead.

On Friday morning she had got his letter. The post had been late that morning, so by some devilish chance she had opened it in front of both children at breakfast. She had been feeling so peaceful about Felix that it was just lovely to see his handwriting, and she had ripped it open with no more thought than that she must read it impassively with Cressy there. The first sentence had stopped her cold. He announced baldly that by the time she got this he would be in uniform, training somewhere in England. He had volunteered for the Royal Marines. She had folded up the letter without reading any more of it, and put it back into its envelope with clumsy, trembling fingers. 'Was it from Daddy?' Emma had asked. She had simply not taken in the fact of her father's death – interpreted it as some different kind of journey which she constantly alluded to in a challenging manner. Now Cressy said: 'Of course not, Em. He's gone – he's not coming back.' 'He's gone to London for the weekend?' 'No,' said Cressy and Emma had looked up at the sound of such a tormented voice and then dug viciously into her boiled egg. 'He *is*.' The egg had overflowed, and tears had begun to spurt from her eyes.

She had put down the letter and got to her feet to comfort Emma: her throat was aching as though it was burned, but Cressy was before her. '*I'll* explain to her: come on, Em.' And she had swept Emma out of the room, leaving their mother alone. Really alone. By the time she had read the letter once she was in no doubt about that. What had hurt her most had been the way that the letter had avoided saying that everything was over between them; had relied upon Julius's example, the state of national emergency, the fact that he, Felix, had been brought to the sudden realization that he had been trying to avoid his own responsibility, that his career must come second and so on. Nothing about their situation – simply the firm, constant inference that it was over. He had not even given her the opportunity to reply: no new address (he did not, conveniently, know where he would be sent), but he made it plain that he had cleared out of his London digs. But to begin with she had not really been able to take in the finer points of her misery. All she *knew* with shocking certainty was that he had left her – for good. It was all over: she really *was* alone. The first few months had been the worst of course, just like people – whether anything had ever happened to them or not – always said that they were. She had got through them by a lot of hard gardening, by teaching Emma to read, by struggling with Cressy's unaccountable tantrums of alternate hostility and sulking. It was very difficult to eat; the greatest luxury was being alone at night in her bedroom and able to cry without interruption. After these fits of exhausting grief she would fall into a stupor of dreamless sleep. She wrote six separate letters to Felix, but sent none of them, although she even addressed one or two to his home in Scotland with 'Please Forward' printed and underlined in one corner. But she always burned them in the end, impelled by a mixture of pride and knowing that really, no letter she wrote could possibly make any difference. If Julius had been there she would have told him everything, and sometimes she wondered whether if she had been able to do that, it might not have been a new start for them. For Julius had been an extremely *kind* man. In a sense, she discovered bitterly, the more you take somebody for granted, which at the time seems to equate with any kind of incompatibility and/or dullness, the more you miss them if they vanish or die. People were kind to her: she had lost her husband in the war; nobody had known about Felix and they had no friends in common, but as the weeks went by she came to accept people's kindness on his account: the two losses became inextricably confused.

One really horrible thing had happened which had shaken her out of her enduring stupor for a time, but in the same way that she discovered that nothing mattered for ever, so nothing ever mattered too much: and during the next twenty years she cultivated busyness, attention to detail and other peoole's smaller problems. 'Like planting dozens of little shrubs in a desert,' she thought now as she sat on her newly made bed. 'Things that are hardy enough not to die, and will stand being somewhere where they can't grow.' At least she had made her own bed – properly. She must stop brooding over her life: but there would be time before the others returned to go and examine those new mole-hills, to see which, if any, of the new muscari could be saved. There was plenty to *do*, after all.

CHAPTER 9

EMMA

S HE had set her alarum clock for seven o'clock because she
particularly wanted her hair to be washed and dried by
breakfast time. She didn't want to waste any proper time
of the day doing it; on the other hand, one couldn't change
one's whole life just because one had invited a man to stay for
the week-end. She laughed silently and hugged her knees in
bed: she was certain it was going to be a lovely day. Morning:
walk to Hanwell's with Dan. Smashing Mrs Hanwell lunch
(bags wash that up and then Cressy will have to do dinner).
Afternoon: take Dan to see the sea. Somehow, I'll have to stop
the other people coming too: he'd surely rather see it for the
first time by himself. She wouldn't count as she was his friend.
Back to tea and fireworks, and even good old Jennifer Hammond wouldn't be able to spoil dinner. What on earth had
made her ask him for the week-end? A kind of experiment in
being brave and casual, and also, she hadn't honestly thought
he would accept. But the good thing about him was that he
seemed to know what he wanted to do and immediately do it.
One good thing: not the only one. It was lucky her mother had
invited that rather nice doctor: it took her mind off possibly
disapproving of Dan – she always seemed to think if Emma
mentioned anyone, or had a meal with them that marriage was
in the offing. She laughed again – she was laughing all the time
– poor Mummy always thought of *things* happening to make
life better; she never considered the possibility of life just being
marvellous and *that* making things happen. She sprang out of
bed. Too dark still to see what kind of day it would be, but

there'd been a frost all right. She turned on her fire and seized her old blue woollen dressing-gown which had once been full length and was now too short for her. Her hair was not long – just below the ears – but it was terrifically thick and was quite a job to wash and dry. She settled down to the business of washing it.

Breakfast – in spite of the mushrooms – was spoilt by Cressy. She knew that Cressy was in a bad mood, but it was very unusual for her to take it out on *her*. But immediately after breakfast, Cressy came to her room and apologized. She said that she'd decided to leave Dick, and also that that doctor got on her nerves.

'Perhaps you'll like him more when you've taken him to Battle,' said Emma hopefully. She had a forgiving nature, and was so glad that Cressy was really friends that she wanted everything to be all right for her sister. 'Isn't he rather attractive?' she added nervously.

But Cressy gave an incomprehensible snort at this suggestion.

'He's old, of course,' she said to seal the peace: it was the only derogatory thing she could think of.

'He's not *old*!' cried Cressy: 'That's the one thing he isn't. I think Dan's very nice though. And your hair looks gorgeous.'

'What *match-making* remarks,' she thought, rummaging for her gum boots: 'I do see that what men think about women is right quite a lot of the time.' But her hair did look good. It was a very dark brown and when clean it had what hairdressers called copper lights in it. She had her camelhair jersey and the same old pleated skirt, but she didn't think men noticed skirts so much: legs and breasts were supposed to be the things. Not as though Dan was men though: he was more like a surprisingly intimate friend. Just as well: her breasts weren't up to much. 'Still, breasts aren't necessarily the gateway to happiness,' she thought thinking of Cressy; 'and it doesn't matter what your legs look like in gum boots.' Her coat was in the hall, and he

131

helped her into it like he had at the office yesterday – *ages* ago – and then lifted her hair and settled it over the top of her collar. 'See? I'm up to all the fancy moves,' he said.

They walked in silence down the drive, and at the gate, she said: 'Would you like to see the farm?' And he said he would. So they crossed the lane and entered a field which had a broad-cart track across its narrow end. She explained that there was a right of way to Hanwell's Farm and on out to a lane beyond his land. To their left was a hazel-nut coppice, and to their right a gently declining, undulating view which went on till the sea – invisible from here, she said. They walked slowly because it was all so nice. The cart-track had short, very green, cropped turf between the ruts which were red, with rusty-coloured ice splintering under their feet, and sometimes there were deeper ruts reflecting the marvellously blue sky. The hedge winked and glittered with rime and frosty old disused cobwebs. The sun was pale and dazzling, not even faintly warm, but the bare woods ahead looked almost fiery in its light. It was a very good year for berries. At the end of the field was another gate and two haystacks by a small wood. The wood had a stile in it, because down in the middle – it was more a wooded quarry – was a small, deep pond: Mr Hanwell had known someone who had stepped into this pond in rubber boots and been drowned. She, Emma, had once seen an adder swimming there on a summer evening. She offered him these pieces of information in case he found the walk boring. Should they go and see? They climbed the stile, and a jay flew angrily over them shouting about their arrival: 'You'd think we had machine guns the way they go on,' Dan said. What was left of the path down to the pond was very steep, and brambles, shrouded in sheep's wool, sprawled across it. But it was worth it when they got there. Half of the pond had streaky ice, and on the other half a pair of mallard floated in a still and secret manner. There was a rotting old landing-stage and the ribs of a sunken boat with rushes growing out through its middle.

'I used to get newts and tadpoles here,' said Emma.

'Have they all left then?'

'How do you mean?'

'Can't you get 'em any more?'

'Oh. Well I haven't tried: I think I got too old for them.'

'Well – it's the wrong time of year,' he said with regret.

The ducks watched them carefully; they had swum a token distance away and were now waiting for them to go, Emma thought. The whole place seemed to be getting quieter all the time. When a cock pheasant squawked, she started. They agreed to go on. 'A nice pond,' he said politely. Better in summer, she said. Things were always more showy then, he agreed.

They walked through three fields' worth of the cart-track to Hanwell's Farm. It lay in a hollow with a steeply banked meadow beside it. There was another pond there and sheep. Geese were loose about the place and some rather dirty white ducks. She led the way to the cow-shed where in a sweet warm twilight three brown-and-white cows were each chewing in their stalls. She took off her woolly gloves for one of them to lick the salt off her hands. Chickens were fussing about in the loft above – in fact everywhere, and a thin black-and-white cat sat looking at them severely. Next to the cow-shed were four pigs in a sty who rushed out to see who might have brought them food.

'He's got a horse as well,' said Emma: 'and Mrs Hanwell keeps bees. Some of everything: not many farmers have that nowadays. I thought you'd like to see it all,' she added rather anxiously. And luckily he said that she was quite right, he would. 'Mrs Hanwell says he's a wonder with animals; it's people he's not so keen on. He never even talks in the pub – just listens. That's their house. It's very pretty inside with a great many things in it. When I was young I used to go to tea and collect eggs and milk the cows with Mr Hanwell: he doesn't mind children nearly as much as people, Mrs Hanwell says.'

The cart-horse was standing apparently plunged in thought,

as it gave a theatrical start when at last it realized that they were there. They rubbed its nose and it tossed its head as though their hands were flies.

'Mr Hanwell calls it Jock, and Mrs Hanwell calls it Brenda,' said Emma: 'she doesn't count gelded animals as male, you see: and she thinks women do most of the work in this world while men just go through the motions. They both agree this horse is a good worker.'

'We had a mule, once,' said Dan. 'And a sheepdog and my sister had a canary. Oh yes, and ferrets. My Dad had a white ferret for a time: *they'd* work for you if you knew how to handle them. But this one went mad and ate what it caught – or mauled it so's you couldn't hardly make a stew of what was left. Eyes like rubies it had. Where does this go then?'

It was a ladder up to the hay-loft above the horse's stall. They climbed it. Bales of hay were stacked against whitewashed walls; an untidy nest was tipsily perched on a crossbeam and there was a very old calendar nailed to the wall. A girl dressed as a drum majorette in a heatwave (tight and scanty green satin) lolled on a polar-bear rug. 'Mrs Hanwell wouldn't have it in the house,' said Emma. 'It's no good to him now though: it's 1944. Let's sit here a bit, shall we? I want to smoke a cigarette.'

'Mind you don't start no fire then.'

They settled themselves on some hay, and she lit her cigarette. Then she said: 'What did you and Cressy talk about last night?'

He seemed both watchful and guarded. He waited a moment and said: 'She made some tea; she talked about men.' Then, added casually: 'She's a tart, isn't she?'

'What on earth do you mean?'

'I mean she goes with men she's not married to.'

'But lots of people do that, without being *tarts*! Of course she's not a tart! Tarts get – paid – for one thing!'

'She doesn't need money though, does she? She wouldn't be doing it for that.'

'Honestly, that isn't the point. She – she just *loves* people. She wants to get married again.'

'She told me she was going with a married man. That doesn't sound like wanting to get married to me.'

'You're just being old-fashioned about it. Perhaps she loves the man. If you love somebody and they want to – want to go to bed with you, if you love them – you do it!'

'Do you?'

She couldn't understand what had got into him. 'Of course,' she said stiffly. There was a silence, and then she said: 'In any case, I'm very fond of my sister and I won't have her spoken about like that.' How awful! Whenever she wanted to sound dignified and angry her voice shook. She smoked her cigarette hard and then said: 'It may be different on canals and wherever else you've been, but I assure you that nowadays people don't get all stuffy and call other people tarts because they go to bed with people without marrying them. People are doing that all the time!' She took a deep breath. 'Virginity's simply uncomfortable and out of date and nobody goes in for that unless they can't help it!'

There was a long pause while she felt the heat slowly dying out of her face and she burned her fingers on the cigarette through holding it badly.

He leaned towards her. 'Give me that,' he said. He took it and pinched it expertly out between his fingers.

'Golly!' she said.

'I'm sorry if I upset you about your sister. Of course you're fond of her. You wouldn't be sharing a flat with her if you weren't. It's natural, after all.'

'What is?'

'Family feeling. Pity you have no brother.'

'If I'd had one, he'd probably be dead from the war. Unless he'd been much younger than me. My father died twenty years ago, you know. I suppose I could have had a brother who'd be about twenty now.'

'You'd have spoilt him between you. One boy and a lot of women. Your sister plays the piano, she tells me.'

'Oh yes: she's awfully good. Well – fairly good, but one judges her by professional standards, you see, and that's pretty high these days.'

'You know a lot about these days, don't you?'

'Well I am *in* them. So are you.'

Everything seemed all right again. Without talking about it, they left the loft. It was likely that people would have different points of view, she thought: it needn't spoil things.

'We could go home a different way, and buy some sweets in the village.'

He agreed to this, and they went on past the farm until they struck the winding narrow lane, sunk between high banks. Wild strawberries, violets, primroses, cuckoo-pint, ragged robin, speedwell, scarlet pimpernel, roses, hawthorn, blackberries and deadly nightshade, lords and ladies, garlic, crab-apples, elder-berries, buttercups, cow parsley, orchids, bugle, daisies, hazel nuts – telling him about these banks she described everything from the point of view of its fruit or flower which was how she had first discovered them. Now the banks looked ragged and sodden, with only old man's beard and briony to decorate the hedges above. 'Still,' she said: 'I expect you know what they're like without my telling you.'

'If you like the country so much, why do you work in London?'

'Oh – well, I have to have some sort of job, and most of them are in London.'

'You don't have to work if you don't want to?'

'Well – I suppose I do want to – in a way.'

'And I suppose you meet more people in London?'

Something in his voice made her look sharply at him; but his face was bland.

'I met you,' she said.

'You meet a lot of writers, I suppose. What are they like?'

'Well – goodness, that's a hopeless question! How do you mean?'

'Am I like them? Any of them?'

'No – you're not!'

'I see.' He seemed disappointed. 'Well – go on: say something about them.'

'Let's see. We have a pretty general list, so there are all kinds.' I'm being frightfully boring, she thought; must try a bit more. 'Well – first there are the terrifically serious ones – you know – they go about looking patronizing *and* tragic; they talk about being writers all the time; they're sorry for you because you aren't a writer but they make you feel that *they* don't feel you have the character to stand being one. As long as you realize that writers are the most important people in the world and they are one of the very best, they're quite kind and democratic. That's one kind. They write poetry and rather obscure novels. Then there are rather bluff but shy tweedy ones who always live somewhere where the post takes three days to get to them, and only come to London about twice a year wearing a lot of clothes they're too hot in. They write historical novels and books about animals. Then there are the academic ones who speak so quietly you can't hear a word they say, and never meet your eye and always bring bulging brief-cases which they always leave behind. They write books about Shakespeare or Milton, or detective novels. Then there are rather dashing ones who look like secret agents who are always going off or coming back from some terrifically rare place. They write books about where they've been. Then there are what my uncle calls the overdressed mums who have hats and furs and masses of jewellery – they're very fierce about royalties and advertising: they write romantic novels in which love is all . . .' She stopped to see how he was taking this.

'Sharp, aren't you?' he said; he was smiling faintly, but she sensed his discomfort. 'Aren't *any* of them natural? You know, people you could stand to have a drink with?'

'Oh yes! The best ones are. The best ones are very nice and just like people. I was listing the funny ones: to – to entertain you.'

'You do entertain me. You're the first girl I've met to do that. That's all your education, I suppose?'

'I don't think so,' she said, startled at the idea. 'Here we are, anyway.'

The sweet shop was in sight, and she was glad to change the subject. It would be awful if he counted things about her life that she couldn't help against herself.

In the shop they bought bulls' eyes, and pear drops and extra strong peppermints. Then he saw some sherbet and got some of that.

'I could drink it out of the cup you made me.'

'Did you keep that?'

'Yes.'

'I never like waste,' he said. He seemed pleased.

Clouds had arrived in the sky: hardly any of it was blue now and it seemed colder. They walked home fast. On the way home, and having thought about it, she said:

'Dan, I'm not going back on my promise about the sea. But if we're going to have the fireworks, we ought to set them up this afternoon: posts for the rockets and things. We could go to the sea tomorrow morning. We could take a lunch picnic there, if you like. But of course we can go this afternoon if you like.'

'Just you and me for the picnic?'

'If you like.'

'All right. We'll do the fireworks today, and go off tomorrow. That's a strong promise, then?'

'Of course.' She looked at him to make sure it was all right, and he looked at her back and it was.

Lunch – Mrs Hanwell's fish pie, and dozens of crisp, thin lemon pancakes brought in in relays by Mrs Hanwell – was just as good as she'd expected. Dan ate nine pancakes – she counted them – and Cressy seemed to be in a better mood to their

mother, who seemed, or at any rate looked, rather tired. After
lunch, Cressy said she was going to practise but she'd play to
Dan first as she'd promised. Her mother and Felix King went
to drink coffee in the drawing-room 'like the grown-ups' she
thought, which was a bit silly because Felix King wasn't really
so old. He looked like a nice, intelligent, craggy kind of fox:
that was partly his red hair and high cheekbones, but also his
eyes; she liked foxes so it wasn't at all a rude thing to think.

She was doing the washing up. Mrs Hanwell had gone
home and she had the kitchen to herself. She'd refused offers of
help, from her mother and Felix King because she wanted to be
alone to think about the morning, to understand her feelings
about it. She liked Dan enormously, she began briskly: he was
a much nicer man than any she had met for a long time. He was
intelligent and funny and they seemed to like a lot of the same
things – animals and walks and sweets and talking and just
having fun. He had an extraordinary face, really; because
without one being able to say why, he was sometimes rather
beautiful, although if you took each of his features separately
there didn't seem to be any reason for this. His eyes were quite
large, but pale blue, and you couldn't tell what he was feeling
from them. He had a very long upper lip (just like poets in
books) and a very long, curling mouth – not thin either. He
looked like someone from the country, but then he had surprisingly delicate eyebrows – the colour of sharp sand. A nose
which was quite a good shape but larger than usual. In fact,
most of his features were on the large side, so he must have a
very big face for this not immediately to strike one. It certainly
hadn't struck *her*. When they had been talking about her having
a brother this morning, she had thought that *he* would have
made a very good one. And he didn't pounce on you before
you'd even had a chance to see what he was like. Whenever she
thought of people pouncing on her she got the same sick little
shiver which came always from the one time this had happened.
A friend of a friend of Cressy's – up in London for the evening

– who'd pressed her to go out to dinner with him. She and
Cressy, and Cressy's newest man and this friend of his, had all
been having drinks in their flat. Cressy had awfully wanted an
evening alone with her lover, so Emma had agreed to go out to
dinner with this man; she couldn't at all remember what he had
looked like, except that he had seemed old. He had told her to
call him John and she had done her best. They had had a rather
nasty dinner in Soho where he drank a lot and kept telling
waiters to do things that they were just going to do anyway,
and then he said he knew a jolly good place to go where they
could get drinks all night. He hadn't asked her whether she
wanted to come, but in the lavatory she'd noticed that it was
only half-past nine, so she knew Cressy wouldn't want her back.
So they'd got in a taxi, and in that he'd suddenly screwed her
head round, so that a bone felt as though it was breaking in her
neck, and started to kiss her with his tongue in her mouth. She
hated the smell of him, and she'd struggled. His tongue seemed
enormous and he had huge grasping hands which made her
shrink in her clothes. She couldn't say anything, but she made
some idiotic noise meaning don't, and quite suddenly he
released her and said in his ordinary dinner voice as though
nothing had happened: 'You're quite right: this isn't the place
for it.' And they had sat well apart in the taxi and she rubbed
and rubbed her mouth with the back of her hand until she saw
that he had taken out a handkerchief and was carefully mopping
up his own mouth. 'Can't give the show away to the driver, can
we?' he'd said. By now she was hating him, but it was dark and
she didn't know where they were, and they got out at what
looked like a hotel.

But it wasn't: it was an enormous block of service flats, as
she found a few minutes later when they were in one. She knew
she'd been a fool not simply to run away when they got out of
the cab, but her legs were shaking and she felt sick and she
couldn't think, and he took her arm and they were in the lift.
'You're a very attractive girl, in spite of those funny eyes of

140

yours: they're odd, you know,' he'd added as though she *wouldn't* know unless he told her. In the flat, which seemed to be just one room, he quickly gave her a drink – nearly all whisky, and she was feeling so awful she drank it at once. 'That's the girl,' he said, taking off her coat. She said she had got to go, but he'd offered her a cigarette, and surely she was safe while they were smoking? But he drew her on to the sofa or bed thing, took her cigarette away and literally fell on top of her. He tore a bit of her dress, she heard it; but he'd pinned her face down with his horrible mouth, and *his* face looked so like a nightmare exaggeration so near, that she shut her eyes as she twisted and tried to stop his hands. She heard her necklace break – it trickled down her neck like dried peas, and she felt as though she was sobbing inside but the sobs couldn't get out because of his tongue, and when she could breathe he smelled even more horrible, and he was pinching one of her breasts so hard that she wanted to scream. His other hand was even worse – in a second he would have ripped her knickers; a spasm of rage lasted just long enough for her to jab at him suddenly with her knee. It had worked: he gave a cry of pain and rolled off her clutching himself. Escape. She leapt to her feet and seized her coat – never mind the wretched pearls. 'You're frigid,' he said thickly, 'just a frigid little bitch, out for a good time. You'll never be any good to any man: a sexless little cock-teaser.' She'd stared at him: he'd looked so awful that she said 'I'm sorry,' and left. In a taxi which she'd easily found, she'd tried to cry but she couldn't: she just felt so sick she had to think about not being it in the taxi.

Cressy had gone to bed when she got back. She took off all her clothes and had a bath. She hadn't led him on: she hadn't even wanted to have dinner with him. Of course she'd tried to be polite, and not too dull a person to have dinner with, but it had been difficult to think of things to say. There was a mark like a burn on her breast, and her mouth felt bruised and dirty however much she rinsed it with water. I'm no good with men:

it was quite true, she'd hated him the moment he touched her: she hated even the idea of being touched now, so obviously she must be sexless.

Next morning, Cressy asked her whether she'd had a good time. Not very, she had answered. John was a terribly run-of-the-mill dull old stick, Cressy had then said: she was sorry Emma had had to put up with him, and she supposed that, like all men, he'd made a pass. A bit of one, Emma had said. She couldn't possibly tell Cressy now. If John was run-of-the-mill then she must at all costs keep out of situations that could ever lead to that, because she knew she couldn't bear it again.

She had been just over nineteen when this had happened, and she'd kept out of all situations that could possibly lead to that ever since. Lunch with people, even with one other man – preferably authors she was working with and the like – but dinner only with more than one other person. Whenever she had looked like being pushed into a corner, she'd said that she'd been in love with someone who'd been killed in the war.

Dan wasn't like this: much more like a friend – a new, but deep friend. She'd thought for an awful moment at breakfast that he was going to turn into Cressy's friend, but then Cressy had been nice about it, and then he'd made those distressing remarks about Cressy whom he clearly didn't understand. Cressy had a rather sad and very frightening life, and this made Emma feel protective about her, as well as sort of admiring. She must really be going to leave Dick: wouldn't be practising in the afternoon unless she was serious about that.

She had dried the last glass and put it away. Everything in the kitchen was tidy. Mrs Hanwell's ghastly cat was scorching in a hatbox on the Aga. Cressy was playing Mozart – very good choice for Dan. She decided to make quite sure that her mother wouldn't mind if they put up some stakes on the lawn outside the drawing-room window.

Her mother was reading a letter, and Felix King was leaning

against the fireplace watching her read it. She asked about the stakes and her mother looked up and said in a voice that Emma could hardly hear that they could put the stakes wherever they liked – of course they could. She went out feeling that she'd interrupted something and also it crossed her mind that her mother had been crying. Then of course, she'd left the fireworks in the drawing-room and had to go back. This time they were both laughing, so it seemed all right. How extraordinary other people's behaviour seemed if you didn't know much about them, she thought. If she hadn't gone back into the room, she might have thought that they were having a serious scene.

She waited until the piano stopped, and then slipped into the music room. Cressy was sitting, wiping her hands on one of her tiny white handkerchiefs. She'd just played the first move-ment of the A major sonata – the variations one. Dan was sitting in the leather arm-chair.

'Hi,' said Cressy. 'That's all, I think.'

'Don't stop because I'm here,' Emma said.

'No, I must work now. Was that all right, Mr Brick?'

He got up. 'Thanks,' he said. 'It sounds much better than the wireless. I liked that last piece best.'

They had a lovely time setting up the fireworks. It was cold and there wasn't a breath of wind; the sun had turned orange and there was one blackbird who went on warning them that he was afraid of their presence. She held the stakes and Dan hammered them. Once he hit her knuckles, quite hard, and he picked up her hand and licked the beads of blood as though they were his own. 'If I were your brother, I'd do it,' he said. They nailed the catherine-wheels just right, so that they could spin freely but wouldn't fall off. By the time they had finished it was deep frosty dusk. An aeroplane went overhead and they agreed that it looked practical and mysterious. She asked him if he'd been anywhere abroad and he hadn't. Hadn't had time for it, he said. Where would he like to go? Spain and Mars, he'd answered at once. In the tool shed, while they were putting away the stakes they hadn't used and the bass and the hammer, he said: 'How long does this go on for?'

'The week-end? I have to go back tomorrow evening.'

She thought for a second that he was dumbfounded, but then she thought she must have been wrong, because he said: 'Of course: it's just like week-ends you read about.'

'You could easily stay until Monday, if you liked.'

'I wouldn't want to do that.'

She suddenly remembered asking him yesterday where did he live, and he'd said 'I don't.' He hadn't anywhere; no home and no ordinary work; arriving at Charing Cross on a Sunday evening, what could he do? The bleak uncertainty of it appalled her.

'I got money,' he interrupted her thoughts as though he knew them.

'I know,' she answered quickly. A vision of him slipping out of her life first because he had some money and then because he had none, assailed her.

'Look – London's awful on Sunday evenings, you could come back to our flat if you like: there's a spare bed, and then you'd have time to think what you wanted. If you like, of course.'

'I'll think about it,' he said: 'you know – it's not where you sleep so much – it's the days I've got to reckon with.'

Yes, she said, she did see.

As they walked towards the house, he took her hand.

'Days with *you* are all right,' he said. Her hand was warm and comfortable in his. 'And I'm not making up to you because you have all these houses to live in either.'

The walk to the kitchen door of the house was over in a few seconds, but she thought about it at unexpected but frequent moments for the rest of the day and the night.

CHAPTER 10

FELIX

MEETING her had been much more nerve-racking than, on the journey down from London, he'd kept telling himself it would be. By the time he'd got to Lamberhurst, he'd badly wanted a drink, but the pubs weren't open. Good old England! Oh well, she'd certainly have a drink waiting for him. As he'd got nearer, he'd even thought: 'Supposing I don't recognize her! Don't be a bloody fool – of course you will. And if it's all absolutely intolerable, you can leave after lunch on Sunday.'

When he had finally arrived – after taking a wrong turning out of nervousness, or, he didn't know, perhaps he was losing his memory – she had opened the door to him, but he couldn't see her because of the light. The way she said his name took him back though, and, as he had planned to do, he stooped to kiss her cheek.

In the sitting-room he saw that she was really much as he had expected her to be, although it had been difficult, beforehand, to make a very clear picture of what that was. But he sensed her nervousness, and to help her, allied himself to it. Then the younger daughter had arrived: a grown-up young child with what looked to him like a tubercular farmer, the beguiling Mr Brick – he must say he liked *him*, not sharing Esme's distaste for poetry. What with *him* writing poetry and *her* washing her hair and going for walks all the time, they could lead a really wicked life together. But then, Cressida had arrived and had shaken him so much that he'd only just managed to hold out his hand to her. He thought now, that no wonder: she

145

was the most staggeringly attractive girl he'd ever seen in his life, and what was even more confounding, she seemed to bear no relation to the gawky, silent, dark schoolgirl he'd dimly remembered. Of course, he'd never found very young girls much cop, so perhaps he hadn't looked at her much. It wasn't as though she had been *trying* to look beautiful, although there was a case for saying that women with her sort of figure looked their best in sweaters and jeans. Her hair had been loosely tied back with a little crumpled, dark-blue ribbon – nothing very premeditated about that, but the blue-bottle colour brought out the blue in her very black hair. Thinking of Jack Lewis, he thought: her statistics really are vital – no question about it, and hands and feet like that are just luxury fittings. She had made up her eyes and her mouth, but she'd left the rest of her face alone: she must know something about herself to have done that. In fact, she combined being simple and being voluptuous to an unbearable degree – at least for him. And immediately, she'd started to be childishly rude, unkind, disagreeable. He'd wanted to get hold of her and beat, shake, strike, break her intolerable rudeness. She'd managed to go on being like this all through dinner until he'd have thought that surely Esme or her sister would rebel. But they hadn't. They'd clearly minded, and noticed, but they'd let her alone. He'd thought it would be a relief when she went off to bed before anyone else, but it wasn't. It was merely dull. He'd felt that Esme had just left the door open for them to stay downstairs after the others had all gone up to bed, but he'd pretended to ignore this, because he wanted to be alone – to think a bit, and he didn't want to have his first long talk with Esme late at night. He felt, he knew, that he owed her some explanation, but it had been such a long time ago, and he was afraid that he wouldn't honestly remember, with her there, exactly why he had behaved as he had behaved. The course between what honesty he owed her, and what tact he might find that he needed, was too delicate for a late night session. *She* seemed all right. Funny she hadn't married again:

he'd thought she almost certainly would. But she wasn't a desperate neurotic waif: she didn't seem to be anything he'd been afraid of finding. What a relief for Mary Lewis! Now she would try to marry him off to one or the other of her less attractive, but more sterling girl friends. The funny thing was, she might easily succeed. He had such a desire for some close, continuous, personal contact that he knew he was easy game . . .

In bed that night he wondered whether, in spite of her answer, Esme *had* missed Julius very much. It seemed impossible that she had only felt what she had said: man in the house, father of the children, etc. But then it seemed impossible that *his* life should have been so much affected by a man he had only met once. Perhaps it wasn't Julius's life at all that had affected him: only his death, and the manner of it. It had certainly been the most violent shock of his life – this older man's, this husband's, final gesture. It had annihilated the character he'd invented for Julius: he was no longer anonymous, inconsiderable and boring. It had changed the whole complexion of his affair with Esme; there was a yawning gap between making love to somebody else's wife, and consoling a stricken widow who was clearly in love with one. It had made his excuses about reading medicine (and he'd only been at the beginning of it, after all) – while men like Julius were going off alone at any cost to try and save any English fighting life – petty, irresponsible and an altogether painful reflection on his private view of Felix King. He'd *had* to get out then – at once. And characteristically, he'd done it with the maximum impatience. It had been a second shock to discover Esme's reaction; he had half expected her to be filled with remorse about their behaviour. In fact when she'd cried so much that last night in the flat he'd thought with relief that she was beginning to feel that: that the whole thing would come to a graceful, affectionate close; but the next morning when she had tried to talk about everything, he'd known that he was wrong about her. He'd seen her off on her train, and spent a frightful morning trying to imagine himself married to her, but the facts that she was thirty-eight and he was twenty-four; that he didn't want to marry anyone; that in ten years' time she would be forty-eight; that he hadn't even started his career – let alone the war – that she was fourteen years older than he, who in any case needed more experience of women before he could contemplate settling down, all piled up, overloaded the notion and sank it. He couldn't face marrying her. However irresponsible or self-indulgent he was (and what his mother – who made no bones about anything – would have called 'disgracefully sinful': he had never been able to pin her down about how to sin gracefully), it would surely be far worse to embark upon a marriage so reluctantly? The solution had been obvious, and he had taken it. He had not joined up because he hadn't wanted to marry her; he had joined up because of Julius, but he'd used the joining up as an excuse, and he hadn't had the courage to say good-bye to her. He'd just got the hell out. And not even an active and frightening war, and a subsequent life spent with amateur desperation on the supposed welfare of others, had ever made him feel better about it: however much he'd condemned the idea as arrogant, conceited, wilfully self-dramatizing, he'd been haunted by the notion that perhaps she had been rather more in love with him than he'd chosen to suppose at the time. Seeing her now, surrounded by her family, comfortable home, country pursuits, was a great relief. He opened the windows, turned out the light and at once went to sleep.

Everything had seemed sunny and soothing at breakfast until that damned girl appeared. Looking outrageous, she had managed to upset everybody at the table – excepting Dan Brick, and that was only because she hadn't, in his case, tried.

Her physical presence upset him one way, and her manners another, and between the two he was divided between wanting to tear down her jeans and beat her, or just tear down her jeans. She was old enough to know better, he told himself grimly with what Jack would call his *most* Scottish accent. Going to Battle with her would give him a chance to speak his mind. Put her in her place at once.

Now he sat beside her in her scarlet Mini and she was driving them at a speed which precluded any serious conversation, he told himself; but really, glancing at her profile with the dramatically tilted chin, eyes firmly on the road, so that he got a fine view of her eyelashes – like sooty fur – the down on her upper lip and one small, neat mole just below her cheekbone, really when he looked at her, he could think of nothing to say. It was she who began it.

'You don't *really* want to see the Abbey, do you?'

'Why are you always so offensive?'

He saw her start to smile, and with evident satisfaction she said:

'*Am* I?'

'You're one of the most offensive people I have ever met in my life.'

'With you, I should have guessed that that was some accolade.'

'I asked you a question.'

'So did I. I asked you one first.'

'You know the answer to it. Of course I don't want to see the Abbey. I wanted to talk to your mother.'

'Exactly!'

'And you prevented me. So – I ask you again: why are you always so offensive?'

'Perhaps you bring out the worst in me.'

'Like your mother! And your sister! In fact everybody I've seen you with. You're not a child!'

'Would it be better if I was? Oh yes, then you could ignore me.'

'What on earth are you talking about?'

'You're not married, are you?'

'No.'

'You never have been?'

'What the hell's it got to do with you? No, I never have been.'

She slowed the car and then stopped it, her hands still gripping the steering-wheel.

'I'll tell you. Because it's people like you who go around ruining other people's lives. And the funny thing is you're too selfish and *stupid* to see more than a fraction of the damage you do.'

'I say, are you sure you're not over-estimating my powers a bit?' he said mildly, concealing both irritation at her melodramatic manner and the faint desire it provoked in him to laugh.

'I don't think so. I think people are divided into those who try to help other people and those who try to help themselves. Where have you been for the last twenty years? Have you got a cigarette?'

'Here you are. Ignoring your asinine distinction, let me turn to the far more interesting subject of my life. Well – first there was the war, you know. I was a Commando in the Royal Marines. I ended up as a Major with a DSC. And if you think that that was entirely because I was trying to help other people, you'd be wrong; I was quite keen on my own life as well. Then when I came out, I read medicine at Aberdeen until, in due inexorable course, I qualified. Don't know who that was for, other people or myself. A bit of both, I'd say. When I'd qualified, some idealistic bug drove me to a rehabilitation camp in Korea. I spent six years there. That was the only time I had the mistaken view that whatever you were like you could help other people. I've grown up now. It's time you did the same.'

There was a long silence. Then, in a much smaller voice, she said: 'I see. I suppose I owe you an apology.'

'Not at all. If I hadn't been a fairly destructive sort of chap with an eye to number one, I wouldn't have got the DSC. I'd have got a VC. And I'd be dead. One had a kind of licence to ruin other people's lives in the war, but I don't think I've made a habit of it.'

There was another long silence. Then she just said: 'Oh.'

Then he said: 'Look here, I can't have you caving in like that. You must have had some reasons for your sweeping assertions about me. Since frankness is the hallmark of this conversation, you needn't feel in the least inhibited.'

This roused her: 'Of course I have reasons. What about my mother? What about my father? What do you think that was like for Emma and me?'

'What do I think *what* was like?'

'Now you're simply hedging. I know perfectly well that you were having an affair with my mother.'

'Yes?' He felt his heart beginning to pound.

'You can't possibly argue that that was a good thing to do.'

'I'm not arguing about it.'

'Well – I don't suppose, either, that you've the faintest idea how much damage you did.' There was a pause and then she said: 'Have you?'

'Look – I'm not trying to defend myself at all costs: but when one is twenty-four one doesn't think in terms of damage much. I was in love with your mother. She was in love with me. You must know what I'm talking about. There was never any question of her leaving your father or breaking up your home or anything like that.'

'That's exactly what happened though, isn't it?' She wound down her window and threw out her cigarette stub.

'No, it isn't.' He was beginning to get angry with her. 'How on earth do you arrive at that?'

'My father went off and got himself killed. Why?'

'Your father went off to try and collect some of the BEF off the beaches at Dunkirk. That's why he went. He was a brave man who wanted to do something to help. It had nothing to do with me, *or* your mother at all.'

'It *had*! You see – you *don't* know what you are talking about! My father knew about you! That's why he went!'

This was worse than the worst he had suspected.

'To begin with I don't see how you can possibly know that he knew . . .'

'I tell you I *know* that!'

'To go on with, he wasn't the kind of man who'd deliberately get himself killed because of anything he knew or found out about his private life. *How* did he know, anyway?'

She turned quickly to him and then looked away.

'*I* told him,' she said.

He swore violently to himself, counted three, and then said as calmly as possible: 'What on *earth* – made – you – do – that?'

'I thought he ought to know. It was wicked to him. My mother had absolutely no right – *I* don't know. I – just told him – that's all.'

'But why didn't you talk to your *mother*, for heaven's sake, surely that would have been a more honourable way of . . .'

'Honour!' She was trying to sneer but her voice broke. 'That comes well from you, I must say – *or* from my mother. What good do you think that would have done? She wouldn't have given you up, because *I* talked to her. She would simply have been more careful, told even more complicated lies – including me in them – and stopped you coming down here!'

'Well – you would have done better to talk to me.'

'Why should I? You treated me like a child! Worse than that: like somebody treats a child who isn't even fond of children.'

He gave them both cigarettes and lit them, thinking, but she *had* been a child – well, seventeen, not much more than one: and except that she'd been very intense and silent, and Esme had said she was musical, he couldn't remember anything about her. No – he had to admit that it would have been difficult for her to approach him. He said so.

'How did your father respond to being told this tale by you?'

'That was what was so awful! I simply couldn't tell at all. He treated me as though it was all happening to some other people.

He sort of *generalized* about it. He kept telling me not to worry about it. The only thing he made me promise was not to say anything to Emma about it! As if I would have! She really *was* only a child; she couldn't have been made to understand. But Emma was *the* child to *him* you see – he loved her most for being that. He was always trying to protect her. He said that people over-estimated their personal importance and this made them get things out of proportion. He said there wasn't time to interfere with what separate people did – that they were responsible for far more than their immediate, personal actions . . . I can't really remember any more. Except that I tried to tell him that he'd got me, but he didn't seem to understand. So I left him. But afterwards, because he seemed so quiet in there . . .'

'In where?'

'His study: the room he was sitting in,' she said impatiently, as though he ought to have known, 'that after I'd been away from him for a bit, I went back and listened at the door, and I couldn't hear a sound, so then I went out into the garden to see him through the window, and he was sitting at his desk, leaning over it, with his hands over his face. So then I knew that really he was very unhappy.'

'And then what?' He thought he knew, but he had to ask or rather, she had to tell him.

'Then about a week later he went. Then I really *did* know.'

'Know? What?'

'That I shouldn't have told him, of course!' she said, in a voice so used and worn with guilt that for a moment he felt a third and quite different feeling about her. 'If I hadn't told him, I don't think he would have gone. He would have been alive now.'

After a bit, he said gently: 'Have you told anyone else this?'

And she said immediately, and between her teeth:

'Of course I haven't! Of *course* not! I did it: the least I could do was bear it. And I could protect Em a bit. The awful months afterwards – you wouldn't know – you'd disappeared pretty smartly – when my mother was being a grief-stricken widow and I wanted to kill her for pretending about something so important – I did what I could about Em because he'd asked me to. My mother used to cry at night, you know, without making the *slightest* effort to be quiet about it; and one night I found Em sitting up in bed with her teeth chattering: she could hear my mother and she was terrified. *She* was crying, and she kept saying "It's horrible: I hate her doing that: I hate it", so then I moved her to my room, which was farther along the passage where she couldn't hear. But it didn't stop me feeling to blame.'

She had thrown the second cigarette away – seemed to be watching it burning out on the verge – then she said: 'If something has gone wrong – you know the feeling, that at the time it doesn't seem to matter what you do, everything's burned up anyhow – but then afterwards, without you being able to help it, you find it *does* matter, just as much as if nothing had gone wrong in the first place.'

He didn't know the feeling, but he thought he knew what she meant, so he said yes.

'That's how life has seemed to me ever since. I got married like that. I seem to have done nearly everything like that.' She made some small sound, like a sigh – he could only just hear it.

'We must get on with going to Battle,' she said, and started the engine.

He wanted to say so many things to her: and it was necessary, he thought, to say something to lighten this load she had carried alone for so long.

'Interesting, what your father said about there not being time to interfere with other people. I suppose when he said that they were responsible for far more than their personal actions, he meant that if you worried too much about any one of them, you became irresponsible on the larger scale.'

'I think he was talking about the war then.'

'Oh well, war shows that sort of thing up – like emergencies do.'

'But if you want to – be any use in the world, surely you have to start with a clean slate?'

'You can't. People aren't born with clean slates. At least, I don't think so. When I'm born I don't think that I've no right to a smallpox vaccination until I've isolated the bug and prepared a home-made vaccine. We've got to accept that that has been done already. Well, then there are the disadvantages: the nature of man, many of his actions and so forth.'

'But we all know that babies are innocent. They don't *know* . . .'

'That's the Christian view of innocence – calling it ignorance of evil – dangerously idealized, if you ask me. The time to assess innocence isn't with a baby, it's with an old man. Everybody wants to be a little fallen angel – that's the trouble: that leads you slap into the stalemate of guilt.'

He stopped: he hadn't meant to say anything like as much as that; but things that he'd been dimly trying to think about alone, had suddenly become clear to him in her company: he'd had nobody to *talk* to for years, he realized.

'Go on about guilt: I want to know what you think *that* is.'

He looked at her beautiful hands, much more relaxed now on the steering-wheel – her curtain wedding-ring glinting in the sunlight.

'Guilt,' he said slowly: he had to be a bit careful here. 'Guilt is just the failure to live up to an arrogant self-made image. It hasn't got anything to do with being sorry for what you've done. It's only being sorry for what you find you aren't. But it's a great preventative from getting on with the next thing.' Then, with a touch of what he hoped would be psychological cunning, he said: 'I feel much better. I must say, you're wonderful to talk to, offensive though you are.'

155

And that, for the time, was that. They did all their commissions in Battle, and he bought a bunch of dahlias for Esme. On the way home she asked abruptly:

'What made you come here after all this time?'

'I wanted to see that your mother was all right.'

'What could you do about it, if she *wasn't* all right?'

He thought about this for a moment, and then laughed. '*I* don't know. One doesn't always think these things out. I expect I would have indulged in a bit of guilt.'

'Good old guilt. You see? It comes in handy. Well, she *is* all right, isn't she?'

'She seems to have managed very well. It can't be much fun to be widowed at thirty-eight with two children, and one of them fairly hard on her.'

'If she hadn't been all right, you weren't thinking of marrying her or anything like that – to improve the situation, were you?'

'There you go again. No – I don't consider that marriage or "anything like that" with me is the answer to everything. Just as well, isn't it? I couldn't go around doing that with everybody.'

'Well – I'll try not to be so hard on her,' she said, as though he had specifically asked her. 'If only to give you the chance of minding your own business,' she added, more, he felt, to keep his concession in character, than for any other reason.

'What are you going to do now you are in England?'

'I'd like to go into general practice. I've had enough of hospitals and institution life for a bit. Like to do things on a smaller, more personal scale.'

'But surely, even in a hospital, a good doctor has to have a personal relationship with his patients? Otherwise, they might not get well?'

'Not where I was. If you dared to start caring what happened to any of your patients, you would have gone out of your mind.'

'Why?'

'Because most of them had nowhere to live, no work, and

all of them were in varying degrees of starvation. And there were thousands of them, and thousands more we couldn't do anything – or much – about, beyond a bowl of rice or soup a day. If you start feeling personal about a rice queue for people too weak to stand in it, too weak to brush hordes of flies out of their wretched, sickly babies' eyes, whom you can't speak to – you'd go mad. And even the ones you can afford the equipment to treat can't be given any sort of future that would make sense to them.'

'What's that? Go on. Tell me what they want for a future.'

'They would see it as their own village back; their own patch of land, their own paddy fields, the piece of country they've known all their lives. But really, I mean a future of any kind. You know they all talk about things like travel shock, and territory for animals? It applies to those people as well. They're in deep shock most of them, and if you add acute malnutrition to that, multiply them past the point where you can envisage the numbers at all, you can get a rough idea of the situation. I've spent six years trying to feel impersonal and certainly being inadequate. I had to stop before I lost the chance of being able to care for anyone.'

He had felt her listening intently to him: now she was frowning. 'Are you frowning because you don't approve, or because you don't understand?' He was surprised at how anxious this sounded.

She glanced at him, and he saw that she'd been frowning because she was moved.

'I was listening. I was thinking about it,' was all she said. There was a silence, and then she said: 'Even nomads have territory to be nomadic in. I do see that.'

They were almost home, and after driving in silence from which much of the tension had gone, she said: 'Would you like to stop at the pub?'

'Very much.'

He thought she had done this because there was more that

she wanted to say, but she gave no sign of it. They had one drink in the empty saloon; he told her about the Lewises and his temporary job, and he asked her about her professional life.

'It's not up to much. I could say that it's an over-crowded profession dominated by too few power-ridden agents; but honestly, I'm not good enough to complain. I get a few – very few – engagements, just enough to make me have to go on working: and occasionally I pluck up enough courage or exhibitionism or what-have-you to give a recital in London at the Wigmore Hall. I'm supposed to be working up for one now.'

The thought of her career seemed to make her lack-lustre and restless. 'It's exciting playing with an orchestra, but I don't get much concert work, so when I do I'm far too nervous to enjoy it. I don't know why I go on with it really,' she finished.

They'd drunk their drinks: he offered her another.

'No – we'd better get back before your dahlias are dead.'

He sensed the return of her hostility then, and in the silence with which they drove the short way back.

Just before they got out of the car, she said: 'Please, for God's sake, don't tell anyone what I told you this morning. You know what I mean,' she continued irritably, before he had time to say that he did or didn't: 'about my telling my father. I can't think why I told *you*.'

She burrowed in the back seat of the car, almost threw a number of awkward, ill-wrapped and heavy parcels at him, and, laden herself with two shopping baskets, stalked ahead of him into the house.

Esme met them in the hall. She was wearing gardening gloves and carried a plate of orange peel. Cressy went straight to the kitchen.

'I said moles to Hanwell, and this is what I get! No earthly use for them at all.'

'What would it be some use for?' Felix asked, glad of her friendly preoccupation.

'It's supposed to spell death to slugs, but I think they've come to love it.'

He handed her the dahlias. 'These are for you.'

'Oh Felix – how *sweet* of you!' She took them, and put them automatically to her nose. 'Of course – how silly of me, but they're *marvellous* colours, like the Russian Ballet.' There was a brief silence while she went on looking at them, and to his discomfort, she seemed to be blushing. But then she took them away from her face, and he thought it was simply a reflection of the flowers. 'Help yourself to a drink,' she said: 'I'll go and get something to put them in.'

He went gladly: he thought he was going to be glad of a respite from Cressy, preferably to be alone, to sort things out a bit, but Dan and Emma were sitting on the window seat playing a game of draughts in a spirit so competitive as to verge on the cantankerous. It was clear that neither wished the other to win – or to come anywhere near it – and to this end, they took back moves and accused each other of cheating. They took no notice of him. Almost at once, he began to wish that Cressy would prowl into the room helping herself to drink and cigarettes and kicking the fire about. 'Because you can't see someone properly if you're sitting beside them in a car. That's for when you know them much better, or never wanted to in the first place.'

He picked up a copy of *Country Life* and went and sat in a chair with it. 'If I could just get a bit more *used* to her appearance,' he thought, staring moodily at a blurred photograph of the Queen presenting a cup to some winner of a jumping competition, 'then I wouldn't have to keep trying to remember it when she wasn't there.' Perhaps, he thought, finishing his drink without noticing it, it would be easier if she was *there*.

Esme came in with the dahlias, and Daniel clearly won the game: 'Good thing for you,' Felix heard him mutter triumphantly: 'I don't half lose my temper if I lose,' and Mrs

Hanwell came in and said that lunch would spoil if they didn't have it.

She was late for lunch: she'd changed into a scarlet flannel shirt with pockets over the breasts, and put silver rings in her ears. These were easy to see, because she scraped her hair back. Emma said: 'What a posh shirt! When did you get that?' and she answered: 'I've had it for ages. It's not *new*.' Suddenly he *knew* that she was lying – in which case . . .

In which case – what? The whole situation was uncomfortably inbred.

After lunch, she said she was going to practise, so that was that. Later, he realized that Dan Brick had somehow wormed his way in to be played to: this made him feel obscurely irritated. Esme seemed very keen on them having coffee in the sitting-room, so that is what they did.

Almost at once, she asked him how he had got on with Cressy.

'Very well.' He knew at once that he didn't at all want to discuss Cressy with Esme.

But what, Esme persisted, did he think was the *matter* with her? She added, rather pathetically: 'I mean, her whole life can't be out of joint because she doesn't much like *me*. She is nearly thirty-eight, after all.'

'She's astonishingly young for her age, isn't she? I mean, she not only looks it – she *is*.'

'Does she seem much younger than I used to be?'

'How can I tell that? You see, I'm much older myself – so of course she's bound to *seem* younger.

'I think she's depressed about her career,' he added after a short silence during which he began to feel that somehow he had said the wrong thing.

'She's never taken it seriously enough. I think she's been far too involved with her private life. More?'

She brandished the coffee pot, and he held out his cup, resisting the vulgar and violent urge to ask about Cressy's private life, as Esme called it.

'Anyway, she wasn't rude to you?'

'Not exactly. No – she was perfectly all right.' There's package mendacity for you, he thought. 'She wasn't rude to you at lunch, either,' he returned.

'No – I must say, you seem to have a good effect upon her. 'Tell me, what are your plans, now you're back?'

He told her, but his mind was only half on it, and she seemed to sense this, because when he came to a decent interval, she did not press him. She's an immensely *tactful* woman, he thought.

'This is the only job I've actually been offered – apart from being a locum.' He felt in his pocket and found the letter from the eccentric old lady in the Hebrides who implored him to apply for her brother's job of GP there. He got up to look what kind of day it was – very grey now – and put his coffee cup down. One quickly missed the fire. He moved back to it. Emma came into the room, asked her mother something, and went out.

'You're not taking it seriously, I hope?'

She looked up at him. 'You mean, you've no intention of going up there?'

'Good Lord, no. If anyone ever managed to make a job sound uninviting, it's Miss McPherson. That bit about the people regarding one as a foreigner and never having to go more than forty miles to a patient is enough to finish me.'

'Felix – you frightened me. I thought because it was Scotland, you might go.'

'Not me. I've a marked aversion to being a foreigner for a bit. It was my fault for advertising. I should keep running out of petrol and running over sheep.'

Emma came in again and collected her fireworks. He had the impression that Esme resented interruption, and wondered what she had in mind which could make her feel that.

She collected some sort of tapestry thing which she seemed to be embroidering in wool, and he asked politely what it was.

161

'A chair seat.' She held up a bilious beige square of canvas in the middle of which was some indeterminate flower. The colours suffered the dual disadvantage of being 'antique', i.e. faded and muddy, and unrealistic – the flower had large prussian-blue leaves. The background was khaki. It was mostly background.

'It is horrible, isn't it? It's the embroidery equivalent of what the Victorian architects did to village churches. I suppose everybody does it because it's practically the only needlework that requires no real talent. That's why I do it, anyway.'

'What else do you do?' It wasn't so much that he terribly wanted to know, as that he suddenly simply couldn't *imagine*. She'd always seemed to him an urban creature; somebody who went to theatres and parties, and had her hair done and took pieces of stuff to her dressmaker. Not a countrywoman at all. And particularly alone in a house week after week.

'What do I do?' she repeated. 'Well – I read a lot, and I've become very passionate about gardening. It's one of the best things to do by yourself. Friends come and stay, and the girls most week-ends – Emma, anyway. Then I do some work for the WVS, and in the summer I help with a holiday camp for convalescent children out of hospital. At Easter I go and stay with Mervyn – Julius's brother and his wife, in Somerset. About once a month I go to London. I do the flowers for the church every other week. I listen to the radio a lot; friends come and stay – oh, I've said that – well, that's about all, I think.' She looked at him with a little smile which was engaging and uncertain, and added: 'Not at all how you imagined I'd be, I suppose?'

There was a pause, and then she said, 'I'm fifty-eight, you know?' It sounded like a question.

'I don't know why – I was sure you'd marry again. If that is an impertinent remark – ignore it.'

'I expect you simply hoped I would.' Then, to take the edge off this she went on: 'It never came my way, and therefore, being me, I never considered it. I was always very practical, you know – particularly about pleasure. Also, you know, I was very much in love with you. Perhaps you didn't realize that?'

'I thought I did: I don't know.' He wanted to explain – what? Why he'd written that letter and run away – but even now he found it impossible to put his motives in order of their priority. And they were not quite as cosily *dead* when they were alone together for it not to matter uncomfortably what he said or how he put things. 'I'm sorry,' he said lamely.

'Is that what you came here to say?'

'Good Lord, no! I mean – it's not what I thought of when I asked myself here.'

He knew she was going to ask him why he had come, and desperately wished she wouldn't.

'Why *did* you come, Felix?'

'I – wanted to see how you were. In every sense, I wanted to see that – to know that for myself. Will that do?'

'People always say that when they are speaking exactly half the truth don't they? But I can guess the rest . . .'

'I want to ask you something. *Did* Julius know about us?'

She put down her embroidery and looked him straight in the face.

'Yes: he did. Wait a minute. I didn't know that on the last evening that we met. I really had no idea of it. It was afterwards. The lawyers had a letter for me from him – to send me if he didn't come back. I got it the same day I got yours. Rather ironical.'

'Have you kept it?'

'Oh yes,' she said wearily. 'I've kept everything. Mervyn started to try and collect all the facts about his brother's venture. He wanted to publish a little book – privately. He went to a great deal of trouble. He tracked down the two men who got back alive in Julius's boat. The mother of one of them wrote to me. He wanted that letter and anything else that I had. He saw the owner of the yacht, he did everything he could. He was very hard hit by his brother's death. Julius had written to *him* as well.'

'*Did* he print the book?'

'No – he couldn't. He wanted to see the letter that Julius had written to me; he didn't try to force me, of course, but in the end I felt it would be dishonest not to show him.'

'That was very brave of you.'

'It wasn't. I really felt I had nothing to lose: but I did know that Julius would have hated a distorted account of his – his end to have been even privately printed. I saw Mervyn and told him, and then showed him the letter. He was extraordinarily nice about it – really astonishing. He'd always admired his brother, you see – not that this made him admire Julius any less, but it somehow changed the whole thing in a way which made it much less simple. He – Mervyn – knew that you'd gone – perhaps that made him kinder to me. Anyway he *was*: we're much better friends than we were when Julius was alive. He gave me the folder with all the material to keep. I keep it, but of course, I haven't shown it to anyone – not even the girls.'

'May *I* see it?'

Without answering, she got up and went to her desk. 'Of course, it's locked.' She fumbled in her bag and found the key. Then she opened a drawer and pulled out a dark-green folder which was tied with tapes, and handed it to him. 'Don't read it now,' she said. 'I don't think I could bear it. Read it in bed tonight.' For once, her voice was almost acid. He supposed that the document made her feel very emotional, even now.

CHAPTER 11

CRESSY

A FTER Dan and Emma had left the music-room, she opened her Haydn at the third movement, changed her mind and went back to the first. At least there had been one thing she hadn't told that wretched man. She must have been *mad* to tell him such a lot. 'The trouble is, that the moment I'm alone with *anyone* I talk far too much. I'll be a crashing bore when I'm old.' She'd only gone on because he'd been unexpectedly sympathetic and much more serious than she'd thought him. Of course, she'd been quite wrong about him being just some kind of glamorous layabout. He certainly wasn't that. In a way, he'd been interesting to talk to – in a way. She turned to Haydn, and as she did so remembered Dick. Sunday night would be the end. She felt calm and poised about it: obviously it couldn't matter if that was all she felt about it. She rolled up her cuffs to get them out of the way and settled down to work.

At the end of an hour the muscle was hurting again. She got up from the piano and had a cigarette. Apathy was attacking her about going on working – a sensation she associated now with the weeks before giving a recital. At least he was trying to help people who badly needed it when there wasn't enough help to go round, instead of coercing a few unwilling people with too much time on their hands to pay upwards of a pound to listen to her. Put like that, there was no earthly point in her going on with music. No music, no Dick – it would certainly be a clean sweep: it would make her *have* to do something. Perhaps Ann would have her in some very humble capacity. Presumably, for charitable enterprises – like any other kind –

you need twice as many people in humble capacities as you needed the other sort. Perhaps *she* ought to go to Korea or that place in Africa where Dr Schweitzer had his leper colony . . . Silly and dramatic. If she wanted to help people she could do it perfectly well in Uxbridge or Liverpool.

She wandered to the window: it was nearly dark, but she could just see Daniel and Emma working away at their fireworks – talking to each other only about what they were doing she betted, like children. She supposed the other two, her mother and Felix, were having a cosy heart-to-heart by the fire – God! What could that be like? It made her feel savage to think of it: it was so – so *unsuitable!* Perhaps he really *had* just come back to see that her mother was all right. Couldn't blame him for that. She seemed to be the odd woman out. Better get used to *that*. She went back to the piano and shut it. When she turned off the working lamp, the room seemed enormous and nearly dark, and she wanted to stay there and be sad; not to turn on the sadness exactly but to let it out. But then if she did, she had an even worse fear that there might be nothing left of her – nothing at all. Should she make tea for everybody, as a way of marking this new leaf? She decided against it: they would all, in their different ways, regard this kind of help as an interference – 'which a lot of help is, after all,' she thought. She decided to go and have a bath.

In the bath she decided to give up any idea, hope or prospect of love: and she thought that this would probably and naturally rule out sex. If she found that after all she couldn't do without sex she would seek it from a position of strength. Like a man, she thought with triumphant austerity, she would not confuse it with anything else – an accusation which had been constantly levelled at her in the past. Life would then be very much simpler: would it turn out to be dull? Not if one filled up one's life with prolonged good deeds. If she managed to keep this regime up for a year or two, she might become one of those understanding, untouched confidantes: a woman to whom the poor wretches still struggling with the confusion she was now renouncing would come. She would explain it to them and they would not understand and she would understand. She would care so little that she would get a tremendous reputation for kindness. She would also be able to help those people who confused love with getting married from it: who acted on the basis that if you shared enough houses, motor cars, a name and a routine everything must be all right. This she had always distrusted: but generally speaking, these people *were* all right, since they had been aiming at the houses and motor cars and called it love because they really couldn't feel any better. 'I should never have had a private income,' she thought: 'It makes you feel you ought to take short cuts before you are old enough to know how.' If she had ever *had* simply *had* to earn her own living, she would have learned the primary lessons. As it was, she felt as though she had been pushed into a high form much too young and then had to stay there because she had never understood the homework. But now, she would at last be able to use this to advantage. She could afford to pay for a training so that she *would* be some use to somebody: she need not be accepted simply as someone who could address envelopes. Usually, when people had the reputation for knowing a great deal about life, they knew about a lot of things going wrong, so it oughtn't to be difficult for her to acquire the reputation. In the end she would become quite famous and people would come to interview her to find out why she was so wise and calm. 'Mrs Egerton received me simply in her simple flat: it was simply furnished with the barest essentials . . .' (What were *they*? Urban simplicity, in her experience, was very, very expensive except for white walls and Penguins and blue jeans.) *Anyway*. Some sort of old flat – jolly simple and nice. 'I was immediately struck by her simple manner – the aura of calm wisdom which seemed to emanate from . . .' She stared down the naked length of her body trying to think where the hell wisdom and calmness were most likely to emanate from. Nothing that she could see.

There was a knock on the door: 'It's me,' said Emma's voice: 'I've brought you some tea.'

She got out of the bath and wrapped herself in a towel to unlock the door. Emma came in with a huge mug.

'I thought you might like some.' Her face was pink and her eyes shining. 'Do you want to get back in?'

She shook her head and sat on the rim of the bath. 'Thanks awfully. Where's Dan?'

'Eating crumpets,' said Emma proudly. 'He doesn't look as though he could possibly eat so much, do you think?'

'I suppose he doesn't. Perhaps he just eats at week-ends.'

'You do like him, don't you?' Emma had perched on the clothes basket and seemed to want to stay.

'Of course I like him. I think he's a honey. A remarkable man,' she added, seeing Emma's face.

'So do I. I say, could you lend me something for this evening? The thing is my long flannel skirt is here, but there's nothing to put on top.'

'You can have anything I've got. Except I wouldn't take a shirt because you look funny in mine. Try the jersey shelf. You'd better let me do it with you. Fit you out.'

'Yes. One other thing.'

'Eh?'

'Would you mind awfully if Dan came back to Lansdowne Road just for Sunday night? Or would it be awkward with Dick there?'

It *was* awkward: but Emma almost never had anyone to stay — had never had a man there at all, as far as she could remember.

'No — it'll be all right. Dick won't be there for long. I'll need the sitting-room to talk to him in though.'

'Oh, Dan won't mind what time he gets to bed. We could go out to a film or something. It's just that he hasn't *got* anywhere. We'll find him somewhere on Monday.'

'Don't bother to go out.' It was the law not to ask questions:

Emma never did – always waited to be told; but she couldn't help saying: 'I've never seen you like this, Em.'

'I'm not like anything,' said Emma, seized her mug and went.

Cressy dried, realized that she hadn't brought her dressing-gown, and wrapped in the bath towel she wandered to her room. On the way she came face to face with Felix who dropped some sort of file he was carrying and said 'Christ!'

She glared dreamily at him: her future had reached the point where she was gracefully, humbly refusing to be made a Dame . . .

'Sorry,' said Felix.

In her room she thought that the new regime must already be having some effect: if anybody was to try and make a pass at her now, they'd have to try about fifty times harder than they'd ever tried before. That showed you something.

She had nearly finished a tremendous clearing out of clothes in her room – a lot of them were not going to be suitable for her new life, and others she was simply tired of – when Emma returned to be fitted out.

'Are you having one of your clean sweeps? Or are these all for me to choose from?'

'They're all things I've no need of. You can choose all right, but I'm not going to have you wearing things that don't fit you.'

'All right,' said Emma meekly. 'I won't have me doing that either.'

'Where's the skirt?'

'In my room.'

'Well get it, you halfwit. How can you see what will go best with it, without it?'

'What are the others doing?' she asked when Emma returned with her skirt.

'Mummy's doing the table. Felix is making an enormous jug of martini. Dan's playing solitaire. Do you know, he can easily end up with one marble, but now he's working out how to leave the marble in whatever hole he's planned. We thought fireworks after dinner. They'll be a terrific show. Black news. Jennifer Hammond is coming to dinner.'

'She's not!'

'She is. And Major Hawkes.'

'Major Hawkes *and* Jennifer Hammond! How do you know?'

'I was looking for some paper for scoring and saw it in Ma's diary. You know what: I think he wants to marry her.'

'He may want to. But think of straining to hear every word he says in his soft brown voice and getting too near and being spat at.'

'She calls him Brian,' said Emma primly, holding up a scarlet jersey against herself. 'I think if you married someone like that, you'd be entitled to ask them to speak up. Or get him some new teeth.'

'You'd be *entitled* to – but he never would. The thing to do would be to steer the conversation off foreign place-names: they're the wettest.'

They started to play their Major Hawkes game. 'What's Major Hawkes's favourite drink?'

'Sarsaparilla,' said Emma after some thought.

You played the game while you were doing other things. Now Cressy ripped the scarlet jersey away from Emma. 'You *know* scarlet doesn't suit either of your eyes, you fool.'

'Which does Major Hawkes call the bravest little country in Europe?'

'Czechoslovakia. Damn Jennifer Hammond. Let's make her sit next to him. What's Major Hawkes's worst trouble when he gets ill?'

Emma thought. 'Can't do it. Could I have this? Not for tonight – '

'Septicaemia,' said Cressy triumphantly. 'Yes, you can. Put your skirt on – let's see. What's his favourite English county?'

'That's easy. Somerset.'

'It's a very good blue – your skirt. Not Somerset, you fool – Sussex!'

'This is what you should wear.' She held up a tobacco-brown cashmere. It was sleeveless – 'Sleeveless,' hissed Emma as she put it on. 'Who's his favourite composer?'

'Rimsky-Korsakov . . .'

'Shostakovich.'

'Stravinsky . . .'

'Saint-Saëns . . . He simply loves music, doesn't he?'

'Mad about it. You know I think our mother is seriously lacking in social sense.'

'No she's not. It's just that you get to like more boring people as you get older. How do I look?'

'Not bad: keep still. Wait a second – I want to try tucking it in.'

'It's so like life,' Emma said pensively. 'The only person who could *do* anything about his teeth is his dentist. And when he goes there, either *they're* out for the count, or else *he* is. So the poor dentist would never know.'

'You either need a wide belt or else have it outside. As it's a bit big for you I recommend the belt. You don't think *she* wants to marry him, do you?'

'I think she's a bit lonely,' said Emma after some thought. 'And she's so keen on us marrying people, she must think it the best thing to be.'

'Not necessarily,' said Cressy darkly. 'Try this.'

'I'll have to make a new hole.'

'Your waist's indecently small: you're always lifting belts off me! I can't wear them after you've punctured them all over the place. Why don't you ever have any of your own?'

'They get left on the backs of chairs in restaurants whenever I'm having an expensive meal. What's his favourite river?'

'*What* is it? I don't know.'

'Mississippi,' said Emma crossly: 'you're not trying. Can I

171

go through these things quickly, before you cast them on the
WVS?'

'Help yourself.' Cressy lit a cigarette and sat down to brush
her hair.

'What's Felix like?' Emma asked some minutes later.

'All right. Better than I thought.'

'How does Ma know him?'

'Met him before the war, I think.'

'He's much younger than she is.'

'Yes,' said Cressy, 'he is, isn't he?'

When Emma had taken away her loot, and Cressy had back-
combed her hair a bit for her and had a final inspection, Emma
went away. She really looked very nice; the skirt was straight to
her ankles and a beautiful blue: the cashmere fitted surprisingly
well and anybody with a twenty-two-inch waist looks good in a
belt. 'I don't think she's ever been in love before,' she thought,
with a twinge of protective anxiety. But she couldn't be sure:
Em was very secretive sometimes, and one reason why they got
on was never trying to find things out about each other.

Now *she* must dress. Her earlier, and distinctly lofty, feeling
about her appearance from now on, was mitigated by the news
of Jennifer Hammond coming to dinner. She wasn't going to
look as though she'd tried very hard, but she wasn't going to
look a frump, either. She set about it. It was seven o'clock when
she started (drinks were always at seven-thirty) and of course
she was bound to be late.

When she got downstairs her mother, Felix, Dan and Emma
were all drinking, and Major Hawkes was most rashly being
given a whisky and soda. Felix poured her a martini, and she
asked where was Jennifer Hammond?

'There they are now,' said her mother, and they all heard the
car in the drive.

'They?'

'The Hammonds, dear. Richard could come after all, as the
fog was too bad for him to go abroad.'

Oh God! It only needed that. The last person she wanted to see, now, in this company, was Dick. She put her glass down, then picked it up again and drank a lot of martini.

'Cigarette?' said Felix.

She stared at him feeling trapped and furious. Why hadn't her mother *said*? She heard the front door – Jennifer's maddening high-pitched voice. She took a cigarette without speaking: it was too late to get out now – why on earth hadn't he told her? He *couldn't* love her if he simply turned up to dinner in her own home *with* his wife ... where was Em? *She'd* understand: she did. Their eyes met for an instant, just before the Hammonds, ushered by Esme who had gone out to meet them, came in.

'Had a frightful time persuading him to come at all ...' Jennifer was saying.

'Finish it, so I can fill you up,' said Felix's voice.

She focused on him: he gave her a small, cool, but friendly smile. If she didn't know he couldn't know, she would have thought he knew. She finished her drink and he refilled her glass. She knew Dick had seen her, and didn't look at him. Instead she turned to Major Hawkes who had been amazing Dan for some minutes. Major Hawkes said something lengthy which she couldn't hear, and Dan retired thoughtfully rubbing his face.

Esme was introducing people, ending with 'And there, of course, are Cressy and Emma.' Why of course?

Jennifer, who had been given a martini by Felix, was coming up to her.

'I suppose you've been frightfully busy on your concert tours, and that's why we never see you.' She was wearing a low-necked beaded sweater and a terrifically hairy skirt.

She smiled. It felt like a smile – and offered Jennifer a cigarette.

'How *super*! I'm not in the least musical, but honestly, I should adore to hear you play. I'm so stuck with the children these days, that nothing ever improves my mind.'

'Be good sweet maid, and let who will be clever,' said Major Hawkes audibly and unexpectedly.

'There you are!' cried Jennifer. 'Oh darling, could you lend me your hanky?' She looked round wildly for her husband and he came over and handed her one. Dick.

'Good evening,' he said to her.

'Good evening,' she said back.

'Darling, why on earth are you drinking martini if you think you are getting a cold? Why don't you have a whisky?'

'I'm quite happy with martini.'

'You may be, but I'm not for you. *Could* Dick have a wee drop of whisky?' she pleaded to the room in general. 'I'll drink your martini, darling,' and she whipped it away from him in one expert swoop.

Felix got Dick some whisky. Major Hawkes muttered something about whisky making the heart grow fonder, and then, most distressingly, laughed. Jennifer laughed too, and started talking to him about ear canker: they both kept dogs.

She looked at Dick, trying to pretend that she'd never seen him before. A handsome man with a dull face. But handsome. How could you be both, she thought irritably.

'Better?' It was Felix. He was offering her another cigarette.

'Than what?' she said as rudely as she could.

'Than ever, of course,' he said smoothly.

Her mother was wandering about filling up people's glasses. She watched Jennifer have her third martini and knew, from the expression on Dick's face when he looked at his wife, that Jennifer was drinking herself out of a row. She realized then, that apart from hating to be Jennifer, she did not want to be in Jennifer's position. One of Dick's tricks was to make out that his relationship with his wife was a much more formidable business than, obviously, she could now see that it was. To Cressy he had always maintained a married position composed of his protective, manly compassion for a good, sweet, dull little woman who had given him the best weeks of her life and to whom therefore he owned his painful loyalty. Now she could see, and hoped that he knew it, that he was just comfortably bored enough with a woman whose notion of marriage was to preserve external possession at any small price of tact or dignity. She suddenly remembered René in the middle of her affair with him. She had asked him why he had chosen her, and he had answered: 'Well, you see – my wife *understands* me; and that, my dear, you may discover, is a piece of French realism.' Dick's boredom was exactly of the kind that enabled him to justify his infidelities. Jennifer was not a disappointment to him: she was just what he had expected, and this made it possible for him to have affairs with a smooth romantic conscience. You couldn't love somebody who wanted so little. She felt so good, that when she saw Jennifer spilling some of her drink on to her beaded sweater, she offered *her* handkerchief for mopping up. Jennifer took it with cries of gratitude, mopped, then smelled the handkerchief. 'What a marvellous scent! What is it? Don't tell me – I know I know it somehow.' But she couldn't think of its name, and eventually, Cressy had to tell her.

Mrs Hanwell came in to say that she couldn't hold back the goose any longer than it would take them to eat their melon, so everybody finished their drinks and started to go in to dinner. Her mother, who had Major Hawkes explaining the differences between the Industrial and French Revolutions to her, asked her to make up the fire: Felix seemed to have taken charge of an even more high-pitched and unsteady Mrs Hammond, and Dan and Emma had gone ahead to light the candles on the dining-room table. Thus Dick was able to hang back, and as she straightened herself up from the fireplace, he made a quizzical face – helpless and conspiratorial dismay. She met it with an expression of impassive good humour. He tried harder.

'You look so wonderful, darling: God, I'm sorry about this: she insisted on my coming . . .'

She brushed the lichen off her hands and said: 'Don't let it worry you,' as she started to move for the door. He tried attack.

'You shouldn't have told her what your scent is. She suspects me anyway, and if she found out, the fat would be in the fire.'

'You've got to keep your home fires burning somehow,' she said and went ahead of him through the door. She felt about ten feet high and fifty miles away. Good heavens, it was *easy*.

CHAPTER 12

FIREWORKS

EVERYBODY had drunk more before dinner than he or she usually did. Jennifer Hammond had perhaps gone further than anybody else in this direction; Dick had been simply awful about coming out to dinner, and considering how little fun she got nowadays she thought this very mean. They had had a sort of a row; not really one, but she had told him that he never did anything *she* wanted, and he had sulked and said all *he* wanted was a quiet evening at home – nothing wrong with that, was there? She had thought one martini would pick her up and it hadn't, so she'd had another, and then she felt so marvellous she couldn't resist a third. Felix had given Dick two enormous whiskies to make up for him being made to drink it. Felix himself had drunk rather a lot to keep his mind off Cressy, who was wearing a black sheath dress which made it impossible for him to keep his mind off her. Cressy had drunk a lot out of shock, and Felix giving her drinks all the time. Emma had drunk more than she usually did because she felt indefinably excited. Dan had drunk a lot because he couldn't find a drink which he actually liked. Esme had had two martinis which she never usually drank, because she had felt so anxious about Cressy being rude to the Hammonds and/or Felix. Major Hawkes drank a lot for him, because his pension wouldn't run to more than one bottle of whisky a month at home, and a splendid doctor he knew had said that alcohol was good for his arteries.

Conversation at dinner was therefore gay and general, in Major Hawkes's case so general as to be downright confusing.

'So you see, my dear Esme,' he had gone on and on, 'the French Revolution lost France a whole class of their society, and the Industrial Revolution *instigated* a whole class of our society, and my view of French being a diplomatic language has always been based on the theory that the fellers talked French *in order* that nobody should understand what they were saying. Diplomacy's always been a shifty business, it wouldn't be the slightest use a general issuing his orders in French – his officers wouldn't understand him. Unless they were French in the first place, poor fellers,' he added kindly. He lived alone and was rather short of people to talk to. Esme was carving the goose and listening to him. Felix was pouring burgundy, and Jennifer was telling Emma how marvellous it must be to work among books – she never got time to read a thing nowadays. The others were willy nilly listening to Major Hawkes who was dealing with French painting and the oversight of the Allies in not bombing Japanese spectacle factories – a cinch! Every little Nip has his specs although you need dark glasses for some of this abstract stuff the French keep knocking up – beauty wasn't in the eye of the beholder *there* – he'd found better things to look at in his time – American legs were better than French ones at that – Esme headed him off here by offering him a whole tray of sauce boats. His eyes glistened: he was very fond of food, too, but his dog ate so much that he spent a lot of his time making do. He looked up at her. 'Thank you m'dear. Having the time of my life,' he said, with the unusually succinct and simple gratitude which made Esme go on asking him to dinner. 'Where were we?' he asked daringly. 'Roving camera reports,' muttered Felix to Cressy, but Esme, who felt that all was not well in the Hammond direction, began asking Dick about his foreign trips, and Jennifer began cross-examining Daniel on his life. 'But what do you *do*?' she was practically screaming. Daniel said he walked about, and had meals, and played with things . . . '*What* things? How do you mean – play with things?' Emma, in an agony of

furious protection, said that Mr Brick was one of their authors
– a poet.

'Poetry's gone to the dogs,' remarked Major Hawkes
through his apple sauce. 'Fellers can't write anything but bibs
and bobs. I like a poem you can sink your teeth into. Patriot-
ism's a good subject, or *was* – I read a lot so naturally I bump
up against the odd poem now and then: a cracking battle with
everything going wrong's another good subject. But who cares
what some young feller thinks about dandelions or what it was
like when he was a child? Nothing epic about that. That's what
we're short of today: the *epic*.' A cranberry bounced straight out
of a gap between his teeth and landed on Emma's plate. This
had the unexpected effect of making Emma choke, which
reminded Major Hawkes of a time when his dog got a chicken
bone in her throat. 'Treated her just like a woman. Gave her an
awful fright. Bone came straight up on to the lino and everything was hunky-dory.'

More goose was offered. 'Dick – you're off your *food*,' cried
his wife. 'Normally he adores goose – there must be *something*
wrong with you! I wonder what it is?' And Dick answered, with
the minimum of good humour:

'Shut up, darling, there's a good girl.'

The trouble was that every time he said anything like that to
her she looked as though she was going to burst into tears, and
then had a drink instead. Esme battled for the rest of dinner
with the almost impossible task of talking to, or with, Major
Hawkes and Dick at the same time. Major Hawkes, delighted
at the attention, won hands down, and Dick sat looking at him
with an air of faintly weary indulgence that made Felix, Cressy
and Emma all separately despise him. He never found anything
just funny and nice, thought Cressy, as she doled out Mrs
Hanwell's lemon snow – one crystallized cherry each and two
pieces of angelica.

'. . . if it wasn't for the Russians, we shouldn't be faced with rhubarb today,' Major Hawkes was saying when he saw his angelica. 'Starving fellers ate it on the banks of the Don in the first world war . . .'

'It's not rhubarb, Brian, it's angelica.'

'I was only touching on rhubarb, Esme dear. What really worries me is the geographical position of England. The trouble with Europe is' – he dropped his voice – 'that it's nothing but foreigners as far as the eye can see. But then you have to consider the latitude – you *must* do that. England's a damn good climate: wet enough to keep the tourists out; mild enough to stop people getting all those nasty tropical diseases. I've spent hours with an old globe that belonged to my dear wife, and the only possible solution would be to place our island on the east coast of the United States. Not too far in, of course, and not too far north. Can't have our ladies losing their famous English complexions. Nice for the Canadians to have us nearer. The whole thing would be a considerable change for the better . . .'

Felix, who seemed to have taken to Major Hawkes, enlarged upon this tremendous notion, and the tensions submerged for a while. Only Dan, Emma noticed, seemed to have eaten very little, seemed to be more than usually silent. Cressy had tried to talk to him, but he had courteously blocked conversation. Emma, to sort of pay her back for trying, had tried to talk to Dick, but the fact that she knew him in his double life, and that he was aware of and embarrassed by this, made them very stilted. Also, Emma had felt Jennifer's attention instantly veer towards her when she tried to talk to Dick, and anyway, she was worried about Dan. When prompted, Esme explained about the fireworks, and Major Hawkes was instantly so excited at the prospect that Dan was visibly cheered. It was agreed that everybody should have coffee and some brandy first, and then watch the show from the sitting-room windows. Black coffee, Esme thought, would do Jennifer good.

Emma stayed to clear the table, and Dan lingered with her.

'Are you hating it?'

'They're not nice together, are they? What's wrong?'

'*I* don't know.' (How could she say?) 'They won't spoil the fireworks, will they? I wish they'd go home, though.'

'Poor girl,' he said unexpectedly: 'she's just foolish: he's a real swine.' He said that word as though he had invented it after some thought.

In due course Esme had them all assembled rather scrappily in the drawing-room. As soon as Major Hawkes had grasped exactly what was entailed by the forthcoming firework display, he took some sort of charge and started arranging a line of chairs in front of the french windows. But this took so long – because he kept thinking of fresh things to explain to Esme about the history of gunnery, and he declined offers of assistance from Dan and Felix so firmly – that, by the time he had got three chairs lined up and Esme and Cressy installed in the ones on each flank, the others were settled elsewhere in the room. Jennifer Hammond, by now looking a little bewildered, sat by the fireplace and was dealing with brandy-glass, coffee cup, handbag, cigarette and lighter. Out of the corner of her eye, Cressy saw her grab Dick's hand – no mean feat considering her other manual commitments – and pull him, against some resistance, to a stool at her side. He said something indistinguishable in a slow level undertone Cressy hated like hell, or would have done, she felt, up to a few hours ago.

Dan was by the window looking into the garden. He said to Felix with some dissatisfaction, 'They won't get the benefit from in here, you know. I've tried to put as many off the ground as possible but there's some you can't. And there's the rockets. The take-off's nothing compared to the burst.'

'Well, it's up to them,' said Emma. 'They can come out if they want to. Anyway, *we*'ll see the best of it.'

'That's true. Come on, then.'

'Can I give you a hand?' asked Felix. 'Or watch, anyway.' Fireworks for him meant boredom, plus sharp uneasiness if anyone looked like getting himself burnt, but he wanted an excuse for getting out for a bit – away from the couple by the fireplace with their slowly but steadily increasing repulsiveness, also away from Cressy, who a moment before had looked up into his eyes and away again with a twist of her head that showed off the beauty of her neck and collar-bone. Ill temper again? Never mind what – he needed a rest from her: a short one, anyhow. He added hastily, 'We'd better wrap up warm; it'll be pretty chilly out there.'

'I'm wearing my clothes,' said Dan.

When the three had left the room there was silence. Major Hawkes had that moment said he was talking too much again, and whenever he said this he usually stayed quiet for at least a minute. The Hammonds and Cressy were all not looking at anybody. 'Would anyone like another drink?' asked Esme, realizing as she spoke that this was the opposite of what the situation called for. Everybody said they would.

Answering for Jennifer, who he announced would like a change from brandy, Dick wondered if they had any crème de menthe or anything of that sort. Cressy hurried away into the dining-room, knelt down in front of the sideboard and stayed there for a time just looking at it. She no longer felt ten feet high. Remembering what finishing with somebody had been like in the past turned out to be remarkably difficult, considering how many times she'd done it. Was it inevitable to be overwhelmed by plain disbelief that one had done all those things with the person, experienced all that, said all that? She thought it likely that none of the all thats had been very extravagant in this case, but at the moment her power of judging this appeared to have deserted her. Possibly, again, she'd come to find some things out of the last six months that she'd be able to think of as all right or even better, something to salvage, but she sensed gloomily now that what she'd be salvaging would be her idea of herself as one able to draw *some* real distinctions, instead of making self-deception a mode of existence. Unfortunately there was no stage in any situation at which you could know you were seeing it as it really was.

The door opened. 'What on earth are you up to?' asked Dick, trying a smile.

'What are you doing here?'

'Oh, that's all right – we've got a minute. I said I'd left my cigarettes.'

'Christ, what are you *doing here*? Tonight. To dinner.'

'What's the matter with you all of a sudden? I didn't come here on purpose, you know. Just wasn't any way I could get out of it. I could tell it was a bit of a shock for you when I came walking in the . . .'

She asked herself why she'd never noticed before that the skin on his cheeks where his beard showed was semi-transparent, so that it was like wax fruit with stubble. 'Oh, good for you. You'd never have guessed if you hadn't been watching carefully, and anybody else wouldn't have spotted it even if they had, but you know me so well . . .'

'For God's sake stop *kneeling* there like that! What's it supposed to be in aid of?' When she stayed just as she was, down to mouth and eyes, he went brisk in the way that said he was generously and sensibly conceding a point in order to avert a row. 'Well, whatever it is that's bothering you, we'll talk about it tomorrow night when we're at a bit less of a disadvantage.'

It was easy again then. She opened the sideboard door and pretended to consider, although there was only one possibility there, a bottle of Kümmel which she took out and carefully inspected while she rose to her feet. On her way to the door she paused and turned her face in his direction long enough to say, 'I don't want that to happen – don't you come,' before going out. Behind her she heard his long sigh, and the faint slap as his horizontally raised arms fell to his sides.

Back in the sitting-room Jennifer said loudly, and more nasally than ever, 'And where have you two been sneaking off

183

to like a couple of . . . What have you been up to?' She was very close to not being funny about it at all.

'Getting you a drink.' Cressy found a clean glass and hesitated. Would a great deal or a very little be better? She chose a great deal, feeling vaguely it was more malicious, more like poisoning someone.

'Fetching my cigarettes – I told you. I freely admit to having run into Cressy and exchanged a few words with her.' Dick considered that this was a case of a tricky situation bringing out the best in him, and thought his voice sounded bantering or could have been taken so, when he went on: 'Of course if I'd known you were going to take this line I'd have been as silent as a monk and then we'd all have been happy.'

Outside, a rocket fizzed and flared briefly before disappearing. 'I take it that means they're ready,' said Major Hawkes. 'Dowse the glim, eh?' He turned off the lights and settled himself in his chair, rubbing his hands together slowly.

At his side, Esme strained to hear and see what was going on over by the fireplace. She was used to the idea of drink bringing out the worst in people, but the actuality was still worrying, and there seemed no guarantee that the worst in Mrs Hammond was yet out. And whatever was wrong with Cressy was more than embarrassment. The light of two Roman candles from the garden showed the Hammonds comparatively quietened down, with him talking emphatically but inaudibly at her turned-away face, but nothing was to be made of Cressy's profile.

'Brilliant people, the Chinese,' said Major Hawkes. 'Wonderfully gifted. Taught the Japs everything they know, of course. There must have been a very high proportion of first-class brains about at that time. Look at that, now.' He indicated a multi-coloured upward shower just ignited by Dan, accompanied by a muted hissing roar. Esme gripped the sides of her seat. When the bang came it was less bad than the totally unexpected shrieks and whizzes made by whatever the things were that came shooting out. One of them thudded lightly against the window. Esme flinched and Major Hawkes laid his hand on her arm for a moment. 'That's a modern one, I suppose,' he said. 'New to me, at any rate. I think I'd call it rather crude – not much beauty there. That's always the trouble, my dear Esme – fellers just don't seem to know how to leave well alone. Ah, now this' – a large double catherine-wheel, slowly accelerating, began to throw out jets of changing light – 'this is nearer the kind of thing I look for. Imagination at work for a change. This sort doesn't go pop,' he added more quietly.

It didn't, and neither did the next, but during the one after that – another Roman candle – there was a sharp bang only a few yards away. It was no louder than the earlier one, but it was unexpected. At any rate, Esme heard a rattle of china and a sort of yelp and gathered that Mrs Hammond had spilt her coffee over herself. Then, 'It's all *right*, I can use this,' she heard her say.

A Golden Rain spurted brilliantly in Emma's hand and she ran about waving it aloft. Her face, sporadically illumined, and the movements of her body, conveyed the wild freedom of a much younger Emma. Dan lit another of the same at the guttering Roman candle and bounded towards her, gesticulating with it. The two began a rudimentary capering dance. Then Esme saw Felix a little farther off, stooping down by the dark tattered bulk of the magnolia and evidently about to ignite something on the ground. As she watched him he looked up and seemed to stare straight at her, though she realized he could not have seen her through the blaze of reflections on the outside of the window. Then he dropped his head and she saw the small flare of a match.

She was gazing at him so attentively that she missed the first couple of remarks in what she soon recognized as an altercation, if nothing worse. Mrs Hammond was speaking, or rather half shouting, in a voice of varying pitch. 'I know it now all right, now I've had a second sniff at it. That's the muck you come home stinking to high heaven of when you've been up in London for one of your *boring business functions*. Of course it's hers – she gave it to me before dinner to mop up my drink with. It is yours, isn't it? You're not going to deny it, are you?'

In a huge green glow from outside Esme saw Cressy turn and half get to her feet, but couldn't hear what she said because Major Hawkes cut in at his loudest. 'Makes you look at things as though you were seeing them for the first time. It isn't only the colours, it's the light and shade. That what I expect from a worthwhile painting, now. Or a photograph even – they've made great strides with that. Remember how it used to be nothing but orange and green through foggy spectacles? All gone by the board these days.'

By the time Esme had disengaged herself and moved over to where the altercation was, Mrs Hammond was shouting again. Her husband had her by the arm and kept telling her that she was drunk and must shut up and come home, but she took no notice of him. 'Sneaking off. I knew the two of you were up to something. Laughing your heads off about me. What fun to have your *lover* and his poor fool of a wife to dinner and play footie with him under the table and plan your next little dose of . . .'

Cressy was facing her. She said in tones of loathing, 'I didn't invite you here and I don't want you here, either of you, and there isn't going to be a next little anything at all – anyway, please go. I can't see why you're not ashamed to stay.'

'Would you like to go upstairs and lie down for a bit?' asked Esme – sort of lowering the price, she thought.

'No, I wouldn't! I refuse to be shoved out of the way as if I was a . . . a piece of furniture. I'm staying here and we're having this out.'

'There's nothing to have out,' said Cressy in the same tone as before.

Just then the light in the room, which had faded almost to nothing, grew and changed abruptly to a tinny silver, like packaged moonlight. 'Look!' cried Major Hawkes, so sharply and sincerely that all four turned and followed his pointing finger. Esme caught a glimpse of a tiny aeroplane-like object rising in an unsteady spiral towards the tops of the fruit trees. 'Now that kind of job I must confess I do rather admire. Probably a personal thing. It could be that as a child I was given a toy helicopter or whatever it might have been by some relative I particularly admired – or it could just be a primitive desire to fly. Oh, that stuff isn't all nonsense by any means.'

By the time this had ended, Jennifer Hammond might have gone quietly – and quickly – if Dick hadn't told her with a growl in his voice that she had made quite enough of an exhibition of herself, and tried to manhandle her to the door, which brought an assault on his character and habits. Esme stood helplessly waiting for it to stop. She put a hand out to Cressy and it was taken. The thought that her daughter's ordinary life was full of scenes like this, that perhaps tonight was no more than specially annoying and awkward, filled her with fear.

Someone came into the room. It was Felix, about to say – as he explained later – that he was sneaking in for a drink, that Dan had called half-time and was on his way to try to lure them outside for the second part of the programme. As it was he said nothing, because Jennifer Hammond was in the middle of asking Cressy how Cressy could bear to have a brute like Dick make love to her. The room was dark again except for a wan flickering and Felix switched on the light as if to understand better what was taking place.

'But then I don't suppose you care much, do you?' went on that terrible little voice just as before, remaining little and constricted however loud it became. 'Sex is all that counts with your sort. And laughing up your sleeve about how the two of you have got away with it and pulled the wool over my eyes. I suppose that's the best part.'

Felix half-raised his hand and made a sound – he had no

187

idea what he'd been about to do or say, but the result was to draw the woman's attention to him.

'Oh, I can see how any *man* would stand up for her. That's her stock-in-trade, after all. I could see you looking her over earlier on. I'm not so blind as all that. She's a whore. No shame at all – you can tell. Not that you'd mind if you're like *him*. You just don't care, any of you – just . . . don't . . .'

At long long last she was unable to go on. Esme raised her eyes. Emma and Daniel Brick were there now, she with an arm round Cressy's shoulders, he standing apart. Dick Hammond, eyebrows philosophically raised, was concentrating on lighting a cigarette while Felix stared at him with half-shut eyes.

'Stop fiddling with that thing and take her home,' said Emma sharply. 'And don't bring her here again or come yourself. Never mind, darling,' she added to Cressy, 'it doesn't matter. Everybody knows you're worth fifty of *her*.'

Hammond pulled his sobbing wife to her feet and left without a word.

Esme wondered why Daniel Brick, of all present the least involved, should appear to be the most stricken.

For what seemed like a very long moment, everybody left in the room seemed rooted or frozen in their various positions. Then Cressy, drawing in a breath as though she had been holding it before, walked over to the fireplace, and stood for a moment with her hands on the mantelshelf and her back to them. Then, just as she was turning round to face them, Major Hawkes said:

'Cressy, m'dear, I wonder whether you'd be so very kind as to give me a lift home? It's getting rather late for me, and Sophie gets so worried about me she scratches all the paint off the doors, poor dear.'

And Cressy, her eyes brilliant with – gratitude? unshed tears? – said quietly: 'Of course: I'd love to – I'll just get my coat,' and went swiftly from the room.

Emma looked at Dan: he made a dismissive movement of his head and then he too left. With an anxious glance at her mother Emma followed him.

Felix, struggling with some private irresolution, said suddenly: 'Back in a minute.'

Esme, discovering that she was actually shaking, opened her mouth to say *something, anything* which could constitute an apology, but Major Hawkes forestalled her.

'My dear Esme, it was a most marvellous dinner, and I've always had a weakness for fireworks, the twentieth-century view of morality has always been a patchy business, and most families, to misquote that outrageous Frog general, march on their laissez-faire. I'll pop into the Catchpoles tomorrow and ring you up. My coat's in the hall.'

Esme went with him, and helped him into his horribly thin old tweed just as Cressy came down in her coat followed by Felix.

'I'm coming with you, if I may,' he said firmly. 'Here's this back,' and he handed Esme the green file. 'We can take my car,' she heard him say as they started to go. Major Hawkes picked up her icy hand and kissed it. 'Go and have an enormous brandy if I were you: good night.'

She walked vaguely back to the sitting-room – scene of so much disorder and embarrassment – and she had the brandy. It was nice of Felix to have gone with Cressy, but she wished he hadn't: she was already becoming used to the support of his presence. She started to collect the coffee cups and glasses, to give her something not to think about.

Emma couldn't find Dan at first, but the kitchen door was ajar, and although it was dark in the room, she had a feeling he might be in it. He was: standing by the kitchen door which he had already unlocked.

'What are you doing?'

'Never you mind that.'

'No, really, Dan, I *do* mind.'

'I'm off,' he said: he looked strained and almost sick. 'I can't stand this kind of life.'

'Dan – please don't. I – '

But he said savagely: 'Thanks for having me,' and went. Just like that: he was gone.

He couldn't be gone! Where would he go? But that wouldn't make any difference to him, she knew – he'd just got to get away, if that was what he felt like doing. She suddenly realized that she was crying without realizing it. Some kind of mechanical prudence made her run upstairs, still crying, to get her heavy coat and bag and a bag of the peppermints they'd bought that morning. Then she scribbled a note for Cressy, put it on her bed and left the house. She shut the front door very quietly, and Esme did not hear her go.

Esme, bereft of company or any more chores she could bear to do, found herself looking at, and then opening, the green file. *He* would have read it: later, he would want to talk about it, and she simply had not looked at it for years. She adjusted the lamp by the fire, and started to read . . .

PREFACE
by
Mervyn Grace

It is because my brother received no official recognition of his last service to his country that I have ventured to attempt some account of it. To do this, I have had to rely to a certain extent upon my knowledge of my brother's character, and the diary, or log, that he left behind him, but my grateful acknowledgements are due to Lt/Cdr J. S. Vaughan, RN, owner of the yawl *Mavis*, Mr Sam Whiting of the Hamble River Boatyard Company, Mrs G. Watson, mother of Driver F. Watson, RASC, and last, but by no means least, to Signalman N. A. Black of the Royal Corps of Signals: indeed, without Signalman Black's contribution this story could never have been told. He devoted two afternoons of his leave to an account which was taken in shorthand, and without this many salient facts of the story would have been irretrievably lost. Finally, I must beg the reader's indulgence: in spite of having been a reader all my life, and a publisher for a good deal of it, I am no writer, and this exercise has made me very well aware of my failings. I begin with a brief biography:

Julius Edward Grace was born in 1890. The second of three sons, he was educated at Winchester and Oxford. He was three years in the family publishing firm of Speedwell and Grace. On 4 August 1914, he volunteered for the Army with his elder brother Wyndham. Wyndham was killed six weeks after they got to France, but Julius, who later joined the Machine Gun Corps, attained the rank of Major unscathed and was awarded the Military Cross and Bar for his services. After the war he returned to the firm. In 1922, he married Esme Roland. There were two daughters of this marriage: Cressida, b. 1923 and Emma Susan, b. 1933.

On 22 May 1940, at the beginning of the British evacuation of Dunkirk, he sailed a small yawl across the Channel single-handed and collected three men off the beaches near St Valéry. He died on the return journey about two miles offshore of Newhaven. One of the men he rescued died of wounds in the boat; the other two survived to be picked up when the yawl was sighted drifting after her engine had failed.

Perhaps, given the national emergency of the time, my brother's feat does not immediately strike the reader as particularly heroic, or even remarkable. Hundreds of private vessels of every description were making the journey that my brother made in the *Mavis*, but there were several points about Julius's exploit which make it a singular affair, and I am morally certain that it was touched off by my brother's ineradicable guilt at having survived the first world war.

The implications of the possible Fall of France were immediately apparent to Julius, and he worried ceaselessly about whether the BEF would succeed in fighting a successful rear-guard action back to the north coast in order that the majority of it could be embarked. I know he worried because he talked to me about it, and although he never said a word about them, this must have been when he began making his private arrangements. He suffered two severe disadvantages. He knew virtually nothing about sailing – indeed he was almost always sick in ships or boats of any description, and naturally, in view of this, he did not possess a boat. He had to get one, and he had, somehow, to learn how to sail it. He collected a number of books on the subject: manuals, hand-books, teach-yourself-sailing, charts (several were found in his office, and one or two in the boat, and in some of them, he had made notes).

His achieving a boat was attended by that curious combination of ingenuity and sheer luck which so often marks the really private and determined enterprise. He knew a man who was a member of the Royal Thames Yacht Club, and got himself invited to dine there. At this point in the story I am indebted to Lt/Cdr Vaughan who most kindly offered me some of his valuable time, and who was subsequently most generous in his refusal to let me reimburse him for any of the damage done to his boat (for it was his boat that my brother took). Cdr Vaughan said that, in retrospect, he was deeply impressed with how Julius managed to skate over thin ice throughout the evening at the Yacht Club. Having mentioned early on that he was looking for a small ketch or yawl, he was fairly besieged by knowledgeable and enthusiastic boat-owners anxious to sell to him. Most members had no time to go sailing, and nobody liked laying their boat up indefinitely:

he was at once plunged into technical discussions about his requirements and the assets of various yachts he was offered. Julius apparently survived this without giving the show away by saying very little and looking intelligent. Cdr Vaughan said that Julius chose his boat because he had said that the engine was very reliable, and also she was moored in the Hamble River. She was a three-and-a-half-ton yawl, gaff-rigged, and, he assured Julius, a good sea boat. Vaughan had a snapshot of her, and he thought that this must also have influenced Julius: it must have been very difficult to visualize a boat from dimensions and descriptions of rigging, he said, if you knew nothing about the subject. It was agreed that Julius should go and see her, take her out for a trial, and if he liked her, buy her for eight hundred pounds.

Cdr Vaughan took me to see the *Mavis* when she had been towed back to her moorings on the Hamble a month later, and I had the curious sensation of going through some of my brother's experience when he first encountered her. I suppose I must know even less about yachts than with his intensive reading he can have done, but I must confess that my first glimpse of the *Mavis* filled me with a mixture of apprehension and something approaching awe at my brother's determination. To begin with she looked so *small*: it was extremely hard for me to believe that she was big enough to sail any distance. Secondly, I had the ignorant land-lubber's idea of a river – any river – as being a gentle arm of water drifting calmly between green banks until it reached the sea. The Hamble was a narrow and alarmingly fast channel of water which at that time was racing down between steep and horrible-looking mud banks. The *Mavis* was moored at the edge of the channel: to reach her we had to descend fifteen slimy steps down from the landing stage into a mere cockle-shell of a dinghy which, fortunately for me, was rowed by Cdr Vaughan. He was clearly experienced, but he was sweating by the time we reached his yacht. 'It's a devil – this tide,' he said:

'and your brother must have had to make three or four trips out and back with all the stores he loaded. Pretty tiring, on your own. He must have been able to row all right.' I forbore to remark that to my knowledge my brother had done no rowing since he had taken me on the Cherwell when I visited him at Oxford in 1908.

Close to, the *Mavis* was not much more reassuring. She had that extraordinarily desolate air which made it hard to believe that she had been inhabited so recently. The little cabin, with three bunks, was fusty and damp, the port-holes thick with condensation and salt. There was a shelf and two primus stoves where a fourth bunk would have been. The whole thing looked cramped and uncomfortable. Cdr Vaughan unlatched a door and revealed a lavatory which struck me as only practicable for a dwarf. 'Heads in the fo'c'sle very handy.' He then yanked up a floorboard and displayed a trough in which some dark oily water slopped. 'Marvellous bilges: tight as a nut: she doesn't make more than a teacupful of water a month.' We went up into the cockpit in the centre of which was the engine boxed in teak. The decks seemed to have a bewildering quantity of ropes, and there were two masts, main and mizzen, I was informed. The general impression I got was of mystifying confusion and discomfort and I wondered, as I have had occasion to do before, what drove people to exchange comfortable houses where they were warm and dry and did not bump their heads, for week-ends of what seemed to me to be nerve-racking squalor. Cdr Vaughan said wistfully that he had only contemplated selling the *Mavis* because his wife did not *really* enjoy sailing, a fact which he seemed to find wholly astounding: he added that she was a very poor sailor and he thought that that might have had something to do with it. I thought of Julius, and my respect for him grew. I tried to imagine for a moment, that I was he: attempting now to set off on his incredible (to me) voyage. How would I begin? The olive-green water rushed past: I thought of steering; of casting off (the boat was secured fore and aft); of the problems of swinging her head round to face downstream – the channel was a narrow one; of hoisting sails; of navigating miles of open sea so that you ended up even approximately where you meant to in spite of having nobody to help and being sick and night falling . . . Standing in the cockpit, trying to imagine what it was like for him, my mind simultaneously crowded with a host of memories of my brother, I resolved that whatever kind of job I made of writing about his adventure, it must be recorded: he had surmounted and endured and survived too much to fade without a line to his memory. Cdr Vaughan seemed to have some inkling of my feelings, since he said something about it taking a lot of nerve to do a thing like that. We rowed back to the landing stage and went in search of Sam Whiting.

Sam said that my brother had come down to the boat twice: once when he had been shown over by Sam who had agreed to rig her in readiness for Julius's next visit. He had turned the engine over for Julius: showed him where the pump and water-tanks were and told him everything he asked, which, according to Sam, was a great deal. It had crossed Sam's mind that Mr Grace didn't seem to know a power of a lot about boats, and he kept reiterating that if he'd known what Mr Grace had in mind, he'd have tried to find someone to go with him. Not that that would be easy these days. He couldn't understand why Mr Grace hadn't taken anyone with him. He'd wanted as much room as possible in the boat for the men, I explained: she wasn't a very big boat, and he'd visualized filling her. 'Only brought back three though, didn't he? And one of them dead at that?' He had a way of saying that as though he'd caught me out, and I began to find him rather irritating. I asked whether he'd been there when my brother set off. He'd had the day off, but he happened to look in at the yard at about four o'clock in the evening, just in time to see Mr Grace casting off. He hadn't taken his mooring lines on board

– just cast them off: Sam had gone down to the landing stage and shouted that he'd better take in his lines, but with the engine, Mr Grace hadn't seemed to hear what he said: just waved back, and as he was sailing with the ebb he was soon out of sight. Sam thought it was a funny time of the day to go out sailing but none of it was his business: he'd rigged her, and pumped her out: Mr Grace had said that he never knew when he might get some free time to try the boat so he'd done just what Mr Grace said to do. So Julius had had to load the *Mavis* unaided. I realized what that must have meant, because a list was found in his pocket; the petrol alone would have been more than one trip, not to mention fresh water, paraffin, first-aid kit, charts and stores, blankets, lamps, etc.

Late in May, bad news was travelling at a rate that made it impossible, without a map, to keep up with the place names. He spent a long week-end with his family, and came to London on his usual train. In the office, he told me that he heard the guns in France from his bedroom window: we speculated together about the size and urgency of the evacuation: then he went back to his room. About an hour later he looked in on me and told me that he was going away for a couple of days. It never occurred to me to ask him where he was going, but if I had done so, it is possible that he would have told me. He said in his letter to me that the only reason he had preserved such secrecy was that he didn't want anyone to try and stop him. Then he said as though it was an afterthought: 'If I'm not back by Thursday afternoon, there's some stuff in my desk I'd like you to see to for me,' and he took the key off his ring and put it into my hand, nodded to me and was gone.

LOG KEPT BY MY BROTHER IN THE *MAVIS*

It's stupid to call this a log, really; I haven't the faintest idea how to keep one properly. But I do want to keep some kind of record, in case I want to do this again, or, I suppose, in case I don't get back: perhaps someone of the family may be interested in knowing what I was trying to do. Perhaps I just want to keep it. I'm sitting in the cabin now waiting for the ebb tide – due in about fifteen minutes. If I sail dead on it, I shall get the benefit of it on the long haul eastwards. There's nothing more to do now: I've stowed everything – three trips in that dinghy – I've turned the engine over and she starts with reassuring ease. In theory, at least, I know how to hoist these sails, although the mainsail is going to be a bit of a problem. I've eaten a sandwich, made some coffee in a thermos to see me through the night, and I've taken a double dose of seasick stuff – hope that helps, at least. I've laid my course, and it doesn't look too impossible, although it seems much farther than I originally thought it would be. This is much farther west than I would have chosen, but on the other hand, the boat is the best I was offered. She is sound, handy, seaworthy, I'm told, with a reliable engine, and I should be able to get ten or a dozen men in her: they won't be comfortable, but they'll pack in somehow. At the moment, the worst fear I have is that I'll mess up getting under way: the channel's so narrow and the tide so fast that one has to do everything right and quickly, or I'll run the boat aground and have to sit there until the tide floats me off. I've made a gadget for lashing the tiller: it looks Heath Robinson, but I think it will work. The water is hardly eddying round the mooring buoys now: I think the tide is on the turn. I shall sail down the river; make for open sea leaving Ryde Pier well to my right, and then lay my course as planned. The river channel seems fairly well marked and anyway it will be light . . .

Eleven p.m. I've come down into the cabin to try and drink some coffee with brandy in it. Been sick so much that I need to get something down for next time. Anyway it will be warming. I'm well out to sea now: no land in sight, but there is a moon between small clouds and I don't suppose any real sailor would call this a heavy sea. The *Mavis* is undoubtedly a sea boat. She seems to enjoy the waves and at least I now have confidence in her ability to ride them. Saw people on Ryde Pier: that was when I wished I had somebody with me. I could have hoisted the mainsail with help, but have had to abandon it alone. Got the foresail and mizzen up, and with the engine, we're doing about six knots I should guess. That's enough, and if I did get the mainsail up, I couldn't reef, or get it down quickly if I needed to. The point is to get there: I'll have plenty of crew for the return. It's a most desolate and beautiful sight, the sea at night. Phosphorescence; the sky is darker than the sea: stars are much more cheerful than the moon. That coffee isn't going to stay with me . . .

I want to sleep, but haven't the courage. Only deserts can seem so immense, endless, as this. There seems no reason why there should ever be land at all. I think the morning is coming, but it is so incredibly slow that I'm not sure. But there is the faintest change from clouded, moonlit dark: the horizon is just marked by silver. Writing to keep awake. Or for company.

Notes on sunrise. (Poem?) Been done so much: I'd never do it well enough to warrant the initial cliché. But colours!

Horizon warm silver: stars going out: the sea is becoming darker than the sky. A streak of pale, piercing green; changing from green to yellow chartreuse. Not a streak now – bleeding up from the farthest edge of the sea. Water like dark molten lead, as though it would be heavy to touch. Above the yellow the sky like dog violets: yellow warmer. Apricot. Yolks of gulls' eggs: violet turned to rose colour: like no rose – more rose-coloured than any flower. A deep golden flush on skyline; the sun is coming up. Very slow, majestic; colours violent and dazzling: herald the sun like trumpets? God, I'm cold: I can just feel the sun and it's made me realize how cold I am. Must fill petrol tanks, check course and try some soup if I heat it.

Had to alter course two points south. Foresail jibbed: took in sheet; set nicely now. Saw two fighter planes. I waved and shouted, it was so wonderful to see them and I didn't feel alone. Providing air cover: I feel marvellous now I've survived that interminable night: clear-headed: now I can afford to think whether I stood a good chance last night of pulling this thing off: fifty-fifty I think. More planes. Guns audible. Watching for French coast. Dear little Emma will still be asleep. Soup wonderfully warming. Haven't been sick now for over four hours, and am a better helmsman – judging by the bubbles in my wake. Two destroyers? Big ships anyway on a course parallel to mine. Guns louder: or sharper? I want to get there now. Extraordinary drumming sound: v. powerful engines. Six MTBs roaring towards France. 'Everybody's *doing* it.' (Who used to sing that?) More planes. One limping home by sound of engine. I keep imagining I can see the coast now: look away a bit and see I was wrong.

Coast! No doubt of it. I've looked away: it's still there. Remains to be seen what bit I've hit, but I'll check once more. Thank God, it's a fine day . . .

There is a gap here which cannot be filled in. Julius did not record the time of his sighting the French coast, and there are no witnesses to what happened between that time and when he finally picked up Corporal Godden, Driver Watson and Signalman Black. Signalman Black takes the story from here. I cannot do better than leave it in his words.

SIGNALMAN BLACK'S ACCOUNT

It must have been about four when Mr Grace picked us up out of the water.

M. G. Could you say something about how you came to be there?

BLACK. Oh yes. Well sir, the situation in or around St Valéry was a real old muddle. That's the only way you could describe it, really. I'd lost my Section: been ordered to destroy stores and equipment some way inland and meet at an assembly point. It's surprising how long it takes you to destroy that sort of stuff, sir – so's it's no good to anybody else, I mean. I got to the assembly point, all right, but no one else was there, and I knew we was making for the coast so I kept on walking and sometimes there were people I could ask where my Section was, but nobody knew. And the other two. Driver Watson had simply been told to drive his truck north, and he picked up Bombardier Godden on the way. He – Godden – had lost his battery and he couldn't do anything about trying to find it 'cos he'd been wounded and he couldn't walk. I suppose we spent about two days at the coast: more and more men were arriving all the time, and we kept being told to wait in cellars, march down to the beach, march back to the cellars, dig ourself into a bit of shore there, etc. You know – they kept saying ships were coming and we'd be embarking at oh-bloody-oh hours and then it didn't come off. In the end it did though. We was put into transports to be taken out to destroyers – they couldn't come inshore as it was too shallow for them – miles out, they looked. I didn't meet Watson and Godden till after our transport was hit – she was badly hit, sir – killed a lot of people and it was clear the boat was sinking. The officer told all men who could swim to jump for it and disperse – they'd get picked up by other transports, and those who couldn't swim to hang on. I jumped, and then I saw what turned out to be Watson drop over the side of the boat

– she was waterlogged by then – and hanging on with one arm he was trying to hold this man's head out of the water rising in the boat. That was Godden, sir – he wouldn't have been able to move and it looked like he'd drown if it hadn't been for Watson. There was a second burst of fire from the Dornier and that made most people feel it was better to be on their own than hanging on to the target. I'd just reached Watson when I was suddenly aware of this small yacht bearing down on us. She seemed to come from nowhere. One minute she wasn't there, and the next minute I thought she'd ram us. The yacht was towing a dinghy, and I yelled at the man on board (your brother, sir) to cast her off for us. I swam for the dinghy, and he got the point just in time and I heaved myself into it. Well then we had to manoeuvre Godden out of the transport into the dinghy and that was tricky. We could float him out of the transport by then – it was full of water – but we had to rock and lean the dinghy practically on to one side to get Godden into it. I told Watson to row, but he said he didn't know how to row, so I told him to stay in the water and hang on to the dinghy. That was when I first noticed that Mr Grace didn't seem to have anyone to help him on the yacht. I could see he was having trouble, and the distance between us and the yacht was lengthening too fast. I shouted to him to make a circuit and pick us up and just as I thought he was too far to hear, he started to do just that. Well – he had to make two shots at it, and I could hear Watson's teeth chattering. Mr Grace tried to throw the dinghy's tow rope, but he threw it a shade too early and it fell short. The next time he tried, I stood up: I nearly fell out of the dinghy, but I caught it, and we hauled ourselves alongside. Then we still had to get Godden out of the dinghy. I tried Watson in the dinghy and me on the yacht, but to lift Godden, Watson had to stand: the dinghy rocked and of course he lost his balance and fell over Godden – he made an awful sound sir, and fainted: I don't think we'd realized he was hurt so bad till then. Then Mr Grace, he said lash him to the oars – it'll be easier if we have him rigid, he said, and he was right. Watson went on board the yacht, and when I'd lashed Godden, Mr Grace said to lever him up head first and they'd each take a shoulder. The first part was the worst: he was a big man and the oars weren't long enough to support his head. I suppose the distance from the bottom of the dinghy on to the deck wasn't more than about three feet, but it was an awkward angle and of course we was trying not to hurt him. The last part was worse for me, because I had to mind his bad leg, and standing in the dinghy was a risky business. In the end we managed it with one final heave – quickly, while he was still out – we wouldn't have had the nerve to get on with it when he'd come to. We'd been so taken up with getting him on the boat, we hadn't noticed that the Jerry plane had gone. Mr Grace – he told us his name then – pulled a flask out and offered me some brandy. I had a swig, and I said what about giving him some to pull him round, and Watson his teeth were chattering so much he could hardly talk said we had to get him on to the big ship: he needed a doctor badly, he'd said so when Watson had picked him up. Mr Grace said we'd better make straight for the destroyer, and then we could come back for other people. He revved up the engines and we set off – miles away the destroyer looked and the other transports had already got there. We must have been quite a time with the dinghy and all. I made Watson have a drink – he was only a kid and he didn't want to, but he'd got much colder than me because he couldn't swim. Mr Grace said there were blankets in the cabin, and Watson started getting Godden's wet clothes off him. When I brought up the blankets, Watson said: 'He has a tourniquet: it has to keep on being done.' He set about it, and I thought you never know I'd better watch. His trouser leg had been cut: the wound was high on the inside of the thigh – Watson looked scared when he loosened the stick, and said: 'He says it's a compound fracture and damage to the artery.' The moment the stick was loose, blood – you could see the blood coming out on the dressing – a lot of blood it looked to me. Watson tightened it up. 'I couldn't find no one to do better for him. When my truck give out, I couldn't leave him for long enough to find anyone.' He had eyes like a dog we had at home when we were leaving to go out. 'He a pal of yours?' I asked. But he said he only see him on the road. 'You done your best,' I said: 'let's get him into a blanket and give him a spot of brandy.' We had to cut his clothes off him and Watson found a spoon for the brandy. Mr Grace said there were some oilskins and a jersey in the cabin and to change into them, so I did. I was still in the cabin when Mr Grace gave a shout. When I came up I saw that the destroyer – she still looked bloody miles away – had embarked all the men off the transports. 'She's making ready to leave,' Mr Grace said. He said he couldn't get any more speed out of the engine. I asked if he had a torch, and he had, and I went to the front of the boat and made a signal. Wounded on board wait, wait, wait. I made it three times, but they didn't answer – the battery was low in the torch and it can't have been very strong to see.

Then the destroyer just moved off, sir – nothing we could do. I had a job trying to explain that to Watson, though – that there was nothing we could do, I mean. For some daft reason, he seemed to think that the smaller a ship was the faster she could go: he thought we could catch the bloody destroyer up. When at last the penny dropped, he burst out crying with a lot of naughty language. It was all on account of his pal, but I had to speak sharply to him to pull him together. I told him to go below and change his clothes and be quick about it: he was hysterical sir, but he hadn't worried about number one when he was in the water. He went off, snuffling like some kid. Well, I asked Mr Grace what he thought we should do now. Godden was round, but he didn't look so good, and I could see Mr Grace thought that too, because he said we'd better make for England. We decided to carry Godden down and put him on a bunk where he'd lie softer. Mr Grace said he had a first-aid box and that cheered Watson up: he said he'd put a dry dressing on Godden's leg. He did too. He had hands like a bunch of dirty bangers, and he said he didn't know anything about first aid, but he bandaged him up as gently as a woman doing it, sucking his teeth and breathing deep the whole way through. Well, we heated some soup on the primus and we all had cigarettes – it was quite a party then. It was then Mr Grace told us he'd come from Hamble. 'Charley comes from Portsmouth,' Watson said. He was feeding Godden with soup, I couldn't believe at first he'd come on his own, sir. I mean by then, it was clear he was no sailor if you'll excuse the expression. Well, he said that. He said: 'I'm sorry, I'm not really used to boats.' That made Godden smile and Watson grinned and said: 'You're feeling better, aren't you Charley? Charley can sail a boat all right,' he went on. It was amazing what a lot Watson seemed to have picked up about Charley: they'd had nothing to do but chin in the truck, I suppose. Godden said we'd do better with our mainsail. He seemed better then, he had quite a bit of colour in his face – it was fever, but we didn't know it then. Well, Watson stayed below with Godden, and Mr Grace and I got the mainsail up O.K. and then we took turns to steer, and talked. It's a funny thing, sir, your brother was in a world apart from me; I mean he was old, and he'd had the education; he was the kind of man who I wouldn't have had much time for if he wasn't a teacher or a doctor – you know what I mean. But we were on our own and everything wasn't normal for either of us, and I don't think I've ever talked to anyone so much in my life before. We had talks that went on past argument to finding out – I can't explain it, it wasn't a normal experience – well, that's how it was . . .

M.G. What did you talk about?

BLACK. Well, of course, he asked me about myself – you

204

won't want to hear that – where I come from, my life and times you might say . . .

M.G. No, we should like to hear that. What did you tell him?

BLACK. Oh well, sir . . . I'm twenty-four; I'm a Londoner; made the grammar, always had a passion for everything to do with electricity: my uncle had a small shop and I worked for him in holidays. As soon as I left school I got apprenticed to the GPO. By then, I'd got this thing about electrical faults – I had a kind of feel for them without testing through the book for it, so I did quite well. I volunteered for the army and got drafted into the Royal Corps of Signals. After eight months I was made a lineman – that's good going in a way, but I don't think your brother understood. I tried to explain a circuit to him, but I could see he couldn't understand what I was talking about, so I give up. But it's an interesting job, and a lot of people depend on you when you're doing it. That's all there is about me, sir – and I'm not saying your brother wasn't interested – I just couldn't make him understand. No more than I could understand his job – he told me about that – it seemed funny to me spending all your life on communications and not be able to understand a circuit. We're both in the communication business, I told him, and he laughed. We had one argument though – I wish we'd finished it. He said that the reason he minded about language and communication was because it was the only hope for humanity and what did I feel about that? Humanity, he said, sir. 'Must look after number one,' I told him. That tore it. He said that after this war, we all had to be responsible for everybody else – had to think about them and all that. I said: 'Look, I had a good job and a nice young lady. I give it all up to fight this war. *I* don't hold with war: *I* didn't make it. Here I am – would have been dead today if it hadn't been for you most likely. And that won't be the end of it,' I said. 'I reckon when this war is over, I'm entitled to my life in my own country and a good job and

a house, and it's my kids I'll be worrying over – not a whole
lot of foreigners. I don't expect to worry them – and they'd
better not worry me. I'm doing my bit now.' He kept saying
that it wouldn't be like that. The world would get smaller and
much more crowded and we'd all have to think of everybody
else. 'Look, sir,' I said: 'you get this boat and come over to
France to rescue me and those two. Right?' He said 'right'.
'Well,' I said, 'if you hadn't looked after number one coming
over, you wouldn't have got here, would you? That proves
you have to start with number one, doesn't it?' He said a
whole lot more, then, about humanity – we rather lost the
thread there, sir. We started having trouble with the mainsail
after that, and he went to ask Godden what to do. He told us
to let it right out and we'd run, and we did that, and Godden
was right. He had a bit of nerve, your brother, because he
didn't know half the time what he was doing. Then Watson
came up and said Godden was so thirsty he kept drinking
water and now he wanted a piss and needed help propping
up a bit. We got a can and I helped, and I didn't like the look
of him at all. He was flushed, and his skin was dry and
burning hot. I asked him how he felt and he said all right, not
so good, but he'd taken against Watson loosening the tourniquet and Watson said he wasn't getting to do it as often as he
should. Mr Grace said to give him aspirin to bring down the
fever and make him sweat, and he'd go and talk to him about
the tourniquet because he knew Watson was right to loosen
it. 'I should have brought a book on First Aid,' he said. He
was a great one for books. I told him I thought Godden
would have to have it off – it looked poisoned to me – puffed
up, and a nasty colour. '*We* can't take it off,' he said: 'we've
nothing to do it with, and he'd probably bleed to death.'
'Christ!' I said: 'I know we bloody can't. I wasn't suggesting
anything so daft.' He said that people used to do this kind of
thing in the Napoleonic wars, but I hadn't the stomach for it.
I said I'd try to get a bit more out of the engine, although

engines weren't my line. He went down to look at Godden's leg, in case there was anything he thought he could do, and a bit later, he came up, and vomited over the ship's side and said there wasn't anything. I'd coaxed a bit more out of the old engine, but she was running very hot, and I told Watson to come and look at her. He sat over her, but he said it was nothing like his Bedford, and he didn't know no more than his Bedford. I sent him back down.

There'd been planes over from time to time, and Mr Grace he thought maybe we could attract one of them. I found a small sail in a locker, and with his pen I drew out a big SOS on it. Then I had to find something dark to do the writing with. It's funny, what beats you. I tried everything. The pen was no good – the canvas was too rough and the area had to be too big if we had a hope of anyone seeing it. I burned a slat of wood that Mr Grace said went in a sail to make a kind of charcoal, but it came out pale grey. Not a blind bit of use. I even tried some of poor old Godden's blood, but it only showed up rusty. Mr Grace lit the lamp but it was a sunny evening for making a signal with not much power. In the end I tore my shirt in strips and pinned it on the sail with pins out of the First Aid Box. We'd just got it hoisted on to the top of the mizzen mast when the wind, which had been dropping, died right away and it hung down, as much use to us as a sick cat.

Mr Grace said he'd plotted what he hoped would be the shortest course back home, but I began to wonder why we'd seen no other ships. He showed me how he'd done the plotting, and he said he was sorry not to know more about navigation – he had no side about him at all, your brother. We thought we'd ask Godden if he had any bright ideas, but he was having a bit of a kip, and Watson said not to disturb him. Then we started having trouble with the mainsail boom – Mr Grace was very keen on the right words for everything – he'd read a book about it, he said. He seemed to spend his life reading, *I* don't know. We had some corn beef and some tea, but Watson said Godden wouldn't fancy corn beef, so we heated up some soup for him. They was talking quite a bit; Watson was asking Charley all about his peacetime job. He worked for a timber firm in Southampton, lumbering logs on the river. He tried to get into the Navy, he said, he'd always liked the sea, but he hadn't passed the medical for it, so he'd ended up in the RA. He had a wife and kids; he was old: he must have been about forty. After the food, I couldn't hardly keep my eyes open, and Mr Grace he was yawning too, so we agreed to have an hour's kip in turn. When I came to, Godden was raving: telling Watson his wife wouldn't pay the HP on the three-piece if he wasn't there to make her, and Watson was telling him not to worry, he'd soon be back; and Godden didn't notice if Watson loosened the tourniquet or not – just kept harping on what the Hire Purchase companies did to people like his wife who couldn't see that just because she'd got the things in the bedroom she didn't own them without she paid the six bob a week. He went on and on about it, and it didn't make a blind bit of difference what Watson said to him.

It must have been about seven when we saw the plane: we knew at once that it had seen us, because it made a circuit high up and started to come down in on us. Black against the sunset it was, coming in fast and looking as though it would be low enough for it to be worth waving. I was going to use the torch, but Mr Grace said he'd do it, and he went and stood right out at the back of the ship – the counter, sir – he stood with one arm round the mizzen mast and he started waving the torch and shouting, but the noise of the plane was so loud they couldn't have heard him. I thought, Christ, it's so low it's going to hit us – like those bloody dive bombers, I thought, and then all at the same moment, I saw its markings and heard the machine gun. I threw myself flat on the floor of the cockpit, and it roared away climbing again and heading due east. Bloody Heinkel, I shouted to Mr Grace, and he didn't answer at once, but I could see him standing there clutching the mast so I thought he was all right: the torch was smashed though. He didn't make to move, so I went to him and asked if he was all right. 'I think they must have hit me,' he said, and I saw the bullet marks all over the sail. I took his arm, and as he moved, he said: 'Can't be serious: I feel all right. Sorry, I didn't realize it wasn't one of ours.' 'We'd better have a look,' I said. I could see his jacket had a kind of ragged hole in it. I sat him down in the cockpit and told Watson to come and steer. As soon as I undid his jacket, I could see he'd been hit. I got him down to the cabin – so I get his clothes off and have a proper look. He'd gone rather white, but he could walk OK. He was wearing a lot of clothes: a thick jersey and a shirt, but the blood was through that. The bullet had gone in the right side of his chest, but I couldn't see it had come out. The blood was very light red, but there didn't seem to be all that much of it. I got a dressing and a bandage and put them on, and he said he'd like a spot of brandy. When he drank it, he tried to cough, and I could see that hurt him. 'I'll put some water in it,' I said. He had some brandy and water and he said it done him a power of good. I got his shirt and jacket on him again, but I didn't like to try getting him into that jersey.

He said he'd go back to the tiller – he could steer and he knew Watson wanted to go back to Godden who was very restless and nattering on about his three-piece and his wife. I said I'd steer, and he could have his kip – he'd never got it due to the bloody Heinkel. But he said he wanted to watch the sunset, then he'd have seen the whole thing for once in his life: he told me he'd watched it come up. That's when he told me he'd kept a log of sorts coming over, and that's when I realized he'd been up all night, hadn't slept now for nearly two days. We started to have engine trouble about then: she was missing and I stopped her to clean the plugs and then I had a right time starting her. After that she kept going for a bit and then stalling, and each time it was worse starting her. It was flat calm now – the sea looked as though you could walk on it, and the sky was red and a whole lot of other colours – like Fairy dyes I said, but Mr Grace didn't seem to know about them. Mr Grace said it was very close – stuffy, he said, and how he would love a breath of fresh air, but it seemed cool enough to me. That's when I began worrying about him: he was very quiet. I asked him if he had a family: somehow I'd thought he was on his own, but he told me he had a wife and two daughters. What did she think about his larking about the Channel at his age, I asked? She didn't know, he said: he hadn't told anyone. I told him about my young lady, and he showed me pictures of his kids: one was quite old, but then *he* was old – too old for what he'd taken on with his ignorance and all, I thought, but I didn't like to say so. After a bit, he asked for a cigarette, and I didn't feel he should be smoking, but he said he'd find it soothing. I lit it for him and he had his first draw, and then he started to cough and there was blood all over the fag, and he looked at me and tried to smile and dropped the fag over the side. There was a teacloth by the primus and I gave him that, but the blood was still coming up, and I called Watson, and *he* didn't answer. I got some water out of a fancy bottle he had and wet the towel and helped him mop up. I wanted to lay him down, but he shook his head, and when he could speak again, he said: 'I can't breathe – must sit up.' So I propped him up and gave him a cup of water to rinse out his mouth, and he kept still awhile. Then he said: 'Is all the blood off?' He'd nearly stopped bleeding, and although it wasn't, I said pretty good. 'Good,' he said, 'she said I looked awful with blood on me.' I suppose that was his wife, sir. The engine was playing up all the time, and what with trying to start it, and then keep it going, I had my hands full. 'Any coastline yet?' he asked. He was speaking so quiet, I had to watch him and

210

guess, but that was plain enough. 'Won't be long now,' I said
to keep his spirits up. He sat quiet again, mopping his mouth
every now and then. Then he said: 'How's Godden?' I said I'd
go and look. Watson was still sitting by him, but Godden
wasn't talking now, just moving his head from side to side,
and Watson looked at me – like our dog again – and said:
'He's going: he doesn't know me any more.' He knew about
the Heinkel, and Mr Grace, but he didn't seem to take it in.
The engine cut again, and I thought I'll never get this lot
home, and I felt awful, angry – as though everything was
against me. I was kneeling by the engine, having another look
at the plugs, when Mr Grace made a noise like choking and
blood was bubbling out of his nose and mouth. I got the
cloth and held his head up while I wiped him up, his forehead
was all sweat with him trying to breathe: the buggers got his
lung, I thought – I was frightened now. I couldn't stand the
idea of them getting him somehow. He was a dreadful colour,
sir – not grey or white – somehow worse than either. It can't
have been such a bad haemorrhage as it looked, because it
stopped again. I slung a can over the side and got some sea
water to rinse the cloth out and clean him up, and when he
could speak he said: 'I'm very grateful to you, Black. I seem
to have made rather a mess of things.' I said he'd done a
wonderful job sailing the boat by himself and all, and if he
hadn't collected us we'd all have had it. He started to say
something about not having filled up the boat and then that
poor silly sod Watson come up out of the cabin and said:
'He's dead!' and burst out crying like a kid. I couldn't stand
it: I yelled at him to shut his mouth: I said if I heard another
sound out of him I'd clip him over the ear-'ole. It stopped
him cold. He kept on wiping his face with his sleeve, and I
ordered him to have a go with the engine to keep his mind
off Godden. When it was clear he'd no idea what to do with
the engine, I said to get below and make us all a cup of char.
Mr Grace roused himself – he seemed drowsy – and said:

'Sorry, Black, to leave you with all this.' 'Never say die, sir,' I said without hardly thinking. He smiled and said: 'Won't the engine start?' I said I was giving it a rest to cool off: I'd started lying to him, so I must have known he was right out of it. 'What about the lamp? Can you make that work? You might get picked up if you carried a light. Get it as high as you can, so they'll see you.' I said I'd look at it in due course. The sun was nearly down, and it was cool, but he was perspiring all the time now. 'I think we're nearly over the other side. Hang on sir: we'll make it – you'll see.' Watson come up with the tea, and I offered him some, but he shook his head. I knew I ought to look at the lamp, but I couldn't leave him then. He asked, was Godden dead, I told him yes. 'It's still two of you,' he said. 'That's more than one, isn't it?' 'Don't you worry,' I said. He *was* worrying – I could see that. The last thing he said was: 'Tell them all I'm sorry.' Then he had another haemorrhage and before it seemed to be over he was dead. Watson came up with the teapot and I told him Mr Grace was dead and to help me carry him down to the cabin. Watson was shivering, and when we'd put him on the bed, he just looked at me and I knew I'd frightened him and he was only a kid.

I said, 'What's your name then?' and hardly above a whisper he said Fred. 'We're on our own now, Fred,' I said. 'We've got to make it. I expect you've got a girl back home haven't you?' But he said he'd only got his mum, and he wished he was with her now. 'We'll both have a fag,' I said, 'and we'll finish the brandy.' That done him good and sitting in the cockpit while I was botching up the lamp, he said: 'It's worse than they tell you, ain't it?' 'They don't tell you nothing,' I said. 'That's right,' he said.

Well sir, I rigged that light, and lashed it as high up the mast as I dared climb, like Mr Grace said, and he was right; it saved us. We was picked up by a gunboat two miles off Newhaven. But I'm sorry your brother had to die sir, without knowing he got us back.

LETTERS

My dear Esme,

I don't suppose you will need to get this at all, but I have to write it, just in case. I am taking a boat across to France to try and collect as many men as possible. I feel that this is something that I *can* do, and one must do what one can. I hope you will understand. Keep the children in the country. I expect Cressy will want to do some war work when she is a little older which of course would be right, but the child should stay away from possible/likely bombs. If the threat of invasion becomes serious, as I think it may, take them to Mervyn's in Somerset. It probably won't be any safer, but it will feel it, and Mervyn will look after you all. In *any* trouble, apply to him.

One more thing – difficult to say, but against the possibility of it being my last chance, I must try. I am *not* trying this venture out of jealousy, pique, or any sort of retaliation. I haven't liked your situation, and curiously, what I have most disliked has been putting you to the necessity of lying to me. This is my fault as much as yours, I think. I was afraid of what the next step might be if I made you tell me the truth: told myself it was for the children's sake, but really *I* couldn't face it. But any lie is never about itself – it always seems to discolour everything near it. You will have to be very intelligent and careful with Cressy: in some ways she knows too much for her age; in others not enough. I love them both. Thank you for them. Be happy.

Julius

Dear Mrs Grace,

I just want to take the liberty to offer my condolences for your loss. My boy Freddie was in the boat that your husband took, and he says he would have drowned if your husband hadn't picked him up – like a miracle. He is my only boy and

213

I am a widow my husband being dead some years now so you can see how gratefull I am for what your husband did and I hope you are manageing to bear up alright. We shall all be glad when this dreadful war is over and Hitler is where he belongs. My boy would write but he is not given to writeing but sends his best regards, yours sincerely.

Mrs G Watson

That was really all. She sat for a long time, with her hand over her eyes.

The last bit, she knew, was simply Mervyn, dear anxious creature, pompously dotting the i's, and making one feel, with every sentence, that writing must be very difficult. No need to read it. She blew her nose, supposing that it was a good thing that a few people *knew* they couldn't write. Where were the others? Surely they had been gone a very long time? By others, of course, she meant Cressy and Felix: she assumed, without thinking about it, that Emma and Daniel had gone to their beds. She wouldn't wait up for the others. She'd have one more cigarette, and then go to bed. Cressy was probably unburdening herself. The thought vaguely disquieted her. She finished her cigarette, but she did not go to bed: she continued to wait.

PART THREE

SUNDAYS

CHAPTER 13

DANIEL

H E walked fast down the drive because he was angry and wanted to get well out of that set-up. Then, in the lane, he slowed down a bit, till his eyes could get accustomed to the dark. It was cold: his feet were quiet on the road since he wore rubber soles, and there was nothing to smell – the temperature had dropped so even a fox would have had trouble winding a hen coop. The banks of the lane were high each side of him; he could see now where the sky began above them. In the house, he had been shivering in the hot, rotten atmosphere: now it was clean and quiet – he could get on with his life. What he didn't like about it all was these people turning out to lead lives like that. All that room and money and three hot meals a day and what did it amount to? The older girl was a tart, and the pair who came to dinner had no manners or consideration for anyone else at all. And that doctor. Everybody tied up with everybody else – like people in decadent books they were. None of those women knew their place and you could see that they weren't happy out of it. A shocking waste. A shocking waste, he repeated miserably to himself. When he thought of *her* – not only putting up with it, but actually standing up for her sister, he wanted to hit her until she promised never to be like it again. How did she manage to seem like a child then, with all this going on? She must be sly about it: well, when she'd come mincing into the room in her long skirt, he'd wondered. Her not seeming to be like the rest of them seemed now to be mere treachery. Perhaps she had only pretended to enjoy the fireworks. Why had she asked him? To get him in some sort of trap – she probably collected men like her sister. Women were notorious for looking one thing and being another. Vampires, witches, ghosts, mermaids, the more wicked they were the more beautiful they had to be to get the chances. But *she* wasn't beautiful: she had a funny face when you came to think of it; standing on her dignity so you had to smile.

It wasn't her fault that she'd been brought up with that rotten lot. What he couldn't stand was all his notions of splendour being smashed up. If she'd been sixteen, he would have taken her in a little boat, just the two of them, with cold chicken and chocolate swiss roll and anything nice she fancied and he would have put a ruby ring on her finger and bought her a brand new hat with a bunch of cherries and of course they would have got married; she wouldn't need white gloves and all her accessories to match like Dot had. She wasn't sixteen, though. Far from it. She was too old to know better by now. And if he'd known her when she was sixteen it would have been no good – it was even before he was ill – although that seemed to have gone on for such a long time that he felt he could hardly remember before it. And here he was still with all this time in his life to be filled in: she'd been a false start, that was all. Maybe if he'd gone straight for her from the start, he wouldn't be feeling so filled with anger now. Probably that was what she'd expected. To be thrown on a bed and have her clothes ripped off her: sex and excitement and then one of those elaborate drinks and on to the next one . . .

A car was coming down the lane, which was so narrow that instinctively he stood still, pressing himself against the bank. It stopped beside him. It was her.

'Dan?'

He couldn't see her face properly: but she sounded dead anxious.

'I'm not coming back,' he said.

'I'm not asking you to. Let's go and look at the sea.'

218

She was trying to sound as though nothing was the matter. Or perhaps she was trying to sound as though something *was* the matter when really she didn't think there was. She won't trap me, he thought, and got into the car without a word. At the bottom of the lane she turned left. It was a much wider road with cats' eyes in the middle, but they were going too fast to count them. He shut his eyes and thought about Violet so that he didn't have to *think* not to think about *her*.

Violet had been at the sanatorium with him. She'd had the same things done to her, three months before they did them to him. When he began to get better, they used to sit in deck chairs in a huge dull garden and talk. She looked frail – thin and weak like a small plucked bird, but she never stopped talking. She'd had a packed and mysterious life and she kept telling him things but he never got them in the right order. She'd been to prison – twice, and in countless hospitals, an approved school, a hostess in a night club, to the Isle of Man, a chambermaid in a big hotel, she'd had a baby but it died; when she was young an old man had given her ten bob a week to go to the pictures with him without any knickers; she'd been in a train accident; to Ostend for a naughty week-end; all her hair had been burnt off by an electric fire. She had told him everything in exactly the same way; nothing was different from anything really, she said: it was all all right, only she'd hated being at home: her father had – you know – when she was fourteen and he'd always been hard on her after that. There were too many of them, and Mum used to get so depressed for months on end she didn't count for much. He never discovered a single thing which he considered to be nice that had happened to her, her life seemed to be simply a series of wicked shocks. She had a seedy little face with beautiful eyes, hair like dry hay, and her small sharp bones stuck out everywhere although she ate everything she could lay hands on. She liked the sanatorium – didn't want to leave it – she'd seen enough of life to last her, she had said. It was weeks before he discovered that she was twenty. She liked someone to chat with and everything nice and regular meals. He slowly fell in love with her because she had made him want to be angry on her behalf: she was bright without being above herself; she didn't blame anyone or make excuses; she was wonderful, extraordinary company, and he could not help imagining how charmed she would be by a life jam-packed with good events. He felt that he would be able to transform *things* for her – it wasn't a matter of wanting her to change in the least. She was entirely friendly and he began to want her badly. There was a lot of chat in the sanatorium about people getting randy – convalescent energy the prissier nurses called it – and it was all quite true, he found. He wanted someone, and more particularly, he wanted her. She wasn't a flirt; she never edged up to sex and backed off giggling like some he could mention – it just didn't seem to cross her ways at all. Then one day, they'd gone for a little walk in the grounds and sat on a piece of rough grass out past the borders, and she'd said: 'You want me, don't you?' And such was the ease between them that he'd simply nodded. 'Well, go on, then,' she said: '*I* don't mind,' and she'd lain down with her hands behind her head until he'd taken off his jacket and made her a pillow. He'd had her, and it had been like all the feeling in the world *without pain* to his body, and after the weeks of feeling pain this was like water on a scorching desert. Afterwards, she said: 'Did you like it?' And he said: 'Yes, I liked it all right,' and then, looking at her face, friendly still but unmoved, he said: 'Thank you,' and then her face did move, and she said: 'Nobody's ever thanked me before,' and he thought she was going to cry. So he'd told her that he was going to make life so she'd never have to thank him, never be grateful, and she wouldn't go on doing kindnesses and not know what they were. He told her that he loved her and wanted to marry her and they'd have a wonderful life, and she lay there listening – smiled all the time but she never said a word . . .

'. . . thinking about.'

'You shouldn't ask that question: it's dull – and rude.'

'I'm sorry,' she said humbly.

He looked at her straight little nose as she drove without looking at him: she wasn't pretending to be anxious, but that wasn't the end of it.

'You can catch an early train from Hastings if you want,' she said. 'You could have the key of my flat and sleep there tomorrow – in the daytime, I mean.'

'I don't know. I may go abroad.'

'But you *can't* . . .' she began.

'What can't I do?' He was instantly on his guard.

'I mean – you'd have to go to London first.'

'Why? If I get to the sea, it seems a bit silly to go the journey back to London. The sea's where you go abroad from, surely. I take no interest in air travel,' he added, in case she thought he didn't know about that.

'Well, you have to have a passport for one thing.'

He ground his teeth. He'd honestly forgotten that: it seemed to him that life was fixed so that you couldn't have one: you had to think ahead about every single thing you did – surprise was knocked out, and you ended up doing things long after you'd stopped wanting to.

'It wouldn't take you long to get one, though.'

He looked at her suspiciously. Was she trying to get rid of him now? He wasn't going to be fobbed off unless he felt like it.

'Once you've got a passport, you can go to a lot of places without making plans,' she said.

'Have you got one?'

'Mmm.'

She'd got everything – of course. She was probably *born* with one.

'We're nearly there,' she said.

There was the feeling of the land stopping: 'I know,' he said. He tried to open the window to smell if the air had changed: he wasn't used to cars and it seemed stuck. She reached across him and undid some catch and the window slid back. It was foreign air: you couldn't say it was salt, like they did in books, but it had an oceanic flavour.

'Will it be too dark for me to see properly?'

'I do hope not. Anyway, you'll get some sort of feel out of it. The sea is never the same whenever you look at it,' she added.

'Never?'

'Honestly not. It's about as much the same on the same sort of days as people who are supposed to be like each other look like each other. That's not the same, is it?'

'I'm not sure that I've seen enough people to know that,' he said cautiously: he was liking her again against his judgement: she's *deep*, he told himself furiously: you can't judge her by the things she says; she just *wants* you to, of course. Why?

She was driving more slowly – down a steep hill: he expected the sea to be at the bottom, but it wasn't.

'About half a mile,' she said. Sometimes he wondered if she couldn't hear what he was thinking: a dangerous notion and not one he took kindly to.

They seemed to be driving through a small desert – sandy banks with rough grass and little windswept trees. 'What's this then?' he asked after a bit.

'A golf course. Here's the beach.'

She turned sharply to the right and stopped the car in front of a field gate. 'You pull the string on the door to get out.'

She'd turned out the lights of the car, and for a moment they both stood in the dark. There was just enough moon for them to see where it was, bedded in yeasty-looking clouds. He waited till he could see better, and then turned to the sea. It lay neatly all along in front of him – very dark with oily glints. He liked the sound of it reaching the shore.

'Let's go down to it.'

She led the way round the gate and he realized that she'd still got her long skirt on under her coat.

'Watch out for sea holly,' she said: 'or perhaps it won't hurt you.'

He stumbled a bit, because all his attention was on the sea. They walked down the sandy scrub to the shingle. There was a strong sea smell now. A row of huts, for bathing, she told him when he asked, but she wasn't chattering. He could see the whites of the waves a few yards from the edge, but he couldn't see the horizon, the sky just seemed to come down into the sea. The noise was continuous and irregular – there was a strong air rather than wind. He went right down to meet the water, stooped and put his hand to it: it felt cold and thick, and tasted very nice. A wave came over his shoes – nearly – he jumped back and turned to see if she had seen, but she was sitting on the stones looking up at the sky: the moon was doing better or else his eyes were getting used to everything. He walked along a bit, and found a bit of sand covered and recovered by water: there were big sunken pebbles in it, with the sea swooning out round them and the sand glistening new each time. He stood for a bit, trying to imagine the country beyond. It ought to be very different – black cliffs with neat green on top, or sugar-coloured sand and great forests. It was different this way round, here it was just the end of England, you couldn't expect any excitement. He thought of going there – France that would be. He had a moment's panic about all Frenchmen being like sheep – looking exactly the same because you weren't used to them: then he remembered Charles Boyer and thought it would be all right. Except he *wanted* them to look different really – but different from each other as well – to *him*. He enjoyed the animal air in his face and wished it was light. The sun coming up at sea would be good. He went slowly back to where she was sitting, and sat beside her. She sat quite quietly not saying anything.

'I'd like to be out in a boat on it. That where your father went?'

'Yes. Not there, exactly, but somewhere out there.'

'Does that make you sad?'

'I can't really remember him. Only a kind of regret. Have you known anyone well who's died?'

'I may have.' That snubbed her, and he stared resolutely out to try and find the edges of sea and sky.

Violet had died. She'd left the sanatorium very soon after that afternoon: she was cured, they said; she must get back into life. She didn't want to leave. Leaving meant going back to her family, and she didn't know how she was going to stand that. She wasn't strong enough to do a full-time job yet, and she needed a home life, they said. He told her that he'd be out in a matter of months – she'd only got to hang on until he was out and he'd see to her. 'You're an invalid yourself,' she said, 'you can't look after no one.' He asked her to write to him and she said she might. He begged her to write to him and she said she'd think of it. He said he'd write to her: she looked as though he'd changed the subject away from the practical problems of living in four rooms with Mum and Dad and three brothers and sisters. It won't be for long, he'd said. 'It won't be,' she said with a return of her usual energy, she'd go clean out of her mind if it was for long. Mostly she seemed stunned at having to go; it left her with nothing but a kind of lifeless despair. She'd gone, on a wet morning in the station taxi – she hadn't even looked back to wave at him, but he knew she'd been trying not to cry.

Ten days later she was dead. It was in the papers: the nurses told him before he'd seen it. Of course they hadn't known about him and Violet. The papers just said that she'd been found in an hotel bedroom in St Pancras, near where she lived. She'd taken the room for one night, and they'd found her at noon the next day when they'd gone to clear out the room. She'd smoked twenty Craven A, drunk a bottle of Australian port and taken a boxful of her mother's sleeping pills. She'd left no note. He hadn't understood how much she hadn't been able to stand home; he'd never realized that she'd never believed him: perhaps it wouldn't have made any difference if she had. He hadn't known, till then, that you could love somebody, without knowing the important things about them. He blamed himself; he blamed the sanatorium; he blamed her – until he remembered that she didn't go in for blame: never had done. She always hated being alone, and he couldn't bear to think of her going to that room by herself. He couldn't stop thinking of it. That was when he began to write poems: they weren't *about* her at all, but they were about the things he'd wanted to show her – ordinary splendours, pleasures of the world that hadn't come her way. He'd tried to put it so that she would have known what he meant, and then he'd got fascinated by doing it, and the poems stopped all being for Violet. They weren't for anyone, he just felt like doing them, which was a bit like laying an egg with the whole adult bird in mind: when you first thought about a poem it seemed neat and easy like an egg, and then you had to grapple with all the bone structure and feathery detail with the whole bird in mind until you could go mad with irritable anxiety. Other kinds of writing seemed too like talking to him – not worth the dull trouble . . . Still, Violet had started it, and his Special Nurse had made him send some stuff to Speedwell and Grace, and here he was at the seaside on a November night with *her*.

'What's the matter?' he asked – back to noticing her.

'I'm awfully cold,' she said, but she was crying. She was huddled in her coat and he could see the track of tears on her face.

'Let's go then,' he said. He put out a hand to help her up, but she pretended not to notice. Two can play that game, he thought, and pretended not to notice she'd pretended. They both walked to the car in a huff and got in and slammed the doors rather hard. In the car she sat quite still for a moment and then said:

'Dan! I'm sorry about the awful evening, but it honestly

wasn't my fault. I don't see why you have to be beastly to me about it. It wasn't anybody's fault, really – except, perhaps, Jennifer Hammond.'

'What about your sister?' he interrupted. 'Didn't she have anything to do with it?'

'Of course she didn't. She didn't know they were coming to dinner; she didn't know *he* was coming until he'd actually arrived. It was a frightful shock to her – you must see that.'

'It was a shock to Mrs Hammond too, wasn't it? *She* didn't know what she was in for, did she?'

'I see that – and I do see it was awful for her, too, but she needn't have made that awful scene and embarrassed everybody.'

'So you think it doesn't matter what people do as long as they aren't found out? How would you have felt if you'd been Mrs Hammond?'

'I don't know. Terrible, I expect. Yes – of course I would have.'

'But you might easily have been in your sister's position? It just happened to be her?'

'What do you mean?'

'I mean that you don't see anything queer about your sister having affairs with your neighbour's husband? That's normal behaviour in your set-up, is it?'

'Look – it's not my business to pronounce upon other people's arrangements any more than I think it's yours. And I don't like the way you go on about Cressy. She's a perfectly normal, good, kind, rather unhappy person: she's my sister and I care about her. But in that respect there's nothing unusual *or* wicked about her which is what you seem to be implying.'

'If you fancied someone, you'd go to bed with them?'

'Of *course* I should!'

'No need to shout,' he said. 'I just wanted to know. You're twenty-seven – you should know your mind by now.'

'Of course I should,' she said more quietly, but with the same defiance. 'I'm tired of talking about this. Let's go.'

She started the car, and drove jerkily off. After a few minutes she said: 'Shall I take you to Hastings?'

'Eh?' He had been plunged in gloomy thoughts.

'Do you want to catch a train from Hastings?'

'I'd rather go in the car with you.'

'To London?'

'Why not?'

'Oh!' She seemed to relax again. 'That's a good idea. We can have a very early breakfast at home.'

'Why not? If you consider that I was rude to you – I beg your pardon.'

She turned to him, her face glowing. 'That's all right, Dan.'

'That's all right,' he repeated. He might as well get something out of it.

CHAPTER 14

FELIX

OUTSIDE the house he said: 'Let's take my car: we can all sit in front in it,' and she simply nodded. 'You turn right, outside the drive,' she said.

Major Hawkes climbed in, and after one or two shots, succeeded in shutting the heavy door. 'This car is so well made, that either you've had it for years or it must be second-hand,' he began.

Felix said it was second-hand and he'd hardly had it a minute.

'I often wonder,' said Major Hawkes dreamily, 'what on earth that's being made now will actually be nice to have in thirty years' time. Up till now, nearly everything has a use and value: furniture, cars, houses, books – but there you are, a second-hand paperback's not much cop if you take me. Of course second-hand animals have always been tricky: nearly always neurotic with ridiculous standards about food and attention; antique TV sets won't be the slightest use unless somebody turns them into something else, which really brings one straight to slag heaps, industrial waste and do we need to use so much paper all over everything? And of course, if that foreign feller in Switzerland goes on with those monkey glands, the world will be chock full of second-hand people, although they may run short of monkeys and the World Wildlife Fund have far too much on their plates to struggle with the rhesus monkey situation. It even occurred to me whether, when I kick the bucket, I oughtn't to offer my glands to an orang-outang . . .'

'Left,' murmured Cressy.

'Well,' said Felix, grappling with this wealth of subject matter, 'I suppose nature conservation will provide a great many people with interesting things to do with their leisure. One doesn't like to think of one's grandchildren never seeing a giraffe.'

But Major Hawkes retorted triumphantly:

'My grandparents never saw a submarine – so it's six of one and half a dozen of the other.'

'But surely – it's different not seeing something that hasn't been invented, to not seeing something that you knew used to exist.'

Her voice sounded rather odd, but she was trying, Felix thought, and he was just about to support her effort in the conversation when the Major, slapping her thigh by mistake, said:

'Dammit! – so sorry, my dear – I forgot to give Sophie her bone. She *will* be in a state. I don't go out much these days, but when I do, I always give her a bone. Interesting inversion of behaviour patterns: she's beginning to dread bones. Rather like Gregory powders in strawberry jam which we used to have as children: never been able to stand strawberries ever since.'

'That's awfully unfair, isn't it?' said Cressy. 'Trying to compensate for nasty things and then spoiling nice ones.'

'You can't compensate for nasty things. Have to face up to them. They provide the contrast. Can't expect an old dog to appreciate that though. They haven't the intellectual resources – nor have most people actually – but it's accepted in dogs. We still employ the feudal system with dogs, and they need it. Democracy would mean nothing to a dog thank goodness because one couldn't afford to keep one if it did.'

'Major Hawkes's house is the third on the left, past that tree,' said Cressy.

'Bungalow,' said Major Hawkes cheerfully: 'and hideous at that. It is so frightful to look at that I called it Ypres, as I had a bloody awful time there like many more I could mention only you wouldn't know them.

'I think,' he went on, as Felix drew up beside a jig-saw gate, 'that for its size it is the most god-awful bungalow that has ever been built. My poor wife liked it though – she was a great stickler for convenience, and there are some nice roses in the garden.'

An hysterical barking began the moment Major Hawkes opened the car door.

'I'm extremely obliged to you: it's a bit of a walk after dinner. Good night, my dear. Tell your mother I'll be in touch with her.'

He attempted to shut the car door, which swung insolently back into his chest. Both he and Felix apologized for this, and Felix imagined the car blinking its headlights at the exchange like a giant sneering cat.

Major Hawkes negotiated his horrid little gate with difficulty and stumped up his uneven crazy-paving to the door, behind which were the increasingly frantic barks. They watched him unlock the door and saw him nearly knocked over by the largest spaniel Felix had ever seen. He waved feebly with one hand and was gone. It was not a relief when he went.

They both turned from looking after Major Hawkes to looking at each other, then Felix said quietly:

'Are you in love with that man?'

'Look,' she said: 'for goodness' *sake* drive away from his gate, or he'll think we're in trouble or want to come in, or something.'

We are in trouble, he thought, as he started the car. There was no confusion about pronouns, he went on bitterly – none at all. He drove rather fast for a few minutes until he came to a turning into a lane which he took. He pulled up on a piece of verge, switched off the headlights and stopped the engine.

'Now,' he said: 'are you in love with that man?'

'No.'

Relief made him more belligerent. 'Then what the hell did you get yourself in such a mess for?'

'That seems to me entirely mine and Dick's business.'

'Oh no it's not. We all had it spilled all over us tonight. There was nothing private about it at all!'

'I didn't *know* he was coming with her to dinner. He was supposed to be in Rome. I've always avoided anything like that before.'

'Bully for you.'

'I don't see why you need to hector me. I was going to apologize – to all of you, after the Hammonds left – but you don't make that easy to do.'

'I can't see why you got yourself involved with a man like that. He's not just married – he's *dull*! An unpleasant bore, I should have said, with a stupid, unattractive wife. Where on earth do *you* come in?'

'Where I always come in,' she said wearily. 'People like you always talk as though I've gone out and deliberately chosen the dullest, most squalid situation I can find. It's never like that. If you're – free – ' he noticed she hesitated with discomfort over the word, 'you can't help wanting not to be. You want somebody to matter; of course you start by thinking you know what you want. Then you can't find it. Then you wonder whether there is such a person, and whether you'd still want him if you found him. And meanwhile – and meanwhile stretches into years – there you are, all the time – obviously free, and obviously wanting to fall in love with someone. And when you get to my age, most men are married, and a surprising number of them are looking for someone to have an affair with. Well – some of them find me. I sometimes think I'm in love; I nearly always hope I will be. Of course, I hope they will be too. And don't give me any of the you-must-be-highly-sexed stuff. I don't get anything out of that side of it except at the beginning – sometimes it's before the first time in bed, when I can imagine that it's real, before I start the hoping and pretending to hope.'

She stopped quite suddenly, and there wasn't a sound except the faint ticking of the engine cooling off.

He said carefully: 'What is it you hope?'

'Oh – that it's a matter of loving – the whole thing: not simply choosing bits of somebody that you're short of, or putting up with them because of being lonely.'

'You're talking about marriage, aren't you?'

'*Everybody* always says that!" she said angrily. 'I'm so *tired* of everybody saying that! I've stopped wanting to talk about it to anybody! The marriage part isn't what I'm talking about. Millions of people get married without what I mean. And if it isn't there, you can't make it. You can pretend, or you can settle for doing without it.'

'And which did you do?'

'I won't do either. That's the whole point!'

'But you've *been* married. What did you do then?'

'I started by pretending – not knowing – I don't know which it was – and just about when I'd settled for doing without it, Miles got killed. Have you got a cigarette?'

'No,' he said, after looking: 'I'm afraid not. So what did you do after that?'

'What everybody does, I suppose. Lived alone: tried to get on with my work. Met somebody: had an affair. And so on.'

'But have you ever really thought you were in love? For more than the beginning with anyone?'

'Once,' she said. 'I met him at a party. He was older than me – very intelligent and concerned with the state of the world. He asked me to marry him. I said no. He asked me to go and live with him for three months and then marry him. I said I'd live with him for three months. I was very nervy – unsure of myself – I don't know – I expect a frightful bore. He liked to run everything. He liked me to be nervy so long as it didn't inconvenience him. He hated me using birth-control – anything. One night he said I was a fool, and it was the safe time in the month for me, and it was time I stopped knowing better than everyone else – especially him. He made such a scene about it that I didn't want to be with him at all, but I was so tired I just stayed – no, *weak* – thinking perhaps that if he'd been so beastly he'd make it up to me in bed. So then of course I was pregnant. I knew it would worry him, but I thought as he'd wanted to marry me, he might possibly find he was pleased. He was furious! He managed to make me feel squalid and entirely to blame. He started ringing up anybody he knew who could, as he put it, "help us". Then a friend of a friend of a friend said that there was a man in Mayfair – he wasn't a doctor and he would fix it. All we had to do was get in a taxi – abortion while you wait. I stuck at that. They were my insides, I said, not his. We had a frightful row. I said I'd find someone, and I did. But all the time – the weeks while I was waiting to see the doctor I found, and then waiting for him to do it – I had the feeling that I must be mad. This man was supposed to have loved me: he wrote books about people and ideology – he was regarded as a pioneer, a humanitarian, someone of great integrity who cared what happened to society – a responsible and courageous man – one in a million. And yet there I was pregnant, honestly because he bullied me about knowing better, and all he wanted to do was be shot of the situation – never mind what became of me in the process. A lot of women die or are permanently damaged by those sort of operations, you know.'

'Yes,' he said, 'I do know.'

'Well, I felt I must be mad to have thought that he loved me: to have thought that I could love him: that was one part of it. But in a way, the other part was worse. You know – finding that someone who went about being so publicly responsible was so craven inside. I expect I was a bit mad at the time: you know, feeling sick, and feeling it's all to no purpose, and being frightened of the operation, but also when I was alone I kept saying "*Who* is *good*?" which sounds a terribly silly question, except that I could not answer it, past saying "Well *you* aren't for a start – look what you're doing – what you're *conniving* at."

But I couldn't get any further than that and that was what was so frightening. You know when you have something that seems so important you can't think of anything else, *and* you find that you can't *think* about it at all?'

'Did you want the child?'

'That was all part of what I couldn't think about,' she said, after a silence. 'I knew that *he* didn't – that he regarded the idea of it with panic-stricken loathing. That didn't seem a good start for it. I knew I couldn't have had it, and then got it adopted. I couldn't face it much more than that. I didn't want to be with *him* any more, so it would have meant bringing up a child by myself with everybody knowing who the father was.

'I couldn't – can't – argue ethically about any of this. I couldn't get past wanting him to want it, or at least being calmer – more indifferent . . . I'm not trying to justify myself. I'm just telling you. I can't think why.'

'I asked you: that's why. So you went through with the abortion?'

'Yes. I only saw him once after that. He made one more scene – a smaller one, because I clearly wasn't up to the full-sized kind. He said I was dramatizing a perfectly ordinary situation. I expect I was. Then he went to stay with friends in the country, because he needed a rest after all the strain I'd put him to. He wrote to me saying he thought it was better if we didn't meet for a time. He was right there. And that was that.'

After a long pause, she said: 'I do wish we *had* got a cigarette.'

'You know, don't you,' he said, 'that most men aren't like that?'

He felt her shake her head.

'He was a bastard,' he insisted. 'Most men simply don't behave quite as childishly and brutally as that. You were just damned unlucky. Whatever most men thought about wanting a child or not, they wouldn't be so irresponsible or obsessed with their own panic.'

'I chose him,' she said dully: 'that's where this all began. I got myself involved with a man like that. What you said. That was *my* responsibility.'

'But you couldn't have known this about him.'

'Anyway, hundreds of women are made pregnant by people who never even know. Just go off – leaving the woman to do what she can.'

'It's no good saying that. You know perfectly well that those are all people who don't think what they are doing – don't believe it will happen to them, and don't care.'

'You don't see the point. I don't go to bed with people casually like that. One-night stands of somebody I meet at a party and never see again. I was looking for something much more than that. And if you have a prolonged affair with somebody, eventually there comes a time when you *know* that in no circumstances do they want your child, and then you're finished. It's a kind of primitive vanity thing, I suppose. Like a man being told that the woman had never really wanted him at all: she just liked his company, his affection, or something. I don't suppose he'd find it easy to go on with her sexually if he absolutely *knew* that. It isn't that I'm simply looking for someone to have children by: it might sound like that, but it isn't. It's just that what I wanted would include the possibility of children – they'd just naturally have to be there.'

'Aren't you still looking for it?'

'I wouldn't be talking about it if I were. I was going to stop seeing Dick this Sunday anyway. He was coming back from Rome to see me, and I was going to tell him then.' Then she said: 'I suppose I *do* dramatize things. I think one does that when one isn't sure whether the other person has the slightest idea what they're like. It makes me want to shout and underline things.'

'I know.'

She was instantly defensive.

'How do you mean?'

'I mean about shouting when one doesn't think people are hearing. Usually, of course, it's just that they don't want to hear.'

He wanted to put on the light in the car to see her face, but he didn't.

'Well,' he said, as lightly as he could, 'what are you going to do besides get rid of Mr Hammond?'

'That's the question. Give up playing the piano merely rather well as well, I think. Then I think I ought to get a different kind of work to do.'

'Such as?'

'Well – *don't* laugh at me,' she added, as though he already had, 'I thought it would be a good thing if I did something for other people. I mean, I never have. I think if I felt a bit more responsible for other people, I wouldn't get into these morasses.'

'What had you in mind?'

'Oh, I know you think I couldn't do anything. But apart from training to be useful, there are thousands of dull jobs that anybody could do.'

'But how long do you think you could stand doing one of them for?'

'I don't know, till I try, do I? And anyway, it's absurd to think that anyone who has a public conscience has it from a position of strength. If that was so, there wouldn't be all these jobs going, and all these thousands of people who need help. It might be better for them if everybody who helped them was all right Jack, but if three-quarters of the helpers are doing it to help themselves where's the harm? And how can they choose anyhow? I mean, the people who need helping.'

'They can't, of course. But you've left out one thing. All the people who are any good at this sort of work believe that where it really matters people *are* the same, and that they *are* one of them.'

'Of course . . .'

'No – wait a minute. I don't mean the democratic intellectual: they're deeply dishonest about it all. If you push them, they start talking about intelligence, degrees of it, and so on. They operate a secret double standard, which means that they're judging themselves against other people all the time. To go on doing most of the work you're talking about you have to love everyone you're working for, and the moment you start judging people, the love breaks down.'

'That sounds unbelievably priggish to me.'

'Yes? Well – you try talking about this sort of thing, meaning what you say, and avoid that little trap in your nature. I don't say *I* love people. I've just spent six years finding that out, at enormous cost to my self-esteem. What I mean is that it's very difficult to go on slogging away unless you do care.'

'So – what do you do?'

'Well, *I'm* just going to try simply earning my living without too much self-conscious regard for my character. I don't think I can do much on a larger scale until I've got the basic conditions of my own life straight. I can't love millions of people anyway – but as I haven't made a success of loving even one person, that's probably the place to start.'

'Oh!' She started to laugh, unconvincingly. 'Oh – God! Don't you see? We're back where we started! In two years' time, I shall be saying to you: "How on earth did you get yourself involved with a woman like that?"'

'I can just see your flashing social worker's eyes. Why don't you start your career of self-abnegation by doing something for me? Go on – say what?'

'All right, what?' She said it with genuine wariness.

'Come and be my secretary for the next two weeks. Help an over-worked GP new to the job. You can answer the telephone, and drive me all over London on calls. It might make the difference between life and death for quite a lot of people: I've forgotten my way about London and my sense of direction is a bit underprivileged.'

'What else would I have to do?'

'Well – I don't know. Of course, a GP doesn't have ordinary hours, like other people. I think you'd have to live in my friends' flat with me.'

She said nothing to this. He said:

'I've fallen in love with you, you see. So I should prefer you to be there all the time.'

She said: 'You can't have!'

'All right. I'm madly attracted to you. I want you. And if you came and lived with me for a couple of weeks, I might get it out of my system.'

'Oh *that*!' she said, and sounded like an aggressive twelve-year-old.

'Yes! That. What's wrong with it? "How can I know what I think till I've said it" stuff! Got to start somewhere, haven't we? Do you think I ought to begin by admiring your character? Well, maybe I ought – but I haven't. Anyway, you've been running down your character most convincingly ever since I met you, but you've most properly remained silent on the subject of your physical charms. All doctors are very keen on bodies, you know, and some doctors prefer women's bodies. I'm one of them. A woman's body seems to me a very good starting point indeed.'

'So you think I'm the kind of person who'd go to bed with the first man who asks me?'

He drew a deep breath of mock patience: really he was thinking very hard. 'To begin with you've made it quite clear that I'm far from the first man. To go on with you didn't seem to take to my falling in love with you. And – a few passing remarks about your character – apart from being intermittently offensive, romantic to the point where any discrimination you may have isn't the slightest use to you, you sometimes strike me as moronic. Finally, don't you think my enlarging upon the reasons why I love you when we hardly know each other and haven't been to bed is just a weeny bit old-fashioned?'

238

There was a pause, and then she said, hardly audible: 'If you think all that, how can I know that you like me?'

'You can't be *sure*: it has to be a bit of a risk. This is where somebody ought to say that we're neither of us children. Do you mind if I turn on the light?'

He turned it on before she could answer, to see her, and she looked back at him, deeply uncertain, openly waiting and afraid, poised for some kind of emotional flight – an expression which, with a sense of shock, he suddenly remembered and recognized as belonging to her.

'You looked like that when I left after staying that night in your house at the beginning of the war! Exactly like that! You said: "Good-bye, Felix. Take care of yourself." Do *you* remember?'

She made some minute movement of denial, frowned, and then, unaccountably, to him, she started to blush: a painful business, he knew, and only facile in literature. Oh – God; Esme, he thought: surely that can't ruin everything now? He turned off the light.

'We're going back now,' he said: 'and tomorrow I shall take you away – if you'll come with me?'

He heard the faintest sound of assent and took her icy and trembling hand.

'Are you going to kiss me?'

'No,' he said. 'I can't simply kiss you, and I don't want us to begin like this.' He raised her hand and kissed it. 'You're frozen, darling, but you needn't be afraid.'

He looked at her, huddled in the dark beside him, took off his scarf and arranged it, under her hair, round her neck.

'There; now we *must* go, or all my good resolutions will fail me.'

He asked her to tell him the way, but otherwise they were silent the short journey back. He drove slowly because his mind wasn't on it. Declarations, of any kind, he reflected, were illuminating. They didn't simply crystallize whatever it was you had thought you were declaring about: making them revealed a whole lot more. He had known that he *was* falling in love with her, that he wanted her more than he had ever wanted anyone in his life. He hadn't known that he would feel overrun by this mixture of elation, belligerent desire to protect her, awe at the thought of living an everyday life with someone who looked as she did, amusement at how much better he understood her than she realized, anxiety that, when it came to the point, she wouldn't choose *him*. He glanced at her, lying back in her seat – her eyes were shut. One way and another, she had had an exhausting evening, and if she felt better about anything at all now, she might have gone to sleep. That scene with the Hammonds, in front of her mother, would have taken it out of anybody, and then, on top of that, the effort she had put into telling him about the abortion, not simply of truth as to facts, but care about her responses to them. She had never taken the easy way out, even to the key question of whether she had wanted the child. That swine! For a few minutes he indulged in a hate fantasy about Mr X. He was in court; the charge was private irresponsibility: he was face to face with John Freeman (briefed with all unsavoury facts) for half an hour under glaring television lights. He was walking up and down Oxford Street every day for a month with a sandwich board saying 'I am a neurotic bully' on it. He was face to face with Felix King, the world heavyweight champion boxer. There was something wrong with his balls and he was being forcibly driven in a taxi to some unqualified quack by a friend of a friend of a friend . . .

Steady . . . it was all in the past – all over. But at least, whatever he was like, he wasn't as bad as that. There were other things in the past, though, which weren't over enough. There was Esme. Somehow, he knew she would be waiting up for them, wanting him to talk about 'things'. The green folder, Julius, herself, him, them. It wasn't going to be easy, somehow, to say 'I've fallen in love with your daughter.' But at some point he was going to have to say it. Or was he? He wished they need not go back; could drive straight to London. What was more important, Esme or Cressy? Starting right with Cressy, of course, and that involved not leaving a mess in Sussex. Perhaps she would even be pleased about it, relieved that Cressy had found somebody who was, if nothing else, reliable and kind . . .

He came upon the drive, which he recognized just in time. When he'd switched off the engine, he turned on the light again. She *was* asleep, and for some seconds he watched her, learning her face. She was very pale; her hair and her eyelashes looked black. Her mouth was just beautiful – there was nothing else you could say about it. She had that simply gentle, ageless appearance of someone deeply engaged with sleep. Here she is, he thought, how extraordinary to have found her. I suppose everybody feels like this at some time in their lives, he thought, feeling that nobody had ever quite felt it. He didn't want to touch her, had the notion that she might vanish or break, but she had to be woken up.

'Cressy, Cressy. We're home.'

'I've been asleep,' she muttered, in tones of faint accusation, as though he had *put* her to sleep.

'You're awake now. Come on. You can go straight up to bed. I'll deal with your mother, if she's still up.'

'I didn't sleep last night either,' she said, as though this was his fault too.

In the house, he said: 'Go straight to bed, then.'

She accepted this without question, and started to go upstairs.

'Cressy!'

She turned.

'Everything's all *right*.'

She gave him a fleeting sleep-ridden smile. 'Good.'

He waited until she had gone, and then went to the sitting-room. Except for the remains of the fire which still gave a dim rosy light, it was dark, and Esme was not there. She'd gone to bed, he thought, thank God! Tomorrow everything will somehow be easier – the morning – *I'm* not at my brightest now, but in the morning . . . she's a woman of innate tact, after all. Cressy can go out somewhere with Emma and Dan, and I'll talk to her alone . . .

He shut the door, turned off the hall lights, and went quietly upstairs. He had just reached the door of his room when she called him. Her bedroom door was ajar, and the second time that she called, he could not pretend that he had not heard.

She was sitting up in bed in her peachy Tudor room. She wore a bedjacket edged with swansdown and her daytime face and hair.

'I thought I heard you. Shut the door, darling, and have a nightcap with me: it's so cold, you must need it.'

She indicated her dressing-table, on which stood a tray with whisky. His heart sank.

'What a thoughtful idea,' he said, and shut the door.

CHAPTER 15

ESME

SHE had made half a dozen resolutions not to wait up for them: she'd smoke one more cigarette and then go; she'd wait until a particular log had burned out on the fire, until the clock said half past, until she'd finished looking at all the houses in the current *Country Life*, until she'd finished the brandy she was now drinking with soda, until she'd finished a last cigarette – and so on. But in the end she had gone up. Then an idea had occurred to her, and she had come down again to fetch a tray with brandy and whisky and soda. This would be better, really, because Cressy would go to bed, whereas if she waited in the drawing room, Cressy would certainly come in with him, and they would have a nervous, three-cornered conversation about the Hammonds and so forth. And what she wanted was a really good talk alone with Felix – to 'catch up with him', to 'establish things' – she repeated the desire to herself in various, innocuously vague ways. She had undressed, done her hair, powdered her nose, had another little nip of brandy, and got into bed to wait. But waiting for somebody while they don't come, not only changes the manner of one's waiting, it can change the actual reasons why one is doing it. The more she thought about him, the more certain she felt that he had probably, certainly, *must* have come back for the reasons which she had suspected – although she had not allowed herself to think of them – all along. She had reached a stage where it seemed to her simple, courageous and necessary to indulge in a little plain speaking. A little before she heard them eventually

243

arrive this had assumed proportions of duty in her mind and she was longing – simply longing – to get it over.

She heard Cressy come upstairs and go straight to her room. An agonizing pause, and she heard his step. He'd probably looked in the drawing-room to see if she was still up. More confirmation.

She had to call him twice before he heard her. He looked so wonderful, standing in the doorway, that her heart lurched with the old familiar excitement, but she welcomed him casually – with just the right touch, she thought.

'Give me one too,' she said, while he was pouring the drink. 'Brandy,' she added; 'it's years since I drank so much brandy.'

He seemed to take a long time over the bottles, and she filled in the gap with questions – she did not want the tension of silence.

Was it very foggy? Not especially. She supposed it was colder, then. Yes – it was – a bit.

He brought her drink over, and she patted the bed. 'Sit here, it's much comfier, and we can talk more quietly and not wake the others.'

She drank some brandy, and wondered how to start. 'I seem to have done nothing but drink all the evening. Did Cressy make a scene in the car?'

'No – not exactly – not at all, in fact. She talked quite a lot.'

'It probably did her the world of good to get everything off her chest to you. She's gone to bed now, hasn't she?'

'Yes.' He looked suddenly dreadfully shy – embarrassed – as though he wanted to say something and didn't know how to begin. She remembered that look so well. He leaned forward.

'Esme! I . . .' But he stopped – he seemed quite unable to go on.

'Look,' she said gently: 'let me do the talking. I think I know what you are thinking about. Although it is usually the wrong way round, *I* want to speak first.'

'I don't think there is any special way round, is there?'

She put down her glass carefully without replying. Then she looked at him. He was eyeing her anxiously, but when she smiled, he seemed to relax, and smiled back.

'I'm full of Dutch courage,' she began. 'I was so thrilled when you came back to see me. At first I thought perhaps you'd just come out of curiosity – to see what I'd turned into after all these years. Then, when you were actually here, I felt you'd come to make friends. And *then*, when I saw how much you seemed to fit into the situation – how wonderful you've been with Cressy, for instance, how you made me see what a nice young man Emma has brought down – how much you seemed to *care* about what happened with Julius and what it was like for me – it occurred to me – ' she looked at her hands on the eiderdown and then put them out of sight, 'well – I know you know what I mean, my dear – and all I want you to be sure of is that *I'm* not standing in your way!'

There was a silence, which somehow seemed very full. He didn't say anything, but after a bit, he took her hand. His touch was too much for her.

'I've *never* changed!' she said, feeling tears rush to her eyes. 'I was afraid you'd think it – oh – perhaps just a bit *absurd*! I *know* I'm older than you, but it seems to me that the difference is not what it was. Neither of us is a child: we've both had a great deal of experience one way and another. But we've also had experience together – we know about that – and I assure you that nothing about that has changed!'

She could hardly see him, he was blurred by her tears.

'In a way, I suppose that's what I've been waiting for, all these years. I haven't looked at anyone else – I haven't been to bed with anyone since that last night with you! That's not as easy as it sounds to say, even though it was *you* I wanted – not just anybody else!'

'What I'm trying to say,' she said, fumbling for a hanky (he had released her hand much earlier), 'is that I'm in love with you – always have been – it hasn't changed at all.'

245

He got up from the bed and was pouring himself another drink. 'I'd like one, too,' she said, and held out her glass. He took it, and she could not tell at all from his expression what he was feeling (*shouldn't* she be able to? but any distant, uncertain warning from the hazy depths of her mind was useless now: she felt like someone who was exactly half-way up a steep, slippery slope – just as dangerous to look down and go back).

'There was one thing about the last night we spent that you don't know,' she said, and saw him jolt to attention although his back was turned. Then, he said, in a voice she hardly recognized as his:

'Did I make you pregnant?'

He had brought the drinks over, and she took her glass. His hand was shaking too, she noticed. She had reached a stage where she knew perfectly well that she had drunk too much, but she wanted another drink, and she also felt that it was *better* if she went on drinking.

He had taken her dressing-table stool and was slumped upon it, a few feet now from her.

'I didn't realize it for weeks and weeks,' she said. 'There was a lot to do – Julius dying so suddenly – I had to keep going to London for family meetings and lawyers and signing things – closing the flat and so on. The children were upset – particularly Cressy, and I couldn't leave them for more than a day without me. I seemed to spend my life in trains. I couldn't sleep much, and I was so unhappy about you that I thought I was slowly dying from it. I mean I felt ill, and I knew I was unhappy, and the unhappiness got like some ponderous disease which was making me feel sick all the time and dizzy and I kept finding it difficult to eat. For days and days I'd only say things to people like "Return ticket to London, please" and "The children can finish up the cottage pie for their lunch" and "Do I have to initial every single alteration?" to lawyers. You know – as though you are really entirely alone – you don't talk *to* anybody – you just keep life going by arrangements and questions. Then, somehow, you can talk far too fast to yourself, so you have too much time even after you've said the same things over and over again. Anyway, I didn't realize for ages what was the matter, and then, the moment it occurred to me, of course I knew.'

He was staring down at his glass of whisky. He said: 'What happened?'

'I had an abortion, of course.'

'Why "of course"?'

'Well – what else do you think I could do? I couldn't creep away somewhere and have it and get it adopted, because I couldn't leave the children. I didn't know where on earth you were: you had simply made it very plain to me that you were vanishing from my life. I couldn't write to your home with that piece of news. I was afraid simply to have it and brave it out with Julius's family and everyone. Mervyn was so desperately upset about Julius and so kind to me, that I felt I couldn't face him with a baby – red hair and your eyes, probably. I can see that sounds rather dim of me, but I was so depressed and feeling so frightful that *everything* seemed too much for me – let alone a fatherless baby. I just couldn't face it: I'm sorry, Felix.'

He made some gesture – she didn't know what it meant: 'Never mind' was the nearest that she could get. He looked stricken – but after all, it had happened to *her*, not to him; if she had had to do it, he ought to be able to stand hearing about it.

'Go on,' he said.

'There's not much more to tell.'

'There must be.'

'Well – a friend of a great friend of mine knew somebody. I got the address by pretending it was for a friend of mine, and went to him. He'd been a doctor. He said the best thing was just to come one Sunday morning, with a hundred pounds in notes; he'd do it, and I could walk away. I sent the children to Mervyn's for a week, and went to this man's flat. He had a nurse there. I lay on a kind of table thing and he gave me an injection.

When I came round, I thought I was still waiting for him to do it. But it was all over. I had to get back here, though, and that was awful. The man told me to go straight to bed and I'd said I would – I hadn't told him that I lived in the country. I thought I'd feel much better afterwards, but that was wrong too – I felt much worse. Wicked and miserable, and that it was the last of you somehow. I wished terribly that I hadn't done it. Never felt so hopeless in my life. I came back here and cried and slept and cried until it was time for the children to come back from Mervyn's. Then I had to pull myself together, so of course, I did. That's all.'

There was a very long silence indeed.

'All!' he repeated at last: tried to look at her, and then put his hands over his face. After a moment, he began rubbing the skin over his cheekbones, as though he was trying to think – or trying *not* to think: whichever it was, this gesture irritated her. Everything seemed to have gone wrong: she didn't know – couldn't think – *why*: she simply had this dead, discoloured impression of not being received. She corrected this: he knew, more or less, what she meant; he had no idea of what she felt about what she meant.

'I've no idea, really, why I told you all that.'

'Because I asked you to.' He sounded very tired, and miles away. 'But there's nothing I can say back. Nothing adequate. I do see that, between me and Julius, you have had a bad time.'

'How do you mean – between you and Julius?'

'Oh! – He was worrying about the state of the world. I was worrying about the state of Felix King. From any woman's point of view those are untenable extremes.' He got up. 'Apart from it being no good now my saying it – I *am* sorry. And that's only part of it.'

'It's the smaller part, now, isn't it?'

He looked up and found her looking at him steadily.

'It's no good,' she thought: 'absolutely – no – good.'

'No, you don't,' she said quickly. 'You needn't say any of it.

We don't feel the same any more, do we? I've realized that – much too late, of course. It *is* the larger part, though. If – if – you had wanted to be with me now, then everything else would have been all right, somehow – not washed out exactly, but just part of our history. But I know you don't. I had to drink far too much to find this out, but I did need to know. I think you're in love with someone else.'

Why did almost everything she said sound like an accusation instead of an appeal? Because that was what hopeless appeals turned into. 'Never mind,' she said. 'I expect you came down here meaning to tell me about it, and I made it difficult for you somehow. That would be very like two people with good intentions and different requirements, wouldn't it? I drank too much: inhibitions are much more than convenient when one gets old: they're vital. You – or anyone else – would lose me without them. I expect tomorrow I shall feel terribly ashamed of myself, and one of these years we'll both be laughing about it.' She tried to smile, but it hurt her face like sticking plaster on a cut, and she looked again at the freckles on the backs of her hands – only this time she did not hide them.

'Bed,' she said brightly. 'It's high time we both got some sleep. It must be awfully late.'

He had been standing at the foot of her bed, and she wanted him to go now, without any gestures of affection – or pity. But he came round to her, picked up one of her limp hands, and kissed it. She shut her eyes and endured this kindness in a man's world. Then he went, and the instant he shut her door, she turned off her light, and the dark, like an airless, salt sea, engulfed her. In all these years while she had been growing old, she had not learned what to outgrow. When she suffered pain, fear, or any misery, her age became meaningless; she was a child, a young woman, in the wrong body: her throat ached as it had always done before tears; her reason vanished and the same, crying question recurred; tears scalded, sobs racked, injustice rankled, pity was too close for comfort: she could have been six, or sixteen: not, surely, nearly sixty. But the side-tearing, inescapable joke was that she *was* nearly sixty. Too old for what she wanted from her life. She suddenly remembered Julius, that last morning – *crying* because he was too old to fight, and the conscious cruelty with which she had said: 'There's nothing *you* can do.' So he had gone quietly off to do something he thought he could do and died in the process. She knew a bit what he felt like, now, she thought. Perhaps *she* should devote herself to other people: perhaps that would fill her bleak mind and the ache, like a burn, in her heart? The thought made her suddenly so weary that she felt she never wanted to move again.

Like everyone, she supposed, at some time in their lives, she just wanted to be unconscious for ever – starting now. She turned slowly on to her side, drew up her knees, wrapped her arms round her own body – her position for sleep, which occurred almost before she had finished moving.

She was very late indeed for breakfast, but she managed it: both her daughters would have thought it very odd if she failed to appear, and though appearances – so far from being a refuge – were something more like a painful brace, she felt that any kind of dignity was impossible without them.

Cressy and Felix were at the breakfast table. The Sunday papers had not arrived; he was smoking and drinking coffee and Cressy was peeling a pear. They both looked up as she came into the room, and she nerved herself for one of her daughter's sub-penetrating remarks about her appearance – this morning, noticeably worn – and his tactful protective kindness, but nothing of the kind happened. Instead, Cressy said:

'Mrs Hanwell's made masses of delicious kedgeree – do have some or she'll think we don't like it.'

She couldn't face food. Helping herself to an enormous cup of black coffee, she said: 'I drank far too much last night for my age. Got the wrong kind of hangover for kedgeree.' Then, seeing their empty places at table, she added: 'Emma and Daniel will eat it up.'

'They seem to have gone to London. Emma took my car last night. She left a note in my room. Said she'd ring you up later today.' She was peeling the pear like an expert waiter.

'I hope they didn't have a frightful drive. Oh no – the fog wasn't so bad, was it?'

'The forecast is bad today, though,' said Felix. 'Fog *and* frost. In view of the fact that I've promised my friend to take over his job from midnight tonight, I think I'd better start back in the light.'

'He's kindly offered me a lift,' said Cressy. 'Have this?' She was holding out an elegant glistening quarter of pear.

Mrs Hanwell came in with the papers, just as Esme was accepting this gift, and wondering with vague misgivings whether her daughter had noticed what had been going on, and was trying to be particularly kind. The idea produced mixed feelings – none of them comforting.

Mrs Hanwell had examined the sideboard, and discovered the remaining mole-hill of kedgeree. Esme explained about Emma and Mr Brick having had to go to London, but this only made Mrs Hanwell sniff.

'Won't Hanwell like it?' asked Cressy.

Mrs Hanwell looked at her reproachfully. 'Fish turns him: except for the odd pilchard he's never abided fish.'

'Whiskey will be pleased though.'

'He won't touch rice; and give him a bit of hard-boiled egg and he only plays with it.'

'Never mind,' said Esme. 'I'll have it for supper: you know I can't resist your kedgeree. You and I will eat it up and then it won't be a waste.'

'It will be a wicked waste if we don't, Mrs Grace,' said Mrs Hanwell, who only called Esme anything when she was disapproving of her ('madam' was one stage worse), but she relented enough to take Esme's cup and pour her more coffee, remarking as she set it on the table, 'You're looking peaky yourself – I doubt if warmed-up food will be much use to you by this evening,' and on this dark note she left the room.

'She's furious at Em going off without telling her,' said Cressy.

Esme picked up a newspaper without the slightest curiosity about its contents. 'They did go off rather suddenly,' she said.

Cressy leaned forward with another section of pear. 'I'm afraid that was my fault. I gathered from Em that Dan was horrified by the scene last night. I do apologize for my part of that.'

Esme looked up to meet her daughter's anxious and melting eye, and thought: 'She really *is* very beautiful,' at the same moment as she felt her own eyes fill with tears ('I can't stand anyone being nice to me – not yet'). 'That's all right, darling,' she said as steadily as she could and buried herself in the paper. Perhaps, she thought, unable to see the print, perhaps we shall become friends at last – perhaps *all* relationships change, not just the ones that hurt like . . .

'Cigarette?' said Felix. She shook her head. After a decent interval, she found her handkerchief and blew her nose a little.

'Fur trousers will be worn this Christmas,' said Cressy dreamily. 'I'd love to go about as half a leopard: a leopard woman: mock, of course, but you couldn't tell by candlelight. That shows you spots don't camouflage the shape, doesn't it?'

'Does it?' said Felix. There was such a complete silence that Esme looked up from her paper.

'Wasn't Major Hawkes a *dream* last night?' said Cressy rather quickly. 'I do think he's one of the nicest men I've ever met. His mind is like a very *good* junk shop – you know, crammed with marvellous things you've never thought of wanting, but once you see them!'

'He's a dear,' said Esme absently. 'But you and Emma have always been naughty about him,' she added, remembering what they were talking about.

'Well, we shouldn't have been. He's mad about you, too. I think the only reason he doesn't propose to you is pride. He's so much poorer than you that he'd think it dishonourable.'

Esme, looking at her, suddenly realized that Felix was doing the same.

'All I meant,' said Cressy who seemed unhinged by their joint attention, 'is that if you want to marry him, you have our consent. Em's and mine I mean. I think it would be a splendid arrangement.'

That was when she knew. Without the slightest warning – absolutely at once. It was as though somebody had hit her very hard on the back of the head, and instead of becoming unconscious, she stopped noticing anything she had been noticing before, and was made aware of one, new fact; was jolted, dislocated into a piece of entirely new knowledge which spread and bled over everything. It wasn't a steep slope any more: it was another twenty years of sand – changing colour with the days and nights but always, always feeling the same. 'I'll walk beside you through the passing years' – that song had been fashionable when she had not been alone, but she had never liked it – had never even disliked it enough to find it funny. In two years' time, without anybody walking beside her, she would be only sixty. Desolation – warded off by illogical preservation of health and frenzied obsessions with any trivia in reach ... A feeling of helpless terror, like the beginning of drowning, was succeeded by all the evidence edited, linked like film. He had gone to Battle with Cressy; had offered to go with her and Brian last night; had come back hours late; had tried to tell *her* something last night; but she, she had been too wrapped in the courage of her own convictions to listen, to have saved herself the final humiliation. Now that she could see nothing else, she felt she must have been mad not to see it. Her own daughter! Why not? Perhaps that, too, would be a splendid arrangement. A feeling of hatred for her daughter came – and went.

Felix was speaking: '. . . what frightful nonsense you talk.'

And Cressy answering like a child (she was no child!), 'I don't!'

She said: 'At my age, one has to make one's own arrangements: they can't be made for one.' That was splendid, too. A splendid answer – considering everything. Which, she suddenly realized, Cressy couldn't be doing, or she wouldn't have said that in the first place. She *didn't know*. Earlier this morning, she would have thought she was already so unhappy that this couldn't matter; now it seemed to make – not all the difference in the world – but a difference.

'You and your age,' said Cressy affectionately: 'you know perfectly well you're marvellous for it.' She got up from the table. 'If Felix wants to be off, I think I'd better pack.'

About an hour and a half later, they left, in his car. She spent that time, which seemed both long and crowded, trying to keep unobtrusively out of their way – particularly out of his way. She didn't want his confidence – or couldn't stand it. She tried to mollify Mrs Hanwell, but Hanwell was having some castle puddings in the kitchen and wearing his Sunday suit, in which, for some reason, he seemed unable to bend his knees at all. He started violently when she went into the kitchen, and half a castle pudding rolled slowly down his rigid legs on to the floor, pounced on by Mrs Hanwell – like a fat little cat.

'There,' she said, brushing him down with a tea towel as though he was only his suit. 'There! I told you golden syrup was silly on Sundays. He doesn't like Sundays – doesn't even care for newspapers unless there's a war, which leaves him under my feet all day . . .'

Some things stayed the same. She explained about being alone for lunch, and suggested the kedgeree for it. The steak and kidney puddings were on, she was told, but they would heat up nicely during the week. She knew, for Hanwell's sake, she must go, but Mrs Hanwell was sorry she had been cross about the kedgeree, which made her want to go on talking. Did she realize that Miss Emma had gone to London *again* without a single one of her winter vests? She'd come down in one, because Mrs Hanwell had washed it on Saturday morning, but now it was lying in her drawer with the other three. It was much worse to leave vests off than never to start them. Men or no men, you couldn't go taking off all your underclothes in winter. She knew men nowadays expected the moon, but people had been known to pass away from taking off their vests . . .

She got away in the end and went to fetch the papers from the dining-room, decided that this was the safest room to be in, and, very slowly, cleared the breakfast table. She was longing for them to go now, and they seemed to be taking an age about packing. She heard him coming down the stairs, and hastily opened the hatch into the kitchen.

He came into the room, saw the hatch and Mrs Hanwell's hands receiving crockery; stood waiting a moment, and then very quietly said: 'Esme?'

She pretended not to hear: she felt him watching her and for a second she wanted to scream at him: 'Get out! Shut up! Don't try to put anything right or be honest with me – just go!' but just then Cressy came down, wearing a dark-green Austrian jacket over her yellow sweater. She clicked her fingers and said: 'My music!' and went to get it, but Mrs Hanwell put her head through the hatch and said what about the eggs and tomato chutney for Miss Emma, if they were going to take them she'd get them but if they weren't she'd let them lie. They'd take them. Felix said he would get the car. Mrs Hanwell said she'd pop up for the vests – she'd found a carrier for them: the departure, like most, was assuming the frenetic unnecessary flurry that characterized the end of so many week-ends. It was never nice when people went, she reminded herself; there was always the moment of walking back into an empty room, and feeling that the house was too big. She tried pretending that it would just be like that.

They all met again in the hall: farewells exchanged: nothing about why Cressy had to get to London so early: he simply thanked her and said he'd enjoyed himself, hesitated, put a hand on her arm and turned away. Cressy unexpectedly kissed her: she was wearing a delicious scent, but then she usually was. Mrs Hanwell had disappeared. 'I'll ring you,' said Cressy. An icy wind into the hall: his car was running. He opened the door for her and she climbed in. 'Good-bye!' 'Good-bye,' he said. 'Good-bye,' her mouth ached with smiling.

She watched them round the bend of the drive, listened as they slowed down and eased into the lane and she shut the door before she could not hear them any more. Cressy's scent was still in the air; she walked away from it into the drawing-room with its log fire, berries arranged in an urn, and her desk, neatly crammed with letters she had already answered.

CHAPTER 16

EMMA

O F course she was glad that he had changed his mind – so suddenly too – but after that announcement, he said that he was going to take a short nap so they didn't talk any more, and as she drove steadily, so as not to wake him up, she had time to worry a bit about the whole thing. She didn't in the least understand why he had changed his mind: why, after all the haughty stuff about going abroad and slashing at Cressy, he had suddenly changed into being nice again – and begged her pardon. Of course she had forgiven him – of course. But getting close to anyone was not at all the illuminating business she had supposed. It was much more like being shown a slide under a microscope – the leg of a beetle or a human cell: it gave you a startling fractional close-up which made the whole beetle, or person, far more mysterious than they were before. 'I prefer the bird's eye view,' she thought. And yet, didn't some philosophers say that a part of the truth was not only better than no truth at all, but the way to discover the whole? At this rate, she'd never find anything out, because on top of there being so many million cells to one person, they reputedly changed all the time, and it would be a good many years before she could get cosy enough with the microscope to say 'a typical cell' or anything soothing like that. The power to relate and apply, she felt, was not hers, and she suspected that it was not a particularly enjoyable gift, since she could not, off-hand, think of a philosopher who seemed to have become actually happier as a result of his findings. But she did feel, rather stubbornly, that understanding *anything* ought to make one feel better about it; that even *trying* to understand something was a good deal better than nothing. Anyway, she *wanted* to understand Dan. She thought now that he was the most interesting person she had ever met, and that was not a light thing to say, because by her age she had naturally met a good many people, and could be expected to know what she was talking about. This sober and worldly assessment of her feelings pleased her and showed her that she was not being carried away. She didn't think he was especially glamorous; she couldn't think it was because he was a good poet since she hadn't read a word that he had written; he wasn't famous or rich or powerful (she was arguing from a long way outside here, but still, that was what people did); she simply felt the same as he did a lot of the time. If she had had a brother, she thought that ideally she would have felt something of the sort about him. So she wasn't in the least carried away. But naturally, if you met the first person in your life about whom you felt these things, you didn't want the relationship to stop. 'I wish he *was* my brother,' she thought, 'because then it wouldn't be *able* to stop, whatever either of us suddenly thought or did.'

She glanced at him. His head was sunk forward into the turned-up corners of his jacket collar. His eyes were shut, and the glimpse of him was like the casual work of some famous artist drawing his friend in a railway train. 'I'm not in love with him,' she thought, as the idea (overloaded with other people's interpretations − naked bodies, the airless agony of incomprehensible requirements − a kind of grab and clutch at being together at any cost) occurred to her. And the notion − of any consummation being oblique, imperceptible; that the other person's eyes, voice, would always be dominating a situation which would only be rounding off her life with them − came, and seemed real and true. She wasn't like Cressy. She had told lies to defend her: but *her* body was inadequate, out of touch: she couldn't rely upon it: and nobody else ought to try and make her.

A little red light began winking on her dashboard: petrol. She slowed down instinctively, and then hastened on for a garage. The first two were closed: it was miles before she found one beside a lorry drivers' café. She asked for three gallons, and hunting in her purse, discovered half a crown and her return ticket. Dan had money: she didn't want to wake him up, but she knew he would hate her trying to take ten-shilling notes out of his pockets. So she woke him.

He didn't seem to mind too much. 'It's a dull way of parting with your money,' he said, but she so much agreed with this that she couldn't blame him. When they had started, she remembered the peppermints, and they both had some. 'How far are we?' he asked. About half-way; perhaps more, because there wouldn't be bad traffic going into London at this time of night. She had a cigarette and he told her that soon he would be an uncle. Was he pleased, she asked. Not when you consider the father, he replied. Was it his sister? How did she know that? She had just guessed: he didn't seem to be the kind of man who had brothers. She was right there. What was his sister like? What, he had repeated with scorn. What indeed! She was all right: she simply had no taste in men. Perhaps if one loved somebody, one saw things in them that other people didn't. (She was thinking of the microscope again: perhaps that was where it came in handy.) No – he didn't think that. He simply thought that one stopped noticing some of the awful things, and with Alfred, that would amount to being nearly stone blind. He described Alfred to her, and she did see. What a pity, she cried. What's a pity? he asked, on guard with her. To think of her being tied to him for life. Oh – you regard it as life, do you, he asked – what she is tied to him for, I mean? You said she married him. Yes, he said, after some thought, he had said that. He hadn't expected her to see it in that way.

'They were good fireworks,' he said, just before he went to sleep again.

'I just want to *be* with him,' she thought. 'Thank goodness I don't have to go to work tomorrow.'

It wasn't until they were crossing the river that she began to feel apprehensive: and even then, that was probably too strong a word. Perhaps he wouldn't like the flat. If he didn't like it, he would just go – she knew that. Mrs Moffat would have cleaned it up, so it would be tidy, anyway. For the first time, she hoped that Cressy wouldn't be cross at her pinching the car – a thing she had never done before in her life.

When they arrived in Lansdowne Road, she said nervously: 'Here we are,' and 'We have to be quiet going in because of the other people in the house.'

She locked the car, and they pushed open the stiff gate and crept up the path. She had her key out: she was now in an agony of impatience for them to arrive. Fires must be lighted, coffee made, and eggs cooked, if he wanted them; they had to get settled.

He stroked the badger's head silently and mounted the stairs. At each landing, he was always the immediate step below her. They reached her door, and he bumped into her while she fumbled with the key. After her front door, the carpet gave way to coconut matting, but the lamp-shades were nicer, she thought. She felt anxiously critical of the whole place. She rushed ahead, and, seizing a box of matches, started lighting fires. He walked into the sitting-room and stood in the middle of it looking carefully round him, at the piano, the large sofa where people sometimes stayed the night, the large lamps with dark shades, and the jar of wilting chrysanthemums, at the bookcases, and piles of music and a fur hat of Cressy's lying on a round table. 'Big, isn't it?' he said.

She was just about to say 'Not very' when she saw his face. 'It's an attic,' she explained. 'I mean, it used to be – before the house was turned into flats. Would you like some breakfast now?'

He nodded. 'Can I look round all this?'

'If you want to.'

Immediately he started prowling round, but she didn't see where he went exactly, because she rushed to the kitchen. She felt at the same time very restless and very tired.

There were eggs and some bacon, the heel of a loaf and two modern tomatoes. She put on a kettle. The bacon rashers were frozen together: she put them on the cooker to thaw, and realized that *she* was very cold. She'd have a boiling hot bath after breakfast before they went to sleep.

He arrived in the kitchen carrying two small glasses filled with dark, reddish-brown liquid. 'I made us a drink,' he said. 'Warm us up.' He held out a glass. She sipped it. It tasted like cough mixture for a witch, she thought: very nasty, *and* burning. 'What *is* it?' she gasped.

'I don't know. I just used what bottles you had to hand. Drink it up. It'll do you good.'

They looked warily at each other, and drank at the same time. She tried to visualize the bottles in the sitting-room – some very old cooking rum, a lot of French vermouth, and the dregs of some pure Polish spirit that Cressy had been given.

'I put a spot of cherry linctus in for the colour,' he said complacently. 'Want another?'

'No thank you. I'm making scrambled eggs. Would you like tea or coffee?'

'It surprises me that you can cook,' he said. 'I'd rather coffee. You couldn't make a decent cup of tea in that pot.'

When she had made the meal, he helped her carry it to the sitting-room, which was now much warmer. She remembered about the gas fire in her room, but he said he'd lighted it for her.

'Kind of you.'

He looked up. 'It wasn't particularly kind.'

In spite of the warmer room, and the comforting familiarity of breakfast food, the situation wasn't at all how she'd imagined – or hoped. There was an edge to everything which made her feel awkward and shy. And it wasn't that he seemed unconscious of it: he almost seemed to be making it on purpose. She tried to talk about things like they had on their walk this morning – ages ago! – but he didn't respond; kept watching her. Perhaps, she thought, *he* is shy: often when you feel awful, the other person is feeling it too.

As soon as she had finished, she said she was going to have a bath. Would he like one? she inquired. Not in winter, he said firmly, and for a moment, everything was all right.

'Is that what you usually do?' he asked.

'Yes,' she said, puzzled. 'It'll warm me up, and I always feel dirty after a long drive. Go to bed if you want to – don't wait for me. You can have Cressy's room or the sofa – whatever you like. There are blankets and things for the sofa in that oak chest.'

'You like me, don't you?'

He hadn't moved from the floor where he was sitting – was staring fixedly up at her – not as though he was seeing her, but as though he was blind.

'Of course I like you. You wouldn't be here if I didn't. I like you very much,' she added nervously. He laughed and stopped looking at her. 'I'll finish that drink, then,' he said: 'I made rather a lot of it,' and he held up a flower vase. '*Sure* you won't have another?'

'No, thank you, Dan.'

She undressed in the bathroom while the bath was running. She and Cressy had bath wraps which served as towels and dressing-gowns: hers was white and Cressy's was pink. They were quite decent, she reflected, because they had towelling sashes – you could answer the front door in them, which, as Cressy had pointed out, stopped them being a luxury at once. The bath was good: the whole evening had been rather a strain; and it hadn't stopped being one when she'd expected it to. Perhaps Dan was worried about being alone in the flat with her: he had his decorous side, and in fact, so had she. There wasn't anyone else she would have thought of inviting here alone, now she came to think of it. 'I wonder whether I *am* falling in love with him?' she thought as she soaked, but even in the bath, this made her shiver. She wanted him to like her very much and talk to her about it, so that she could feel if it was going to be all right: she could explain to him about her body not seeming to work, and perhaps, if he loved her, he would understand this and then things might be better . . . Time, and feeling the other person was very fond of you – but perhaps he didn't like her enough for that. Perhaps he would *get* to like her. Time was the thing.

The door of Cressy's room was open and she could see clearly that he wasn't in it. She went to the sitting-room door: most of the lights were out but the door was widely ajar.

'Emma?'

'Yes?'

'Come here. I want you.' He laughed, sounding strange, and repeated: 'I want you.'

As she went into the room, he seized her round the waist from behind and she had hardly time to make a sound before she found herself being carried to the sofa, on to which he flung her. She started to exclaim, protest, but he put one hand over her mouth, and with the other undid her sash. Then, with his hand still on her mouth, he said softly: 'You were too long having that bath. If you scream, I'll strike you. I mean what I say.'

There was a pause, and then, watching her, he slowly withdrew his hand. She felt like a petrified doll.

'You remember what you said?'

'What about?' Her voice seemed so small, she could hardly hear it herself.

'About if you fancied someone, you'd go to bed with them?'

'I didn't mean . . .' she began, but kneeling on the sofa he stopped her. He wasn't wearing his shoes.

'No need for any of that routine. If you start lying to me, I'll give you a bad time.'

'I *wasn't* . . .' She stopped again, because with one sudden movement he ripped open her bath robe so that she was entirely naked except for her arms in her sleeves. At once, she started to shake – her heart pounding and the shaking were shatteringly out of time with each other.

He ran a hand pressingly over her – upward – ending on one breast: instantly it felt like stone. He was smiling, but it was a menacing smile.

'Dan . . .' She thought she was shouting, but it came out a whisper. He leant down over her, until his face was nearly touching hers.

'Yes?'

But she couldn't say anything after all.

'Say something,' he demanded.

She moved her head and his hand closed more firmly on her breast.

'Your heart's pounding: you're excited: you love me, don't you?'

She started to shake her head and tried to move, but he put his mouth on hers then, and it was like a clap of lightning – as though her spine recoiled from the shock. Utterly unknown, overwhelming; she felt suddenly a stream of sweetness in her mouth – but lighter than sugar, and at once he kissed her more gently. He smelled of summer grass. A lock of his hair fell over her face; she seemed only to be breathing through his mouth. He had put one hand round the back of her neck: anywhere that he touched she felt was going to break or burn. He stopped kissing her, tilted her head with his hand and gazed at her: she felt so much that he was searching *her* that she hardly saw him; she was simply the thing he was looking at.

'You love me, don't you?' he said again.

'Let me talk to you – please, Dan.'

'We'd never meet *there*,' he said with scorn. 'I take no account of how you've conducted things in the past. We'll do this my way.'

'I haven't conducted anything . . .'

At once he hit her cheekbone with the flat of his hand – not hard, but it made a lot of noise. 'I've *told* you – I meant it – I won't stand you lying: not to me – about this. I warned you . . .'

Of course she was very frightened: but why don't I scream – or try to run away? Or something like that? Instead, infuriatingly, she felt herself weakly smiling. *Smiling!* She said: 'I won't tell you any lies – I promise. I just want . . .'

'I know what you want. Be silent then.' He knelt upright, and took off his jacket and laid it deliberately on the floor. Then he rolled up the sleeves of his jersey. His forearms were muscular, very white, with dark-blue veins. 'That's better. I'm used to this out of doors – I haven't lived your kind of life.' He put his arms under her shoulders and eased off the bath robe. Then he laid his head on her breasts and started kissing them and her spine kicked again with the shock.

When he stopped, he lifted his head to look down at her. 'You're ready for it now, aren't you?' He touched a breast. 'It's like a hard little raspberry. Beauty. Don't you move then.' He stood up and without taking his eyes off her, undid his belt and stripped off his trousers. 'I'm ready for you too. See?' And before she could have answered, he laid himself full length upon her; she could feel that part of him hard against her stomach, then against her thighs. 'Shift then,' he said; 'make room for me,' and as though she had done this all her life, she moved her legs apart. He put one hand round her head, began kissing her mouth. His other hand was touching her down there, parting her, pressing in till it hurt. 'You're resisting me! Don't do that. You want me. You can't stop me now.'

He drove into her suddenly – and she cried out, she felt she was breaking inside with the violent pain; she arched her back under his weight as the pain flowered to torture, until she thought she was going to die from it, and instantly he came in her, and she cried out again and could not stop crying. Then she did not know what happened until she found him stroking her forehead and moving away the tears streaming down her face with his fingers. His face came into focus, and he looked quite different, and it was he who was whispering. 'You hadn't done it before?'

She tried to shake her head, and managed only to turn away from him.

'You tried to tell me: I didn't believe you. You really are mine!'

'Listen to me. I love you. It won't ever be like that again.' He turned her face towards him and kissed her with such gentleness that she dissolved into more tears.

'I want to marry you, *dear* girl. Wait. I've got to come out of you. I don't want to hurt you any more.' But she was hurting so much that however he moved it was like a burning bruise; and now she sobbed childishly, for much more than the pain, as though it was the only thing she could do.

'You must have loved me, to do it.' He looked anxious now. 'I'll take care of you. Don't cry any more.' He got up and arranged the bath robe round her carefully. 'Look at me. Don't I look funny like this? You have to smile – seeing a man without his trousers.'

She looked at him: he didn't look funny to her. Just familiar – the only person she could be with when she felt so broken and weak. She tried to smile and he noticed it, knelt by her, and mopped her face with the edge of the bath robe.

'You need a good sleep now. I'm going to take you to your bed. You're worn out, poor little thing. Relax, now.'

He lifted her up and carried her to her room: pulled back the bedclothes and laid her in the bed. Then he pulled the bath robe, and she felt him very gently drying between her legs. 'Don't worry now. I'm mopping you up: I won't hurt you.'

The sheets felt very cold and she *was* tired – the kind of tired where she wasn't sure whether she had the strength to shut her eyes.

'I'm coming in with you,' he said, and then, watching her face: 'Just for the warmth and to be friends.'

She heard him taking off the rest of his clothes and then he got into bed, and turned her on to her side. He put one arm round her, stroked her softly and said: 'Off you go.' And she did. She must have fallen asleep on the instant, as she couldn't remember any more.

When she woke, light was coming through the rusty marigold curtains, and it was lovely and warm, because he had left the gas fire on. She moved, and felt him move against her, and remembered everything at once about them, and she turned round to see him and he said 'Good morning, Emma,' and she said 'Good morning, Dan,' and then they didn't say anything, just looked at each other for a bit. Then Dan said: '*This* is what Sunday mornings ought to be like. You *are* a beauty, you know. I'm not making up to you now – I'm telling you. And you smell nice.'

She said: 'So do you,' and then, because she felt suddenly shy, she buried her face in his shoulder, pretending to smell him.

'Am I the first man you've ever brought here then?'

'Yes.'

'I'm sorry I hurt you last night.'

'It's all right. Honestly.'

'Honestly,' he repeated, in her voice.

He sat up in bed, and at once she saw the long, white scar which ran right round one side below his breast bone. 'What's that?' she wanted to say, and just managed not to. He had picked his vest off the chair and was putting it on, as he said:

'Don't worry about my scar. I had a bit of chest trouble once, but it's all over now.'

'You had an operation?'

'Three. The surgeon had to saw off bits of my ribs, his wonders to perform. It's not a subject I take much interest in talking about. Don't worry – I got my strength back.'

They got up, and she tidied things while he made a list of all the things they wanted to do. Then they found it was two o'clock, so they had some sardines, some shortbread, half a banana and a pot of tea made by Dan. There wasn't any other food, but they both enjoyed it and ate everything up. Dan's list turned out to read: 'Get married. Go to the Zoo. Go to Spain. Get bloody passport first. Get suitcase out of station.' Which station? she asked. He couldn't remember the name, but he could find it by starting from his sister's flat. Anyway, they should take things in order. He got rather cross about not being able to get married at a moment's notice on a Sunday afternoon. He thought it ought to be in the public interest to be ready for that sort of thing. They might be having a child. This side-tracked them on to their children's names and it turned out that they would have to have a good many to accommodate both their tastes in names. It was too late to go to the Zoo, so they decided to get his luggage. She left a note for Cressy asking if she could have the flat to herself for a day or two and telling her how good everything was. He was standing by her bedroom window while she wrote it.

'There's a seagull out there; standing about on a pear tree.'

She joined him.

'It's the same one. He always seems to be there.'

'That's how I used to feel,' he said. 'Wondering how to fill in the time. Till I met you.'

CHAPTER 17

CRESSY

IN the car she decided to be passive – to do no more about anything than allow it to happen. This seemed to be a good decision, but having made it, she couldn't think of anything to say. I've been horrible to my mother for years, she thought irrelevantly. Her mother had been very good about that awful dinner party last night, and then good about them all leaving so suddenly, but Felix didn't seem to want to discuss her mother, so outwardly she became silent. Inside, she was having one of those spiky, jeering duologues that always seemed to crop up when she was nervous. Why was she here? Because love mattered more to her than anything else. How did she know that being here had anything to do with love? How *could* she know that till she tried? But could she tell the difference between having the courage to try something and being a sucker? *Could* she? Or couldn't she? Perhaps you have to have the courage to risk being a sucker. Her mother had looked rather lonely when they had left. Breakfast had not been comfortable, but perhaps it was always difficult if you suddenly felt different about someone you have known for a long time: trying to change your behaviour simply made you a stranger talking to them.

Felix was driving slowly, and when she asked why, he retorted that he wasn't used either to English traffic or her company and caution was the thing. They lunched in Sevenoaks, and he told her more about his friends the Lewises – adding that he was supposed to be dining with them that night and did she mind? Oh no, she lied at once (was she not used to this?), but he went on, 'with you, of course,' and then she really hadn't minded. They had had a long, rather horrible lunch which they noticed, without criticism, ending with tepid, muddy coffee in a draughty passage labelled 'coffee lounge'.

Then, in the car again, he said: 'I'd like to take you to an hotel tonight. I'd like to have you entirely to myself, after we've had dinner with Jack and Mary. It's her treat, this dinner, and I don't want to let her down. Will you do that?' It was his plan and she agreed.

When they arrived outside the Lewises' flat, she said: 'You go in and tell them you've got me with you. I'd much rather.' But actually meeting the Lewises turned out to be one of the least straining moments of the day. Mary had been ironing everything both children possessed, and Jack said he'd been reading the papers and snarling at her about the state of the world. The baby was in a pen with some saucepans. Barney was apparently in a tent under the kitchen table where he was eating biscuits and spilling milk. The Lewises were friendly, tactfully unsurprised. As soon as Felix felt she liked his friends, he went away to ring up an hotel. It had turned out to be full. At this point they were being discreet about their plans: Felix simply took the telephone into another room. After he had tried six hotels that were also all full, he came back saying so, and the Lewises were unembarrassingly helpful with telephone directories and sensible suggestions. But trade conferences, a cat show, and some vast exhibition optimistically connecting the arts and sciences seemed to have used up every hotel in London – even the very expensive ones that Felix resorted to. It became a kind of game for Jack and Felix to take turns with the telephone – and she still was not taking it seriously: if they were going to an hotel, an hotel would be found; the actual night seemed far away. By this time they had all had tea and flapjacks made by Mary and the baby had been put to bed. She rang Emma – perhaps they'd better go there, she had thought, wondering whether the ground would be comfortably familiar or too familiar, but Emma, when she finally answered the telephone, sounded incoherent about everything except that she frightfully wanted the flat to herself for that evening. She added that as soon as possible she would be married if not in Spain and *then* Cressy could take over the flat as she, Emma, would not need it any more, as she thought that Dan would rather live in a boat as he wasn't keen on a lot of space indoors . . . Here her breath had run out, and Cressy, who understood the rules (had she not made them, after all?) said that it didn't matter in the least; she was delighted about Dan; she might come and collect some clothes tomorrow – she'd ring up first, of course.

They all had a drink, and Jack took over the hotel-ringing. Barney was put to bed, the baby-sitter arrived, and Mary was changing. She was left with Felix and Jack. Felix slept on a camp bed in the box room, Jack explained, and due to his wife's *incomprehensible* shape, they could not move from their present bed into the camp one. 'She's already broken a chair,' he said affectionately: 'she'd spell instant death to a camp bed with me in it as well.' They assured him that no thought was further from their minds, that they would not dream of Jack even considering this, and for a moment they all felt slightly uncomfortable. Mary came back into the room wearing a brown velveteen tent dress which enhanced the air of splendid bravado she had noticed before in happy and very pregnant women. 'Well, *I* don't know,' Felix had said, putting down the receiver for the hundredth time. 'I've never had so much trouble seducing a woman in my life. Britain's state of economy *must* be flourishing if all this is going on in November on a Sunday evening.' Seducing her? Perhaps he was joking to conceal his meaning just that. But he looked at her with such warmth, and as though he knew what she was thinking, that she had felt better again. She offered to ring Ann Jackson, but Ann proved to have two blind children staying the night with her. It wouldn't have been the right place to go anyway, and it meant she would have made the plan.

Dinner – Jack and Mary treating them with that blend of

indulgence and envy that steadily married couples so often slip into with lovers. This was accompanied by Mary clearly enjoying what Cressy recognized was a rare treat, and also by the distinct feeling of strain between herself and Felix about what *was* going to happen to them that evening. Perhaps they would not find anywhere. But, she had realized, this still did not solve *her* problem. If she couldn't go back to Lansdowne Road, where could she go?

They took the Lewises home, were provided with a key in case they utterly failed to discover any other roof, and Felix started driving aimlessly about. Then, without any warning, she had felt utterly despairing – that she did not want him, did not know him, that everything augured badly – they weren't meant to be together – that the whole business was stupid and unnecessary – it was mad of him to drive about the streets in this pointless manner. He had no idea where he was going. 'I *always* believe people,' she thought angrily. 'It's time I stopped.' She said she wanted to go to Ann's who would be able to put her up somehow or other, and he could go back to the Lewises. They would both go back to the Lewises, he replied. She didn't want to. Why not? She felt humiliated by the whole situation and not inclined to share it with those who, for her, were nearly strangers. Well, *neither* of them would go back to the Lewises. They had a row and that was awful, too: idiotic and awful. It ended with her crying, and him grinding his teeth, giving her his handkerchief and then *laughing*! 'The point is,' he said, 'it *is* funny: it's ridiculous that we can't find one double bed in the whole of London – the largest city in the world. It's absurd that just when everything ought to be smooth and romantic and dreamy we should spend so many of our first hours together trying to find somewhere to be alone. It's an incredible coincidence that Emma should have embarked on an affair the same night. It's idiotic that you should be sitting beside me crying on our first proper evening; that we should apparently have to conduct our entire emotional life in a *car*! Isn't it? Now. Cheer up – because at last I've had an idea.'

It worked. He found a cab rank, and then consulted the drivers on it. They were directed to some back street in Pimlico which proved to be lined with small, sleazy hotels. The third one produced a room. They were in to the Hotel Ronald. She followed him through a stained-glass door to a narrow hall where a large tired woman in a flowered overall waited for them. Felix signed some name in a dog-eared exercise book, handed over two pounds and was given a key. Number three on the third floor, the woman said, eyeing them with a knowledgeable lack of interest, toilet on half-landing, and breakfast was from eight o'clock.

She followed him upstairs, thinking: 'This is the *last* time I ever do anything *like this* again. In my life. The last time. Never again.' The stairs were very steep and covered with linoleum designed to look like marble chips. The landing lights were as dim as electric lights could possibly be. Felix was carrying their luggage, and had given her the key, but when they came to the room, she resented being the one to open the door, and handed the key to him. The room was adequate. There was a wash basin and a small double bed covered by a maize-coloured slippery counterpane. The walls were porridge with a frieze of what looked like tinned fruit. The curtains were not drawn; he drew them, and a curtain hook fell down. There were two chairs and a dressing-table with face powder spilled on it. There was a gas fire that needed shillings in a meter. There was a picture of two puppies tugging a ball of wool over the mantelpiece. She could no longer avoid looking at him. He was looking at her, but he said immediately: 'I'll light the fire and we'll have a drink.' She watched him kneeling by the fire. 'I really am back where I started,' he said. 'This is just the sort of room I had when I first came to London: only smaller, of course. Are there any tooth glasses?'

There was one – dirty. Only the cold tap worked. She washed the glass and then found there was no towel. She unpacked her paper handkerchiefs while he opened his bottle of whisky. 'We'll have to share the glass, darling. Do you mind that?' She shook her head, thinking irritably, 'What an idiotic question – considering what else we are to share.' The fire made any of the room not near it seem very cold, and standing by it scorched her legs but she stayed there because she was trembling, and if he noticed she could say she was cold.

He pulled the chairs up to the fire and handed her the glass.

'I'm sorry it's here. It's wildly unsuitable for you. I'd like to have taken you to Paris, at least, or Morocco or a Greek island: Pimlico is far too near a cry. Have a cigarette? You know you want one.'

She found her cigarettes and he lighted one for her.

'You have the most beautiful hands of anyone I've ever seen.' (But someone had said that to her before: they might have meant it, but they hadn't loved her.) 'At least we're alone here: at least there's that about it.'

She did not reply. She did not feel that it was at all 'at least'; being alone with him was looming so large that she didn't think it would matter much where they were. She drank some more whisky and handed him the glass. 'It's stupid, really,' she thought. 'I've done this kind of thing dozens of times before: I can always escape tomorrow. I don't owe him anything at all.' And she imagined herself working with Ann: humbly learning how to care about other people so much that she never had time or inclination to care about herself: an exhausting, pure life, with one's conscience like milk – no more hangovers like she had about her mother – even, in a way, about Jennifer Hammond. She, too, might keep an animal as her sole emotional luxury. Anything to get away from these precarious, nerve-racking experiments. People always thought you did these things because you got paid, or loved sex or being flattered: they never seemed to think that you might just do them because

274

you knew that they were the ropes and you wanted to get into the ring, or go on the voyage or whatever the ropes were supposed to be about. An added disadvantage to these thoughts was that they didn't use up any time – he'd barely taken a swig of whisky.

And what the hell do we do when we've finished the whisky? That was when she realized how much of her life she'd strung along with people; as they seemed to know what they wanted, things had generally gone their way. That her natural responses had gradually withered under their collective indifference had not struck her at all until now. But oh God, it did now. She had not managed to love any of those men – not one; she'd wanted to, just as much as she'd wanted to feel that they loved her, but the moments that she had known that they hadn't and wouldn't, it had all become the lonely game of pleasing people and fitting in with their requirements.

And here was a man whom she liked – very much: even more than that: but the situation wasn't better because of that – it was much worse: worse than it had ever been with anyone else. She couldn't face the dreary, routine embarrassment of taking off her clothes, let alone getting into bed with him. With him, of all people.

'Can I have some more whisky?'

He said yes, of course she could, and poured it. Then he added: 'It's not just this place. You wish you weren't here with me, don't you?'

She shook her head, half aware that this was ambiguous.

'All right. I won't tease you with questions. Let's pretend we *have* to be here: we've just got no choice. I'm going to get out of my clothes and into bed. You finish the whisky.'

She sat by the fire with her back to him, hearing him rummage in his suitcase and then the movements of undressing. Her cigarette was burning her fingers and she flung it into the hearth so that she wouldn't have to turn round to find an ashtray. She heard him get into bed, and then he said:

'Cressy!'

Without turning round, she said: 'Yes?'

'Come over here. Please. There's something I want to say to you.'

She got up and walked reluctantly over to him. She was horribly afraid he was going to tell her she was making a fuss about nothing. Then she could cease to make the fuss and it really would be nothing.

'Sit on the bed, or you'll give me a crick in my neck.'

So she sat.

He took one of her hands. 'Listen. I know you don't want to take off your clothes with me staring at you: I know you don't feel like that. So you go and undress by the fire and I'll leave you in peace. You do that.' He gave her hand a friendly pat, and turned on his side towards the window.

'All right,' she said gratefully. All the time she was getting her things out of the suitcase, and putting them by the fire, scarlet silk pyjamas (she looked at them doubtfully, but they were all she had), slippers, dark-blue man's dressing-gown (better), she thought how kind it was of him to say that. A piece of affection, but she had to watch out not to confuse affection with love. She took a long time to undress, clean her teeth, brush her hair, go to the lavatory on the half-landing. When she came back she switched off the light at the door. He said: 'The bedside one doesn't work,' but the hot dim light from the gas fire seemed to her enough. She walked over to her side of the bed, and took off her dressing-gown.

After a moment, he turned over and put his arms round her, and she thought then, that when he kissed her, everything would be all right. But it wasn't: her body remained tense and unfeeling; the gabble of being cold, selfish, and incapable began in her head. He was stroking her shoulder, her breast: he stopped for a moment, and she steeled herself for the first accusation, but he was simply undoing her jacket so that he could touch her skin. He was gentle: it was all her fault. This was the moment to give in, or give up. She said: 'I'm sorry.'

'That's all right,' he said. 'You're too tense for anything to be all right with you yet. Don't be so anxious.' He settled her head in the crook of his shoulder. 'I love having you like that.'

His kindness brought tears to her eyes. 'If only it was always like this,' she thought, 'I could manage it.'

'Is that all right for you?'

'Yes.'

'You're not secretly madly uncomfortable?'

'No.'

He stroked her head. 'That's good.'

They lay for a while and she had begun to feel soothed and warmed by his kindness and patience with her. But the moment this second word occurred to her, she knew it could not last: people didn't ask you to go to bed with them just so that you could bask cosily in their arms. They expected more than that, and, in the circumstances, more than that was the least she could do. In the end, she made herself say: 'I think it would be all right now.'

Without a word, he made her sit up, and took off her jacket. Kindness was not unique to him: most people made a few, rationed gestures at the beginning. Once, she had been taken in by them; had believed that they were not just a part of the full treatment, but she had learned worse than that. Everybody tried at the outset to be nice about getting their own way. He pushed her, still gently, on to her back and began kissing her breasts – both, and then one, and she felt her whole body start to hold its breath again. He *wasn't* different from anybody else; it was just that from some distant, romantic notion she had wanted him to be. She knew that once the worst of her desolation had swept over her, she would be able to pretend – to write him off and let him have her. He put his hands round her waist and held it hard: this, because he enjoyed it, was supposed to excite her. She *hated* him for doing it – for just being like everyone else. The nearer people got to you, the more like everyone else they turned out to be. She could get it all over, if she tried, so that he would fall into a complacent stupor, and she would be able to escape. She shut her eyes, and waited for him to undo the cord round her waist – impatient, fumbling, still pretending to care for her. Why didn't he get *on* with it? If she was only allowed a ration of kindness, then he damn well ought only to be allowed a ration of time – of her passive availability. She began to undo her trousers herself but his hands stopped her. He sat up, gazed at her intently for a second, and said:

'How many times have you let yourself be raped in return for a little affection?'

She stared at him: his face was in shadow and she could not see his expression. He repeated: 'How many times?' and she realized that she had whispered: 'I don't know.'

Silence. She was jolted into it: perhaps he was going to be very angry now, in a different way. It didn't matter: she was too despairing to care – there might be something, she thought recklessly, to finding a new way of being unhappy.

He said, very quietly: 'Has it always been like this for you?'

She assented: there seemed no need to speak.

'Then why did you come here with me?'

She couldn't answer that. It seemed too ridiculous, now, to try and explain that. She said nothing.

'Are you in love with someone else?'

She shook her head.

'Is it other women you want?'

She knew that one. 'No,' she answered wearily: 'I don't want women.'

He said: 'I knew that. I shouldn't have asked: I'm sorry.'

Then he said again: 'But why did you come here with *me*?'

So she smashed her final escape route. *Nothing* mattered – absolutely nothing: she'd never known that before. 'Because you were the first man I was ever in love with. When I was sixteen: all those years ago, I thought everything had gone wrong *because* of that. I adored you: I would have died for you. And when I found out about my mother I could have killed her. Then you went away, and there was no point in anything – not even in killing her. I married to get out. It's not difficult to get out of things. The trouble is getting into them. But I've never got out of the feeling that everything would be all right with you – until tonight.'

There was another silence. Then she said: 'There's nothing you could say to me that would make anything worse. You *can't* be angry with me – or make a scene – or anything like that.'

Much more silence.

'No,' he said, and she had never heard anybody sound like that before. 'I can't be angry with you – or anything like that.'

He picked up her scarlet jacket. 'I want to put this on you. At least, let me begin by seeing that you don't die of cold.'

CHAPTER 18

THREADS

O N Monday, Emma went to see her Uncle Mervyn at
Speedwell and Grace. She told him that she was going
to marry Daniel Brick, and could she please have a
month off anyway to get used to this new state? Her uncle said
who was he to stop her: if he tried, she'd give in her notice – all
girls were the same. Yes, said Emma firmly, they were. Then he
said have a glass of Madeira to celebrate and, not to hurt his
feelings, she did. After the toast, he told her that her father had
left three thousand pounds in a trust for her which was to be
hers entirely when she married. This was wonderful news,
because it meant they could buy a boat to live in. Who did she
say she was marrying? Daniel Brick. Oh – Daniel *Brick*. He'd
been reading proofs of his first book of poems and thought he
was jolly good. There was a pause, and then he walked round
his desk and kissed her, and said: 'Your father *would* have been
pleased.' And this seemed to please *him* very much. He asked
them to have dinner at his club and she said could she ask Dan
and ring him up? Quite right, he said approvingly – he could
see that she would make an excellent wife, but he hoped she'd
come back to them part-time for reading, as she was such a
swingeing little reader.

Then she paid a visit to her office and gave an overfed
pigeon on the parapet the rest of the fudge that she had kept
too long, and collected proof copies of both Dan's books – the
poems, and the imaginary/real autobiography. It seemed odd to
be leaving this stuffy little room – perhaps for the last time, and
so suddenly, but she had, she felt, at last achieved more

important responsibilities. On the way home she hoped she wouldn't have more than seven children, because – counting Dan first, of course – she didn't think that she could look after more than eight people properly.

Dan had a smashing day. He got himself polyphotoed – pretending that he was a piece of very old silent film jerking his head like the minute hand on station clocks. This was for his passport. Then he went to see Dot and told her this staggering news and she *was* staggered: put her hand to her mouth and leaned against the door post, and opened her cornflower eyes and hugged him and cried a bit and gave him some caraway seed cake she'd made herself for Emma. He explained about Emma's accent and she said it took all sorts to make a world and one mustn't be snobbish. She kept asking what Emma looked like, and he told her about the marvellous odd eyes and she said, 'Trust you to find someone like that!' but admiringly. So then he said Emma was a secret beauty, and she was clearly impressed. She fixed to slip out to the registry office to see him married without telling Alfred. He said he'd send her a telegram the day before, timed to arrive in the middle of the day but saying: 'Auntie worse', to be on the safe side. Then he left Dot and went to buy presents for Emma. He bought her a box of peppermint creams – good ones – and a dark-blue petticoat with a lot of lace on it, and a box of crackers that said they were each filled with valuable gifts, like rings (he needed a ring), and a bunch of flowers, yellow and white and smelling of honey, and a fountain pen with a golden nib, and two white handkerchiefs with E on them, and a map of Spain, and a cake of Pears' soap and an artificial rose (dark red) to last her when the real ones died, and a black candle because it seemed a surprising colour. Then he hadn't got much more money (he'd saved some for the passport and licence for getting married) so he went back to Lansdowne Road, and she'd brought crumpets and they had a large tea. He didn't tell her about the presents – made her wait until much later, when she was in bed; then he sat her up and gave them to her one by one. They pulled all the crackers and one of the rings fitted her OK. 'I'll be a family man from now on,' he said, watching her dear little pale face looking at the ring on her finger: she was much more than his girl already. He had settled for her from now on.

Cressy spent Monday doing almost nothing. She didn't realize this at the time: it wasn't until Jack and Mary had finally set off for Esher with their children (they had decided to stay the night there, and then go off on their holiday) and she and Felix were alone in the Bayswater flat, that she realized that she had not really listened to Mary about where things were kept: had not gone to Lansdowne Road to collect clothes, had not rung Ibbs and Tillett and cancelled her forthcoming concert, had not, in fact, done anything at all except be with Felix. 'I want you to come with me,' he had said, and so she had accompanied him on his morning and afternoon calls, sitting in the car while he visited patients, waiting, not thinking very much about anything, until he came out of the house, and then driving off with him to the next place. They had eaten sandwiches in a pub and then driven back to the Lewises' flat and tackled the Answering Service that had taken calls in their absence. All day he had been friendly, matter-of-fact, entirely undemanding of anything except her presence. In the middle of the afternoon, she had said: 'I'm afraid I'm being rather dull: I don't seem to have anything to say,' and he had answered: 'I don't care what you're like as long as you'll drive about with me.' At about six in the evening, after he had finished his paper work for Jack, Felix rang him at Esher for a final check-up. They talked for a long time, and Cressy, sitting on the floor by the fire, had felt so exhausted and relaxed that she had fallen asleep.

She woke to find herself on the sofa, cushions behind her

head and Felix bending over her. '. . . a drink and then I'll take you out and feed you,' he was saying.

It turned out to be eight o'clock. 'I put you here, because you'd have felt all stiff and scorched if I'd left you on the floor.'

'I don't remember,' she said.

He smiled. 'Don't you! Well I can tell you that when I picked you up, you put your arms round my neck, muttered a bit, and then croaked something about me not leaving you.'

'I don't remember,' she said again.

'That's all right,' he said. 'The unconscious is supposed to be old hat these days. It takes a nice, old-fashioned doctor like me to pay attention to anything like that.'

She remembered him in the hotel room last night (was it only last *night*?) saying: 'Let's pretend we have to be here: we've just got no choice.' 'I don't want a choice,' she thought; 'I want to pretend I have to be here.'

Felix had been afraid that Cressy would run away from the hotel in the night and so he had not slept very much. For once, he thought, while he shaved in the Lewises' bathroom (they had got up and gone straight there for breakfast), for once, he was actually glad to have been wrong: it made a welcome change from what he had been forced to feel during much of the last thirty-six hours – first with Esme, then with *her*. When she had said: 'You *can't* be angry with me – or make a scene,' he had wanted to do anything for her that would show her – that would make her trust him: he'd had just enough sense to do nothing. He'd dressed her and made her go to sleep. The next day, he'd acted carefully on the apparent assumption that she would *just* come round to the Lewises', that she would *just* come out in the car – and that had worked. She had come with him: had sat in the car, was there each time he came out from a visit (those had been the worst moments – not being sure each time whether she would still be there). All the visiting time he had talked only about what they were doing. For lunch, he had taken her into a pub, and wondered, as he noticed the immediate and widespread interest she caused, whether it was her appearance that made her so confoundingly vulnerable? She did not seem aware of the attention: all day she was very quiet, subdued, acquiescent – a little like someone in mild shock: when they got back she had sat down by the fire with her head on the seat of one of the battered arm-chairs. He finished talking to Jack, and turned to ask her where she would like to have dinner, and saw that she was asleep. He watched her a long time before he lifted her up and carried her to the sofa, and then stood with her arms round his neck before he put her carefully down. Then he stood watching her again. 'The situation has changed,' he thought, 'if three months ago I was still blandly confident of setting a huge rehabilitation camp to rights, and now my heart's in my mouth at the prospect of getting this girl to trust me, and looking after a few people with 'flu. If I can rehabilitate *her*, I'll be doing much better than I deserve.'

Esme stood by her desk for what might have been a very long time – she'd no idea. They would be on the London road by now anyway. She thought she must make some plans quickly which would get her through the day, so she took her memo pad and wrote as fast as possible. 'Clear out desk. Do something about mole-hills. Clear up fireworks: *nothing* is so squalid as their remains. Finish *Pride and Prejudice*. Mark new pillowcases. Background of chair seat. Two square inches? (At *least*.)' Then she thought about all the stacks of food in the larder and wrote: 'Ask Mr and Mrs Fellowhurst meal.' He was the rector, and his wife, an otherwise benevolent woman, starved him practically to death. Since the frightful time when she had come across him dining alone off a rabbit's head and three prunes while he explained with blushes that he hadn't had time that day for lunch, she had always felt that she owed it to the community to get some proteins into its priest. It was terribly boring though: Mrs Fellowhurst talked about knitting all the time and he agreed with her interminably. She looked at the list. The writing looked like somebody else's – all shaky and difficult to read. She put 'Do Accounts' more firmly. Then, looking up from her desk, she saw the dahlias he had bought her in Battle. They were very fresh and were going to last for ages. She took them out of the vase and the stalks dripped quickly all over her new list on the pad. She took them quickly to the fire and thrust them, head first, into it. The fire hissed, the stalks turned black, bubbled with juices but did not burn. She took a poker and jabbed at them, pushing them deeper into the fire: she wanted them utterly burned, and in the end they were. She sat down to watch them be finished, but found this made her cry, so she stood up briskly, feeling a bit sick but stern with herself about it. She found a hanky in her bag and mopped up the green drops off her pad. The telephone rang and it was Brian Hawkes. After thanking her for the splendid meal he said that there was a splendid film in Hastings with Humphrey Bogart in it and he wondered whether she would like to go. 'No, thank you,' she said, and found she was utterly unable to say anything else. There was a brief pause and then he said: 'Sorry, my dear; I just thought I'd ask you. Well – I'll give you a ring next week if I may.' She managed to say yes do do that. Not that she didn't mean it, but she just found it difficult to *say* anything. Talking seemed to make her want to cry, so it was a good thing she was going to be alone, really, at any rate, till she got over it.

For the first time since he had died, she honestly wished that Julius had not tried to save people he had never met because then he might not now be lying, separate, useless, incommunicado, in his grave.

Elizabeth Jane Howard
The Light Years £5.99

Home Place, Sussex, 1937. The English family at home . . .

'She writes brilliantly and her characters are always totally believable. She makes you laugh, she sometimes shocks, and often makes you cry'
ROSAMUNDE PILCHER

For two unforgettable summers they gathered together, safe from the advancing storm clouds of war. In the heart of the Sussex countryside these were still sunlit days of childish games, lavish family meals and picnics on the beach . . .

Three generations of the Cazalet family. Their relatives, their children and their servants . . . and the fascinating triangle of their affairs . . .

'Vivid and compulsively readable' THE SUNDAY TELEGRAPH

'A superb novel . . . strangely hypnotic . . . very funny . . . surpasses even the best of what Elizabeth Jane Howard has written'
SELINA HASTINGS, THE SPECTATOR

'The creation of a vanished historical world . . . engrossing'
VILLAGE VOICE

Elizabeth Jane Howard
Marking Time £5.99

Home Place, Sussex, 1939. The English family at war . . .

'Elizabeth Jane Howard's incomparable imagination, insight and craft
have achieved a work of solid and fascinating reality – and beauty. I read
on with admiration and joy. In due course, this chronicle will be read, like
Trollope, as a classic about life in England in our century'
SYBILLE BEDFORD

The sunlit days of childish games and family meals are over, as the
shadows of war roll in to cloud the lives of one English family. At Home
Place, the windows are blacked out and food is becoming scarce. And a
new generation of Cazalets takes up the story. . . .

'A charming, poignant and quite irresistible novel, to be cherished and
shared' THE TIMES

'Vivid and compulsively readable' SUNDAY TELEGRAPH

'Evocative and gracefully written, this is Howard at her most bewitching'
COSMOPOLITAN

'She writes brilliantly and her characters are always totally believable. She
makes you laugh, she sometimes shocks, and often makes you cry'
ROSAMUNDE PILCHER

All Pan Books are available at your local bookshop or newsagent, or can be ordered direct from the publisher. Indicate the number of copies required and fill in the form below.

Send to: Macmillan General Books C.S.
               Book Service By Post
               PO Box 29, Douglas I-O-M
               IM99 1BQ

or phone: 01624 675137, quoting title, author and credit card number.

or fax: 01624 670923, quoting title, author, and credit card number.

Please enclose a remittance* to the value of the cover price plus 75 pence per book for post and packing. Overseas customers please allow £1.00 per copy for post and packing.

*Payment may be made in sterling by UK personal cheque, Eurocheque, postal order, sterling draft or international money order, made payable to Book Service By Post.

Alternatively by Access/Visa/MasterCard

Card No.

Expiry Date

Signature

Applicable only in the UK and BFPO addresses.

While every effort is made to keep prices low, it is sometimes necessary to increase prices at short notice. Pan Books reserve the right to show on covers and charge new retail prices which may differ from those advertised in the text or elsewhere.

NAME AND ADDRESS IN BLOCK CAPITAL LETTERS PLEASE

Name

Address

3/95

Please allow 28 days for delivery.
Please tick box if you do not wish to receive any additional information. ☐

Elizabeth Jane Howard
Confusion £5.99

London and Sussex, 1942. The English family in turmoil . . .

'Not a shot is fired in these pages but we are made to understand how war invades the body and the spirit. A birth, a death, adultery, a stumbling marriage – an upper middle class family takes shape with cinematic sharpness' DAILY TELEGRAPH

The long, dark days of struggle provide the poignant background to the third book of the Cazalet Chronicle. As the war enters its fourth year, chaos has become a way of life. Both in the still peaceful Sussex countryside, and in air-raid-threatened London, the divided Cazalets begin to find the battle for survival echoing the confusion in their own lives . . .

'This fine saga gets stronger with each passing page . . . one of the literary classics of the 1990s' SUNDAY TELEGRAPH

'A family saga of the best kind . . . a must' TATLER

'In due course, this chronicle will be read, like Trollope, as a classic about life in England in our century' SYBILLE BEDFORD